Praise for L. R. Braden

Winner of:

The Eric Hoffer Book Award for Sci-Fi/Fantasy

The Imadjinn for Best Urban Fantasy (*twice!*)

First Horizon Award for debut authors

On *DEMON RIDING SHOTGUN*: "Braden delivers an expertly paced plot brimming with magic, gale-force fight scenes, and delicious romance. This character will get under the reader's skin, muscle, and bone."
—Hunter J. Skye, Author of the award-winning Hell Gate Series

On *METTLE AND MAGIC*: "This series has been building and building, and the crescendo was absolutely fabulous."
—HookedByThatBook.com

On *COURTING DARKNESS*: "This book was a fantastic second installment to the Magicsmith series. . . . Truly brilliant writing!"
—Richelle Rodarte, NetGalley Reviewer

On *FAERIE FORGED*: ". . . Well-written, engaging, and entertaining. The plot was engrossing, fascinating, and action-filled."
—Pam Guynn, NetGalley Reviewer

Other Titles

by L. R. Braden

The Magicsmith Series

A Drop of Magic, Book 1
Courting Darkness, Book 2
Faerie Forged, Book 3
Casting Shadows, Book 4
Of Mettle and Magic, Book 5
Chaos Song, Book 6
Lies and Illusion, Book 7

The Rifter Series

(set in the Magicsmith Universe)

Demon Riding Shotgun, Book 1
Personal Demons, Book 2
A Demon Faerie Tale, Book 3
Dancing with a Demon, Book 4

Demon Riding Shotgun

The Rifter Series – Book 1

by

L. R. Braden

Magical Realms Press

Magical Realms Press
PO BOX 24
Broomfield, CO 80038

Print ISBN: 978-1-968414-15-3
Ebook ISBN: 978-1-968414-14-6

Published in the United States of America.

Previously published by BelleBooks.

We love to hear from readers!
Contact us at:
MagicalRealmsPress.com
LRBraden.com

Cover design: Debra Dixon
Interior design: Hank Smith/Jim Brown
Photo/Art credits:
Background (Manipulated) © 2009 Susan McKivergan
Woman (Manipulated) © Zegers06 | Dreamstime.com

For David

Thank you for being my partner in every conceivable way.

Chapter 1

Mira

MIRA SHIFTED to keep her legs from going numb and scratched the head of a white cat who'd come to investigate her hiding spot in the bushes at the edge of the construction site. There was a chunk missing from the cat's ear, and one of its front paws was black up to the elbow, as though it had stepped in ink.

<The night's half over. Are you sure this is the right target?> The tinny voice filled Mira's head like an off-key echo of her own.

"It's hit two soup kitchens, a homeless shelter, and a women's rescue." Mira's words drifted into the cold night on a cloud of condensed breath. "This is the next closest place that fits the bill."

Mira rubbed her eyes, blinked, and shifted her tired focus back to the area in front of the homeless shelter—although homeless *resort* might have been a better description. Cafeteria, business center, gym . . . she'd never seen a shelter with so many luxuries. Certainly not in any of the places she'd slept.

<It could've hit that soup kitchen over on Oliver. That was about the same distance from the last attack.>

"And hosted in a church. Most demons avoid those like the plague."

The voice made a soft chuffing sound. <*Most* demons are idiots. Holy ground is no different than anywhere else on the corporeal plane, and priests are just men with titles.>

The cat suddenly went stiff under Mira's hand. It crouched until its belly brushed bare dirt, looked at the area framed by the shelter and the pink insulation board walls of the unfinished building next door, and hissed.

The crescent moon cast only a weak silver light, but Mira had no difficulty spotting the man shuffling along the road toward the shelter with a heavy, uneven gait. He passed beneath the glow of a streetlamp. Mira smiled. Unlike other paranaturals, demons dwelled in the Rift—the chaotic energy that connected all the Realms. They couldn't manifest without a physical body to anchor them. That's where rifters—demon-possessed humans—came in. But such unions usually took quite a toll on the host, and the marks weren't easy to hide.

<Sunglasses at night? Could he be any more obvious?>

He could not *wear the glasses.* Mira responded in the privacy of her thoughts to keep her voice from carrying.

<Well, yeah. I guess there's that.>

The presence inside Mira coiled with anticipation as the rifter moved closer to their ambush point.

Mira shifted her weight to the balls of her feet and checked to make sure none of her muscles had stiffened during her long wait crouched in the shadows. Damp dirt clung to her dark jeans.

She gave the cat one last pat on the head and whispered, "You wait here. This could get messy."

<*Pfft.* He doesn't look like much. That body's nearly done for.>

Don't let your guard down.

The man continued his single-minded march toward the shelter.

Mira took a deep breath. The moment she started drawing energy for her magic, the demon riding that body would know.

The man stepped into the road, preparing to cross. Then he paused. His gaze swept away from the homeless shelter toward her hiding spot.

She tensed.

<Wait.>

The rifter's gaze continued past Mira's patch of shadows to the building on her other side. When he started walking again, his destination had changed.

Grinding her teeth, Mira crept along the wall of the shelter until she could see the front of the unfinished building. A man in faded jeans, a blue plaid shirt, and a bright-orange vest stood in the wood-framed hole destined to become the building's front door. Silvery gray hair ringed the bottom of a hard hat that matched the orange vest. A Santa-worthy beard covered the bottom half of his face.

"*Ay, coño,*" Mira hissed. *The whole point of this ambush was to avoid casualties.*

<Wrong place, wrong time. Sucks to be him, but there's nothing we can do about it now.>

The construction worker turned and vanished through the doorway.

Mira frowned. *What's he even doing here so late?*

<Other than totally screwing up our plan?>

The rifter followed his new target into the building.

Mira darted across the open space between the buildings and crouched under a glassless window opening. Voices drifted out.

". . . area is claimed. You're drawing too much attention."

"There's plenty to go around."

They're . . . talking?

Mira rolled her eyes. Or rather, the demon riding shotgun in her soul did.

<We *can* speak, you know. Well . . . most of us.>

Since when do rifters stop to chat with their victims? Besides, it seems like that old guy is leading the conversation. Mira peeked over the lip of the wooden frame. The construction worker had his arms crossed over his Day-Glo vest. His face was twisted into an unhappy scowl that created deep creases in the skin around his eyes, but his flesh seemed intact—no signs of puppet strain, as Mira called the marks usually created by demon possession. *Could he be a rifter, too?*

<If he is, he's hiding deep.>

Or balanced.

<Don't get your hopes up. What we have is *not* normal.>

But not impossible. She bit her lip. *If there's another pairing like ours . . .*

"This is your only warning." The construction worker uncrossed his arms and widened his stance, planting his feet. "We won't let you upset our plans. Find somewhere else to gorge and die."

This guy definitely knows what he's facing. And did he say "we"?

The rifter sneered, his upper lip rising just enough to reveal grayish teeth and black gums. "Make me."

The rifter Mira had come to kill launched forward, striking the construction worker in the chest. The second man took the impact, leaning forward slightly to keep his feet as they slid a few inches across sawdust-covered plywood.

<Definitely not human.>

Whatever he is, I want to talk to him. Mira vaulted the window frame, calling her magic. She landed in a crouch, one knee touching down in sawdust. Both men turned to look at her. Energy swirled through her, pulled from the air and focused, with the help of her hitchhiker, into a glowing ball on her palm. Tendrils of blue static cracked around a white center. The presence that was always with her but not quite a part of her swelled.

Picturing the result she wanted, Mira flicked her wrist and exerted her will. An arc of pale lightning connected her to the rifter she'd tracked, resting for a moment against his chest before he was blown off his feet.

Two-by-fours splintered as he made a new opening in the skeletal frame of an interior wall.

Mira didn't rise from her crouch but pivoted to face the second man. Maybe another rifter. Maybe a practitioner. Maybe someone like her. . . . "Who are you?"

The man's gaze shifted between Mira and the broken wall. He pursed his lips. Then he stepped through the doorway behind him that led deeper into the building.

The downed rifter sat up amid snapped beams and a cloud of dust.

She'd come to end him—she needed to end him—but what she'd overheard from the mysterious construction worker had raised more than a few questions, and Mira wanted answers.

Racing past the stunned rifter, she darted after the second man.

He was on the far side of the room, passing into the next.

Mira charged up another bolt of energy as she ran—strong enough to knock him down but not enough to permanently injure him if he turned out to be mortal.

"Wait," she shouted. "I want to talk to you."

She launched herself through the next doorway, hand raised to throw her charged bolt.

The construction worker was only halfway across the room this time, facing her. His gaze met hers The metallic bronze of his eyes sent a shiver down her spine. A dark shape clung to the man's body, draping him like a liquid shadow.

Before she could release her energy, an invisible wall slammed into her, throwing her back through the opening. She connected with something that offered a moment of resistance, then hit the ground in a tangle of limbs as she and the recovered rifter rolled together across the floor.

She tried to break away, but the rifter pulled her down. His glasses had come off during their tumble. Jagged fissures radiated from his eyes, cracking his skin like dirt in a desert, and in the depths of those wounds flowed lines of radiant darkness like the cooling trails of a lava flow. The hands that clutched at her bore a similar texture—skin flaking around the fingernails, inky veins snaking just beneath the surface.

Mira elbowed the rifter in the teeth, knocking him back hard enough to crack his head against the floor. She twisted to follow up with a cross jab, but the rifter's foot found her gut with a painful shove.

Mira grunted as she rolled backward, but the shot had given her enough distance to glance into the other room.

The construction worker was gone.

Mira clenched her fists. She wanted to go after him, but he had magic and a head start. Her chances of catching up to him at this point were next to nothing, and she still had her original target to deal with. If she didn't finish this rifter, more people would die before she tracked him down again. She didn't need any more deaths on her conscience.

Growling like an angry bear, Mira opened herself fully to the flow of energy around her. A pale glow coated her skin, encasing her like a suit of ethereal armor. The constant presence in her mind swelled along with the energy, growing stronger, more dominant. A gnawing hunger filled her.

I want to question him, she warned.

<Then let's get him in a talking mood.>

Power surged through Mira's body as she closed on the rifter. The first punch she landed cracked his jaw.

The rifter's response was a roundhouse aimed at the side of her head.

She managed to block, but the impact sent knives of pain through her arm. She wasn't the only one with a demon amplifying her strength.

The rifter's tongue slithered along his upper lip, licking at the new split Mira had put in his skin. "I'm gonna eat you up."

Mira had seen the crime-scene photos of this freak's handiwork. He liked tearing people apart, but those victims had been human. Mira hadn't been human for a very long time. She planted her feet and waited for him to come at her.

She didn't have to wait long.

He snatched at the collar of her black leather jacket. She knocked his hand aside and snapped a quick jab at his nose. The two exchanged a flurry of blows, neither doing significant damage. Mira took an elbow in the face and a knee to her ribs. She returned an uppercut to the gut that lifted the rifter's feet off the floor. As they fought, the dark film clinging to the rifter grew thicker, more opaque, just as the swirling energy around Mira grew stronger.

Mira grabbed for the rifter's throat but was knocked aside. The rifter snatched at her wrist. Mira twisted free.

<Enough of this,> the demon snarled.

Heat poured into Mira's fists. Tendrils of flame licked over her fingers.

Are you crazy? Panic flared through Mira, along with the memory of her mother's eyes, wide and accusing. She flapped her hands until the flames vanished. *You'll burn this whole building down.*

The rifter's fist connected with Mira's cheek while her guard was down, and she stumbled back into the metal frame of a scaffold. A hammer clattered to the plywood floor. There was a familiar hiss. The white cat who'd found her in the bushes earlier was crouched beneath the scaffolding, hair raised like the bristles of a toilet brush.

The rifter grabbed one side of the scaffold. His arms strained. The frame tipped. The materials on top shifted and started to slide.

Mira tensed, preparing to jump clear of the collapse, but the cat was still crouched, eyes wide, fur up, claws dug into the plywood subfloor at the base of the scaffold.

With a noise somewhere between a grunt and a curse, Mira changed directions.

She dropped over the cat like a net and stiffened the energy above her into a hardened dome.

The poles of the scaffold bucked and bent. Boards snapped. Sheets of drywall waiting to be hung crushed and crumbled around her. Beneath her, the cat clawed and slashed in a panic to get away, but Mira held on tight, wincing as burning cuts opened on her face and arms. Protecting the fierce little maniac was like hugging a blender.

As soon as the scaffold and its contents settled, Mira sat up with a gasp, shaking debris off her back. Freed, the cat sprang to the nearest windowsill and vanished.

Mira pushed to her feet.

"Ungrateful little—" The splintered end of a two-by-four slammed into her upper arm, smashing her into the wall. She bounced with the impact, cratering a piece of freshly mounted drywall. The two-by-four swung back for a second strike, but this time she got her arm up to block.

She took the impact and grabbed the board with her left hand, holding it in place. With her right hand, she created a gravity sink that brought a section of ceiling down on the rifter's head. Beams split. Planks splintered. Drywall dust sifted down like powdered sugar, turning the room into a snow globe of suffocating particles.

<I thought we were trying *not* to bring the building down.> The demon's voice rolled through her with a chuckle.

Ignoring the gibe, Mira stepped toward the rifter. His lower half was trapped beneath the collapsed ceiling.

He twisted and pushed, but Mira had her fingers around his throat before he could wiggle free.

"Who was that man you were talking to?"

"Go to hell." He spat a glob of blackish goop into her face.

She wiped it on her forearm and tightened her grip. At the same time, she sent a trickle of magic into her fingers. The skin on the rifter's neck began to blister.

"What plan was he—"

<We're out of time.>

Mira tipped her head to the side, finally processing the noises at the edge of her awareness. Sirens blared in the distance. Closer, voices argued. People had taken notice of the commotion, called the cops. Would they work up the nerve to investigate before the police arrived?

Mira clenched her jaw. The last thing she needed was some curious rubbernecker taking her picture.

She shook her head. *Finish it.*

<With pleasure.>

The energy in her swelled once more, and Mira felt herself shrinking, settling into the passenger seat as hunger and instinct took the place of thought and reason. The cuts the cat had given her sealed. The aches in her body subsided. She took a deep breath and felt as if she'd just woken from a long and pleasant nap.

Ribbons of white, black, and gold surged around Mira's body like a whirlpool. The inky darkness clinging to the rifter shrank back, but there was nowhere to hide now. The rifter screamed as threads of the demon possessing him were siphoned off, pulled into the vortex. Most of the darkness was drawn up to the point where Mira's fingers were wrapped around the man's throat, but some wisps of shadow snapped and faded to nothing.

A face, stretched and strained, emerged in that darkness to overshadow the man's features.

"Traitor." The voice sounded like a million clawed feet scrabbling against stone.

Then the face was caught in the current and became just another black ribbon coiling around Mira's arm.

The man's skin sank and shriveled as the possessing demon's tendrils drew every drop of energy from the shell of its mortal host as it was ripped free. For a split second, the rifter's copper gaze cleared to reveal the murky green of pure, terrified, human eyes. A choked gurgle bubbled past Mira's grip as the man—no longer a rifter—died.

She opened her hand and let the corpse fall.

Have a little care, Mira snapped. She wished she could feel sick or sad about the man at her feet whose leathery skin now clung to his bones like an excavated mummy's, but the familiar rush of power and pleasure that followed a feeding had already taken root.

She straightened, stretched, and smiled.

We need to get out of here.

"Right, right," the demon spoke aloud with a purr Mira was certain wasn't present in her normal speech.

Now.

"Should we take the body?"

Mira glanced down, but she wasn't sure if that had been her impulse or her demon's. Their usual routine was to find a secluded area to dispose of their victims by magical means, but the sirens were closer now and there were definitely more voices.

No time.

She shrugged and sauntered toward the empty window frame where the cat had disappeared. Shapes moved in the darkness of the night, mostly crowded near the front end of the homeless shelter.

Wiggling her fingers Mira grabbed hold of a shadow and pulled it around her like a cape. Then she slipped out the back door through which the construction worker had fled and walked away from the scene of her latest crime.

Chapter 2

Mira

TWO POLICE CARS raced past her a block from the homeless shelter.

"What shall we do to unwind?" Her hitchhiker practically skipped as she walked, reveling in the euphoria of her recent feeding. Energy pulsed through her veins, making her body sing.

There was that junkyard full of old cars, Mira offered. *No one would notice if we smashed a few.*

She paused, considering. "That was what, five miles east of here?" She shook her head. "We passed a tavern just to the south. Let's go there."

Mira cringed. A workout was the best way to bleed off the excess energy of a feeding—something they needed to do fairly quickly to get back in balance before Mira's body started showing the strain of a full possession—but while Mira preferred solo activities, her companion had a more social approach.

We did that last time.

"Not my fault there are more bars than junkyards." She continued along the sidewalk, shaking debris out of her hair and wiping her face to make herself more presentable. She even started to hum.

Can't we just go for a run?

"Maybe if you stopped pretending you *like* being a sulky, lonely wretch, you might actually enjoy these encounters."

We can't all be as codependent as you.

"Ouch. Just for that, I'm gonna find someone ugly."

Yeah, right. Remember that guy in Vegas you vetoed because he had a big nose? Or that fox in Arkansas you insisted smelled like olives?

"She *did* smell like olives. Your senses just aren't as good as mine."

We use the same nose.

"I use it better."

Whatever. Let's just get this over with.

Only a faded sign above the weathered red door distinguished the pub from the rest of the row houses on the block. The interior was dim and cramped, with tables lining one wall and a full bar dominating the other. Orange globes hung from the ceiling, casting a warm amber glow over the room that softened the scene like an aged photo.

A few couples sat together at tables, but Mira had no interest in them. One woman sat alone near the back, but the way her skin clung to her gaunt features spoke of addiction and desperation that Mira knew to steer clear of. A pale, middle-aged man in a business suit with a loosened tie sat at one end of the bar, already so deep in drink he could barely keep his head up. At the other end was a man in plaid flannel with wrinkled leather skin and wispy white hair. He cradled a frothy mug and stared at nothing. Between the two, separated on either side by empty stools, sat a man whose broad shoulders stretched the wool of his terracotta-colored coat. He had rich sepia skin highlighted orange by the hanging globes, short, black hair, and a well-trimmed goatee. The tattooed woman behind the bar filled a shot glass in front of him, but there was already a full one on the counter.

Not a lot of prospects in here.

<The one in the middle's not bad. Strong features. Big hands. Looks like he has stamina.>

He looks like he's about to jump off a bridge.

<Maybe because his drinking partner didn't show up. We shouldn't let the extra shot go to waste.>

Or maybe his girlfriend is right around the corner.

She shrugged. "No harm checking."

Mira let her awareness recede as her body moved forward on the demon's impulse—the equivalent of sticking her fingers in her ears and humming. She'd seen this play out often enough. She didn't need a front row seat to what came next.

Ty

TY SETTLED HIS weight on a cracked vinyl stool and called to Tina, the bartender of this hole-in-the-wall establishment he'd discovered his second week after moving to Baltimore. "Two shots of Jack."

Ty's cell phone buzzed, and he pulled it out to read a new text from Billy—an especially outgoing officer in his new department who seemed to have made it his personal mission to befriend Ty.

Didn't see you leave. Bunch of us heading to O'Sullivan's on Lafayette. Want to come?

Ty's gut clenched at the thought of joining his brothers in blue at the local cop bar. He pictured Billy's smiling face. Then the face morphed, growing wider and darker until his best friend grinned at him from his imagination.

Blinking to clear the image, he pushed the phone back in his pocket, leaving the text unanswered. He picked up one of the shot glasses Tina set in front of him and clinked it against the second. "Happy birthday, buddy."

He tossed the drink back, hissing at the burn that erupted at the back of his throat and seared its way through his chest and down to his stomach. Then he set the empty glass beside the full one and waved for a refill.

A gust of frigid air surged through the bar as the front door opened and closed.

Ty shivered, grabbed his topped-off glass, and brought it to his lips. He closed his eyes and savored the numbness seeping into him on a tide of amber liquid. He sighed, opened his eyes, and set the glass down. The shot he'd left untouched on the counter plunked down beside his, equally empty.

"It's not good to drink alone."

Ty stared at the empty shot glass he'd never intended to touch. His jaw tightened. He followed the dainty fingers wrapped around the glass along the black leather sleeve of a motorcycle jacket, over a silver chain that dipped below the V-neck collar of a tight red shirt, to the face of the woman beside him, and swallowed the words he'd intended to say. She stood at maybe five foot two, coming barely up to his shoulder. Her smooth skin was tawny beige, accentuated by dark, glossy lips. Her eyes shone like the burnished gold of a sunrise framed by long lashes. Wild brown waves fell to her jawline with a wide streak of pure white on one side.

He licked his lips and gave himself a mental shake. "That drink wasn't meant for you."

The woman did a slow scan of the bar's other occupants. "I don't see any other takers."

Ty followed her gaze around the room. A few couples. Mostly single drinkers, like him, looking to drown their sorrows. But this woman was different. Vibrant. Energy rolled off her, infectious, intoxicating. Just looking at her made Ty want to sit up straighter, and his back wasn't the only part of him stiffening.

He shook his head again and shifted his focus to the empty glass in his hand.

"You prefer to be alone?"

The words stung. He didn't *want* to be alone. He *wanted* to be celebrating with—"I prefer to avoid complications."

"Then you're in luck." The woman slid onto the stool beside him, brushing against him in the process. "I'm the opposite of complicated." A strange expression flashed across her face—like she was about to laugh, then suddenly annoyed—but her features smoothed so quickly he might have imagined the change. "No games. No strings. I'm just looking for a little company to help me unwind. You seem like you could use the same." Her golden gaze swept over him in slow assessment.

He shivered as cold guilt warred with the heat of his body's reaction. He'd intended to reflect on what he'd lost and find oblivion at the bottom of a glass. Did it matter if he found it instead in the arms of a stranger?

"If you're not interested,"—the woman took a deep breath that strained the fabric across her breasts—"I'll leave you to your wallowing."

She began to rise, but Ty's hand flashed out and grabbed her wrist, stilling her. He looked down at the connection, noticing a scuff of dusty white on the black leather just above his grip, then returned to the golden orbs that never wavered from his face.

"No strings?" His voice was rough and lower than usual. Hopefully she'd attribute the change to lust rather than any deeper emotion.

She smiled. "One night, no strings, and you'll never see me again."

He released her wrist. "Let me buy you another drink."

Ty

THE DOOR TO Ty's apartment thumped against the wall of his narrow entryway as he and the woman who'd accompanied him home stumbled inside, lips locked together. They'd downed three more rounds before stumbling out of the bar, during which Ty had learned next to nothing about his companion—not even her name. Though truth be told, he hadn't tried very hard. A nameless, no-strings encounter was just what the doctor ordered to take his mind off his troubles.

They twisted through the doorway, and her hip bumped the small table just inside. Ty pulled back enough to swing the door closed and throw the deadbolt.

"Very . . . clean." The woman was looking at the kitchen and living room, both visible from the entryway. There were no pictures on the walls. No knickknacks on the shelves. Just a bowl of fruit on the gleaming island, a single leather recliner, and the blank screen of the television.

"I just moved in." Six months might be a little more than *just*, but that answer seemed easier than explaining his aversion to clutter.

"A loner who avoids complications and keeps a tidy house." She quirked her lips in a not-quite smile. "I've got a friend you should meet."

She laughed—though Ty didn't get the joke. The laughter rolled through her body and into his where they were pressed together.

Dropping his keys in the ceramic tray by the door, he pulled her through the stark emptiness of his home to the apartment's single bedroom. She stepped out of her sneakers, grabbed the collar of his coat, and used it to guide his mouth to hers, where she explored him with her tongue. Then she slipped the fabric off his shoulders. His coat fell to the floor.

"One second," Ty gasped.

She stared into his eyes from inches away, her breath puffing in warm, moist bursts against his face. "You want me to stop?"

He shook his head but stepped back to pull the Glock 22 out of his holster and lock it away in the small safe beside his bed. He also tucked his wallet and shield in there for good measure.

"You're a cop?" The laughter was back in her voice.

He stepped close, sliding a hand around her waist to feel that rolling vibration against him again. "That a problem?"

She pressed her thigh between his legs and pulled out the hem of his shirt. "Not for me."

Her palms slid up his back and around to his chest. He tensed when her fingertips brushed the thick scars on his side, but she didn't hesitate. His heart raced. Heat engulfed him. He lifted his arms so she could tug the blue fabric over his head. Her coat joined his on the floor, and he copied her movements to slip her clingy red shirt up and off.

He pressed a kiss to the edge of her jaw. Her pulse raced beneath his lips, and his own quickened in response. He followed that rapid flutter down the side of her neck, over her collarbone, to the swell of one satin-clad breast.

The woman reached behind her, and her bra fell away.

Ty trailed a hand along the silver chain around her neck to a pendant nestled in the valley of her cleavage. A saint medallion, though not a saint he recognized. Questions about the woman in his arms sprang to mind, but he pushed them aside. She was beautiful and soft, warm and inviting. He didn't need to know more than that.

Ignoring the watchful eyes of the saint, Ty braced his partner's arched back and slid his hand down the tight plane of her abdomen until he reached the button and zipper that kept him from what he wanted. A second later he found the warm, wet welcome he was looking for.

The woman twitched as he moved his fingers, and a small moan escaped. She tossed her head from side to side, waves of hair spilling over her face. When she met his gaze again, her golden eyes glowed with a feverish intensity. She bared her teeth in a snarl and dragged her fingers over his chest and down to the belt that trapped him.

Tearing the leather off his waist, she had his pants and hers in matching piles on the floor before he could blink. Then she gripped his upper arms, fingers digging into his biceps, and pulled him onto the bed.

Ty supported himself on one arm as he found where he fit, though the woman clung to him as if daring him to crush her. Their bodies moved in unison, finding a rhythm and upping the tempo until his breath came in ragged gasps and sweat slicked his body. The woman panted, clawing at his shoulders and back.

He tensed, grunted, and found the quivering release he hadn't shared in more months than he cared to count.

As the tension left his body and his muscles grew slack, so too did the weight of guilt and the pain of memory he'd been drowning in all day. A heady euphoria filled him. Far from being tired from his exertion, he felt energized, as though every nerve in his body was charged and singing for more.

He relaxed his grip on the curve of his companion's knee and let his hand slide up her leg but paused when his palm encountered an odd texture—a series of parallel scars like ladder rungs on her thigh. The investigator in him perked up, but he moved his hand to her hip and safer ground. He smiled down at her, entranced by the golden light that danced in her eyes. "That was . . ." He shook his head, at a loss for words.

She rolled him over, straddling his hips. "Oh, we're not done yet."

Chapter 3

Ty

TY STARTLED awake to the synthesized imitation of a classic ringtone. He groaned, rolled over, and reached for the nightstand where his cell phone should have been. He found only the disconnected charger cord. Wiping grit from his eyes, he blinked sandpaper eyelids and looked around. The room was dark. He clicked on the bedside lamp.

The ring persisted, coming from the floor past the foot of his bed.

He blinked again and looked at the rumpled covers beside him. He frowned. Where was the girl?

The cell phone ceased its noise, then immediately started up again.

Ty rose, dug in the pocket of his discarded pants, and answered the call. "Ty Williams."

"This is Detective LaRosa. Sorry to wake you, but I need you to meet me on scene for a case I just caught."

He glanced at the bedside clock and frowned. He couldn't have been asleep for more than a few minutes, but he felt surprisingly well rested. He looked around the empty room again, then peeked in the bathroom. No sign of his guest. He rubbed a hand over his face. "Address?"

Ty jotted down the location on a notepad.

"I'll be right there." He disconnected the call and did a quick search of the rest of his apartment. Other than the clothes littering his floor, nothing was out of place. He dumped them in the laundry basket, pulled on a fresh set, and headed to the bathroom for the fastest grooming he could manage.

As he splashed water in his face and brushed his teeth, he considered how strange it was to sleep with a stranger and wake up alone—as though the whole encounter was a dream. He must have dozed off after their marathon of lovemaking, but he didn't remember getting tired. In fact, he felt invigorated. And he was normally a light sleeper; he should have noticed her leaving.

He gargled some water and spit into the sink.

One night, no strings, and you'll never see me again.

He stared into the dark gaze of the man in the mirror. "No complications, exactly like she promised."

He ran a hand over the scruff on his scalp, retrieved his gun and badge from the safe, and headed for the crime scene.

Pale dawn bloomed on the horizon, blue pushing back the black of night, as Ty approached the homeless shelter LaRosa had told him to look for. A pair of uniformed officers bustled around a framed and insulated apartment building marked off with police tape while another spoke with a rail-thin woman with lank, brown hair and a tattered gray jacket that hung to her knees. The woman gestured toward the unfinished building with one hand as she conveyed her story, and the officer dutifully took notes.

LaRosa stood near the police-tape barrier that marked the scene, sipping from a paper cup. Her dark braid and thigh-length, navy-blue coat blended with the night, but her golden skin picked up the yellow highlights of the lamps and headlights illuminating the area. Dark circles shaded her eyes, but the tight line of her mouth spoke more of irritation than exhaustion. She straightened when she spotted Ty.

"What've we got?" He ducked under the police line.

"A slew of witnesses from this homeless shelter who say they heard crashing noises and saw plumes of dust coming from that building." She pointed to the incomplete apartment.

A shiver raced down Ty's spine as he looked again at the building. A slight tremble shook his hands, and a tingling numbness spread through his fingers.

"First officers on the scene found one corpse inside, half buried in rubble from a collapsed ceiling. There are signs of a struggle, but no one saw . . ."

LaRosa's voice faded into the background as a high-pitched ringing filled Ty's ears. The moisture left his mouth, replaced by the suffocating desiccation of drywall dust.

"Hey." Fingers snapped an inch from Ty's nose, bringing his attention back to LaRosa. "You listening?"

Ty swallowed the dry lump in his throat and nodded.

"We've collected all the evidence and are working on the witness statements, but you need to take a look before we move the body."

Ty frowned. LaRosa was a seasoned detective with her eye on a captain's chair. She didn't need hand-holding and wasn't one for sharing glory, especially with an upstart transfer like him. "Sounds like you've got everything under control. Why'd you call me?"

"Just take a look." She motioned toward the nearest entrance. "We'll talk when you come out."

Ty walked slowly, stiffly. His boots skimmed the raw dirt, dragging trails. His jaw was so tight he felt like his teeth might crack, but that tension was nothing compared to the pressure building in his chest.

LaRosa hadn't just contacted the next detective on the duty roster, she'd called *him*. The only thing that set him apart from the other detectives was his background with the Paranatural Task Force—the organization responsible for investigating incidents involving fae, practitioners, and all those things that went bump in the night. A background he'd done everything he could to get away from.

As if walking into an unstable building wasn't nightmare enough.

There was no door, just an opening of framed wood. The windows were equally absent, but dawn's weak light couldn't penetrate the interior, so a portable floodlight had been set up to illuminate the scene.

Ty froze on the threshold.

White dust coated everything. Small yellow tags with bold black numbers dotted the room. One beside a spatter of blood. One next to a smudged shoe print. One marking an indent where something, or someone, had impacted drywall.

Ty stepped inside. His pulse shot up. Blood pounded in his ears.

"I can do this." He took a moment to steady his breathing, then centered his focus on the body in the middle of the room.

The man's lower section was buried by broken sheets of drywall, splintered beams, and chunks of plywood.

A sympathetic ache of searing heat and stabbing needles roared to life in Ty's leg and side.

"Old scars." He took a shaky breath. "Focus on the present."

One man. Pale. Gaunt. Mid-thirties.

The man's skin grew darker before Ty's eyes until it was a deep umber. His cheeks and jaw swelled to a familiar square structure. His nose flattened and spread. His lips thickened. Then the fogged eyes cleared, and Ty's best friend looked up at him.

"I can't breathe." The apparition's voice was ragged and airy, just as Jamal's had been as he choked on the blood seeping into his punctured lungs.

The room dimmed, the floodlight of the physical world no match for the darkness of Ty's memory. He wiped his hands against his pants but couldn't tear his gaze away from the specter before him to verify that the sticky moisture coating his palms wasn't blood. He took a deep breath that failed to ease the burning tightness in his lungs. There wasn't enough air.

The shadow of his friend lifted a hand. A phantom touch gripped Ty's arm. "Tell Jen—"

Tell her yourself. Ty barely kept himself from saying the words out loud. This conversation was old, a looping record.

Ty shook his head and slapped his palms against his face, relishing the sting. "Focus on the present. This isn't real." He repeated the mantra three more times, whispering the words lest any nearby officers overhear and come to witness his predicament. As he chanted, he reached in his pocket and found the small stone he carried there—a river rock worn smooth by years of erosion save a scratch on one side just wide enough to slide his thumbnail into. He clutched the stone and traced the familiar contour of that scratch, marking its length, width, and depth, cataloging every imperfection, just as his PTF supervisor had trained him.

Don't show your anchor to anyone. He imagined his CO strolling among the recruits, hands clasped behind his back, as they all fought to break free of the illusion he'd trapped them in. *The fact that it can't be recreated is why it works. If you focus on your anchor, you can find your way back to reality through even the strongest illusion.*

As he repeated the words and focused on the stone, light seeped into his vision, chasing away the shadows until the features of the man before him shrank back to reality and the specter of his lost friend was once more tucked away in Ty's subconscious.

Maybe not the situation he'd envisioned all those years ago during PTF training, but what worked against fae illusions worked against flashbacks and bad dreams as well, though the technique was far from a sure bet in either case.

Once he was sure he was seeing what was really in front of him, Ty crouched to get a better look at the victim. A ring of blisters wrapped the front of his throat in the shape of a hand—a small hand with thin fingers. He sniffed the air. Beneath the pervasive dust was a faint electrical odor, like ozone after a lightning strike. There were cuts surrounding the victim's eyes, like fractures radiating from a point of impact, and the skin around his fingernails was peeled back and blackened.

Ty pulled on a latex glove and lifted the victim's upper lip. His teeth were gray and cracked. Either this guy had the worst dental hygiene in the world, or he'd been rotting before he died.

He took one last look around the room. Too much damage for just a weak roof or a single spell gone wrong. Definitely some kind of fight.

Something bumped his leg—a white cat with a single black paw.

Ty scratched its arched back as it rubbed against his boot. "Hey, buddy. You see what happened here last night?"

The cat purred. Then trotted outside.

"Yeah, I hear you." Ty straightened and moved with steady intent toward the door and the wide open world. Morning air filled his lungs, and he let it out with a sigh. He'd survived. He'd overcome his flashback. He'd even managed to gather the necessary data to confirm LaRosa's suspicions.

His steps grew lighter and faster as he moved farther from the building until he was once more standing in front of LaRosa. He peeled off the glove he'd used to check the victim's teeth, holding it inside out to prevent contamination. "There was definitely magic involved."

"Figured as much." She tipped her face toward the lightening sky. "Looks like we'll be partnering up on this one."

Ty shook his head. "Magic's outside our jurisdiction. Kick it over to the PTF."

"The Paranatural Task Force has their hands full thanks to that necromancer shit show in D.C. 'No agents available.'" She made air quotes with her fingers. "So, Captain gave me you."

Ty rubbed the headache trying to take hold just above his eyes. Having resigned months ago, he hadn't been present for the sorcerers' rebellion or their subsequent march on the U.S. capitol, but he knew plenty of men and women who would've been. At least he hadn't had to watch them die.

"I don't work magic cases anymore."

LaRosa lowered her gaze and crossed her arms. "That's not up to you. I'm point on this case, and I'll use whatever resources I have at my disposal. Right now, that's you. Got a problem with that, take it up with the captain."

Ty bunched the crumpled glove in his fist.

LaRosa held his gaze.

A car door slammed, making both detectives flinch.

Ty used the distraction to turn and walk away. He tossed the dirty glove into a blue, plastic trash bin at the edge of the construction area, climbed into his silver Ford Super Duty pickup, and headed for the station.

Chapter 4

Mira

MIRA PARKED HER Ducati Scrambler beside a blue-and-white plumber's van at the edge of the Walmart parking lot. At least, it *looked* like a blue-and-white plumber's van. Anyone who really knew their vehicles might notice this one was a little longer than the standard cargo van it was pretending to be, but most people wouldn't give it a second glance.

Stepping around to the back, she reached carefully for the handle she could see, making sure her fingers connected with the real latch hidden beneath. Then she fed a little magic into the lock and pulled open the retrofitted barn door on the back of the truck. The door of the plumber's van moved with its real world counterpart to maintain the illusion for anyone who might be watching, and Mira slipped inside.

"Home sweet home," Mira said as she hung her black leather jacket on a small hook bolted to the wall. The sides of the renovated U-Haul that served as her base of operations and sometimes mobile home were lined with shelves and cabinets, all bolted in place to keep from shifting like the furnishings in the captain's cabin of an ancient ship.

Moving through the narrow central space, she knelt beside a cupboard, pulled out a can of Cafe La Llave ground coffee, popped the lid, and inhaled deeply, savoring the scent.

She spooned the aromatic grounds into the filter of a small espresso pot, took one last whiff, and put the can away. Then she filled the bottom of the pot from a half-full jug of water. She pulled a small propane stove out of its cubby, turned on the gas, and set the espresso pot on to boil while she stripped out of her dirty clothes. Within seconds, the truck was filled with the bold smell of coffee.

<That guy from the bar reminded me of you.>

"Don't want to hear about it." Mira dropped her shirt in the laundry bin hidden under a flip-up countertop.

<A brooding loner with an unnaturally tidy apartment.>

Mira tugged off her pants and socks.

<A beautiful body housing a damaged soul. Did you notice the scars on his leg and side while you were *not* watching? Clearly a troubled past.>

"He's a cop. I imagine it's an occupational hazard."

<And limber . . . very limber.>

Mira popped open a can of evaporated milk, poured some in a small sauce pan, and swapped it for the coffee.

<You can't honestly tell me you're not even *a little* interested in the details.>

"Your exploits are none of my business."

<I thought humans were supposed to be all need and hormones. How did I end up in the only body that doesn't care to be touched?>

"This body gets touched plenty."

<But *you* don't.>

A lump caught in Mira's throat. "I don't need that kind of complication."

<Like the guy at the bar. Didn't stop him from having a good time though.>

A very good time, if the looseness in Mira's joints was any indication.

She shook her head and stirred sugar into half a mug of coffee, then poured in warm milk to it top off. "Just let me enjoy my café con leche."

The demon was silent for a moment. Then, just as Mira brought the first sip to her lips, she said, <I bet you peeked.>

Mira spluttered. Her cheeks warmed. She'd done her best to remain distant while the demon burned off the excess energy from last night's feeding, but it was impossible not to notice *some* things when they were happening to their shared body. And Mira might have snuck a peek or two.

The demon chuckled.

Mira took another drink, then set the steaming mug on the counter and opened a drawer.

The demon sighed, if such a sound could exist without breath.

Mira pulled out the X-Acto blade she kept in the drawer, along with two butterfly bandages and a pad of gauze.

<Why must we go through this every time?> All the levity had drained from the demon's voice.

"You have your rituals. I have mine."

<He was a rifter. We saved lives by ending him.>

"He was also a person, and we killed him." Mira lowered the blade to her thigh, measuring out the distance from the bottom scar. "Remember, don't heal it."

<I won't interfere with your perverse penance.>

The knife pierced Mira's flesh. She inhaled sharply, then dragged a steady line, splitting her skin. As she cut she recited, "Hail Mary, full of grace. Blessed art thou, and blessed is the fruit of thy womb. Pray for us poor sinners, now and at the hour of our death."

She lifted the knife. Blood welled along the line, marking the newest addition to her death toll. She wiped at the drips, sealed the gap with the two butterfly bandages, and pressed the gauze to her leg until the trickle of blood stopped. Then she raised the medallion that rested against her chest and brought it to her lips. "Saint Jude, faithful friend to Jesus, I hail thee now in glory. Grant help to the despairing when hopeless seems the task. Be ever by my side that I need not face my troubles alone." She kissed the image of the saint. "Amen."

<Why continue with these prayers? Nothing ever comes of them.>

"They brought me you."

<*I* came to you. There were no gods, virgins, or saints involved.>

"So you say. But to find me in all the chaos of the Rift—an endless expanse that fills and overlaps all the Realms—at exactly my moment of need?" Mira shrugged.

<Whatever.>

She pulled on a fresh pair of jeans and a bright-pink sweatshirt decorated with white and yellow flowers, then opened the door to the under-counter refrigerator. She found a jar of dill pickles, half a loaf of bread, a quarter stick of butter, and a container of peanut butter with only dregs clinging to the sides.

Pursing her lips, she grabbed the bread and butter and heated a slice over the stove. While the butter was melting, she pulled out the futon folded into the shelf above the cab and set it, still folded, in the aisle so she had a comfortable place to sit.

She settled down, sipped her coffee, nibbled her toast, and let her head rest against the metal wall that separated the truck back from the cab.

"That second rifter last night"—she rolled her head from side to side—"he wasn't normal."

<He might have been possessed by a slightly stronger demon, one with a sense of patience. That doesn't make him like us.>

"He talked about a plan." She cradled her coffee cup between her palms. "Demons sow chaos. They burn, and destroy, and kill. Sometimes they stick around long enough to sink a company and spread financial ruin, but long-term plans? Defending a territory? That goes against everything it means to be a demon. And the idea that he was trying to *stop* another rifter from killing . . ."

<Killing *there* anyway.>

"Exactly. He said the area was 'claimed,' which makes it sounds like he's been here for a while and intends to stay."

<Definitely not standard rifter behavior.>

"Even we don't linger long in one place. Speaking of which . . ."

<I thought you'd want to stick around a while, find out what was so weird about that rifter.>

"I do, but after leaving that body in the open . . ." Mira took a bite of toast. *We should move before anyone takes notice of us.* She swallowed. "But we've never seen behavior like that in any of the rifters we've faced."

<There was that necromancer who led the raid on D.C. He certainly had a plan.>

Mira stiffened. "You think we could be dealing with another necromancer?"

<No, but maybe an ameeri-level demon, like me. Maybe even a sovereign.>

"Hmm." Mira stared into the bottom of her mug.

<A strong demon does *not* mean a balanced partnership.>

"I know, I know. I just . . . Isn't it *possible?*" She looked up at the textured metal ceiling. "Surely we can't be the only one?"

<We certainly can be.>

"So you're in favor of skipping town?"

<I didn't say that. I'm all for hunting that rifter down. I just don't want you to get your hopes up . . . or hesitate at a crucial moment.>

Mira set her empty mug aside. "We should follow our normal routine—gone within twenty-four hours of dropping a body."

<If the rifter that got away *is* like us—>

"Which you keep pointing out isn't likely."

<—you need to know. You'll never stop wondering, so you might as well investigate before the trail goes cold.>

She hugged herself and rubbed her upper arms. The urge to find someone like her had consumed her during the early years of her possession—someone who could understand what she was going through, maybe even teach her to control the terrifying powers that made her so dangerous to be around. But after years of failing to find even a rumor of another balanced pairing, that desire had turned bitter. The hope she once felt was now a dark, empty hole . . . but she couldn't deny the treacherous flicker of light kindled by last night's rifter.

<Even if he isn't like us, he wasn't a common demon either. We don't want to leave someone like that running loose. So we'll either make a new friend or have a nice meal. Win, win.>

"That's not what that means." She sighed and ran a hand through her tangled waves, considering the threat a long-term rifter without her *somewhat* functional moral compass might pose, both to the city and to the delicate truce between humans and paranaturals. It wasn't until the Faerie Wars a decade ago that most humans even became aware of the many magical beings who shared their world, including practitioners—human magic-users sometimes called witches or sorcerers, the fae—on whom the ancient myths of many cultures were based, and most recently werewolves and vampires, though the vampires still clung to their secrecy. And demons were in a league of their own. The PTF—the human agency established to monitor and control those magical beings who frequented the mortal realm—was an infant organization compared to what they were trying to deal with, and more often than not in over their heads. That's where people like Mira came in. Capable, discrete, and able to do what the bureaucrats couldn't . . . get shit done. It was thanks to people like her that the things hiding in the shadows of the world hadn't overrun the mortal realm while humans were still trying to convince themselves they were at the top of the food chain.

"We've still got half a day of our twenty-four hour window. I guess it wouldn't hurt to poke around."

Leaning forward, she opened another drawer and pulled out a battered laptop. The screen was cracked along the top edge and the cord was patched with electrical tape, but the machine still worked for what she needed . . . usually. She waited for the computer to boot up, then opened a browser using the unrestricted network from the nearby McDonald's that shared the Walmart parking lot. The battery icon in the lower corner blinked red despite the machine being plugged in. Mira glanced at the ceiling and cast a silent prayer that the power would hold out long enough for her search. With all the overcast winter days lately, the solar panels mounted to the roof of her truck were barely enough to keep the lights on and run the space heater that kept her from freezing in her sleep.

"The guy last night was wearing a construction vest, so let's see what company is building on that site."

She typed in the name of the homeless shelter that had been part of the development and hit enter. After digging past PR pages talking about the need for decent low-income housing, the rising numbers of the city's transient population, and testimonials from various politicians and community leaders, she found a page documenting the site's history. The project had originally belonged to a company called Doxon and Feyer, then passed over to KBU Construction after some kind of disagreement with the land developer.

She clicked the "contact us" button and pointed at the screen. "KBU Construction has a local office not far from here. What do you want to bet we find our mystery man there?"

Chapter 5

Ty

TY PUSHED THROUGH the station door, nodded to the desk sergeant, and headed for the CID office. A dozen desks sat in nose-to-nose pairs with narrow aisles between each set. Most were stacked with papers or folders. Some held potted plants, family photos, or other personal touches. Ty's gaze flicked to his own station, bare except for his computer and a tidy stack of files on one corner.

"We missed you last night." Billy, fresh-faced and impossibly young, stood with two other rookies near the coffee station set up at the far end of the shared space.

Ty continued his approach, eyes fixed on the captain's office behind them.

"We're meeting again tonight if you want to—"

Ty walked past the group and opened the captain's door without knocking. The captain glanced up from his phone call, furrowed his eyebrows, and waved Ty to enter.

Ty closed the door on Billy's faltering smile.

He stepped up to the captain's desk, directly behind the brass nameplate that read CAPTAIN W. HOLTZ in bold, broad letters. He planted his feet shoulder-width apart, clasped his hands behind his back, and lifted his chin.

The captain's burly frame filled the space behind the desk. He'd been a fighter in his youth, but now his sun-stained skin sagged along his cheeks and jaw, its elasticity stolen by age. He raised one finger and said into the phone, "I know, John. You said that last night."

There was a long pause. The muffled voices of Billy and his companions filtered through the office door, making it impossible to pick up anything from the other end of the captain's call.

"Yeah, you said that too." Captain Holtz sighed and ran a hand through his short, gray-streaked hair. The lines around his eyes crinkled. "All right. Just let me know when the situation changes." He set the phone back in its cradle and looked up at Ty. "Have a seat, Williams."

Ty did as instructed. "Sir, I need to talk to you about—"

"LaRosa's case." The captain leaned back in his worn leather chair. His broad shoulders overhung the armrests. "I figured as much. It was *my* call to bring you in, not hers."

"Sir, when I interviewed for this position I told you I had problems with magic, small spaces, and partners."

"And I said I'd do what I could to accommodate you so long as it didn't interfere with closing cases. This time it interferes."

"Yes sir, but—"

"When you applied to my department, I granted you full detective status because of your previous experience as an investigator with the PTF. Now you're asking me to disregard that same experience out of consideration for your personal comfort. You can't have it both ways. So either take your chances with LaRosa on a case involving magic or turn in your badge and kiss a career in local law enforcement goodbye."

Ty pressed his lips together and took several deep breaths through his nose.

The captain leaned forward, resting his elbows on the desk. "Look, it's not like I don't sympathize with your situation. Losing a partner is never easy, and being buried alive like that . . ." He shook his head. "I understand your reluctance, but with the PTF on lockdown during this"— he waved a hand—"reorganization, they don't have the manpower to take on every case with a whiff of magic. We've got a few PTF-issued toys in the armory, but none of my detectives have experience dealing with magic-users. You were trained for special-ops against the fae in the war and then with the PTF after. You may not have magic of your own, but you understand how it works and you've seen it enough not to freeze when the laws of physics suddenly go out the window."

Ty recalled the way his brain started shutting down when LaRosa recounted the details at the crime scene that morning, then again when he was faced with the partially collapsed ceiling. He clenched his jaw. *Magic aside, I'm already freezing more than a rookie with first-day jitters.*

"Like it or not," the captain continued, "you're our best shot at getting this murderer off the street or finding enough evidence to call in the big guns. If that isn't reason enough for you to face your fears, maybe you're in the wrong line of work."

Ty imagined how it would feel to slam his badge on the desk. He didn't need this job, didn't need to face his fears. He had enough saved up to get by for a year or two, or he could always go home. His family would shelter him for as long as it took to find his feet. By then maybe the world would have changed. Maybe magic would be eradicated. At the very least, maybe he wouldn't have a panic attack every time he stepped into a small space or saw a dead body.

He closed his eyes, but there was no peace in the darkness.

We're gonna protect people. Jamal's grin flashed in Ty's memory. He wore the green fatigues of basic training. A pair of steel tags dangled around his neck. The purple shiner from his dad's last bender was finally starting to fade. *The strong should protect the weak, Ty, and you're strong. We both are.*

Jamal reached out, and a younger, more naive Ty took his hand.

Ty exhaled and opened his eyes. Duty was a weight chained to his heart. It was his fault Jamal wasn't around to help anymore. "I understand, sir."

Captain Holtz nodded.

Ty pushed stiffly to his feet. His mind spiraled with all the reasons taking this case was a bad idea, but every argument hit a brick wall and the persistent whisper, *He's gone because of you.*

"Williams."

Ty glanced back, his hand on the office door.

"Play nice with LaRosa."

Ty turned the knob and stepped into the detective area. His gaze snapped to LaRosa. She leaned against her desk, arms crossed, staring at the captain's door.

"Nice chat?" she asked.

He stalked across the room.

LaRosa straightened as he approached but didn't uncross her arms.

Ty stopped three feet away.

Out of the corner of his eye, Ty saw Billy elbow an officer with rust-orange hair and gesture in his direction.

The two detectives faced off in silence for one tense moment. Then Ty cleared his throat and said, "What's the play?"

LaRosa relaxed her stance. She grabbed a folder off her desk and slapped it against Ty's chest.

He grabbed it by reflex.

"Witness reports," she said by way of explanation. "Lots of speculation, but no one actually saw the crime or anyone fleeing the scene."

Ty flipped through the pages, skimming the text. All the reports were about the same. Sounds of a struggle. Maybe an explosion. No one had been curious enough to get closer with the threat of a building collapse. He couldn't blame them.

"There were dozens of footprints around the area, but only two sets in the most recent covering of dust that came down with the ceiling." She handed him another folder. "It seems our killer wore nine-inch sneakers. Techs are analyzing the tread pattern, but it's pretty generic."

"Did you ID the victim?"

"I've got a rookie running his prints through AFIS. In the meantime, I thought I'd pay a visit to the foreman of the construction site, see if anyone noticed our vic hanging around earlier in the day. Care to join me?"

He dropped the folders on the desk and motioned her to lead the way.

Ty settled in the passenger seat of LaRosa's black Dodge Charger and snapped his seat belt. "Where's the construction company?"

"Their main office is up in Wyndhurst."

"I'm still pretty new to this area."

LaRosa clicked her seat belt and started the car. "About twenty minutes north of here. Which means you've got time to fill me in on what kinds of magic could mummify a fresh corpse. Have you ever seen a victim like that before?"

"No."

"Care to speculate?"

Ty watched buildings slide past through the side window. "I can think of a half-dozen species of fae that might be able to do something like that."

"For example?"

"A water elemental could suck the liquid out of a body. That might make it shrivel like we saw. There was also charring, so maybe a fire fae. Succubi drain energy from their victims through arousal. I've heard that wraiths can absorb not only a person's physical essence but their soul. There's a sub-species of sidhe, the leannan, that will exchange magical inspiration for years of life. The yamachichi are known to drain people, but they're native to Japan, so we rarely see them here in America. We're still learning the limits of practitioner magic, since so much of their documentation is guarded by the Church, and I've got no idea what a demon-possessed rifter might be capable of."

"So basically . . . you haven't got a clue."

Ty glanced at LaRosa, then went back to staring out the window. *A clue, huh?* He moved his hand to trace a small, square box in his pocket—another holdover from his time with the PTF. "Maybe I can get one."

She glanced at him.

"Let's make a detour. There's something I need to check at the crime scene." Something he should have checked when the scene was fresh, but his fear had made him sloppy.

Ty

"WAIT HERE," Ty said as he climbed out of the car.

"Yeah right."

He scowled at LaRosa as she followed him to the unfinished apartment building. The last thing he needed was for her to witness one of his episodes, but the scene didn't look nearly as imposing as it had the night before. Yellow crime scene tape still marked the area, but the body had been removed and the room didn't feel nearly so confining in the light of day.

Reaching in his pocket, he pulled out the box of matches he carried with him out of habit.

"What are you doing?"

"Testing a theory."

He removed one match and struck it on the side of the box. It flared and went out, leaving a charred stick in its wake. Ty hissed and shook his stinging fingers. "That can't have burned for more than a second or two."

LaRosa crossed her arms and gave him an *Are you stupid?* look. "It's a match. That's what they do."

"The average time it takes one of these matches to burn all the way down is thirteen seconds."

"Fascinating," she said dryly. "And this matters, why?"

"The speed a match burns is an indicator of how much ambient energy exists in a place. Faster burn, less energy. The fae use their own, innate magic. They don't drain the land like this."

Now she perked up. "So we're looking for a practitioner."

"Maybe." Ty tipped his head toward the rubble where the dead man's corpse had been cleared away. "Our victim might have been the practitioner, which leaves the second person's nature open."

"Right back where we started."

Ty shrugged. "We've got another piece of the puzzle. That's not nothing."

LaRosa walked to the exit. "Let's get to KBU Construction, see if we can't find a few more pieces."

Chapter 6

Mira

MIRA'S SNEAKERS touched down on either side of her motorcycle. She looked through the tint of her visor at the plain, brick building in front of her. A wide, white sign with the red KBU logo in the center dominated a patch of dry brown grass ringed by sidewalks.

"This is the place." She cut the engine by using magic to twist the snapped-off key fused in the ignition—a modification she made to all her vehicles after too many instances of losing her keys. Before pulling off her helmet, she channeled a little extra energy.

<What are you doing?>

He saw us last night. No reason to put him on guard right away.

She slipped off the helmet and squinted into the bike's small side mirror. Her skin was several shades lighter. Her hair was straight and blond. "What do you think?"

<You look like you, but pale.>

Mira rolled her eyes. *Gimme a break, you know disguises aren't my strong suit.*

<How about . . . >

She felt another pull of energy, this one directed by the demon. In the mirror, her eyes turned fuchsia.

<That's better.>

You can't be serious.

<They're pretty.>

They're pink. She shook her head. "The point is to be *un*remarkable."

<Fine.> Another surge of magic and Mira's eyes returned to the warm brown of a dark ale.

Mira set her helmet on the gas tank, swung her leg over, and headed for the front door of the construction office.

A bell jingled on the glass door, and a man who resembled nothing so much as a pencil looked up—narrow cheeks, narrow jaw, close-set eyes, and a spindly frame. His close-cropped brown hair made a rectangle of his head, and a thin bar of fuzz decorated his upper lip. He squinted in Mira's direction, then sat up a little straighter. His gaze drifted down, then up, tracing the swells and dips that Mira's tight jeans and leather jacket did little to hide.

When his inspection made it back to her face, he cleared his throat and tugged at the edges of his brown suit. "How may I help you, miss?"

Mira lowered her gaze and smiled. "I'm afraid I don't have an appointment." Mira added a slight southern drawl to her words.

The secretary waved his hand, marking her concern as meaningless. "We can always make time for new clients."

Mira glanced side to side as she approached the desk. The robin's-egg walls were decorated with large canvas prints, each highlighting a scene of the company's accomplishments—everything from ground-breakings and ribbon-cuttings to demolitions. Men and women in safety vests with KBU logos like the one she'd seen last night smiled beside satisfied customers and waved for the camera.

<There he is!>

In the second-to-last picture on the right, the man she'd chased last night stood beside a woman in a pinstripe business suit with a smile so white it practically glowed. The two were standing in front of a towering office building, sharing a grip on an over-sized pair of scissors frozen against a thick red ribbon.

Mira pointed to the man in the photo and turned her smile back on the secretary. "I'm here to see him."

"Mr. Nowak?"

"Is he in?"

"Well, yes." The man rubbed a thin-fingered hand against the back of his neck. "But Mr. Nowak has his hands full with a big redevelopment project right now. One of our other project managers would probably—"

"I want Mr. Nowak." She stretched her smile. "He comes highly recommended, and my project's time frame is flexible."

The secretary relaxed on an exhale. "In that case . . ." He lifted the phone receiver on his desk and pressed a button. "Mr. Nowak? I have a prospective client here to see you." He listened, nodded, and hung up. "Mr. Nowak will see you." He gestured to the white door on his left. "Third door on the right."

"Thank you." Mira gave her hips an extra swish as she walked through the door.

The hallway was lined with plain wood doors, each sporting a brass nameplate. She passed the first few and stopped in front of A. NOWAK.

<How do you want to play this?>

Let's start slow, put him at ease. See if you can tell anything about his possessing demon.

<And if he recognizes us?>

Then we subdue him and get our answers the old-fashioned way.

<Two meals in as many days. You spoil me.>

Remember, if he is like us, we don't want to hurt him.

<*If.*>

Mira reached for the doorknob, but a voice from inside the office made her pause.

". . . interrupted by some vigilante practitioner."

Mira let her hand drop and leaned in closer to the door.

"Yes, but it was sloppy work. She left the body at the site."

<He's talking about us.>

Shh.

"Of course." There was a pause, then, "Understood."

Mira strained to hear through the wood, but nothing more came.

Whatever plan this guy is involved with, I don't think he's in charge.

<Does that mean there's *another* rifter involved?>

Only one way to find out.

Mira took a deep breath, rapped her knuckles lightly against the wood, and pushed open the door. "Mr. Nowak?"

The Santa Claus look-alike she'd chased through the construction site last night looked up from a clipboard on his desk. His blue-plaid shirt had been replaced with red, and the hardhat was missing, leaving his short silver locks to stick up at odd angles. His eyes were a dull brown.

"Please, come in." He stood and indicated two black plastic chairs on the near side of the desk. "You have a project to discuss?"

Mira closed the door behind her.

A coat rack holding a long beige coat, a bright-orange vest, and a blue hard hat stood to one side; the opposite wall held a narrow bookcase with the sort of leather-bound books office decorators bought for the look but had probably never been opened. Behind Nowak, light snuck between the blinds of a medium-sized window. Her sneakers scuffed against hard wood that didn't have enough character to be real.

<I don't sense any magic in him.>

Which only means he's not casting. What about the demon?

There was a slight strain behind Mira's eyes, as though she were squinting really hard.

<There's a small concentration of rift energy inside him but not

enough to account for even a weak demon. More like what we'd see in a vampire.>

Mira frowned. *He's not a rifter?*

The demon hesitated. A twist of discomfort tightened Mira's chest.

<I think . . . it might be a tether. Like how I keep only a small piece of myself active most of the time to avoid damaging you.>

Mira's pulse quickened. *So he* is *like us.*

<Just because another demon has figured out how to tether to a body without burning it to a crisp does *not* mean they're anything like *us.*>

But they're not like any other rifter we've come across before. Mira lifted her chin, and before she could think better of it or chicken out, she said, "I know you're a rifter."

<Are you insane? What happened to take it slow? Put him at ease?>

Mira crossed the room and set her palms flat against the polished red wood of Mr. Nowak's desk. "How long have you had a demon inside you?"

A bronze sheen flashed in Nowak's eyes, and with it, a hint of recognition.

A tingle raced over Mira's skin, and the small hairs along her arms and neck pricked up.

<The demon's coming.>

"I only want to talk," Mira said.

Mr. Nowak tipped his head to the side and smiled, but he didn't look at all like the solicitous businessman who'd greeted her when she entered. "You're quite brave, coming at me head-on in broad daylight."

"You've put a lot of effort into fitting in here. I don't think you'll throw that away."

He raised his palms in a shrug. "An impasse then." Nowak frowned. "Who are you?"

"I asked my question first."

"An answer for an answer?"

Mira straightened and nodded.

"I've been in possession of this body for . . ." He rolled his gaze toward the ceiling. "Eighteen months."

Mira gasped. "You must have been a strong practitioner to be showing no signs of wear. How do you maintain your energy balance?"

"Ah-ah-ah." He waggled a finger. "My turn. Who are you?"

Mira shifted her weight. She could lie. She *should* lie. But the idea of another person like her—a rifter who hadn't lost their humanity—made her want to connect with this man in a way she'd long since convinced herself she didn't need. Loneliness welled up in her like a spring rushing toward the surface. "Mirana Fuentes. I've been a rifter since I was eleven."

Nowak took a step back, his eyes growing wide. "That's—"

"Impossible?" Mira chuckled. "That's what I used to think about ever finding another stable rifter."

<You're sharing too much.>

He's like us.

<That doesn't mean you can trust him.>

"Last night you mentioned claiming this area. You talked about a plan. What plan?"

Nowak smiled. "Would it surprise you to learn we are not the only ones"—he made a sweeping gesture up and down his torso—"like this?"

Mira leaned onto the balls of her feet. "There are others?"

"My . . . employer . . . has great plans for this world."

"And your employer . . . he's like us? How long has he been a rifter?"

"Many years. Though perhaps not so many as you."

"What does he intend to do here?"

"First let me ask you, how do you feel about this world and the humans who inhabit it?"

Mira sank back on her heels and frowned. "What do you mean?"

"Your human body possesses the conduits to channel magic, does it not?"

"I'm a practitioner, if that's what you mean."

"And your *demon* self? How strong is that?"

<Don't tell him.>

"Ameeri."

<I told you not to tell him!>

Nowak nodded. "As am I, though this shell holds only the barest traces of magical control." He slid a finger over the surface of his desk. "When you look at the people of this world, do you feel a kinship to them?"

The wellspring of loneliness bubbled and boiled inside Mira as a lifetime of shallow encounters and casual betrayals played out in her mind. She dropped her gaze.

"I see you do not."

"I just . . ." Mira shifted her weight. "Life's easier on my own."

"But what if you didn't have to be on your own anymore? What if this world was filled with people like *us*."

Mira looked up into Nowak's stare. The metallic glint in his eyes reminded her of a crazy vagrant she'd seen ranting about Armageddon on a street corner in Detroit. He'd sounded almost believable to a child whose world had just ended, but now she knew that look meant danger. She wouldn't be tricked by promises of salvation from any earthly source. Never again.

"What exactly does your employer intend to do?"

Nowak raised his arms. "We will all be free."

<That's the demon talking. He means they'll make more rifters.>

"Normal humans can't survive possession. At least not for very long."

"Not yet. But that won't be a problem once the work is done. Then humans and demons, and even the half-breed races that scurry about this world, will all be equal, and it will be the fae traitors who are locked out."

Do you know what he's talking about?

<No. And physically stable or not, this guy is definitely unbalanced.>

"Who's your employer? What's his human name?"

Nowak stepped around the side of the desk. He watched Mira with a predator's eyes, cold and calculating. "The rifter at the construction site. You were hunting him?"

Mira nodded.

"Why?"

"He was murdering innocent people."

"Humans." He pursed his lips. His bronze gaze pierced her like a spear. "Why do you care about them?"

Mira frowned. "Because I am one."

Nowak nodded. The corners of his mouth turned down. "That's too bad."

He was on her before she could react, before his words even registered. His fingers closed around her throat, and the weight of his body colliding with hers sent them both to the floor.

Bluish-white flame erupted from Mira's skin. She might have been caught off guard, but the demon within her wasn't.

Nowak hissed and reared back, shaking his hand to extinguish the flames. The light danced in his now entirely metallic eyes.

Mira pulled energy in through her left hand, but her concentration scattered as Nowak's fist connected with her cheek.

"If you're not with us," he growled, "you're against us. And I can't allow you to interfere with the great work."

Mira bucked her hips and rolled to the side to dislodge Nowak, and together the two tumbled across the floor in a tangle of limbs as they each struggled to hold the higher ground.

As Mira rose to the top, she sent a tendril of magic into the floor. Imitation wood sagged like wet sand under Nowak's back. She braced her knee in his gut to push him deeper, then snapped the floor back in place, encasing his midsection, half his chest, and one arm.

"Play time's over." She pinned his remaining hand and pressed her free palm to his forehead. "Tell me who you serve."

Nowak laughed. "Unshackle me from this realm, and I shall simply return to the Rift. Do what you will to this body."

The corner of Mira's mouth twitched up in a wicked smile. "Oh, I don't unshackle demons." She leaned in close and whispered in his ear. "I eat them."

She opened herself to the hunger of the demon within her and pulled at the rift energy infecting the man like a doctor drawing poison from a wound.

Nowak twitched and seized, but the floorboards held him tight.

"Who are you working for?" Coils of writhing energy lifted free from Nowak's body, pooling in the palm of her hand.

"Stop." His voice was breathy with strain. "You're one of us. You should be working *with* us. Don't you want a world in which you can be true to yourself? A place where you can live without feeling like an outcast, hunted and despised?"

"Not at the cost of innocent lives. Now tell me who you work for."

Nowak opened his mouth to scream, and Mira shifted some of her focus to squeezing off the cords in his throat before more than a peep could escape. She glanced at the door.

The flow of magic shifted. Pain lanced through the hand holding Nowak's arm down.

She gasped and recoiled. Blood ran down her wrist from a dozen holes punched through her skin by the needles Nowak had grown in his.

He punched at her side, but what connected with her ribs wasn't the flat surface of a fist. A long, thin blade pierced her skin and angled for her lung.

Mira steeled her body, reinforcing organic matter with magic.

The blade stopped an inch into her side.

White light, swirled with black and gold, poured over Mira, coating her like honey as the demon who usually kept such a careful foothold filled her to capacity. Mira's body began to vibrate, as though her very cells would shake apart under the strain. Warm liquid seeped from the corners of her eyes, and the world took on a hazy film, as though she was looking through a gauze blindfold.

She pressed both hands to Nowak's temples and yanked with the part of herself dedicated to moving magic.

Wait. I still need answers. Mira's voice was a whisper in the torrent of her mind. The demon was done playing second fiddle in this interrogation.

Energy rushed toward her, and with it came tendrils of purplish-black smoke that rose from Nowak and streamed up Mira's arms, blending with the misty light already clinging to her.

The shadow of a second set of features rose above Nowak's face, mouth agape in a silent scream. Bronze eyes blazed from deep pits. Spikes erupted along the bridge of his nose and formed a ridge along his forehead. Then the features blurred and smeared as the smoky form was dragged away from the sagging flesh of its physical shell.

Nowak, the human part of him, shriveled like a deflating balloon under the strain of the demon pulling free.

When the last trickle of bronze-streaked purple was absorbed into the swirling light of Mira's demon, she released the sides of his face and sank back on her heels.

We weren't done talking.

<He was.> She sighed and looked at the ceiling. "We can find this 'employer' on our own."

Let's just get rid of the body.

Mira nodded. Together, woman and demon drew on the scattered energy remaining in the room. They'd used a fair bit in their struggle. She pressed her palms to Nowak's chest. His ribs were distinct ridges under her palm. She focused on separating the bonds within his body. If she'd cared to study, she might have been able to name the individual elements a human body broke down into—she'd certainly decomposed enough of them—but all she needed to know was that rearranging organic material was an effective way to hide a corpse.

Holy Mary, Mother of God, pray for us sinners, now and at the hour of our death.

The air took on a tangy scent. The pressure under Mira's palms gave way. Between her knees, where she'd been straddling Nowak, was a pile of grayish dust. One more burst of energy, and the floorboards absorbed all that remained of Mr. Nowak.

Ashes to ashes, dust to dust.

She rose and brushed off her palms. "Shall we see if last night's partner is still in bed where we left him? I'll bet he's good for another round or two."

A vision of tight, sweat-streaked skin, straining muscles, and soft lips filled Mira's mind. *No. It's my turn to choose, and I say we do a solo activity. Let's head for that junkyard.*

She reached for the doorknob, but there was a sharp knock on the wood before her fingers made contact.

She darted aside as her adrenaline spiked and pressed herself flat against the wall behind the coat rack.

The doorknob turned.

She grabbed a handful of shadows from the corner of the room, infused them with magic, and dragged them over herself. So long as she held very still and didn't draw any attention, the gaze of whoever was about to walk in should slide right over her.

The door opened a crack.

"Mr. Nowak?" The speaker's voice was deep and rich . . . and familiar.

The door swung fully open and the nameless fling she'd left sprawled on his bed in the predawn light stepped into the room. He wore the same coat as he had at the bar and tight jeans that hugged his thighs and the curve of his butt, then flared over the tops of tan work boots.

What is he *doing here?*

<Well, he *is* a cop. Maybe he's investigating the death at the construction site.>

But why would he be working that case? He clearly wasn't on duty last night.

The demon gave a mental shrug. <Whatever the reason, he's here now.> Warmth flooded Mira's body, relaxing some muscles, tightening others. <And he looks even yummier in the daylight.>

No. That guy is officially off limits. We should have cut and run as soon as we found out he was a cop.

Mr. Yummy walked over to Nowak's desk. He glanced around the room. Mira held her breath. His gaze slid over and off her, then swung back to the door. "Where is he?"

A woman walked in. She was a good half foot taller than Mira, nearly as tall as the man, but her form-fitting coat and pants showed plenty of curves despite her slender waist and limbs. She had a warm olive complexion that made Mira think of sunbathers on the Mediterranean coast. Dark mascara and a light coating of bronze eye shadow drew attention to her hazel eyes, and shiny gloss coated her full lips.

<Looks like we have some competition.>

She can have him. I just want out of this room.

"The desk clerk said he was in his office." She stepped around the desk. "With a woman." She separated the blinds over the window behind the desk and peeked out.

"Maybe they stepped out." The man also moved toward the desk, but stopped mid-step and crouched down. He pulled a latex glove from his pocket and used it to lift something from the floor, but his broad torso blocked Mira's view.

His focus was on whatever was in his hand. The woman was looking out the window. Both their backs were turned.

Mira shifted as quickly as she dared toward the open door.

The woman moved.

Mira froze. Just two more steps to the hallway.

The woman's attention swung down to the crouching man. "Find something?"

"I don't know. Maybe." He stood, and she joined him to inspect what he'd collected.

Mira used the opportunity to bolt through the door.

<What do you think he found?>

Who cares as long as he doesn't find us?

Mira turned away from the lobby and followed the hall until she spotted a gray security door with a steel push bar. The word EXIT glowed in pale green light on a sign above it.

"Bingo."

Chapter 7

Ty

TY TILTED THE pendant pinched between the loose material of the latex glove so LaRosa could see it. The broken ends of the chain dangled over the edge of his hand. He studied the raised figure of a saint—the same unknown saint he'd found nestled in the cleavage of a stranger last night. The figure was draped in cloth and seemed to be holding a small disc in one hand. He gripped a walking stick in the other.

"A saint necklace?" A small crease appeared between LaRosa's eyebrows. "It's not Mary or Michael. Those are the only ones I know."

"Not a clue," said Ty. *But I'm damn well gonna find out.*

"Bag it for evidence. Maybe we'll get lucky and pull a print."

He slipped the necklace into a clear plastic bag and tucked it in his pocket. Then he pulled out his box of matches and gave it a shake to make them rattle. "Any predictions?"

LaRosa just crossed her arms and watched as he retrieved a single match and struck it against the side of the box. The flame flared and raced down the wood.

Ty shook it out when his fingertips grew warm. "Seven seconds." He returned the box to his pocket. "Someone's been using magic in here."

"You think Nowak is our killer? Maybe he used his magic to escape when he heard us coming?" She glanced at the closed blinds over the window.

"Maybe. But what about the woman we should have found in here with him?" He tapped the pocket with the broken necklace. "Let's have another chat with that desk clerk."

Ty led the way back to the lobby and stopped in front of the desk. "Nowak wasn't in his office."

The clerk's eyes widened. "Are you sure?"

"I think we would have noticed a grown man. And didn't you say you'd just sent a woman in to see him?"

"Yes. Barely five minutes ago. They should both have been in there."

"Might they have gone out a back way?" LaRosa propped her hip against the man's desk and crossed her arms. "Or maybe found a quiet broom closet?"

"No. I mean, Nowak is old. And the girl"—he glanced at LaRosa—"woman . . . she couldn't have been much over twenty."

Again Ty's hand went to the slight bulge of the pendant in his pocket. "Can you describe her?"

"Blond. Shoulder-length straight hair."

Ty pursed his lips. "How tall was she?"

"Oh she was a petite little thing. Maybe five-three."

LaRosa raised a finger and drew a circle in the air. "You got security cameras in here?"

"In the lobby. Not the offices."

She pushed off the desk. "Show us."

The three of them entered the first room on the way back to Nowak's office. The label on the brass plate read FILES. Bare, beige walls reflected every sound, and metal filing cabinets with short, wide drawers lined the walls and split the room into aisles. In the back corner, a monitor that looked at least two decades out of date sat on a chipped Formica desk.

The clerk settled at the computer.

"The woman you sent to Nowak's office," LaRosa said. "Did you notice anything odd about her? Was she behaving strangely? Nervous? Excited? Angry?"

He shook his head and pulled up the security footage, showing the empty lobby. "But she was insistent."

"What do you mean?" Ty asked.

"She said she'd only work with Mr. Nowak, even though I suggested another lead might get to her project sooner." He clicked rewind.

Ty watched LaRosa and himself walk backward through the front doors. A moment later, a woman backtracked from the hallway leading to Nowak's office.

The clerk paused the recording with the woman pointing at a picture of Nowak on the wall. "That's her."

Ty squinted at the woman in the image. Her hair was longer than that of the woman he'd met in the bar, and as the clerk said, straight and blond. Her complexion also seemed lighter than he remembered, but that might just be the difference between night and day. The height and build were about right, and her features seemed similar.

He closed his eyes and tried to bring his lover's face into focus. He could remember the press of her lips against his, soft and yielding. The smooth curve of her cheek. The tickle of her eyelashes against his neck as she kissed his collarbone. Heat swelled inside him as dozens of remembered touches blazed across his skin.

"Hey." Fingers dug into his upper arm—not remembered phantoms, but solid.

His eyes snapped open.

"You still with us?" LaRosa released his arm.

"Yeah." Ty cleared his throat to get rid of the husky cadence of his reawakened desire. "Just . . . thinking."

LaRosa watched him for a moment, then turned to the clerk and handed him a business card. "Send a copy of that footage to my email. And call the second you hear from Nowak or if you see that woman again."

LaRosa gave Ty another glance, lips pursed, and led the way out of the office. Once they were both settled in the Charger, she pulled away from the curb, took a deep breath, and said, "Spill."

Ty glanced sideways. LaRosa had both hands on the wheel. She stared straight ahead as she guided the car through traffic. "Excuse me?"

"The woman in the surveillance video. You've got a lead."

"More like . . . a question."

Her gaze flicked to him, then back to the road.

He sighed and settled deeper into his seat. "You know the necklace we found? Well, I met a woman who wore one just like it."

"Like it, or the same necklace?"

He shrugged. "Can't be sure."

"Was she the woman in the video?"

"Can't be sure about that either." He glanced at the people on the sidewalks as they passed through a shopping district. Their faces went by in a blur, too fast to register any details. "The hair was wrong, but the build was right."

"Hair's easy enough to change. Let's pay your friend a visit and see if she's still got her necklace." She shifted gears. "At the very least, we can put your mind at ease so you can stay focused."

Ty grimaced. "Easier said than done. I . . . don't know her name. Or where to find her."

LaRosa cut her gaze to him and raised one eyebrow.

"We met at a bar in Midtown last night. Shared some drinks." *And more . . .* Ty schooled his expression and thanked the heavens he had a complexion that hid the heat in his cheeks.

"What time?"

"Late. Last call late. I'd just come off my shift."

"First responders arrived on the scene at one forty-eight."

"You think she murdered a man, dropped a building on him, then stopped for a drink at a bar up the road?"

She shrugged. "You tell me."

Ty grumbled and rubbed a hand over his fuzzy scalp. "She's worth talking to."

LaRosa's phone vibrated, and she pressed a button on the steering wheel to connect the call. "LaRosa here."

"Detective." Billy's voice was even higher and more energetic sounding through the speaker than it was in person. "We got a hit on your vic's prints in AFIS."

Ty leaned forward. "Who is he?"

"Rodney Temple. A high school math teacher from Delaware. His boss reported him missing when he didn't show up to teach classes the day after the attack in Wilmington. No one's seen him since."

Ty nodded. Just over a week ago rogue sorcerers led by a necromancer had marched down the U.S. coast from New York to D.C., wreaking havoc along the way. A lot of people had died in the clash at Wilmington—cops, PTF agents, civilians—but the really disturbing part had come when the fighting stopped. The necromancer who'd been leading the rogues brought all those casualties back to life in the form of demon- driven undead. The sorcerers' coup of the PTF council had failed, but they'd left a lot of bodies in their wake, and not all of those bodies stayed down.

"Good work, Billy." LaRosa shot a glance at Ty. "We're on our way back to the station now. Call in a sketch artist. We may have a lead." She pressed a button to disconnect the call.

"There's a good chance our victim was a rifter." Ty remembered he wasn't working with a PTF agent and shifted in his seat to focus on LaRosa. "A person who's had their will overwritten by a possessing demon."

She frowned. "I thought demons only possessed magic-users. Billy would have mentioned if there was any record of Mr. Temple being a practitioner."

"If he was registered," Ty amended. "Remember, school teacher is one of the jobs paranaturals are restricted from holding. And while practitioners may be the preference, a demon will take any body it can get. It's the only way for them to have a physical presence here." He studied her profile. "How much do you know about the rogue sorcerer attacks?"

She raised one shoulder in a half shrug. "I was pulling double shifts, same as everybody. There was a lot of fear, a lot of rumors . . . a lot of panicked calls to dispatch. And the PTF—the people who were *supposed* to be handling the situation—were holed up in their conference rooms debating bureaucratic bullshit while the sorcerers strolled right up to the capitol gates."

"Did you see the fight at Wilmington?"

"Not firsthand, but I caught a recap on the news."

"They were led by a necromancer. Demons normally infiltrate practitioners through the magic they draw, but a necromancer can force artificial pathways into a person with his magic. Basically, he opens the door and a demon walks through, practitioner or not."

LaRosa shuddered. "No wonder you hate magic."

Ty lowered his gaze. Demon possessions didn't scare him. Not any more than a human gangster with a gun.

"If our vic was a rifter, could the 'fight' the witnesses overheard have just been a demon on a rampage?"

"Maybe. Demons are unstable, chaotic. And they come with their own magic, so even a non-practitioner can do magic when they're possessed. He certainly could have lost control and brought the ceiling down on himself."

"Which I might actually believe if not for the extra footprints and the marks around his neck."

Ty nodded. "*Someone* walked away from that scene last night."

LaRosa eased to a stop at a traffic light and twisted toward Ty. "What if the woman on the security footage was a witness? Maybe she saw Nowak kill our victim last night, then went to blackmail him this morning."

"Blackmailing a killer who won a fight against a rifter? That'd take guts."

"Or desperation—remember, that was a homeless shelter next door—and I've seen people do dumber things for money."

Ty nodded. "Nowak freaks, kills the girl."

"Or subdues and moves her. Killing someone, disposing of the body, and cleaning the scene would take time. That necklace probably broke in a struggle, but the room wasn't a mess and the clerk didn't hear anything. So whatever happened, happened fast."

A horn blared. Both detectives looked up to see the light had turned green.

LaRosa shifted into first and hit the gas. "Or maybe she's the killer, Nowak was a witness, and she dropped by this morning to tie up loose ends."

Ty tensed at the idea of possibly sleeping with a murderer not twenty minutes after she'd killed a man. Was that why she hadn't wanted to share her name? Why she'd reacted to the sight of his badge and gun? That white streak he'd noticed on her jacket . . . could it have been drywall dust?

He hadn't been at the top of his game since . . . in a while, but were his instincts really *that* bad these days?

He sighed and shook his head. "There are too many variables, and we don't have a motive for either theory. We should dig into Nowak. If he was a witness, we should be able to find a reason why he stayed quiet. If he was the killer, or working with the killer, maybe we'll find some connection to our vic."

LaRosa swung a right toward the station. "We'll put out a BOLO for Nowak, the woman from the video, and your friend from the bar. Hopefully we'll get a hit on at least one of them."

"Before another body turns up." Ty went back to watching pedestrians and trying to recall the details of his lover's face. Was she the woman in the video? Was she a killer? Would she be the next corpse he was called to investigate? He imagined the silky soft skin he'd caressed last night replaced with the desiccated remains he'd inspected this morning. The coffee in his stomach turned sour.

Chapter 8

Mira

“*SABÍA QUE QUEDARME haría un desastre.*” Mira tossed the pretzel-shaped steel bar she was holding into the dirt and ran her fingers through her hair, snagging several tangles and coming away with clinging strands. Sweat coated her forehead and stained her shirt, making her shiver when the breeze picked up.

<Messy or not, at least you got an answer.> One camouflage spell, a super-human hop over a barbed-wire fence, and a pile of torn and twisted metal later, Mira’s demon was safely back in the passenger seat—their balance restored so the overflow of energy didn’t rip Mira’s physical body apart molecule by molecule.

“And more questions.” Mira kicked the steel again before releasing the energy she’d been channeling to amplify her strength. “That bearded bastard was middle management at best, and if what he said is true . . .”

<There are more rifters who’ve discovered the secret to a stable—at least semi-stable—relationship. I never would have thought it possible.>

Mira shook her head. “I knew we couldn’t be the only freaks out there.”

<Just remember, figuring out how not to self-destruct does *not* mean they’re friendly.>

Mira sighed, plopped down in the scuffed dirt, and leaned back against the rusted frame of a gutted car. “The question is, what do we do now?”

<You’re worried about Mr. Yummy.>

“I’m worried that a man, a *cop*, who’s seen our face is investigating at least one if not two people we’ve murdered. This city is getting too hot.”

<So let’s leave.>

“And miss the opportunity to find a group of hidden rifters operating long term for some specific goal?” She shook her head. “You know we can’t.”

<I know you *won't*. We absolutely *could*. And we probably *should* if you want to maintain your anonymity and this whole Lone Ranger persona you've got going. Sticking around here, hunting rifters who can blend at least as well as we can . . . *someone* is going to take notice.>

"What do you think about what the foreman said? About the rifters wanting to create a world where people like us could belong?"

There was a thoughtful silence in Mira's head as the demon considered.

<I don't see how anyone could manage that. Humans and demons . . . they're too different.>

"You and I do okay."

<You're not normal for a human, and I'm not normal for a demon.>

"All the more reason to find out how multiple other rifters have managed not to self-destruct." Mira stilled as a thought hit her. "Do you think they could be necromancers?"

<That guy in the office went down way too easy for a necromancer. Besides, necros are crazy rare. The fact that we've met one in your lifetime means we probably won't meet another.>

Mira exhaled. A necromancer would be more than she could handle on her own. "I think we should stay and figure out what's really going on around here."

<Fine by me. Where do you wanna start?>

"We don't know how long this investigation will take, but I'm guessing long enough to need easy access to a bathroom and shower." She pushed to her feet. "So we start by finding an inconspicuous place to stay."

<We should find a hotel with a pool.>

"I doubt anything we can afford will include a pool."

<You could always magic some money.>

"No. We've talked about this."

<You used to do it all the time.> Mira's lip jutted slightly to match the pout in her demon's voice.

"Only for emergencies."

Mira experienced the mental equivalent of an eye roll. <Then your whole adolescence must have been one giant emergency.>

Pretty much. "Anyway. We don't want to make a trail of counterfeit bills after leaving that body at the construction site. The cops are already too close for comfort." She braced her legs, pulled in a trickle of magical energy, and vaulted the barbed-wire-topped fence that encircled the scrap yard. Once on the outside, she released the energy—becoming once more visible and of average human strength—and strolled across a patch of weeds to the alley where she'd left her motorcycle. "We'll just have to find somewhere cheap."

Mira

"HI." MIRA PLASTERED on her friendliest smile and set her hands on the motel's check-in counter. "I'd like to rent a room. Preferably on the end."

The clerk looked her up and down. He had long, thin features, narrow, russet-brown eyes, pale, yellowish skin, and a shaved head. The dark-blue flannel he wore over his gray T-shirt was rolled up to his elbows, revealing a Japanese-style sleeve tattoo on his right arm and what was clearly supposed to be a demon writhing in flames on his left.

Mira nodded at the image. "Nice tattoo."

The man slid a form toward Mira. "Fill this out."

<Can I pick the name?>

Fourteen years and you haven't even settled on a name for yourself. We don't have all night.

<That's different. I don't want to be *stuck* with a name. This is just for fun.>

She smiled. *Fine. Who should we be today?*

<How about Bethany? There was a character named Bethany in that movie trailer we saw yesterday.>

Do I look like a Bethany to you?

<Does it matter what you look like?>

Whatever. Bethany, it is.

Mira lied about her name, her age, her contact information. When the form asked for the length of stay Mira glanced up. "I'm not sure how long I'll be in town. Can I just settle up at the end?"

"Most people do. I'll run your credit card now and charge it when you check out."

"I'd rather pay cash."

He frowned. "Then you'll need to pay each night in advance. Sixty-eight per, due by noon."

Mira's smile tightened. She pulled out her wallet, dropped the required cash on the completed form, and pushed both across the counter.

"And I need to see an ID."

She pulled a driver's license out of her wallet and smudged her thumb over the surface, simultaneously drawing power. When she handed the ID over, its information matched what she'd put on the form.

The clerk studied the ID, looked up, down, up, and handed the forged document back. Then he picked up a plastic key card, ran it through a machine, and slapped it on the counter. "Number twelve. End of the line."

The door jingled as Mira stepped into the parking lot. Her motorcycle was parked in the farthest spot from the office, right next to a dented, green garbage bin chained in place by thick steel links attached to the property fence. She'd left her truck two streets over in a residential neighborhood after tweaking the exterior to make it look like a landscaping service vehicle.

She followed the sidewalk to the end and stopped in front of a beige door with a brass number twelve screwed to it. Then she slid her key card in the lock, waited for the light to turn green, and stepped into her temporary home.

The switch near the door turned on a red, ceramic lamp in the corner that cast an orange glow over the room. The bedspread was thin, the seams frayed, and the blue-and-green floral pattern was faded. The mottled gray carpet felt like walking on a layer of fabric laid directly over concrete. A dinged-up wooden chair with peeling varnish sat in one corner under a small television mounted high on the wall.

"Not exactly the Four Seasons."

<At least it has a bathroom.>

Mira pushed open the door at the back of the room and found a standard ceramic tub with a basic shower faucet, a toilet, and a sink.

"It'll work."

Withdrawing from the bathroom, she slipped off the shoulder strap of the pack she'd brought with her and unzipped the bag. She pulled out her laptop, set it on the night stand, and plugged it in to charge. She dropped her jacket on the bed, grabbed the small first aid kit she'd packed, and headed back to the bathroom. Stripping off her jeans, she sat down on the lid of the toilet and pulled out the X-Acto blade she used for atonement.

<Here we go again . . .> The demon's attention drifted away.

"Loving Mother of the Redeemer, gate of heaven, star of the sea, assist your people who have fallen yet strive to rise again. You who received Gabriel's joyful greeting, have pity on us poor sinners." Mira drew the blade across her skin, splitting it apart in a straight, thin line directly below the previous mark. Then she set the knife on the edge of the sink, reached up to her neck, and froze.

Where . . .? She groped around the collar of her shirt, panic rising. She yanked the fabric over her head and twisted to stare at herself in the mirror. Her sternum was bare. No pendant dangled between the curves of her breasts.

The demon's focus came roaring back, drawn by Mira's distress. <What's the matter?>

"It's gone."

<What is?>

"My Saint Jude necklace."

Mira's posture sagged slightly as the demon relaxed. <Is that all?>

Mira stared back at herself in wide-eyed horror as she replayed the morning's events. When had she seen it last?

<I know you were fond of it, but really, it was just a hunk of not-very-pure silver with a face stamped into it. We can get you another.>

She pounded her fist against the sink. "It was more than that."

<Fine. You wanna go back and look for it?>

She shook her head, picturing the struggle in Nowak's office. "That cop must have it."

<Mr. Yummy?>

Mira rubbed her sternum as though she could feel the void that seemed to be eating through her chest, turning her anger to numbing cold. "How could I not notice?"

<Look, we'll go shopping tomorrow, get you a new necklace. Maybe one with a little color.>

Mira pressed her palms over her eyes. "You don't get it."

<What will make you happy?>

"Forget it. You can't help."

Irritation rippled through her. <Humans are so moody.>

"Yeah, well, demons are no picnic either."

Removing the last of her clothes, Mira stepped into the tub and blasted herself with hot water. Her fresh wound and the slightly older cut from that morning stung under the beat of the shower, and she focused on that physical pain to distract herself from the ache in her heart. She stayed under the water long enough to clear the grime of two murders and a one-night stand off her body, but her soul still felt dingy when she toweled off.

<Are you still moping?>

Ignoring the demon, Mira pulled on a fresh set of clothes from her backpack. Then she started collecting and folding the clothes she'd left on the bathroom floor in her panic over the missing necklace.

<Uh oh.>

Mira paused, shirt dangling from her fingers. *What?*

<You're doing your obsessive cleaning thing.>

It's called being tidy.

<You're *folding* dirty laundry. That goes way past tidy. Next you're gonna start scrubbing the porcelain.>

She rolled her eyes and set the folded shirt on top of her jeans on the toilet seat. She glanced at the sink but resisted the urge to wipe off the soap scum collected around the drain. She would *not* give her demon more ammunition.

"Paying for this room used pretty much the last of our cash. If we're staying more than another day, we'll need a paying gig."

<I thought you wanted to lay low while we investigated.>

"Not if it means starving." She sat down on the bed and grabbed her laptop. "Besides, a side job gives us a legitimate excuse to be in town. Might even provide an alibi in a pinch."

She opened the lid and smiled at the full battery icon in the tool bar. Then she saw the symbol that meant she had an unread email. She clicked the icon to bring up the mail client software that routed her various accounts—each registered to a different user and shared with a different contact. The email was from her *abuela.*

Mira opened the email. The text was in Spanish—Mira's *abuela* always preferred to communicate in her mother tongue. Mira had grown up bilingual in Florida, but when her mother moved them to Detroit she'd spoken English almost exclusively. It was comforting to see the Spanish words, like a breath of home.

My dearest Mira,

I hope this letter finds you well. I haven't heard from you in ages. Are you getting enough to eat? I know you won't tell me where you are, but I pray you're warm and comfortable. Remember, you are always welcome with me, for however long or short you need.

A tightness squeezed Mira's chest at the thought of her *abuela*'s small but tidy home with its bright walls, fully stocked fridge, and lace doily coasters. Mira had spent the best years of her life in that house, and the plea in *abuela*'s letter echoed the ache in her own heart.

I'm writing because I want to let you know the doctor has recommended a new treatment for Maria.

The warmth created by thoughts of home turned to ice and a sour flavor at the back of her throat at mention of Mira's mother. Eyes too wide and bright to be sane stared at her from her memory. A face engulfed in flames. Skin like melted wax. The smell of burning hair momentarily overpowered the Lysol scent of the motel room.

She's become increasingly agitated lately. I had to have tio Luis help me when she became physically violent. The doctor asked me again to consider releasing her to a hospital, but I will not send her away. She is family. I think that seeing you would do her good. I think it would do you both good.

Please come home soon, even if only for a visit.

Love, always.

Abuela

Mira tipped her head back to prevent the liquid in her eyes from spilling down her cheeks. A brown stain in the shape of a duck discolored one corner of the otherwise cream-colored ceiling and was working its way down the equally bland walls.

<We could visit when we're done here.>

No. Mira sniffed and closed her eyes. *We can't.*

Visions of her last "visit" swirled through her head. Not just the screaming rage her mother had gone into when she'd seen Mira, but the horror at the school where Mira had briefly entertained the dream of finishing her education. Six teens in total . . . carried out on stretchers . . . because Mira lost her temper.

<We have much better control now.>

That's what we thought last time. I won't risk hurting them again. She opened her eyes and took another look at the email. "Besides, *Abuela's* wrong. Seeing me wouldn't help my mother . . . it would only make her worse." She sniffed again and wiped her fingers over her dry cheeks. "What I *can* do is send money to help pay for whatever new treatment they're trying."

<Sure, because we're rolling in cash of the non-magical-counterfeit variety.>

Mira rolled her eyes. "We needed a side job to pay for this room anyway. We'll just have to find a desperate client with deep pockets." She closed the email and pulled up one of the job boards for private investigators where she often scouted for work when in a pinch. "The more desperate a person is, the more they're willing to pay to get the job done."

<Those jobs usually end up being more work, too.>

"Not always. We'll be selective." She scrolled through the first page and half of the second before pausing to point at the screen. "There."

The listing read: *I'm convinced my girlfriend is cheating on me. Had her followed, but previous P.I. failed to find evidence. I need to know the truth! Will pay handsomely for photographs confirming my suspicions.*

<An insecure lover looking for dirty pics to confirm their paranoia.>

"Exactly." Mira usually avoided domestic affairs, but cheating lovers were pretty straightforward—a little tracking, a few pictures, and a paycheck—and this client definitely sounded desperate enough to pay well.

She clicked the link to open a private chat with the prospective client and typed, *Interested in your job. Meet to discuss specifics?*

If the client was truly desperate, they'd respond quickly. She glanced at the clock next to the bed. She'd give them five minutes before moving on to the next job. In the meantime, she continued to scroll through the postings, searching for other likely matches. Before she reached the bottom of the third page, the chat alert chimed with a message. A few quick exchanges and Mira was all set to meet her client later that afternoon.

"Now down to business." Mira rolled her neck, cracked her knuckles, and shifted the laptop on her thighs. A few keystrokes later and she was back to the site documenting the history of the construction project where this all began.

She pulled up the website she'd skimmed before, but this time she didn't click past the documentation of the construction site. The disagreement that had caused KBU to take over the contract for the original construction company had been instigated by the land developer, Bressett International. The site had started out as a multi-billion-dollar gentrification project involving a handful of luxury apartments surrounding an exclusive clubhouse with top-of-the-line amenities. Then the company's CEO—a man named Reed Decker—had shocked investors and workmen alike by turning the whole project on its head shortly after breaking ground on the site.

The central clubhouse was redesigned as a homeless shelter, keeping all the base amenities but adding two stories and one hundred beds. The four surrounding buildings were changed from forty luxury condos to nearly two hundred low-income apartments.

There had initially been a public outcry against the changed plans. The company, and Decker in specific, had to jump through a lot of hoops to get approval. Eventually—with the backing of some powerful politicians—the changes were approved, the contract transferred, and construction resumed. The clubhouse-turned-homeless-shelter was finished first, followed closely by the first apartment building. Of the five buildings on the site, only the final apartment was still under construction, and according to the leasing office the others were already full to capacity.

"Why would a CEO scrap an approved development that would have brought in millions to build what more or less amounts to a charity project?"

<Good PR? A sense of moral obligation? Maybe he had a religious epiphany.>

Or maybe he was suddenly possessed by a demon.

<Turning a company's plans on end would certainly appeal to a demon's sense of chaos. Especially if destabilizing the company would have a ripple effect.>

A few more clicks brought up a listing of Bressett International's job portfolio.

"They've done work all over the world, and they're involved in over a dozen ongoing projects."

<So maybe the project shift was to undermine the company with their Fortune 500 clients.>

"But they've handled charity and humanitarian efforts before." She enlarged an article. "Check out this school they built in Venezuela after a flood. They made zero profit off that."

<But they planned that from the get-go; they didn't flip-flop the plan for seemingly no reason.>

"It looks like the driving force behind the change was this CEO, Decker." She tapped his image on the monitor. "That makes him the prime suspect for the foreman's boss." She clicked another link. "He's got an office downtown."

<Can I pick the disguise this time?>

Mira shook her head. "Unlike Nowak, no one at Bressett should recognize us, and we may need to go back more than once. Keeping track of aliases is hard enough without trying to match faces to names."

<What if Mr. Yummy follows the same bread crumbs and goes to see Decker?>

Mira pictured the cop's jacket stretched across his broad back as he crouched on Nowak's floor and discovered her Saint Jude pendant. She sighed. Her demon was right. It was just a cheap hunk of metal with a face stamped on it—like a million others. He couldn't connect it to her. And yet, she felt like he'd stolen a piece of her.

Hopefully we can avoid crossing paths again until we've verified if Decker is a rifter. Once we've sorted out what's really going on around here, we can hightail it outta town. Mr. Yummy will be left chasing shadows and rumors.

Chapter 9

Mira

BRESSETT INTERNATIONAL claimed the sixth floor of a glass-and-metal high-rise in downtown Baltimore, the lobby of which looked like an airport lounge.

Mira took a moment after passing through one of the wide, glass doors that spanned the front wall. The vaulted ceiling coupled with bright- white walls and chrome accents created a stark, futuristic feel, as if she'd stepped into a high-tech lab or the scene of a science fiction film. Eighty percent of the walls were actually windows, so there was no shortage of natural light, but globes of pale white hung from the high rafters like dew drops on spider silk in case the ambient light should drop below blinding.

A long, curved desk of polished wood dominated the middle of the lobby, and three uniformed guards sat behind it, glancing alternately at the comers and goers and the bank of monitors Mira assumed showed surveillance footage of various locations around the building.

Many of the people passing through the lobby paid the desk and guards no attention at all. Some waved or called a greeting. One or two approached to ask a question, but most headed straight for the four elevators set in the back wall. Mira followed the crowd.

Seven people packed into the elevator with her, and if not for the fact that she was shuffled to the back she might have jumped ship and taken the stairs.

<What is that godawful smell?>

Cologne.

<I've smelled cologne. This is . . . worse.>

It's because we're stuck in this tiny space with a bunch of different colognes, and perfumes, and body sweat, and . . . Mira closed her eyes and tried to breathe shallowly.

The elevator jerked and paused on the third floor. Two people stepped out. Then the doors closed and the ascent continued. Three more people got off on floor four. When the elevator reached the sixth floor, Mira squeezed between the remaining two women who had placed themselves directly in front of the doors. She waited until the elevator sealed behind her to take a deep breath.

The room she'd stepped into was small compared to the vast expanse of the main lobby below but a welcome improvement over the elevator. The wall behind her was dominated by the four elevator bays and a door that would lead to the stairs she'd definitely be taking on the way down. The opposite wall was decorated by four huge landscape paintings depicting a city skyline, sparkling ocean, tropical jungle, and mountain peaks. Something for everyone.

The shorter sides of the room each held four black, cushioned chairs and identical doors. In the center of it all was a desk and the second line of defense Mira would have to breach to reach Reed Decker.

The carpet on the sixth floor muffled her sneakers as she walked over to the smaller but equally polished wooden desk that mirrored the security station in the lobby. This one, however, was occupied by a single man with long, drawn-out features, streaky brown-blond hair, and close-set blue eyes that seemed oddly magnified behind a pair of thick-framed glasses. When he glanced up and saw Mira, he smiled so wide it made her face hurt in sympathy.

"Can I help you?"

"I'm here to see Reed Decker. Is he in?"

He blinked twice, looked Mira up and down, then said, "Do you have an appointment?"

Mira plastered on her own smile and stepped closer to the desk. "No, but I'm a big fan of his work. I'm a reporter for the *Baltimore Sun*, and I'd like to interview him for an article about the humanitarian side of big corporations. His work advocating for the transient population and low-income families here in Baltimore is truly inspiring."

The man beamed and nodded as though the compliments had been directed at him personally. "But I'm afraid Mr. Decker is a very busy man. No one sees him without an appointment." He turned slightly and set his hands on his keyboard. "We could perhaps fit you in next Thursday." He hit a few keys and squinted at his screen.

Mira glanced at the doors on either side. There was no indication where either led.

Sighing, she leaned against the desk and reached out until her fingers rested on the back of the secretary's hand.

He looked up sharply, his eyes even more buggy than before.

Mira forced herself to maintain her smile but focused most of her energy on channeling a small amount of magic into the man through their contact. "Mr. Decker wants to see me. He'll be very disappointed if you send me away."

Confusion flickered across the man's expression.

<Too soft.> Mira's magic increased, turning her nudge into a shove.

Stop, we don't want to damage him.

<He'll be fine.> The demon continued to turn up the power on Mira's compulsion spell.

"You need to let me pass," Mira said.

The man's eyes took on a glazed, glassy quality. His jaw went slack. He nodded slowly.

"Where is Decker's office?"

The man's lips parted, came together, parted again. "B . . . ba . . . back." The man's unfocused gaze shifted sideways, toward the door on Mira's right.

Mira released him and walked through the door. Once a layer of solid wood separated her from her victim, her smile turned into a scowl. She cast a quick glance up and down the hallway. A dozen or so doors lined the walls, including one directly to her right that capped off the hallway and bore the label "Storage Closet B." Taking a deep breath, she turned the handle and peeked inside. The room was only slightly larger than the elevator she'd ridden up in. Two walls were lined with wire shelves that held a variety of cleaning and office supplies. Exhaling, she stepped inside and closed herself in darkness.

<Um . . . I don't think we're going to find Decker in here.>

I wish you wouldn't do that.

<Point out the obvious flaws in your plan?>

Butt in when I'm casting a spell. I had that compulsion under control.

<You've got too soft a touch. Especially when it comes to mental control.>

I didn't want to melt the poor guy's brain!

<He'll be fine.> Impatience swelled within her. <Are we doing this or not?>

Yes, fine, just . . . follow my lead. I don't want to raise unnecessary suspicion. We've drawn more than enough attention in this town already.

<Hey, I'm not the one who took the straightforward approach with the foreman.>

Rolling her eyes, Mira opened the door a crack and peeked out. A man in a business suit was in the hall talking to someone in one of the offices that lined the outer wall. The man gestured wildly while he spoke, like he was miming a story. Then he and the hidden audience broke into laughter.

Mira shifted her weight.

The storyteller wiped his eyes, waved, then turned and disappeared down an intersecting hallway. A moment later, another man came out of the office, closed the door behind him, and followed the first.

Mira waited another few seconds before exiting the closet. She straightened her shoulders, tugged her jacket, and lifted her chin. Then she pinned a pleasant expression to her lips and strolled toward the back of the building, trying to project a sense of purpose and belonging. She ignored the office doors along the outer wall, keeping her eyes forward and her pace even. The center of the building was dominated by two large conference rooms. The first was empty. The second was packed. Beyond the conference rooms was a heavy oak door. Resisting the urge to look behind her, Mira inhaled and walked through that door.

A pair of blue-green eyes blinked up at her from the round, pale face of a girl—she looked to be about nineteen—who sat behind yet another polished, wooden desk. A ribbon of freckles stretched across her nose and cheeks like a cluster of stars. Strawberry-blond French braids clung to either side of her head and trailed over her slender shoulders.

"May I help you?"

Mira took a quick survey of the rest of the room—no windows, three chairs lined up against one wall, and only one door other than the one she'd come through. "I'm here to see Mr. Decker."

The girl frowned. "I wasn't aware of a meeting right now."

"The guy at the front desk sent me back to interview Mr. Decker for a newspaper article. You know, PR stuff." She waved a hand to indicate the details were too boring to mention.

The girl frowned, and a small wrinkle appeared between her eyebrows. "I'm Mr. Decker's personal assistant. Randy should have cleared any interview with me first." Frustration bubbled in the girl's words—frustration and a sullen resignation. This clearly wasn't the first time the guy up front had ignored this girl's right to be kept in the loop.

Mira spread her hands. "Maybe it just slipped his mind to call ahead. This interview was arranged on short notice."

The girl shook her head, making her braids bounce and jiggle. "He's trying to undermine me."

Nodding, Mira rested one hip against the desk and lowered her voice to a conspiratorial whisper. "He wants your job?"

"He's already convinced half the office Mr. Decker only hired me as eye candy." The girl's jaw stiffened. "But I'm good at this job, even if I don't have quite as much experience as Randy." Her gaze cast down to where her hands rested on her desk. She picked at the edge of one pink polished nail. "But he keeps setting things up so it looks like I'm not doing my work properly."

<Still worried I damaged that guy's brain?>

Mira gave her demon the mental equivalent of an elbow in the ribs and patted the girl's hand. She'd never had to deal with the dynamics of a corporate setting, but she knew what it was like to be judged on her gender. Luckily in her case, that judgment usually meant the bad guys were underestimating her.

The girl smiled at Mira. "Sorry, I shouldn't prattle on like this. Talk about unprofessional."

Mira shrugged. "I don't mind." She nodded toward the door to the back office. "But I do need to start my interview."

She nodded. "What was your name and which paper are you reporting for?"

"Miranda Hernandez for the *Baltimore Sun*."

She pressed a button on the intercom box on her desk. "Mr. Decker?"

"What is it, Jenny? I'm busy."

"Miss Hernandez from the *Baltimore Sun* is here to do an interview with you."

"Now? I didn't see that in my calendar."

"Yes, sir. The interview was arranged last minute, so I didn't get a chance to add it."

A series of grumbles and grunts drifted out of the speaker. Among them, Mira caught the words *incompetent* and *charity*.

The girl turned a few shades paler.

Mira bunched her fists. *I really hope this asshole turns out to be a rifter.*

The demon smiled.

"I don't have time for an interview right now. In fact, I need you to move my meeting with Darnell to Friday. There's something I need to take care of this afternoon."

"But, sir—"

"Last I checked, your job was to assist me, not argue. Or is that too much for you to handle?"

"Sorry, sir. I'll make the necessary arrangements." When the girl's hand came away from the intercom box, it was shaking.

"I'm sorry you came all this way Miss Hernandez, but I'm afraid . . . well, you heard him." She didn't look at Mira when she spoke.

<We can be through that door in a second.>

And if we're wrong and he's not a rifter?

<Then we scare the piss out of a jerk who deserves it.>

And bring security, and the cops, and probably get this poor kid fired.

<She might be better off.>

Mira couldn't argue with that. She crossed her arms and narrowed her eyes at the subdued secretary. "How can you work for that asshole?"

She glanced up. Her eyes were shiny, but she smiled. "He's really not so bad. It's just lately . . ." She shook her head. "Sorry. I shouldn't be talking about this. We need to reschedule your interview."

You catch that?

<She knows something.>

Maybe we can learn more about Decker without breaking down his door. But not here; she's scared.

<And lonely. We can use that.>

Mira pursed her lips, then said, "I'm pretty new in town, but I've heard the Inner Harbor is a great place to take a stroll. I'd love some company, if you're free after work."

The girl's face lit up like a puppy whose master had just come home. "I'd love that."

<Dang, this kid's almost as desperate to find a friend as you.>

Shut up.

"And I can show you my favorite shop," the girl continued. "It's where I get these." She pushed a small glass bowl toward Mira. "Try one."

Mira lifted a candy out of the bowl. It was bright orange and wrapped in wax paper with a small swirly logo printed on one side.

"Salt water taffy." The girl beamed.

"Thanks, Jenny."

Her smile faltered. "Actually . . ." She wrung her hands and looked away. "My name is Gemma. Gemma Murphy."

"Oh, sorry. I could've sworn I heard Decker call you Jenny."

She nodded. "He misheard me when I first introduced myself and . . . I just haven't had the heart to correct him."

<More like the guts.>

Mira stuffed the candy in her jacket pocket and forced a smile. "What time do you get off?"

"I can meet you in front of the visitor center at five fifteen."

Mira glanced at the clock on the wall—its mechanical *tick tock* echoed like the torturous drip of a leaky faucet. With an hour and a half till her meeting with the client who'd be bankrolling Mira's extended stay, she had enough time for a quick bite before heading across town. Then an hour for the meeting and back before five. She nodded. "See you there."

The meeting in the conference room was still in full swing when she passed. In the office lobby, Randy was staring at his stapler like he was trying to figure out if it meant him any harm. He'd likely recover from Mira's magical intervention in a couple of hours. Whether or not he still had a job after that . . .

Mira smiled and opened the door to the stairwell. She no longer felt bad about messing with him.

Chapter 10

Ty

TY KNOCKED ON the red door of his neighborhood pub and watched the back of LaRosa's car until it turned a corner up the street. She'd be back to pick him up after taking another look at the crime scene and circulating the three likenesses the sketch artist had made for them.

Weathered wood creaked, and a narrow gap appeared between the door and frame. Tina glared out at the daylight world through that gap. "We're not open yet. Come back later."

Ty set his palm against the door to keep it from closing. "I'm not here to drink." He flashed her his badge. "I need to ask you a few questions."

Tina's gaze flicked to his badge, then back to his face. She sighed and stepped back, fully opening the door. "Hadn't pegged you for a cop." She rubbed her right hand over the tattoos that covered her left arm. "A fed, maybe, but not a city cop."

Ty closed the door behind him. "This should only take a minute."

"All good out here, my love?" A man with Mediterranean-blue eyes, a thin, droopy mustache, and an equally thin goatee poked his head out from behind the door that led to the bar's kitchen.

"All good." Tina waved him away.

"Actually," Ty said before the man could retreat, "could you come here for a moment? There's something I'd like to ask you both."

The man emerged fully from behind the kitchen door. He was stocky and pale, with shaggy brown hair pulled into a pony tail. He wore a flannel shirt rolled up to his elbows, a grease-spattered apron, and a gold band on his ring finger.

"What's this about?"

"I'm looking for a woman." He handed Tina the sketch of the woman he'd taken home last night.

She glanced at the drawing, then at Ty. "This is the girl you left with."

Ty cleared his throat. "She's a person of interest in a case I'm working."

The proprietors shared a look that said all too clearly what they thought was going on.

Tina handed back the sketch. "Never saw her before last night. Haven't seen her since."

Ty looked at the man.

He shook his head. "Sorry."

Ty sighed. Returning to the bar had been a long shot, but he didn't know where else to start looking. They hadn't been able to pull any prints off the necklace from Nowak's office.

Tucking the sketch back in his folder, he pulled out a still frame from the KBU security footage and the photo from Nowak's driver's license. "How about these two? Ever seen either of them?"

Again the man shook his head.

Tina squinted at Nowak's picture. "This guy looks kinda familiar. He mighta been in a time or two."

"When?"

She frowned. "Aside from regulars like yourself and those that stir up trouble, I don't mark every face that walks through that door."

"You remembered the woman from last night."

She scowled. "That was, what, ten hours ago? Besides,"—she shrugged—"she was memorable."

That she was. Ty slipped the photos under the image of his mystery lover. His gaze lingered for a moment on the sketch. The artist had expertly captured the mischievous glint in the woman's mismatched eyes, the curve of her lips. He could almost feel their softness and the teasing nip of the teeth beneath.

He snapped the folder shut.

"Do you recall any strange happenings last night?"

Tina and her husband looked at each other, then Tina answered for both. "We chased off the last customers shortly after you left with your . . . friend." She glanced at the folder. "Then we locked up and went to bed. Nothing out of the ordinary."

Ty sighed and tucked the folder under his arm. "Thanks for talking to me. Please let me know if you see any of the people from the images I showed you."

Tina nodded toward the hidden pictures. "This really about a case?"

Heat crept into Ty's cheeks. "Yes," he snapped.

She raised her hands in surrender. "Whatever you say."

Ty tromped to the door and let himself out.

There was no sign of LaRosa on the street, so he turned toward the crime scene and started walking. Halfway up the block he pulled out his cell phone and hit the speed dial he'd added for LaRosa.

"No luck at the bar," he said without preamble when she answered the call. "How's it going on your end?"

"Lots of people recognized Nowak. Guess he was the 'hands-on' type of foreman. No hits yet on either woman."

Ty continued to walk, the *clip-clop* of his footsteps counting seconds against the pavement. *How fast would a woman move if she was fleeing a crime scene but trying to avoid notice?* He picked up his pace a bit. "I'm on my way to you."

"Walking?"

"I want to check the distance on foot."

"In case your drinking partner had just left our crime scene?"

More than a drinking partner. An uncomfortable knot tied itself in Ty's gut, like hunger and indigestion at the same time. His steps slowed as his thoughts spiraled back to the woman between his sheets last night.

He cleared his throat. "See you soon."

He stuffed the phone back in his pocket and picked up the pace again.

Ty

TY SET HIS brown plastic tray on the table across from LaRosa, who took a long pull from her extra-large soda and watched him sit. Two red-and-white checkered, waxed-cardboard baskets—one filled with chicken wings, the other with waffle fries—rested on his tray beside his own soda.

After verifying that his companion from the night before could easily have jogged the short distance from the crime scene to the bar where he'd met her, and more convinced than ever that the white dust he'd seen on her jacket had been powdered drywall, Ty had lost his appetite. LaRosa, however, hadn't. She'd completed her canvass while Ty made his trek, and when he arrived insisted the two of them stop off for lunch before returning to the office.

LaRosa lifted a sloppy nacho and shoved it in her mouth. A string of cheese stuck to her chin.

"You've got a . . ." Ty pointed to the wayward cheese.

"Not a single person recognized the woman in either sketch, or Temple." LaRosa wiped her mouth with a paper napkin, then scooped up another wad of shredded chicken and jalapeños glued together with cheese. "And so many people remembered seeing Nowak on the site that day that the connection is virtually useless. No one could tell me exactly *when* he was there, just that he came and went a lot."

The laden chip went in as soon as her words stopped.

Ty turned a fry over in his fingers, watching the spin of golden, criss-cross lines, and thought again of the woman from the bar. What had made him accept her offer? Sure, she'd been beautiful and he'd been lonely . . . but that couldn't have been all. Red flags had gone up when she didn't want to share her name, or really *anything* about herself, so why had he still taken her home?

"Look, I know you didn't want a partner"—LaRosa's voice startled Ty out of his speculation—"and it's not like we have to be friends, but we're stuck together, so could you please stop treating me like a leper?"

"Sorry, I—" He shook his head. "It's not you."

She took another sip of soda and eyed his untouched food. When the straw left her lips, she asked, "Food not posh enough for you?"

He smiled and again shook his head. Despite his best efforts, he was starting to like LaRosa. She was funny and open. In fact she reminded him of—he shied away from that thought.

"Why so mopey then?" She took another bite. At this rate, she'd be finished before Ty even started.

"Just distracted."

"With?" She drew out the vowel.

"Thinking about the mystery woman."

She nodded. "Wondering if you were drinking with a killer?"

"Wondering . . . if I would have noticed if I was." He sighed and finally took a bite of fry. He waved the remainder as he gestured. "In the PTF good instincts are, if not everything, one of the most important traits an agent needs. Instincts keep you safe when your eyes and ears fail you, when the physical world betrays you. Instincts keep you sane; they keep you alive." He shoved the remainder of the waffle fry into his mouth.

"What are your instincts telling you now?"

He chewed for a moment, thinking. "That the woman from the bar and the one who visited the foreman are the same person, and she's somehow connected with the murdered man at the construction site."

She nodded. "Those sound like good instincts to me."

Good instincts, huh? He picked up another fry and studied it. *I used to believe that . . . before those instincts led me into an ambush that got my partner killed. Now? I can't say for certain the hands that roamed my body last night weren't wrapped around Rodney Temple's neck, choking the life out of him, an hour before.*

Chapter 11

Mira

MIRA RUMBLED down the quiet, tree-lined streets of Ashburton on the west side of Baltimore. This area sported larger, detached homes rather than the row houses that dominated most of the city's neighborhoods. The buildings weren't huge, but they were well-kept, with tidy yards, dormant gardens, and Victorian architecture.

She spotted the number she was looking for and cut her engine in front of a pale-yellow building with baby-blue trim. A set of concrete stairs and a narrow sidewalk climbed the yard to the front porch, which was capped by a second-story balcony. Above that, a set of attic windows stuck up from the otherwise smooth slope of the roof.

She set her helmet on the seat of her motorcycle and started toward the house. When her foot touched the bottom step of the porch, the front door opened.

The woman who stepped out wore black leggings and a blue sweater that matched the trim on the house. The tight coils of her hair were professionally faded from deep brown at the roots to bleach blond at the tips, and the curls were swept up into a ponytail that erupted like a halo around the back of her head. She had chestnut skin and hazel eyes that shifted from deep amber near the pupil to a pale green on the outer edge.

"Are you Mindy Perez?"

"That's me," Mira said, and pulled out her fake P.I. license. "You Shaquana?"

The woman nodded. "Please, come in." She glanced side to side, as though checking for spies, then pulled the door open again and gestured for Mira to enter.

The inside of the house was as tidy as the outside, with clean carpets, polished wood, and well-stuffed furniture. Mira's *abuela* would have approved.

The woman took a seat at one end of a floral-patterned sofa and gestured for Mira to join her. "I want you to follow my girlfriend."

<No beating around the bush with this one.>

Mira settled on a cushion. "So your listing said. You think she's been cheating on you?"

"I know she has. She's out at all hours, sometimes she comes home in different clothes than when she left, and she's been cagey about answering my questions. She even had the gall to say I was being paranoid when I asked where she's been disappearing to." She shook her head. When she focused on Mira again, there were tears in her eyes. "I don't want to lose her, but I won't be made a fool of. I have to know the truth."

Mira nodded. "I'll need your girlfriend's name, job, recent picture."

"Her name is Angela, Angela Dougherty, and she's an event planner for the city." Shaquana grabbed a framed photo from the end table, pulled out the picture, and handed it to Mira. "That was taken six months ago . . . before everything fell apart."

The second woman in the photo had short, spiky blond hair, blue eyes crinkled with laugh lines, sun-kissed pink skin, and a brilliant smile.

<They look happy.>

Yeah . . . till reality kicked in. That kind of closeness can only end in pain.

<You don't know that.>

So Shaquana's crying 'cause she's happy? Mira waited a beat, but the demon didn't reply. *Didn't think so.*

Mira shifted her focus back to her client, who was dabbing her cheeks with a tissue. "How long have you and Angela been together?"

"Almost three years. Our anniversary is next month." Another burst of tears and sniffles racked the woman. "I th-th-thought we m-might even get m-ma-married."

<Human courtship rituals are ridiculous.>

No argument here.

Mira patted the crying woman on the knee. "I'll be as quick and discrete as I can."

Shaquana wrapped her arms around Mira and sobbed against her shoulder.

Mira stiffened.

The demon tensed, gathering energy for a counterattack.

Wait!

Grimacing, Mira raised one hand and patted her client on the back with the mechanical motion of a robot.

The demon stood down, but energy still swirled around Mira, stirred by her agitation.

"I'll need the agreed-upon half up front. Cash."

Shaquana straightened with a shuddering inhale. "O-of course." She stood, crossed the room, and opened a large leather handbag hanging from a hook on the wall. When she returned, her crying seemed more or less under control. She held out a wad of cash. "Please, get to the bottom of this."

Mira stood, nodded, and took the money. Then she practically ran for the front door.

Once she was alone on the porch with solid wood at her back, she gave a full-body shudder to clear the icky, clingy feeling of Shaquana's embrace.

Still think I should become codependent?

<I never said codependent, just less . . . hermity.>

Stuffing the cash into her pocket, she crossed the yard, pulled on her helmet, and straddled the bike. *This is the natural progression of getting close to people. Either they hurt you*—her thoughts turned to her mother—*or you hurt them.* She stomped the kick starter. *We're better off alone.*

Mira

THE INNER HARBOR at five o'clock was a crowded bustle of tourists and workers looking for a place to stroll, eat, or just sit and relax after a long day. Mira snagged a bench outside the visitor center and glared at anyone who looked like they might try to share it. People walked along the wide, red-brick promenade. The three tall masts of an ancient sailing-ship-turned-museum swayed in the wind while more modern yachts cruised the harbor. The chatter of conversation mingled with the threads of jazz and rock that drifted out of various clubs, cafes, and restaurants along the waterfront. The saltwater breeze carried other flavors that fought for dominance as people not yet ready to settle down for a proper meal followed their noses to pretzel stands, vats of kettle corn, and paper-wrapped fish and chips.

"Miranda!" Gemma trotted toward Mira, one hand raised and waving. She plopped down on the bench. "Hope you weren't waiting long."

Mira shook her head. "And please, call me Mira."

Gemma's smile grew even brighter. "Thanks. I've always wanted to have a nickname so I could say 'My friends call me . . .,' but really everyone just calls me Gemma. Except my mom. She calls me Ladybug, but that's even longer than Gemma, and it would be weird to have people on the street calling me Ladybug. But I guess you can call me that if you want."

"And then there's your boss." Mira gave Gemma a significant look. "He calls you Jenny."

Color crept into Gemma's cheeks. "Yeah, but that's not a nickname . . . just a mistake."

"You really should tell him he's got it wrong."

"I know, but it's been so long now. Wouldn't that be weird to suddenly be like, 'Hey Mr. Bossman, you've been saying my name wrong this whole time and I just couldn't work up the courage to correct you, so now we both look like idiots.'?"

<How can she talk so much and breathe so little?>

Good lung capacity, I guess. To Gemma, Mira asked, "Why didn't you correct him right away?"

"Oh, he's a very busy man. The hiring manager introduced me to Mr. Decker as he was on his way to a meeting, and it was my fault for mumbling. I should have spoken more clearly, but I was kind of intimidated. So when Mr. Decker shook my hand and said, 'Welcome aboard, Jenny,' I didn't even register the mistake until he was out the door. And after that, well . . . like I said. No point making us *both* feel like idiots."

"Doesn't anyone else in the office notice he's calling you by the wrong name?"

Gemma shrugged. "No one's ever mentioned it."

<This kid needs a confidence boost. I know! Let's get her drunk and have her take us to Decker's house. She can tell him he's a prick who's been saying her name wrong, and we can find out if he's a rifter.>

And if he is? The last thing we need is a drunk girl to take care of while we fight a rifter.

<Hmm . . . hadn't thought of that. Okay, we volunteer to tell him off *for* her while she waits in the car.>

Mira chuckled.

"I know, it's pathetic, right?" Gemma looked down at her fingers, knotted together in her lap. "I'd laugh too."

Mira shook her head. "That wasn't . . . I wasn't laughing at you."

"It's okay. Everyone else does."

<See? Confidence issues.>

Mira set her hand on Gemma's shoulder and waited until the girl met her gaze. "I'm *not* laughing at you. And I'm the last person you should listen to for advice on how to live your life. If what you're doing works for you, more power to you."

"Thanks." Gemma's smile came back in full force. "Are you hungry?"

Mira pulled her hand back. "What?"

"There's a great place just up the way. Best shepherd's pie. I'm starving. Let's go." Without waiting for a reply, she grabbed Mira's wrist and dragged her to her feet.

Mira resisted the urge to yank her arm free and allowed herself to be led through the gathered pedestrians. It was an odd sensation—unfamiliar but not unpleasant—and for a moment she was reminded of darting through crowds with her cousins during the Calle Ocho Music Festival in Little Havana when she was young.

"Here we are."

Gemma's "great place" turned out to be an Irish bar and grill called Tir Na Nog near the renovated ship Mira had noticed earlier. The bar was packed, as were most of the tables, but the hostess found a spot for them near the back of the main dining room. Mira claimed the chair that put a wall at her back and scanned the crowd. Too many people. Too few exits. Her skin started to itch.

"You like Guinness?" Gemma had to shout to be heard over the chatter of the patrons and the lively jig being played by a trio of musicians.

Mira considered the cash in her pocket. Enough to pay for a few nights in her motel, sure, but enough to splurge on drinks and fine dining? Not so much. "I—" She momentarily choked on a surge of energy as the demon snatched the reins of control. "Sure."

She coughed to cover her discomfort. *What the hell?*

<You were going to say no.>

I know.

<And that was the wrong answer.>

Gemma ordered two beers from a waitress walking past. Lack of confidence didn't seem to be a problem for her outside the office.

<You should relax. Try to have a little fun.>

This isn't a social hang out. We have work to do.

<Why can't we do both?>

"How long have you been in town?" Gemma asked.

Mira struggled to refocus her brain on the companion sitting across the table from her. "Um, about a week."

"Where are you staying?"

"Just some shitty motel." Mira waved that line of questioning away. "How long have you been Mr. Decker's personal assistant?"

<Way to ease into the interrogation.>

Let me handle this.

<Yeah, yeah.>

Gemma looked up. Her eyes skimmed back and forth as though

searching for the information. "Almost two years now, I guess. Boy, time sure does fly."

"Wasn't he involved in a bit of a scandal a while back? Something about turning luxury condos into a homeless shelter?"

The waitress returned and set two dark beers from her overloaded tray on the table. "You ready to order?"

"I'll have the shepherd's pie," Gemma piped without hesitation. She hadn't even picked up the menu.

"Um, sure, I'll have the same."

The waitress nodded and moved to the next table.

"So," Mira prompted, "the scandal?"

"Oh, it wasn't so much a scandal as a . . . a change of heart. And it worked out for the best. Sure, the company lost a few investors, but the project ended up helping a lot more people in the long run." Gemma tipped her drink to her lips. When she set it down again it was half empty.

Mira waited a beat, but when no more information seemed to be forthcoming she said, "I heard there was some kind of crime there last night."

Gemma nodded, a serious expression on her face. "Oh yes, terrible thing. Murder."

"You know anything about it?"

"Just office gossip," Gemma said. "I really shouldn't talk about it."

"What's a little gossip between girls?" Mira lifted her glass, clinked it against Gemma's, and took a sip.

<You're about as subtle as a pink rhinoceros.>

Mira growled under her breath as she set her drink down.

Gemma frowned.

"I have a bit of a fascination with true crime stories," Mira said. "But I get it. We just met. If you don't trust me—"

"No!" Gemma's hand shot out to cover Mira's on the table. "That's not it at all. I just didn't think you'd want to hear about a murder over dinner. But I'm more than happy to talk about it, if that's what you want."

<I take it back. You're clearly a master manipulator.>

A pang of guilt twisted in Mira's chest at using Gemma's obvious desperation for friendship to get her to talk, but getting the information she needed was all that mattered. Right? She couldn't let the fact that she found Gemma's company surprisingly enjoyable distract her. "Do you know what happened? Who was behind it?"

Gemma shook her head. "But I heard the body was really freaky when the cops found it . . . like, mummified. Probably with magic. So I guess the killer must have been a fae. Not too surprising with all the bad blood these days. Still, awful business." She shuddered. "And then Mr. Nowak—that's the construction foreman heading up the project—just up and disappeared this morning. Mr. Decker had me calling everywhere I could think of, but I haven't been able to get hold of him."

Mira tried to look surprised. "Weird."

Gemma leaned in and whispered conspiratorially, "Can you keep a secret?"

Mira nodded.

"I think maybe Mr. Nowak killed that poor man at the construction site, then skipped town. He could have been an unregistered fae hiding in the mortal realm."

"Were Nowak and Decker close?"

Gemma scrunched her nose as though she found the question odd.

"Not like friends," Mira backpedaled, "but they must have interacted quite a bit, working on the same project. Wouldn't Decker have noticed if Nowak was a fae?"

"Once the project was approved, most of the day-to-day stuff was handled by Nowak. He and Mr. Decker met a few times to discuss changes or delays but nothing out of the ordinary. In fact, with this project wrapping up, Mr. Decker is heading out to oversee his next big deal. He and his wife will be in Bangalore by the end of the month."

Mira choked on her beer and nearly spit it out but managed to hold back the cough that would have sprayed Gemma and swallowed instead. "Is that normal . . . to leave before the project is done?"

"Actually, Mr. Decker stayed longer than usual on this one. Once the ink is dry on the paperwork for a project, he's usually on to the next. I think he stayed longer because his wife wanted to be stateside for a while. He even rented a house in Mt. Washington rather than staying in a hotel. Said they wanted more privacy." She cupped a hand to the side of her mouth and stage whispered, "I think she's starting to feel the tick tock of her biological clock."

<Tick tock.>

If Decker's a rifter, sex would be the least nasty thing a hotel maid might walk in on.

"What about you? Will you go with them?"

Gemma nodded. "As Decker's personal assistant, I go where he goes." She downed the last of her beer and held the empty glass aloft for the waitress to see. "It's a pretty sweet deal. The company pays for my travel and living expenses."

"The moving doesn't bother you?"

Gemma set her empty glass down and stared into the dregs. "It does get lonely sometimes, leaving friends and family behind, starting over somewhere new."

<Sound like anyone we know?>

"But I also get to meet a lot of interesting people." She looked up and smiled. "Like you."

Another pang of guilt. Mira knew more than a little about being lonely. "I'm glad. I mean . . . I'm enjoying hanging out with you, too."

<Wow. Did that hurt to admit?>

Mira cleared her throat and reminded herself she was *supposed* to be working. "When Decker had his change of heart, did you notice any other differences? Personality? Secretiveness? Irritability?"

Gemma laughed. "Mr. Decker is always irritable. But now that you mention it, he did seem a little . . . off during that project redesign. Like he was taking orders rather than giving them. When someone asked him *why* he was making a change, he didn't really have an answer. He'd just say that was how it had to be. It was weird."

<Ding, ding, ding . . . we have a winner!>

Weird behavior alone isn't proof of demon possession, but definitely worth looking into.

"What all do you do as Decker's assistant?"

"Mostly it's my job to make sure Mr. Decker's day runs smoothly. That can mean anything from scheduling meetings and following up with contractors, to arranging travel papers and renting cars, or even picking up his coffee order."

"Sounds like you basically run his life."

"Feels that way sometimes."

"So what's an average day look like for the CEO of a Fortune 500 company? Tomorrow, say. What's on the schedule? Cooped up in the office or hobnobbing around town?"

Gemma shook her head. "Neither. Or maybe both? Mr. Decker has a board meeting in New York tomorrow. He flew out not long after you stopped by and won't be back till tomorrow evening."

Mira's thoughts stalled for a moment as the information sank in.

<We should have stormed the office.>

We couldn't risk police involvement. Besides, we didn't know he was going out of town.

<Still, it would have been nice to get confirmation so we at least knew if we were stalking the right guy.>

Yeah.

<On the plus side . . . since there's no chance of paying Decker a visit tonight, maybe you can finally relax and enjoy yourself.>

The waitress returned with another round of beers and two steaming plates of shepherd's pie.

Gemma lifted her fork with a grin. "When we're done here, I'll take you to that sweets shop I told you about, where I get the saltwater taffy."

Mira leaned over her dinner and took a deep breath. It smelled like heaven. She smiled across the table at Gemma, who smiled back. Maybe her demon was right; maybe she should relax a little. Having a friend might be a nice change, if only for one night.

She lifted a steaming forkful and took a bite, murmuring with pleasure. Good food and good company—her idea of a one-night stand was so different from her demon's . . . and much more rare.

Chapter 12

Mira

MIRA STEPPED OUT of the shower and dried off with one of the threadbare towels provided by the motel, then slipped into a fresh pair of jeans and a blue-and-white blouse. When she grabbed her leather jacket off the end of the bed, a sheet of glossy paper fell out and fluttered to the floor.

She stooped down, picked it up, and turned it over.

The thin strip of paper was printed with a series of four square, black-and-white photos—the kind where you feed a dollar into a booth and it takes timed pictures, then drops the prints in a little tray. Before last night, Mira hadn't realized those things even existed anymore.

She ran her fingers over the images, and the corners of her mouth pulled up. In the first, Gemma was grinning but Mira sat with a straight back and a closed expression. Gemma had ambush-tickled her right before the second flash, so Mira's mouth was open and her eyes were shut. Mira couldn't remember the last time she'd been tickled before that. Probably back when she lived with her *abuela*, before Detroit.

Gemma had insisted they make funny faces in the second-to-last picture—Mira had stuck out her tongue and crossed her eyes. The final photo was Mira's favorite. Both women faced the camera with simple, genuine smiles.

Straightening, Mira glanced at the white bag tied with a red ribbon on the motel dresser. The bag held a dozen differently flavored saltwater taffies—a gift from Gemma.

<You liked her, liked having someone to laugh with outside your own head.>

Of course I liked her. She was sweet and open . . . and all the things we're not.

<We should give her a call. See if she wants to hang out again tonight.>

Have you forgotten why we're here?

<No. But there's more to life than just living.>

Yeah, like hunting demons and protecting innocents like Gemma.

<For us hunting demons *is* just living. It's necessary to maintain our balance. That doesn't mean you can't enjoy *other* activities. Get a hobby, make a friend, fall in love—>

"Lose control and ruin their lives." Mira pictured Gemma's laughter as they strolled along the promenade last night. Then that laughter turned to screams in her imagination as Gemma's face was overlaid by the high school kids she'd lashed out at the last time she'd tried to lead a normal life. She'd briefly considered trying to chase the demon off after that incident, but a power struggle like that would have torn her body apart. Besides, knowing what she now did about the Rift, she could never ask her demon to go back there. That would be like abandoning a friend to be tortured. For better or worse, they were stuck with each other.

She shook her head. "Gemma—everyone—is better off staying as far away from us as they can get. We're like a walking toxic dump. I should have a bright-red warning label tattooed on my forehead: *Caution: long-term exposure may prove fatal.*"

<You're exaggerating.>

"I'm not, actually. Or have you forgotten that my mother is a gibbering crazy person with a melted face thanks to us."

<That was . . . unfortunate, but—>

"No. No excuses. I *do* like Gemma . . . which is why we can't ever be real friends." Mira held the photo strip over the trash can, hesitated, then set it on the dresser. She might not be able to have a friend, but she could hold on to the memory. Heaven knew she could use some nice ones to balance out all the shit she'd seen.

<Fine. No friends. Got it.> The demon sighed, and the sound came out Mira's mouth. <Back to demon hunting then?>

"Decker's coming back tonight. We'll stake out his house and confront him when he gets there."

Giddy anticipation swelled inside. <An ambush.>

Mira rolled her eyes. "Remember, we need to *talk* to him. We can't go in there guns blazing."

<Who said anything about guns?>

"Figure of speech. My point is even if he *is* a decent rifter, like us—"

<Which he's probably not.>

"—attacking him without provocation will just ensure he fights back, if only to protect himself. The idea here is to find out how long he's been a rifter and what his plans for this city are."

<Yeah, because that worked out so well with Nowak.>

"Just because Nowak turned out to be an asshole doesn't mean Decker is."

<And just because you're lonely, doesn't mean he's good.>

"I'm *not* lonely."

<Sure. You keep telling yourself that.>

She sighed and pinched the bridge of her nose. "We need to find Decker's address."

<Too bad we're not friends with his personal assistant, who manages his entire life and can tell us exactly which property he's renting.>

"I'm a PI. I find people's personal information all the time." Mira's fingers flew across the keyboard of her open laptop. "Gemma said Decker would be in Bangalore by the end of the month, so whatever house he's renting should be back on the market. We'll do a search of the real estate records for Mt. Washington and compare them to listings from when Decker first arrived in Baltimore."

<Asking Gemma would be easier.>

"It would be quicker. There's a difference."

<Fine. So we look up the address, stake out the property, then *politely* knock on the door. What about the wife?>

"Probably enthralled if she's been married to a rifter for months and hasn't noticed anything wrong."

<Or possibly another rifter, since we're clearly working outside the norms on this one.>

"Until we know if she's a threat or a hostage, we won't hurt her if we don't have to. Bingo! Got it." She jotted what she hoped was Decker's address on a scrap of paper.

<Great, we have a plan. What do we do till tonight?>

Mira closed the laptop, slipped her arms into the sleeves of her jacket, took one last look at the photos on the dresser, and stepped into her sneakers. "We pay the bills."

Mira

MIRA LEAFED through the pages of a magazine without actually looking at the content. Her focus was on the woman across the street. In white jeans and a purple sweater, Angela Dougherty was fairly easy to spot in a crowd.

Mira had arrived at the end of Shaquana's quiet street in Ashburton before the sun rose high enough to burn off the morning mist. When the front door opened a little after dawn, Mira recognized the spiky blond hair from Angela's picture. Since then, she'd followed the woman to a downtown office building, a deli, a landscape supply chain near the edge of town, and a flower shop. Some of the stops lasted only a few minutes. Others, like the flower shop, had been hours.

They were currently at a farmers market near the docks, where bins of fresh produce sat beside stacks of gutted fish on trays of ice. Mira set down the magazine and pretended to inspect a stand of dangling garlic chains.

Angela was deep in conversation with the operator of a stall selling root vegetables, bags of grain, and jars of preserves, and had been for quite some time.

What do you think they're talking about?

<Shaquana said her girlfriend was some kind of event planner, right? Maybe she's, you know . . . planning.>

Flowers, food, décor . . . could be.

Mira moved to the booth next to the one Angela was standing in front of. She smiled at the woman behind the stand, ran her fingers over a pile of hand-knitted scarves, and asked how much they were, but she didn't listen to the answer. She was straining to hear the conversation in the next stall over.

". . . a friend named Dave Rubens who might be able to help you out. Works packing over at the Hermes warehouse. He's on shift tomorrow at four." Mira watched from the corner of her eye as the vendor handed Angela a piece of paper. "Tell him Paul sent you."

<Think she's scheduling a date?>

Mira pondered the question. *Not unless she's moonlighting as a prostitute—too impersonal.*

<We haven't seen any evidence of a love affair yet.>

Maybe she's not horny today.

<Or maybe Shaquana is wrong and their relationship isn't in any trouble at all.>

Affair or no, the fact that we've been hired means their relationship is definitely in trouble.

<Aren't you Little Miss Sunshine. You almost sound like you *want* Angela to be having an affair.>

If it means getting paid sooner, yeah, I do. Besides—three years and no ring? Chances are she is.

<Not that I'd blame her. I've never understood your species' obsession with monogamy. Although, that at least is better than *your* approach to relationships.>

Can we not make this about me?

<See that guy over there?>

Seriously, I'm not in the mood for—

<Seriously. I think he's watching us.>

Mira shifted her attention back to the external world.

Angela was shaking hands with the shopkeeper. A little farther up the street was a man who was a head taller than most of the crowd, giving him a clear view of the market . . . and he was looking straight at Mira.

Time to go.

<Maybe he just thinks you're pretty.>

Or maybe he saw me at the construction site, or Decker's office building, and he's trying to place my face.

Mira started walking toward the edge of the market. She kept her pace to an easy stroll. No reason yet to risk drawing attention.

Mira felt a pull of energy as the demon extended her awareness. She could now feel all the people around her. Each presence was like a ripple in fog, a vague outline of motion as people's movements shifted the hidden currents of the Rift that swirled around them. Most of the disturbances moved slowly as people perused the stalls. A few sped by in a hurry to somewhere or other. One ripple seemed to be matching pace with her.

<He's following us.>

Mira turned down an intersecting street and picked up her pace. If she could just get around the next corner before her stalker caught up. . . . She broke into a jog.

The pressure behind her eased.

The next street up was too far, and people were glancing in her direction now that she was moving faster than the other pedestrians. She slowed and scanned the signs around her. Two buildings ahead on the right was a Goodwill retail store.

Mira changed course and headed for the shop. A digital bell chimed when she stepped inside, but the clerks were all busy at their registers and no one looked up.

She quickly walked to the center of an aisle of winter coats and bent down as though inspecting the material of a long, tan jacket. The door chime rang out a moment later.

Glancing side to side to make sure she was alone in the aisle, Mira cast a "don't look here"—a spell that would distort the air around her, masking her presence and forcing an observer's gaze away without alerting them that anything was wrong with the space. The spell wasn't foolproof—if her pursuer walked down the aisle he'd still bump into her—but few people would willingly endure the headache of breaking through the illusion.

Seconds after the spell settled around her, the man from the market stepped into view.

He was young, probably younger than she was, and wore a blue, button-up shirt and dark jeans. For all his height, he wasn't large; though if he ever filled in his lanky frame, he would be. He had mousy-brown hair, pale skin, and about a million freckles. His eyes, nearly the same brown as his hair, scanned the room.

The man's gaze caught for a moment where Mira crouched. Then he blinked and continued his search. He walked past her aisle, deeper into the store. A moment later he passed again, heading the other direction. The door chimed.

Mira exhaled and let her magic splinter away.

She didn't straighten right away. When she did, she did so slowly, peering above the racks. A woman in the next aisle over glanced in her direction, then returned to her dress comparison. A child wailed near the far wall, pointing to a toy robot while being dragged away by his mother. The man who'd followed her was nowhere in sight.

Mira sighed.

<Who do you think he was?>

No idea. Not someone I recognized. You?

<Nope.>

Let's give him a minute to clear the street. Then we'll head back to the motel.

<What about Angela?>

Even if she's still at the market, I don't want to risk going back. But mention of their target brought another thought to mind. *Do you suppose Shaquana double-booked the job?*

<Another PI? I suppose it wouldn't be the first time.>

That was the downside of working with desperate clients. They paid well, but sometimes they also paid widely, and the last thing Mira needed was to cross paths with another freelance investigator.

<The up-front she gave us is enough to cover our room for a week. We could just dump this job.>

Mira thought of the email from her *abuela* about her mother's treatment costs and shook her head. *We'll just need to be cautious.*

Mira walked the aisles with the other shoppers. She picked up a pair of green corduroy pants with a half-off tag, a white blouse with big, red poppies that was marked down to a dollar, and a pair of dark sunglasses and headed for the register.

When she stepped onto the sidewalk with her bag of purchases, she blended nicely with the other pedestrians. She glanced up and down the street.

No sign of her stalker.

She bit the inside of her cheek and headed back toward the farmers market.

<I thought we were done with Angela for today?>

I want to get another look at that guy.

<Too skinny for my tastes, but whatever floats your boat.>

The lunch rush around the farmers market was dying down, so the crowd was thinner. Mira leaned around the corner of a building. Heat radiated off the bricks. She scanned the area.

No Angela. No stalker. Either he'd called it a day after chasing Mira off, or he'd gotten back to Angela before she left the market and now had a head start on cashing in on this job.

<Maybe he's the affair.>

Mira frowned.

<If he's Angela's on-the-side boyfriend and he saw you following her . . .>

Possibly. Mira left her lookout and turned up a side street. *Just because she's got a girlfriend doesn't mean Angela's lover is female.*

<Should we ask Shaquana if Angela is bi?>

Mira shook her head. "The gender of her lover makes no difference. Our job stays the same."

"Mira!"

She spun at the sound of her name. Gemma was standing across the street waving one arm vigorously above her head. Her other arm was loaded with garment bags.

Gemma waited for a gap in traffic, then darted across the street. "I was across the street picking up Mr. Decker's dry cleaning when I saw you through the window." She glanced at the bag dangling from Mira's hand. "You out shopping?"

"Uh . . . yeah. I was just—"

"Have you eaten? We could get some lunch."

"Um, I can't today."

Gemma's smile dimmed. "Oh, all right." She looked up and down the sidewalk. "Which way are you headed?"

Mira pointed in the direction she'd been walking.

"Me, too." Gemma took a couple steps, then looked back and waited for Mira to join her.

<She's like a stray puppy. You should never have fed her if you didn't want to keep her.>

Rolling her eyes, Mira started walking again.

"Did you not have fun last night?" Gemma's voice was subdued. She didn't look in Mira's direction.

"I had a great time," Mira said, recalling the ease with which she'd laughed as they strolled the Inner Harbor together, that feeling of relaxed companionship. Then she reminded herself that the distance she was creating was for Gemma's sake as much as hers. "I'm just really busy right now."

"What are you busy with?"

Mira shook her head. "Errands mostly. Lame but necessary."

They walked to the end of the block in silence and waited for the crosswalk signal to light up.

<This is awkward.>

You think? Mira shoved as much sarcasm as she could into the thought.

<You should have just agreed to lunch. We need to eat anyway.>

No. I'm trying to discourage her from being my friend.

<With your personality, that's not usually a problem.>

Mira blew out a noisy sigh.

Gemma glanced over, then away.

A spasm of tension squeezed Mira's chest. She cleared her throat and pointed to the pile of clothes in Gemma's arms. "Decker makes you pick up his laundry?"

Gemma adjusted the bags. "He's got a big dinner coming up. Speeches, politicians, the whole deal, so he and the missus gotta dress to the nines."

The walk signal flashed and Mira and Gemma stepped into the street. Halfway across, Gemma blurted, "Are you an undercover PTF agent?"

Mira stumbled and stopped. She stared at Gemma, who turned after taking two more steps.

"What? Why would you—"

A car horn blared as a motorist trying to make a right turn reminded her she was standing in the middle of a street.

She and Gemma hurried to the far sidewalk.

"I've been thinking about our conversation last night, how you kept asking questions about Mr. Decker."

"I was just—"

"And that got me to thinking about how strange Mr. Decker was acting when he changed the designs for the development project."

Mira shifted uncomfortably. She couldn't blame Gemma for being curious after the way she'd steered the conversation last night, but she didn't want Gemma getting involved. It wasn't safe. "I'm sure he—"

"Plus, that was about the same time Mr. Nowak's company replaced the previous construction firm. And that, along with the idea that maybe Mr. Nowak was secretly a fae, got me to thinking that maybe Mr. Decker was under some kind of spell."

<Sharp, but so far off . . .>

Give her a break. Demon possessions aren't nearly as common as unregistered fae.

Mira shook her head. "Look, I really don't—"

"There's something strange going on here, and I think you know more than you're saying."

<Maybe we should run with the whole undercover agent thing. At least that would explain your clumsy interrogation last night.>

Mira didn't like the idea of lying to Gemma any more than she already had, but if that's what it took to convince the girl to butt out and stay safe. . . . She took a deep breath. "Fine. Yes. I'm looking into the construction site murder. You heard how the body was found, right? There's clearly magic involved."

"I knew it!"

"Shh." Mira pulled Gemma into the mouth of a one-way alley. "Deep cover. No one can know what I'm doing here."

Gemma nodded. "Your secret's safe with me."

"Good. Now I need you to drop this. Forget you ever met me. Keep doing whatever it is you do for Decker, just like you have been."

"How do you think Mr. Decker is involved? He's not the killer is he? Or is he?" She looked at the garment bags in her arms and whispered, "I could be holding a killer's laundry."

Mira put her hands on her hips, looked to the sky, and exhaled. "I don't know yet. That's why I'm investigating."

"Maybe I can help."

Mira's gaze snapped down. "What? No."

"But I could be, like, your eyes and ears inside the company. No one knows more about Mr. Decker's comings and goings than me."

<She's got a point.>

"Absolutely not."

<She'd be useful.>

No.

"But—"

"Look, Gemma, this is for your own good. You need to drop this. Promise me you won't do anything about Decker."

Gemma's lower lip turned down. "You're not very trusting, are you? Guess maybe that's part of being an agent? All down in the dirt and blood, seeing the worst of the world?"

"Something like that."

"But it's not all bad. There are a lot of wonderful things in this world, too." Plastic crinkled as she hugged the garment bags tight enough to wrinkle the items inside. "But even the most beautiful sight isn't half so nice if you don't have someone to share it with."

Mira frowned. "This isn't watching a rainbow or sharing a pint. This is dangerous. You could get hurt."

"So could you."

"I have skills you don't."

"But—"

"Look, I don't need or want your help. That's final." Mira sent a thread of magic in Gemma's direction. A gentle persuasion.

Gemma's frown deepened. Her brow furrowed. Then, without another word, she walked away.

<So much for making friends.>

She'll be safer this way.

<Maybe. But did you turn her down to protect her . . . or to protect yourself?>

Chapter 13

Ty

TY TIPPED THE last drop of coffee from his paper cup—his third since returning to the office—into his mouth without taking his eyes off the documents in his other hand. The office coffee left a bitter, burnt flavor in his mouth that matched his mood. Witness statements, the coroner's report, forensic findings . . . none of it led anywhere. He crushed the empty paper cup and tossed it in the wastebasket.

Cause of death: unknown. The autopsy revealed a catastrophic system failure the likes of which the coroner had never seen. It was as if every organ in Temple's body had broken down simultaneously. Every cell was desiccated and depleted of electrical charge—which at least explained why Temple looked like an ancient Egyptian mummy. The estimated time of death was even less enlightening. The temperature of the corpse when the coroner arrived was thirty-four degrees Fahrenheit, which would indicate the victim had been dead for hours, if not days. Yet there were no signs of lividity to indicate the body had been moved, and there definitely hadn't been a corpse on site when the workers left at quitting time.

Witnesses placed Nowak at or around the site all day, but no one could say when, or if, he left.

The skin on the victim's neck was too badly damaged to pull prints. The shoe prints left in the fresh drywall dust told them the second person—probably a woman judging by the shoe size—had an even gait. The same prints had been found in the mud under one of the windows. Nowak wore a size eleven according to the officers LaRosa had sent to search his house.

Ty dropped the folder on his desk with a sigh, leaned back in his chair, and rubbed his eyes. His gut was telling him the crime scene footprints belonged to the woman he'd met at the bar, but he couldn't reconcile her soft, warm smile and tender touch with a cold-blooded killer. Surely he should have had some inkling if he'd been sleeping with a murderer. Or were his instincts so scrambled he couldn't tell the good guys from the bad anymore?

"Got you some kung pao." LaRosa plopped a Chinese takeout carton on his desk. "Any luck with the paperwork?"

"The problem when magic is involved is that all the usual forensic markers mean shit." He reached for the carton but detoured when his phone rang. "Detective Williams."

"I've got a lead."

"Billy? Isn't this your day off?"

"Yeah but get this, I think I just spotted your suspect at the farmers market in Fells Point."

"What?" Ty jerked straight in his chair.

LaRosa froze with a string of lo mein dangling from her chopsticks.

"Which one?"

"The woman from the sketch; the one you stood us up to drink with."

"You sure it was her?"

"Not one hundred percent, but she did a runner when I moved in. Definitely skittish. And she had the white stripe you mentioned."

"Fells Point, you say?" Ty signaled to LaRosa, who dropped her noodles back in their container, grabbed her own phone, and ordered an area search. Ty grabbed his keys. "Tell me exactly what happened."

Ty

TY PARKED UNDER the mottled shade of a bare oak. The street had that "quiet neighborhood" feel Ty recalled from his childhood home back in Roxbury—where he and Jamal had met, played, grown up. Where Ty's family still lived. And Jamal's. Where Ty hadn't set foot since the funeral, choosing instead to run away to a new city and a fresh start. Except ghosts weren't that easy to outrun.

"Hey, Earth to Williams." LaRosa's palm crossed Ty's vision.

He blinked and pulled the key out of the ignition.

"Where'd you go?"

He shook his head. "You want to take the lead here, or should I?"

"Seeing as how I just caught you daydreaming, I'll take point."

Ty stepped out and rounded the front of his truck. A cool breeze rustled brown leaves in the gutter and an American flag hanging beside the door they were heading for.

Billy had been certain Ty's mystery lady was tailing a blond woman at the market. She'd been long gone by the time he returned from his failed apprehension, but he'd gotten her name from a vendor he'd seen her talking to. From there it was only a few keystrokes to get her address and photo from the DMV database.

LaRosa rang the bell. Ty waited on the steps, scanning the street, trying to shake that lingering, hometown feeling.

When the door opened, a woman with chestnut skin and ombré curls stood in the frame.

Ty gave her a quick once-over. *Not Angela Dougherty.*

"My name is Detective LaRosa." She flipped her badge, then indicated Ty. "This is Detective Williams. We're looking for Angela Dougherty."

The color drained from the woman's face. "Why? What's this about? Is Angie in some kind of trouble?"

"Nothing like that," LaRosa assured, though Ty wasn't willing to write Dougherty off so quick. "We just need to ask her a couple questions. Is she around?"

The woman shook her head. "She left for work early this morning, hasn't come back yet."

"Do you have a phone number where we could reach her?"

"Of course, I—wait." She pointed up the street. "That's her now."

A tan Lincoln rumbled up the street and pulled into the narrow driveway by the side of the blue-and-yellow house. A moment later a woman with short, blond hair, wearing a purple sweater and white jeans, stepped out. She matched Billy's description perfectly.

"Hey, babe." Angela waved. "I'm just dropping off some groceries. I stopped by the farmers market today and got some of that mango chutney you love." She opened the back door, retrieved three green fabric bags, and crossed the lawn.

"Miss Dougherty?" LaRosa stepped off the porch as the woman approached. "My name is Detective LaRosa. I need to ask you some questions about your trip to the farmers market this afternoon."

Angela frowned, looked at the woman on the porch, at Ty, and finally back to LaRosa. "What kind of questions?"

"Have you ever seen this woman?" LaRosa held out the sketch of Ty's mystery girl.

Dougherty shook her head.

The woman on the porch leaned forward to peek at the picture. She inhaled sharply.

Ty turned to the woman. "Do you recognize her?"

The woman's curls danced wildly when she shook her head, but her stance was too tense. She seemed more upset now than when she'd been worried Angela was in trouble. *Maybe we're talking to the wrong woman. Then again . . . maybe I'm just imagining things . . . again.*

"Take another look," LaRosa prompted.

Angela squinted at the paper but shook her head. "I've never seen her before. Why? Who is she?"

"She's a person of interest in an ongoing investigation, and she was seen at the farmers market in Fells Point today."

Angela chuckled. "Dozens, hell, hundreds of people visit that market. What made you think I'd know her?"

"We have reason to believe she was following you."

The smile dropped from Angela's face. Her voice cut off mid-laugh.

"Following . . . me? Why?" The first hints of panic crept into her expression.

"We were hoping *you* could tell *us*." LaRosa tucked the sketch back into her folder.

"I . . . I don't know." Angela's eyes were widening by the second as worst-case scenarios flashed through her thoughts. "I'm nobody. I don't have enemies."

"What about your job?"

"I don't—" She glanced at the woman on the porch, then away. "My job isn't important or sensitive at all. I just plan parties, and training sessions, and stuff."

"Do you have any connection to a construction site in Bolton Hill?"

"Those fancy new low-rent apartments?" She scrunched her nose. "No."

"How about KBU Construction? Ever had dealings with them? Or more specifically, a foreman named Anton Nowak?"

She shook her head.

Ty was watching the woman on the porch out of the corner of his eye. Her demeanor hadn't changed at mention of either the construction site or Nowak.

"Ever heard of a man named Rodney Temple?"

Again, Angela shook her head. She was looking more relaxed with each negative answer as the possibility of her connection to this mess grew more remote.

LaRosa glanced at the other woman. "You? Any of this ringing a bell?"

The woman's gaze flickered almost imperceptibly to the folder in

LaRosa's hand. Then she, too, shook her head.

LaRosa looked at Ty, frustration clear on her face. "Looks like this was a dead end."

"Looks like." He pulled out one of his business cards, the ones with his direct number, and handed it to the woman on the porch. "In case you remember anything."

Her hand shook slightly when she reached for the card.

He held it a moment after she pinched it between her fingers so they were connected by the bridge of thick paper.

She glanced up.

He caught her gaze and narrowed his eyes. *I know you're hiding something, but I'll give you this one chance to come clean.* Then he released the card.

The woman stepped back and stared at the card in her hand.

"What was that?" LaRosa asked when they were halfway across the yard and the two women had closed themselves in the house.

"What?"

She hooked a thumb behind her. "That macho staring contest you had with the girlfriend."

"Just a feeling."

"Instincts telling you something?"

Maybe his gut was wrong. Wouldn't be the first time. But then again, maybe not.

"We'll see." He opened the driver's side door and slipped in behind the wheel.

Chapter 14

Mira

ANGELA DOUGHERTY didn't seem to exist on any of the city's online personnel directories.

Mira flopped back on her motel bed and stared at the water-stained ceiling. She'd stopped by the motel office and purchased another night of minimal comfort and running water, but her advance from Shaquana was running thin.

She glanced through the gap in her curtains. Twilight was settling over the city. She'd thought about staking out Decker's office after losing Angela, but chances were slim he'd stop there before going home, and she didn't want to risk bumping into Gemma again. Seeing the girl's hurt expression when Mira said she didn't want her around had twisted a knife in Mira's heart. Once was quite enough.

For now the plan was to wait until night and confront Decker at home after taking his wife out of the equation with a simple sleep spell. Not foolproof, but the best she could come up with. Then she'd either kill Decker or leave him be, depending on his answers, and she would skip town like she should have from the beginning.

<So why are you still bothering with Angela?>

Maybe I don't like leaving a job half-done.

<Maybe you want to prove that your cynicism about relationships is well founded.>

Maybe that, too. I don't like the idea that Angela is lying to a woman who clearly loves her. Either way this plays out, Shaquana deserves to know the truth.

<Even if it hurts her?>

Pain is inevitable when you get that close to someone. Better she face it sooner than later, when she might not recover. She sat up and arranged the laptop on her thighs. "Besides, wherever we land, we'll need money."

The looming debt mentioned in her *abuela's* email hung heavily in Mira's mind, a black storm cloud with occasional lightning strikes of guilt.

"If we haven't caught Angela by the time we're done with the rifter, we'll cut our losses and drop it. In the meantime . . ." She tapped out *event planner* in the search bar on the city's website, which brought up a page heavy with graphics. Colorful ads for upcoming concerts and banquets lined the page. She paused briefly on a face she recognized from another website—Decker. Apparently he was to be the guest of honor at some city award ceremony later that week. Probably the "big dinner" Gemma had mentioned.

<A humanitarian award for a rifter doing charity work. Why haven't *we* gotten one of those?>

Shaking her head, she scrolled through throngs of grinning people until she found the planning coordinator's contact information—beside the image of a smiling woman who was definitely *not* Angela Dougherty. Pulling out the burner phone she'd packed, Mira placed the call.

"Community planning office, this is Cindy. How may I direct your call?"

"Hi, Cindy. I chatted with a lovely woman from your office last month about a concert I want to put on this summer, but I misplaced her number. Her name was Angela Dougherty. Any chance you can connect us?"

<Taking the straightforward approach?>

We don't have time to beat around the bush here if I want that money before we skip town.

The sound of computer keys being tapped came through the line, followed a moment later by, "I'm sorry, but it looks like Ms. Dougherty is no longer employed with the city. I'd be happy to transfer you to our current event coordinator to discuss the details of your concert."

"When did Angela quit?"

"I'm sorry, I'm not at liberty to discuss that with clients. Would you like me to transfer you to—"

Mira hung up.

<If Angela isn't planning events any more, why'd she make all those stops today?>

"More importantly, why does Shaquana still think she works for the city?" Mira pursed her lips. "Angela's lying about more than a secret lover." *Still think they've got a chance at happily ever after?*

<More than you if you don't put yourself out there.>

The laptop chimed, interrupting her thoughts, and an icon appeared in the taskbar. She had a new email.

She clicked on the icon and stared at the single line of text that appeared. The email was from Garrett—a sort-of friend who'd proven himself both trustworthy and reliable. His message simply said, *Call me, now.*

Mira stared at the message and chewed her lip. Garrett had sent a similar message weeks ago, and the result had been revealing her secret to a group of near-strangers and going full demon in view of anyone watching in order to take on a zombie horde and their necromancer controller. She'd ended dozens of rifters that night and sent plenty of demons scurrying back to the Rift, but she'd also risked exposure. Not just to Garrett's partners, who had secrets of their own, but to the soldiers who'd shown up to help.

Garrett and his group of rebel practitioners had gotten what they wanted—a chance to stop hiding, to work side by side with the PTF as equals. But Mira was comfortable with hiding. She had no intention of joining Garrett in the limelight.

<What if he's in trouble?>

Mira thought of the power she'd witnessed in the woman who'd led the charge against the necromancer—a fae-practitioner hybrid named Alex whom Garrett now worked with at the PTF. "Let his *new* friends help him."

<I thought you liked Alex.>

"I did . . . I do." Alex had been more like Mira than anyone she'd met in a long time, but she had a support network Mira couldn't even imagine and she couldn't help the twinge of jealousy that twisted in her heart every time she recalled their time together. She shook her head. "Doesn't mean I want to join them."

<Might be an emergency.>

"How many 'help us save the world' requests am I supposed to answer, 'cause I get the feeling that's going to be a pretty regular occurrence in Garrett's new line of work." After the fall of the necromancer, he'd been made the official PTF liaison to any and all human practitioners working for the PTF, and Mira had no desire to get tangled any deeper in *that* mess. "Whaddya wanna bet he offers me a job? Tries to get me on the PTF's payroll as an upstanding practitioner?"

<No bet. Just make the call and get it over with already. You know you're gonna.>

Mira toyed with the idea of ignoring Garrett's message for another moment, but the demon was right, she couldn't leave him hanging. She dialed the number he'd included below his name at the bottom of the email.

He picked up on the second ring. "Garrett speaking."

"And what exactly do you have to say?"

"Mira? What have you gotten yourself into?"

Mira scowled. "You tell me. You're the one who said to call."

"I just had a BOLO come across my desk with *your* picture on it."

"What?" Mira set the laptop aside and stood up so she could pace. "When? And why?"

"Just before lunch. The BOLO says you're wanted for questioning as a person of interest in a murder investigation." There was a beat of silence, then, "Did you kill somebody?"

"I've been rounding up rifters from that mess at Arlington, which *you* dragged me into."

Garrett sighed. "I know, and I'm sorry, but we never would have succeeded if not for you."

"You could repay me by clearing that BOLO."

"It didn't originate with the PTF. Looks like the contacts on the case are local LEOs out of Baltimore. It got bounced to me from the East Coast PTF office with a request to confirm your identity and current whereabouts. On the plus side, I might be able to offer you some protection. If you were working on behalf of the PTF a case could be made that—"

"And there it is." She placed a hand on her hip and glared at the ceiling. "I'm not joining your gang."

"The PTF could offer you protection, as well as resources you can't get on your own."

"I do just fine on my own, thank you very much."

"We could also offer a stable income. No more scrounging for off-the-books PI jobs."

"The new paranatural division of the PTF is still in its test phase. You don't even have jurisdiction outside of Colorado."

"But we did get a blanket pardon for the actions at Arlington. If your rifter was there, we could argue that you were just cleaning up a straggler from the battle."

"And after that? What? A desk in an office building? Following orders? A partner? A boss?" She sat down on the edge of the bed. "No thank you."

"I know the idea of joining a team is . . . unsettling for you—"

"It's impossible for me, so save your breath." She exhaled and rubbed her forehead, trying to smooth out the crease between her eyebrows. "Look, I appreciate the heads up . . . and the offer, however misguided . . . but I'm fine. I don't need help from you, the PTF, or anyone. Okay? I'm a big girl now. I can clean up my own messes."

"Not every battle can be won alone."

"Not every battle can be won, period."

Garrett sighed again, this time with resignation. "If you want, I could probably get the PTF to take over the murder investigation since the victim was a rifter. With the disorder in the agency right now, it might buy you enough time to get out of town and find somewhere to lie low."

"Thanks, but no thanks. I don't want the PTF anywhere near this one. I've got everything under control."

<Liar.>

"If you say so. But think about my offer. Resources, protection, decent pay . . . it's yours if you change your mind."

"And all I have to do is sell my soul."

<I've got dibs.>

"Don't be so dramatic. It's only a job."

"It's more than that and you know it."

"Yeah, you might actually make a few friends."

She rolled her eyes. "Goodbye, Garrett."

"I'll do what I can to stall the ID. Be careful."

Mira set the phone on the night stand and ran the fingers of both hands through her hair. "Ugh."

<He was only trying to protect you.>

"I don't need protecting."

<Oh really?>

Mira swayed on the bed as images flashed through her mind.

Curled up on the kitchen tiles, lip bleeding, wrist broken. Her mother crying, too afraid to stand up to the man who'd taken them so far from all they knew. The scuffed brown leather of a work boot swinging closer. Pain, sharp and terrible. Coughing, gasping, unable to breathe.

"That's different," Mira snapped, blocking off the memories. "I was a kid. Besides, you get as much out of this arrangement as I do. Or did you enjoy being an amorphous consciousness unable to affect the physical realm?"

<Touchy, touchy. I'm just saying, maybe you shouldn't be so quick to turn down help when it's offered.>

Mira slammed the lid on the laptop.

Flat, orange-gray light filtered through the motel curtains. There were still a couple hours till nightfall. She stood and grabbed the burner phone off the night stand. She'd toss it in the river, grab a bite, then stake out Decker's house. She trusted Garrett . . . mostly . . . but even good intentions could lead to trouble. Best if even he couldn't track her.

Chapter 15

Ty

TY'S KNUCKLES stung under the fabric wraps as his fists met the resistance of the punching bag again and again. He'd left LaRosa poring over paperwork and come to the station's workout room to clear his head and stretch his limbs. Two officers grappled on mats off to one side. Another jogged on one of the treadmills. Ty landed one last punch that rattled the chains holding the bag in place, then straightened and took a deep breath tinged with the stale odor of sweat and deodorant. He grabbed a towel off a nearby bench, wiped down his face and neck, and took a swig from his water bottle.

"Williams."

Ty turned and found LaRosa at the entrance of the stairwell that led up to the station's main floor. He tipped his chin in invitation. "Wanna go a few rounds?"

She shook her head. "That feeling in your gut paid off."

He frowned.

"Shaquana Jones, Angela's girlfriend, is waiting for us in conference room C."

Ty's lips curved up. He hadn't imagined or misinterpreted the woman's reactions. "Give me two minutes to rinse off."

He jogged into the locker room, splashed water on his face, stripped off the faded, gray T-shirt he was wearing for the button-up shirt hanging in his locker, doused himself with deodorant to cover the smell of sweat, slammed the locker closed, and headed upstairs.

Shaquana Jones was fidgeting with a paper coffee cup when he saw her through the wide windows of the conference room. She twisted the cup back and forth between her palms, watching the dark liquid swirl inside. LaRosa was leaning against her desk, arms crossed.

"You talk to her yet?" Ty asked as he strode up to her.

"Your contact, your lead." She pushed off the desk and gestured toward the conference room door.

Ty stepped inside. "Ms. Jones, thanks for stopping by." He sat down across the table from her.

Shaquana nodded, still staring into her coffee.

LaRosa closed the door but remained standing.

"Did you remember something about the woman in the picture we showed you?"

"You said she was involved in an investigation?" The woman finally looked up. "How so?"

"We aren't entirely sure yet. That's why we need to talk to her. Do you know who she is? Or why she was following your girlfriend?"

Shaquana bit one side of her lower lip, then gave one stiff nod. "Her name is Mindy Perez, and she was following Angie because . . ." She glanced at Ty, LaRosa, the closed door, the window looking into the office area, then back at her coffee. "I hired her to."

LaRosa took a step forward.

Ty folded his hands together on the table. "Maybe you'd better start at the beginning, Ms. Jones. How exactly do you know Ms. Perez, and why did you ask her to follow your girlfriend."

Shaquana's lower lip quivered. "Angie's been cheating on me," she whispered. "I wanted to confront her about it, but I didn't have any real evidence. Just a feeling, you know." Her gaze flicked up to Ty, then quickly away. "So I placed an ad on a job site for freelance investigators."

LaRosa pulled out a chair at the end of the table and sat. She took out her notepad and a pen, asked for the name of the site, and jotted down the answer.

"Mindy contacted me yesterday," Shaquana continued. "Said she'd take the job." She leaned forward, gaze suddenly intent. "Do you think she's dangerous? She seemed nice . . . professional, but . . . do you think Angie might be in some kind of danger?"

Ty reached out and covered one of Shaquana's hands with his own. Her skin was sweat-slicked and clammy. "We don't know that Ms. Perez means anyone any harm. We just need to get some answers about an unrelated incident. Do you have a way to contact her?"

"Not directly. We messaged through the site. She said she'd get in touch when the job was done."

Ty pursed his lips.

"I'm sorry I didn't tell you I recognized her right away, I just . . . I didn't want to admit in front of Angie that I was having her followed—didn't want to come across as some crazy, jealous girlfriend." She let out a bitter laugh. "But I guess that's exactly what I am." She set her second hand over Ty's, sandwiching his fingers. "Are you going to tell her?"

Ty squeezed her hand, then tugged his free. "Not unless it becomes absolutely necessary."

Shaquana managed a grim smile and placed her hands in her lap.

"I appreciate you coming in, Ms. Jones. The information you provided should help us get this whole mess cleared up much faster." He pushed back his chair and stood. "And please, if Mindy Perez contacts you in any way, call me immediately."

"Of course." She nodded and stood.

Ty opened the conference room door and waved over a passing officer. "Edwards, please escort this woman out of the station."

Shaquana kept her gaze down as she passed Ty and followed her escort to the front of the building.

Ty closed the door again, leaned his back against it, and looked at LaRosa.

She flipped her little book closed and tucked it in her pocket. "So Angela Dougherty is being stalked by your mystery woman."

"At the behest of a jealous girlfriend. There's no evidence the woman is tailing Angela for any reason other than money."

"You really think she's a PI named Mindy Perez?"

"Not sure, but she seems to be doing the job, and if she's using a PI job site there's got to be a trail we can follow. She'd have to be licensed to get access to those listings."

"So at least we've got a new angle. And we can put a tail on Angela in case Perez tries to finish her job."

"Using a civilian as bait? And here I thought cops had more rules than PTF agents."

She stood. "Not *bait,* covert protection . . . that *may* lead to the capture of a person of interest."

He opened the door for her and followed her out. "Do you want to look into the website or arrange the tail?"

"I'll handle the tail. You get the cyber unit on the line and see if we can track her that way."

Ty reached for his phone but jerked back when it rang. After a second to compose himself, he answered. "Williams here."

"Ty, it's Cameron King. Long time."

Ty groped for his chair and sat down. Cameron King—fellow PTF investigator from the East Coast field office. Ty hadn't seen him since the department memorial for Jamal. He tried to swallow, but his throat was dry. "What . . . uh . . . to what do I owe the call?"

"Your department distributed a BOLO with a 'possible paranatural' tag, so naturally it was circulated to the PTF." Cameron chuckled. "Imagine my surprise when I saw your name listed as one of the contacts. I thought you were done with this business."

"Yeah, well . . . seems the business isn't quite done with *me*."

"Sorry I never checked in after you left." There was an awkward silence. "You doing okay?"

Ty clenched his jaw. That undertone in Cam's question was one of the reasons he'd had to leave the agency. Too many people walking on eggshells . . . and he couldn't even say they were wrong to treat him differently. Losing Jamal had broken him, no doubt. He cleared his throat. "Can't complain."

"I'm sure you've heard about the sorcerer rebellion?"

"I haven't been living under a rock." *Just the bottom of a bottle.*

"The agency's a mess right now, and we've got no practitioner backup for the time being."

"I thought they were trying a new partnership model?"

"In Colorado. The rest of us are on our own, and the bad guys know it thanks to all the news coverage. Anyway, that's not why I called. The BOLO you sent, the girl in the picture matches descriptions of a practitioner who fought in the battle at Arlington."

Ty's intestines cramped. "On which side?"

"Ours. Or at least she fought against the necromancer's troops. I was sent in as part of the cleanup squad to assess any remaining threat and help contain the 'friendly' practitioners who'd come to help. Buddy of mine with the National Guard gave an account of a woman who'd single-handedly wiped out the rifters at the top of the hill but buggered off before backup arrived. He said she was a short Latina with a white stripe in her hair . . . when she wasn't glowing pearly gold and shooting lightning from her hands. I sent your BOLO to the new paranatural liaison in Colorado to see if he can confirm the ID. Haven't heard back yet."

"The people she killed at Arlington . . . what did they look like after?"

"Other than dead? They were all dried out and shriveled like mummies. Never seen the like, even in this line of work."

Ty sighed and rested his forehead against his palm. "Thanks for calling, Cam. I really appreciate it."

"If it turns out your mystery woman really is the chick from Arlington, my advice is to put a bullet in her brain before she has the chance to cast a spell."

Ty frowned. "I thought you said she fought on the side of the PTF."

"And bolted when we showed up. I don't care what hippy-dippy experiment they're running in Colorado—in the rest of the world, unregistered practitioners are still illegal, and this one seems more dangerous than most."

"I'll keep that in mind. And again, thanks." Ty disconnected the call and leaned back in his chair.

"That sounded promising," LaRosa said from two desks over.

"Eavesdropping is a bad habit."

"Not for a cop. So spill. You got a lead on our girl?"

"An old friend from the PTF saw the BOLO—said she matches the description of a woman who fought in the battle at Arlington Cemetery against the rogue sorcerers and rifters."

"Like Rodney Temple?"

He nodded. "If she was hunting escaped rifters, maybe she tracked him here to finish what she started at Arlington."

"Which maybe makes her a hero . . . but still a killer."

Ty rubbed his forehead. "And doesn't get us any closer to finding her."

LaRosa drummed her fingers against her desk and stared at Ty until he grew uncomfortable.

"What?"

She scrunched her nose, then stood and moved next to his desk so they could speak at a lower volume. "Normally I'd say your personal business is none of mine, but your mystery woman is seeming less like a person of interest and more like a suspect. So I need to know . . . how far does your relationship with her go?"

"She's a stranger I met in a bar. We had some drinks. There's no *relationship*."

"Just drinks?"

Ty met her gaze. Sleeping with a suspect would be grounds to take him off the case, just like he'd wanted. Except he didn't anymore. He wanted—he needed—to find Mindy Perez, or whatever her name was, and verify just how effed his instincts were these days. "I have no connection to that woman that would compromise my role in this investigation."

She stared at him for another minute, lips pursed, then nodded. "Okay. Let's focus on how we're gonna bring her in."

He considered Cam's parting advice. The PTF had a shoot-first policy regarding rogue practitioners, but it was awfully hard to get answers from a corpse, and Ty very much wanted to talk to this woman. "We should grab some tranquilizer guns from the armory."

LaRosa raised an eyebrow.

"I know they're not standard issue for police, but you should have a few on hand in case of emergencies. PTF agents use them when apprehending paranaturals that need to be taken alive. The drug is fast acting—designed to drop a target before they can get a spell off."

She nodded. "I'll requisition us some new sidearms."

Chapter 16

Mira

STARS TWINKLED above as Mira rumbled slowly down the street toward Decker's rental. Street lamps dotted either side of the road, creating patchy light that would be hard to avoid. The neighborhood was one of the nicer ones she'd seen in the area, with wide lawns and multi-story Victorian architecture, but it wasn't quite what she'd expected from a globe-trotting CEO. Then again, if Decker was a rifter, he probably needed more privacy than he could get in a gated community or a condo penthouse where his comings and goings would be easily tracked.

She slowed even more as she approached the address she'd found. A grayish-blue house with dark trim sat at the center of a wide yard of pale-yellow grass lined with dormant trees and flowerbeds that, according to the real estate listing, would be full of vibrant colors in the spring. A wooden lattice thick with skeletal vines blocked the space beneath the wraparound deck that circled three sides of the house. Bushes lined the walkway leading up to the front steps, but their branches were bare and patches of snow sheltered near their trunks. A black sedan was parked in the driveway behind a silver Porsche. Lights were on in the first level of the house, but the second floor and attic windows were dark.

A drooping pine in the yard across the street whose branches scraped the dead lawn was the obvious choice for a hiding spot to scope the situation.

She continued to the end of the street, around the corner, and up another street before cutting her engine. Then she backtracked on foot.

<If we're going to ring the doorbell anyway, why bother with all this cloak and dagger?>

I'd like to get an idea what we're walking into before we ring that bell.

She glanced up and down the street as she approached the neighbor's pine tree. She'd purposely waited until well after the standard window for dinner, so the lights reflected in most of the windows were the shifting blues of television screens.

When she was relatively sure no one was watching, she ducked under the low-hanging branches of the pine and hunkered in the shadows beside its trunk. She inhaled the smell of sap and exhaled a cloud of steam that faded into the cold night.

A shadow moved in front of the window on the main floor of Decker's house. A moment later, bright light blossomed in the second-story bay. Two shapes were silhouetted against the curtains. One was tall and thin. The other was shorter and decidedly feminine.

The woman gestured, raising her arms in an "I'm fed up" motion, turned, and walked out of the frame.

<Trouble in paradise.>

The second silhouette followed the first. The sound of raised voices drifted out of the house, not quite loud enough to be clear from Mira's hiding place.

Yet another example of domestic bliss. I don't know why I keep resisting your advice to fall in love.

<You wanna go now or wait for them to finish?>

Mira sighed. *Let's head over.*

She started to rise, but headlights swung onto the street, and she dropped back down. Pine needles crinkled under her knee, and another whiff of resin filled the air.

A tan SUV rolled down the street at a leisurely pace until it turned into the drive one house down from Mira's hiding spot.

She sank a little farther into the shadows.

A woman in nurse scrubs and white sneakers stepped out of the car. Then she opened the trunk and pulled out half a dozen plastic grocery bags.

Come on, come on. Mira glanced back to Decker's house. The upper windows were dark again. No more silhouettes.

<Maybe they went to bed.>

With the front-room lights still on?

<Maybe he's sleeping on the couch.>

The nurse slammed her trunk and walked up the path to her front door. She fumbled her keys, trying to balance the grocery bags, heaved a sigh, and reached down to retrieve them. She got the key in the lock on the second try and pushed inside.

Mira waited, gaze flicking back and forth between Decker's house and the nurse's.

The blue glow of another television turning on filtered through the nurse's front window.

The lights in Decker's house winked out.

<*Now* they're going to bed.>

Not yet they're not. Mira rose again, but again she stopped short as the front door of Decker's house opened.

Oh, come on. She sank into the pine needles once more, hugging close to the sappy trunk.

<What's he carrying?>

She couldn't make out many details, but the man who walked out had a tall, lean frame, wore a suit, and carried a duffel bag large enough to hold Mira's entire wardrobe slung over one shoulder. His lopsided walk made her think the bag was heavy.

Coño. You think he's leaving for another trip?

<Or maybe the couch isn't comfy and he's heading to a hotel.>

Can you sense anything from here?

There was a swell of power from the demon. <There's definitely magic on him, but I can't find the source.>

So he could *be a rifter hiding his presence like Nowak.*

The door to the nurse's house opened again, drawing Mira's attention. The woman walked out carrying a black trash bag. She stopped on the porch and called to Decker.

He paused, then raised one hand in greeting.

The nurse prattled on about the weather, work, and all the inanities that marked suburban small talk while she dumped her bag in a brown, plastic trash bin and wheeled it to the curb.

Decker, for his part, responded in the same small-talk fashion as he crossed to the back of the black sedan, opened the trunk, and heaved his bag inside.

"You going on another trip?" the nurse asked from her side of the street.

Decker slammed the trunk closed. "Business never stops." He waved again and rounded to the driver's door.

<We're gonna lose him.>

What do you suggest we do? Kill the nurse?

<Knock her out.>

I'm not attacking an innocent person.

Decker's sedan backed down the driveway.

<He's getting away.>

The nurse strolled up her walkway, pausing to grab a plastic-wrapped newspaper off the lawn.

Decker shifted gears and drove away.

<Aaand . . . he's gone. Brilliant.>

We couldn't risk the nurse becoming a casualty.

<We could have taken her out in a second. She would have woken up later with a headache and maybe a couple bruises.>

And hypothermia. Do you have any idea what temperature it is out here?

<We could have dragged her inside when we were done with Decker.>

Assuming everything went well with Decker.

<Of course I assume that.>

Mira shook her head. *This is why* I *make the plans and* you *blow shit up.*

<Whatever. So what do you want to do now, oh brilliant one?>

Let's check on the wife. Maybe she'll tell us where he went. At the very least, we can find out if she's enthralled. And if Decker's coming back we can set an ambush.

After double checking to be sure the door to the nurse's house was closed, Mira finally crept out of her hiding spot. She brushed dirt and pine needles off her pants and found a small piece of paper stuck to her knee. She pulled it loose and stuffed it in her pocket.

<What was that?>

Trash.

<Then why are you keeping it?>

I'm not. I just don't want to drop it in the street.

<Why not? There's tons of trash blowing around this city. No one's gonna notice one more piece.>

Exactly. I don't want to add to that.

<So now it's not enough to clean our room obsessively, you have to keep the whole planet tidy?>

Someone has to make up for slobs like you. She climbed the steps to Decker's porch and rang the doorbell.

No answer.

<She can't really have fallen asleep that fast, can she?>

Doubtful. Maybe she just doesn't want to answer the door in her nightgown.

Mira knocked on the door, glanced along the quiet street, then walked around to the back of the house. She knocked on the back door.

Still no answer.

<Guess she's not in the mood for company.>

I'm getting a bad feeling about this.

<You sure it isn't that gas station sandwich you ate for dinner?>

What do you suppose was so heavy in that bag Decker was carrying?

The demon's chuckle cut off. <You think maybe we don't need to worry about whether or not the wife is enthralled anymore?>

I think this house is way too quiet to have anyone inside, and we only saw one person leave.

Pulling some energy out of the air, she set her hand on the doorknob and poured some magic inside. The lock clicked. She twisted the handle, pushed the door open, and stepped inside.

Ty

"I'M CALLING IT." LaRosa pushed back from her desk and stretched her arms above her head with a *pop* and a groan. She stood and pushed the chair in. "This paperwork isn't going anywhere. We can start fresh in the morning."

Ty grunted in response and continued to scroll through the cyber unit's report. They'd tracked Mindy Perez's account to a legitimate PI license, but the registration info she used to acquire it all led to dead ends—empty lots, false IDs, forged records. The licensing department had basically granted PI status to a ghost in the system.

"The cyber guys think they can back trace Perez's IP to a physical location if they can catch her interacting through the job board website again." He looked up and noticed LaRosa standing. "You going home?"

She gave him a deadpan stare. "Yeah. You should, too. Get some sleep."

He nodded. "I'm just going to shoot Shaquana Jones an email . . . see if she'll send a message to Perez asking for a status update on the PI job. Then when Perez responds, we'll have her."

LaRosa glanced out the nearest window. Ty followed her attention. The glass mirrored the station interior, hiding the nighttime world outside.

"Last task, I promise," he said. "Then I'll head home."

She shook her head. "You better not be cranky tomorrow." She set her purse strap over one shoulder, then glanced at Billy, who was manning the phones for the night shift. "G'night Billy."

He waved.

She jerked her head toward Ty. "If he's still here in an hour, shoot him."

Billy laughed.

Ty rolled his eyes.

LaRosa left the station.

"Tick tock," Billy said and tapped his watch. His easy smile exposed a gap in his teeth.

"Yeah, yeah." Ty opened his email and sent a quick message to the address Shaquana had provided. Then he sent another to the cyber crimes department, letting them know the plan. He glanced at the clock, then shut down his computer. "Sorry Billy, looks like you don't get to shoot me today."

He shrugged. "Maybe next time. Have a good night, Detective Williams."

"You too, Billy."

Ty grabbed his coat off the back of his chair, pulled it on, and picked up the tranquilizer gun LaRosa had requisitioned for him.

The phone on Billy's desk rang as Ty headed for the rear exit, and the young officer answered with the standard recitation of, "Baltimore Police Department, Officer Davis speaking."

A second later Billy stood up so fast his chair toppled backwards. "Ty, hold up!"

Ty stopped and waited, studying the young man's face.

Billy's eyebrows were drawn together. His mouth was turned down in a steep frown. The conversation was almost entirely one sided—the side Ty couldn't hear—punctuated by questions from Billy like, "What's your name?", "Are you sure?", and "How long ago?". Billy jotted notes while he listened, but his handwriting was little more than scribbles from what Ty could see.

Ty tapped his foot. He shifted his weight and crossed his arms.

Billy set the phone back in its cradle and focused on Ty. "A woman matching your suspect's description was just seen entering a house in the Mt. Washington neighborhood."

Ty stiffened, then frowned. "Why didn't the call get routed to the northwest station? It's closer."

Billy shrugged. "It was a direct call, not through dispatch. I'll call the northwest station for backup." He reached for the phone again.

"No." Ty took a step forward, hand outstretched.

Billy froze.

"Not yet," Ty amended. He ran a hand over his scalp. "If this pans out, I need a clean shot at her before she gets spooked. Traditional officers won't be much good against magic."

Billy frowned. "I'll give you a five-minute head start, but then I'm calling in the cavalry."

"Text me the address." Ty ran for the back door.

"And I'm calling LaRosa," Billy shouted behind him.

Mira

THE BACK DOOR opened into a kitchen—black marble countertops, stainless-steel appliances, and natural wood cabinets. A single plate and a brandy glass sat on a drying mat next to the sink. A crystal punch bowl half full of fruit sat on the island. The smell of overripe bananas wafted off it.

Mira crept softly across the hardwood floor, past an opening that led to a dining room, toward the front of the house. The hardwood floor continued into the entryway and living room, and up a set of stairs that climbed to the second story. An antique couch with a carved wooden frame and pale upholstery sat beside a curio cabinet full of tiny crystal figurines. Two matching chairs completed the circle around a glossy black coffee table draped with crocheted lace. Framed paintings of tropical flowers hung on the wall.

For a moment Mira was reminded of her *abuela's* house—everything polished and in its place. There was no sign of Decker's wife.

Taking a deep breath, Mira started up the staircase to the second floor. The third step squeaked under her weight.

She froze and waited, watching the darkness at the upper landing, but nothing stirred.

<If Decker's wife is up there, she must be a good sleeper.>

More and more Mira was convinced the duffel bag Decker was hauling hadn't held clothes and a toothbrush. Too bulky, too heavy . . . too convenient.

She reached the second floor and glanced around. Four doors. The first on the right was a bathroom, recently remodeled with a jetted tub and walk-in shower. The next led to the room with the bay window where Mira had seen the silhouettes argue. This seemed to be Decker's office. A wide oak desk dominated one side of the room, piled high with paperwork. Mira flipped through sketches and architecture blueprints. She found a layout for the construction site in Midtown that showed the five proposed buildings and estimates for the number of residents who'd fill them. There was a thick red line drawn diagonally through the property that didn't seem to serve any purpose.

Pushing the blueprints aside, she lifted a piece of card stock printed with fancy script and an embossed, gold seal—an invitation from the mayor's office for tomorrow's awards banquet, where Decker would be honored for all his "good work" for the city.

She let the invitation fall back to the desk, resisting the urge to rip it into confetti.

Using only the soft glow filtering through the window from the street lights below, Mira searched for signs of a struggle, blood stains, anything that might indicate what happened after the lights went out. Everything seemed in perfect order.

Continuing around the upper landing to the other room at the front of the house, Mira stepped into a large bedroom with a king-sized bed and a full set of dark-wood furniture. To one side of the door, a pull-down ladder led up to the attic.

Why would that be left down?

<Let's find out.>

Mira glanced around the bedroom to make sure she hadn't missed anything that was overshadowed by the obvious mystery, then stepped onto the first rung of the ladder. She climbed until her nose was even with the attic floor.

The attic was a narrow room about eight feet high at the peak, then it sloped off steeply to either side. Stacks of boxes filled the shorter areas and created a corridor feeling. The window at the front of the house let in a little light—just enough to make out the shape of a body on the plywood floor.

Mira stared for a moment. The figure didn't move. From her angle Mira could see little more than the soles of a pair of high-heeled shoes and the swells of form that indicated a woman.

"Hello?" she called softly. Then louder, "Hello?"

The figure didn't move.

She climbed the rest of the way into the attic, did a quick survey to ensure there was no one hiding amid the boxes, then edged over to the figure.

The woman was maybe thirty years old. She had black hair that fanned out around her expressionless face. Her arms were at her sides. She wore a satin, cream-colored nightgown. A hunting knife stuck out of her center, just below her sternum, buried to the hilt.

<I guess Decker's wife wasn't in the bag.>

Mira looked the woman up and down. "How tall would you say Decker was?"

<At least six feet.>

Mira laid down next to the corpse and looked up. "This lady's about five-nine."

<So?>

"The silhouettes we saw arguing weren't nearly that close. The woman couldn't have been more than five-six or seven."

<You think there was *another* person in the house?>

"A lover maybe?" Mira sat up.

<Which means Decker's bag still might have a body in it.>

"But is this the wife? Or the lover? And why is there so little blood?"

She knelt beside the body and leaned over to inspect the entry wound. "Cause of death seems pretty straightforward, except there's barely even a stain around the knife. Her nightgown should be soaked with this kind of wound."

<You think maybe Decker drained her, like a vampire?>

"Maybe. There's only one sure way to find out."

Mira held her right hand above the dead woman and drew energy into her left, then she lowered her arm until her fingertips brushed the woman's forehead.

<Wait! There's a—>

There was a flash of light that whited-out the world, followed by searing pain. Mira toppled back, gasping for breath. Several boxes fell around her, bursting open and spewing their contents across the attic floor. She rolled onto her side and curled into a ball, hugging herself tight to ease the ache in her bones and the wracking shivers that juddered through her body. Her vision swam, and she squeezed her eyes closed to block out the world.

Chapter 17

Ty

TY'S TRUCK CAREENED around the corner of the Mt. Washington street where his phone's navigation had directed him. Street lamps dotted the sidewalks. Most of the houses were dark with the exception of an occasional television glow.

Ty scanned the windows. Billy's caller had chosen to remain anonymous, but to have seen Perez entering the building they would have had to be nearby. Were they still watching?

He slowed.

"Your destination is on the right," the chipper phone voice announced.

He parked across the street from the indicated house and verified that the address matched. The front door was closed. The windows were dark. A silver Porsche was parked in the driveway. He squinted at the quiet building, looking for any sign of movement, any hint that all was not as it should be. From where he was sitting there was no reason to suspect a break-in.

If he burst in unannounced and startled a civilian couple from their sleep he'd be in deep shit, but he couldn't let this opportunity pass. He'd burned through his head start getting there; local PD could arrive any minute. He grabbed the tranquilizer gun off the passenger seat.

The front door of the house was locked. He peeked in the window and saw the dim outlines of furniture. No bodies, living or otherwise.

He circled around the deck to the back of the house. When Ty looked in the window set in the back door he found a kitchen. Still no signs of life.

He grabbed the doorknob and turned. The door swung open.

Ty pursed his lips. What were the odds someone living in a well-off neighborhood would leave their door unlocked when they went to bed?

He checked to make sure a tranquilizer dart was loaded, took a deep breath, and stepped into the dark house. He moved slowly, checking shadows and corners where a person might be hiding. Past the kitchen he explored the dining room. Then he stepped into the living room he'd peeked into from the front porch. Satisfied there was no one on the main floor, he headed upstairs.

The second-floor landing was even darker, illuminated only by the street lights filtering through the open doors of its adjoining rooms. Ty trained his gun through the first door and startled when he came across his own reflection in a bathroom mirror. He checked behind the shower curtain, then moved toward the next room.

A muffled *thump* from above stopped him in his tracks.

He looked up. From the outside of the building, he'd seen a third-story window—not high enough for a full floor. There had to be an attic access nearby.

He crept toward the next open door. His senses strained. The night rang with the empty buzz of silence and the rasp of his own constricted breathing. Behind the door he found an empty office with a big bay window that overlooked the street. He glanced out. No sign of backup yet.

He hit the jackpot in the third room. An extended ladder led from the master bedroom to the attic above. The king-sized bed was empty and made—no one sleeping in this house tonight. So the only question was . . . who was in the attic?

Mira

WHAT HAPPENED?

A buzzing silence filled Mira's head.

She opened her eyes. Tears leaked down her cheeks, but at least she could see again. She rolled onto her knees and tried to straighten. Nausea surged through her.

You okay?

The demon didn't respond.

She glanced at the woman on the floor beside her. The nightgown around the knife was no longer cream colored. Bright red seeped and spread from the point of impact.

What the . . . ?

The woman's eyes fluttered open. Her gaze darted around the room until it came to rest on Mira. She opened her mouth, but all that came out was a trickle of blood near the corner of her lips. She lifted one hand a fraction of an inch, reaching for Mira.

Mira grasped the woman's hand with both of hers. "I'm sorry, I . . ." She shook her head.

Blood was pooling around the woman now, inching closer to Mira.

Where are you? She screamed in her head, willing the demon to answer. *Say something!*

She reached for her magic, but found only a sickening emptiness. Somehow, all the energy had been drained out of this area, severing her from both her magic and her demon.

Mira tore her hands free from the dying woman and struggled to her feet. Nausea twisted her stomach once again, but she choked it back. She had to move. She clutched her chest, groping for the comfort of her missing saint necklace as she fought against the abyss of despair. She was alone, without magic, without protection.

"Saint Jude . . . when hopeless seems the task," she mumbled. "Please, help me."

The woman on the floor made a choked, gurgling sound. Her outstretched hand dropped. Blood droplets splashed and speckled Mira's shoe.

"Freeze!"

Mira twisted toward the attic access. The world spun. She staggered a step away from the dead woman.

"I said freeze!"

Mira stared at the gun pointed at her. It wasn't a normal gun. The barrel was too long and narrow. Holding the gun were a pair of steady hands. Hands she remembered. Hands that had been both strong and gentle as they roamed her body. She looked into the face of her demon's lover.

Ty

TY CLIMBED THE stairs to the attic as quietly as he could, keeping the gun gripped in his right hand. When he was one rung from the top, he took a deep, steadying breath and peeked above the rim.

A woman was standing silhouetted by the attic window that let in light from the street below. Her back was to him. She was looking down.

He climbed a little higher.

There was a second person in the attic—another woman—lying on the floor.

The standing figure whispered something Ty couldn't make out.

The prone woman's reaching hand dropped with a wet slap.

Ty cleared the attic hatch and brought the tranquilizer gun up. "Freeze!"

The woman who was still on her feet spun and stumbled.

"I said freeze!"

The woman regained her balance and looked up at him. The light spilling in from the window caught the curve of her cheek, the bridge of her nose. A pair of brown eyes stared at him from a familiar face.

"It *is* you," he whispered.

She raised her hands slowly, palms out. "This isn't what it looks like."

He glanced at the woman on the floor. From the looks of her, it was too late for an ambulance.

"You can tell me all about it back at the station." He shifted his gun slightly so it was centered on her chest. "Are you going to make this difficult?"

She frowned. "What kind of gun is that?"

"The kind that ensures you're on the ground before a spell leaves your fingers."

She pursed her lips. "I'm not your enemy."

"Glad to hear it. Now how about you turn around so I can cuff you."

She turned, hands still even with her shoulders. "You don't understand what's going on here . . . what's at stake." She sounded out of breath—and not the good kind of out of breath he remembered from their time together—like she was fighting to stay on her feet.

He took a step toward her, gun aimed between her shoulder blades, and reached for the cuffs tucked in his back pocket with his left hand.

"I came here tonight because the man who's renting this—"

A loud pounding echoed through the house. "Baltimore PD, open up."

Ty's attention swung toward the attic hatch and LaRosa's voice.

The woman spun.

Ty pulled the trigger on his gun. There was a *fwupt* noise as a red-tufted dart left the barrel. Then a mountain of cardboard boxes stacked to the ceiling toppled onto him. Ty crashed to the floor, buried in darkness, pressed down by the weight of whatever disused knickknacks were stored in this attic and the inescapable cage of his memories.

Chapter 18

Mira

MIRA THREW HER weight against the nearest tower of boxes. Two stacks fell directly onto Mr. Yummy. His gun went off, but not with the bang of a firearm, more like a puff of compressed air. His eyes went wide. Then he was buried under the boxes.

That won't hold him long. Mira pulled the red-tufted dart that shot from his gun out of the fabric of her jacket. The needle had barely scraped her skin.

The silence in her head was deafening. Decker had set a trap for her. But how had he even known she was coming for him? She felt lightheaded, and her thoughts fell strangely flat in a privacy she hadn't experienced since she was a child—like standing alone in the middle of a desert and shouting into the wind.

There was a loud crash below as whoever had banged on the door—probably the woman she'd seen with Mr. Yummy in Nowak's office if the voice was any indication—kicked their way inside.

She glanced at the pile of boxes. Even if they were filled with encyclopedias, it wouldn't take long for him to shrug them off, and she couldn't risk getting pinned between him and the woman below.

She glanced around the room, her vision lagging as she fought the dizziness threatening to bring her to her knees. She needed to get outside, needed to find a source of magic, needed to reconnect with her demon.

She stumbled toward the window at the front of the house and heaved it open. There was a narrow section of roof below the sill. Bracing her hands against the frame, she swung one leg out. A gust of wind whipped her hair across her face and tore at her grip. Her jacket flapped like broken crow wings.

Setting her second foot on the sloping tiles of the roof, she stepped away from the window. Mira moved toward the north side of the house in a half crouch using her hands to help keep her balance. She peeked over the edge. The roof of the wraparound porch stretched below her.

The rough texture of the tiles scraped across her belly as she swung her legs into empty space and lowered herself down until she was hanging, fully extended, from the side of the upper roof. Then she let go.

Her feet connected with the lower roof. Her knees buckled. Then she was rolling.

She skidded and slowed as she approached the second edge but didn't quite manage to grab the overhang.

Her back connected with the ground first, and all the air was forced from her lungs as her chest compressed with the impact. She groaned and rolled onto her side, gasping.

<Get up.> The demon's voice was thready and distant, but there.

Courage and confidence swelled through Mira when she heard that voice. If her demon was back, she was going to be all right. If her demon was there, she could do anything.

She rolled to her knees, paused for a second to let the ribbons of darkness floating across her vision fade, and struggled to her feet. She took three shaky steps across the lawn. There was a silver truck parked across the street and a black sedan on the near side in front of Decker's house.

She hobbled toward the sidewalk. Her ankle was twisted or sprained, but she didn't have time to worry about that right now.

"Freeze!"

Mira glanced over her shoulder and spotted the woman from Nowak's office standing on Decker's porch. She pushed her legs harder and pulled at the energy she could once again feel in the air around her. *Just a little—*

A sharp pain bit into her right butt cheek like the sting of an angry yellow jacket.

Mira stumbled. One knee hit the dirt. Then her palms. Bursts of light and shadow danced in her vision. She lost the thread of magic she'd been channeling.

Seriously? In the ass?

Her chin connected with the concrete sidewalk. Blood filled her mouth. One arm was jerked back, causing a dim ache in her shoulder. Then her second arm was pulled into place.

She twisted her neck until the woman above her came into view, backlit by a streetlight that made her look like some angelic herald come to cast judgment on the wicked. Mira blinked. Her captor was suddenly facing the house, the in-between motion missing like seconds snipped out of a movie scene.

"Where the hell is Williams?" The woman's words stretched and distorted as Mira's brain processed them like a video clip played in slow motion.

Mira blinked again, trying to reestablish her grip on reality, but the ribbons of darkness drifting through her vision spread and merged to block out her remaining senses.

Ty

CARDBOARD BOXES turned to cinder blocks, steel beams, and wood framing as they fell around him. Ty covered his head and dropped to one knee as a chunk of concrete connected with his shoulder. Through the dust and debris, he could just make out his target—a thin boy with high cheekbones and a sharp taper to his ears. Ty had assumed the newly discovered halfer wouldn't have enough power or control to set an ambush, that finding the kid would be most of the task and all it would take was a calm talk or maybe a swift punch to bring him to heel.

He'd been wrong . . . so very, very wrong.

Ty lifted his sidearm. A tranquilizer would've been better, but the iron-core bullets in Ty's gun would slow the boy down until backup arrived.

"Ty!" Jamal tackled him from the side.

The gun went off. A burst of light sparked off a metal beam above the boy's head as he jumped through the open window.

Ty's shoulder hit plywood-topped concrete. Jamal's weight crashed down on top of him, bruising his ribs. The splintered two-by-four that Ty hadn't noticed dropping toward him like a javelin speared through Jamal's chest and tore through Ty's side. Both men howled. Then the rest of the ceiling and a good portion of the upper floors rained down on top of them.

This isn't real. Ty tried to hold on to the present, to remember where he was. The attic. The suspect. The corpse. He reached toward his pocket for the familiar weight of the stone inside. Pain lanced through his chest when he moved. What his hand closed on however, was not the river rock that would save him from this nightmare. He pulled the flashlight off his utility belt.

No, no, no. I don't want to see this.

He pressed the button on the back of the flashlight. Bright light flickered to life, casting deep shadows in the crevasses where the blocks and beams around him overlapped. The light was split oddly by a crack across the lens. Dust continued to sift down like snowflakes in the unsteady beam.

"Ty?" A smear of blood glinted wetly on Jamal's chin when he tipped his face toward the light. "I can't . . . breathe." He coughed, and a gob of black blood splattered Ty's face.

The wet rattle when Jamal tried to inhale probably meant the wood that speared them had punctured a lung. Ty tried to shift his weight, to get a better look at the damage, but moving even a little sent a wave of pain up his leg that pushed him to the brink of passing out. When the agony passed, he noticed he couldn't feel anything below his right knee. He chose to take that numbness as a blessing and focus on the more pressing matter of Jamal's impalement. The splintered end of the wood was wedged tight against the floor. Above Jamal, the wood vanished into a jigsaw of other boards, concrete blocks, pipes, wires, hoses, insulation, and chunks of drywall.

"Hang in there, buddy." Ty set the flashlight down and tugged at the fabric of his jacket. He couldn't tear it at this angle, but he pressed as much as he could into the space around Jamal's wound.

His friend tensed and gasped, but again his breath made that odd, wet, sucking sound.

"Backup will be here any minute. We've just gotta hold out till then." Ty's words bounced back to him, hot in his face and laced with dust. He coughed, which set off a new series of fireworks through his pain receptors.

Jamal's fingers found the collar of Ty's jacket and twisted into the fabric. "Tell Jen . . ."

"Tell her yourself." Ty covered his friend's hand and squeezed. "We're getting out of this."

". . . I'm sorry." Jamal's grip loosened. His cheek rested heavily against Ty's chest.

"Jamal?" Ty slapped his friend's cheek, lightly at first, then harder. He shook his shoulder, heedless of the extra damage shifting his torso might do. Then he screamed until his throat was raw. He screamed until the air in the small space turned toxic and his poisoned bloodstream finally shut him down.

"Williams."

A sharp slap connected with the side of his face.

"Wake up."

Another slap. Now both his cheeks stung equally.

Ty blinked rapidly, trying to clear his vision, to focus on the person in front of him.

Not Jamal.

"Pull yourself together." The woman landed another blow.

LaRosa.

She pulled her hand back again.

Ty jerked away. "I'm awake!"

She lowered her arm. "What the hell happened up here? You were screaming like a banshee."

He jerked his head side to side, scanning the room. Boxes were piled all around him. The attic window was open. There was no sign of the woman. "I lost her."

"What happened to 'drop her before she can get off a spell'?"

Ty shook his head. He didn't want to admit he'd been incapacitated not by a spell but by the nightmare of his own memories. Or that he'd hesitated when confronted by the face of a lover.

LaRosa straightened and offered him her hand. "Come on. This scene is far from secure."

He let her pull him to his feet. He glanced at the dead woman lying in a pool of her own blood. The hilt of a knife stuck out of her torso. He shifted his focus back to LaRosa. "I take it you got Billy's call."

"It should've come from you." She poked him hard in the chest. "I don't know what kind of teamwork you're used to over there at the PTF, but here on the police force we don't run off half-cocked and leave our partner in the lurch. That kind of macho bullshit does *not* fly."

He rubbed the sore spot on his chest. "Sorry, I . . . you're right. It won't happen again."

"You're damned right it won't." She climbed down the attic ladder to the bedroom below. "Now come on. I need help getting our suspect in the car."

Ty grabbed his tranquilizer gun off the floor and followed her. "You caught her?"

"Shot her in the back when she tried to flee."

When Ty stepped onto the front porch he spotted the petite woman from the attic lying in the grass, hands cuffed behind her back. "Good work."

"Just get her in the car." LaRosa was walking up the sidewalk, one arm raised to flag down the two black-and-whites that had just turned onto the street.

Ty rolled the woman onto her back. Her head lolled. Her expression was slack with unconsciousness. She looked just as she had before sleep claimed him after their wildly energetic night together. Only this time she was resting on the cold, hard ground instead of his bed sheets.

He lifted a lock of wavy, chestnut hair off her forehead and rolled it between his finger and thumb. There was no trace of the white stripe she'd had when they first met. Letting the hair fall, he trailed his fingers over the side of her face and traced the soft, supple curve of her lower lip. He still couldn't believe that this beautiful, funny, enchanting woman was a killer. Not that he hadn't met plenty of evil women, but she'd just felt so . . . good.

How could I have been so wrong about you?

Maybe she really had enchanted him, used her magic to befuddle his better judgment. Not that his judgment had been all that clear after downing shots in memory of his fallen friend.

Sighing, he slid one arm behind her neck and the other under her knees. He lifted her in one smooth motion and cradled her against his chest. Even now, having caught her red-handed, his instincts were screaming at him to trust this woman.

He shook his head.

What is wrong *with me?*

Chapter 19

Mira

MIRA STARTLED awake with a gasp. She blinked several times and tried to slow her breathing. Her head was stuffed with cotton balls. The overhead lights stabbed like needles into her eyes. She rolled onto her side and squinted, narrowing her focus to her hands. Dark grime was caked under her nails, and little flakes of ragged skin lined her cuticles. *Abuela would be so disappointed.*

The surface she was lying on was cold and hard, too unyielding to be a bed. She shifted her attention to the world beyond the few inches in front of her face. A dozen feet away was a steel bench that looked like what she felt beneath her. Between the bench and the far wall of the room was a set of bars. She was in a cage.

She swung her legs down so her feet rested on drab concrete and pushed to a sitting position. Her breath caught. Her vision swam. She braced one hand against the bench and reached for her pendant with the other. Her fingertips found only her collarbone.

"Looking for this?"

She twisted sharply and immediately wished she hadn't as her stomach rolled and cramped.

The man her demon had picked up at the bar what felt like ages ago—whom she'd last seen disappearing beneath an avalanche of boxes—was lounging against the wall behind her. He held a silver chain in his fist so the pendant dangled at eye level. Another man, a uniformed officer, was also in the room. It took her a moment longer to place him, since he'd been wearing street clothes the only other time she'd seen him, but she eventually recognized him as the man who'd chased her from the farmers market. He stood just to the side of a beige door and held one of the long-barreled weapons Mira now identified as a tranquilizer gun. It was pointed at her chest.

"Saint Jude."

Her attention swung back to the first man. Mira's pendant spun slowly at the end of its broken chain.

"I did a little research since we first met. Patron saint of lost causes." His gaze shifted from the pendant to Mira. "I have to admit, I'm feeling pretty lost these days. Maybe I should say a prayer."

"Maybe you should." Mira's voice rasped. Her throat was dry as cracked earth. Her mouth tasted of old pennies.

He slipped the necklace into a plastic bag and tucked it in his pocket, then he pushed away from the wall. "Billy."

The guard by the wall twitched and swung his attention away from Mira.

Mr. Yummy walked over and set one hand on the other man's shoulder. "Tell LaRosa the prisoner is awake. I'll bring her to interrogation room one." He held his hand out to Billy, palm up.

The younger man glanced at Mira, then nodded and placed the tranquilizer gun in Mr. Yummy's hand. When the guard opened the beige door, Mira caught a glimpse of more uniformed officers. The din of multiple, overlapping conversations drifted in.

The door closed, sealing her alone with Mr. Yummy.

Mira waited for a joke about him wanting to be alone with them again . . . but silence echoed in her mind. Now that her tranquilizer hangover was fading, she realized that all the thoughts in her head were her own—no snarky comments about her many personality flaws or lewd remarks about the way Mr. Yummy's dark jeans clung to his thighs and butt.

Panic surged through her. She'd assumed the trap she triggered in Decker's house had a limited reach . . . that once she was beyond the affected area her demon would return. Hadn't she heard the demon urging her to run?

Sparks danced at the edges of her vision. She was breathing too fast. She reached again for the place where Saint Jude should have hung, watching over her. She could feel the weight around her neck. She reached higher, above her collarbone, up to her throat. A ring of metal rested against her skin.

She rocketed to her feet and tore at the collar.

"I wouldn't—"

She grabbed for the energy she needed to channel magic, and an electric shock surged through her system, dropping her to her knees.

"—do that."

Mira gasped and panted on her hands and knees. She spat a gob of bloody spit on the floor. She'd bitten her tongue . . . again.

"I take it you haven't worn a control collar before."

She glared at her captor.

Mr. Yummy was crouched near the edge of the holding cell, one hand wrapped around a bar. The tranquilizer gun hung loose in his other hand, pointed at the floor. A deep furrow marked the space between his eyebrows. His lips—those full lips she could still remember kissing—were turned down in a frown.

She looked away.

"The collar can sense the electrical input when you draw energy to cast magic. It disrupts that flow and converts the energy into a charge that's then released into your nervous system. The more power you try to draw, the bigger shock you'll get."

She rested her fingers against the metal around her neck. She'd heard of such collars from Garrett. He didn't like to talk about his time with the sorcerer troop, but he'd told her everything he could about how the Church handled out-of-control practitioners back when he was helping her get a handle on her abilities. She might have expected a collar if the PTF had sent an agent after her, but it wasn't something she'd thought a regular policeman would have. "You keep these on hand?"

"Hardly. The PTF has cases of them, but here we were lucky to find even one among the emergency supplies."

"Yeah," she whispered. "Lucky."

The collar must be preventing me from connecting with my demon. No permanent damage, just a temporary glitch. We'll be together again as soon as I get this off. We'll be fine. Mira rocked on her hands and knees as she tried to ignore the nagging fear that she was, and might remain, truly, utterly alone—something she hadn't been since Detroit and the night of the fire.

"You'll be okay as long as you don't try to use magic."

She took a deep breath. *If I fall apart here, I'll never hear the end of it when she gets back.* "And as long as I answer your questions." She sat back on her heels and met his gaze. "Or are you going to tell me you can't make this thing zap me at will?"

His frown deepened. "There is a remote device, but I would never use it like that."

"Sure." She smiled. "Because practitioners are always treated fairly."

She expected him to look away—she had the high ground—but he didn't.

"I won't." His gaze remained steady. "You have my word."

She was sinking into the deep brown of his eyes, remembering the way the skin crinkled at the corners when he laughed. He was ticklish along his ribs, just above the scars that marked his side.

She blinked and shook her head. "Do all your lovers end up in cages?"

Now he did look away.

Embarrassment or worry? Did his partner know about their nighttime activities?

He rubbed a hand over the back of his neck. "Are you ready to tell me your name?"

She crossed her arms and pressed her lips tight.

"Shall I call you Richard then?" He held up a rectangle of plastic—the driver's license from her wallet. She'd pulled the ID off a drunk in Tucson a few years back. Illusions were more convincing when you had a decent start to provide the basic layout. A few fudged numbers and a face lift on an existing ID were simpler than creating one from scratch.

He sighed. "Look, when we . . . you know . . ."

"Did the dirty?"

"Did you do anything to me?"

She cocked her head. "Wow. That memorable for you, huh?"

"I mean . . . before." He voice dropped to a barely audible whisper. "Did you use magic on me?"

She stared him straight in the face. "You think I gave you a magic roofie? Forced myself on you?" Heat collected in her cheeks as her anger rose. "If either of us has grounds to complain about the circumstances of that night, it's me."

He frowned. "What do you mean? I was just minding my own business at the bar. *You* came on to *me.*"

"I—" Mira snapped her mouth shut. He'd never understand that Mira had just been along for the ride—that who he'd really had sex with that night was an incorporeal consciousness from the Rift who inhabited her body—not without explaining a lot more than she was willing to. "Never mind."

He raised an eyebrow, then stood and unlocked the gate. "Come on. LaRosa's gonna wonder what's taking so long."

The cage swung open, and he stepped inside. He twitched the gun in his hand. "Am I going to need this?"

Mira shook her head. Even if she could take him down without magic, she was in the middle of a police station. She'd never make it out on her own.

Mr. Yummy wrapped one hand around her upper arm, and for a

moment she was ten years old again, being dragged away by a man twice her size. She scrunched her eyes closed. *I'm not a child anymore. Even without my demon . . . without my magic . . . I'm not helpless.*

She stood, winced when her weight settled on her left ankle, and recalled hurting it in last night's fall. Without access to magic, she'd heal as slow as any mortal.

The man hesitated, then leaned close enough to whisper in her ear. She stiffened, expecting a threat . . . or an offer. Which one would depend on whether he'd told his partner about their little tumble between the sheets.

"Did you kill Rodney Temple the night we met?"

She twisted so they were nose to nose. His expression was tight, worried. He searched her face with those dark-chocolate eyes. She got the feeling he was seeking a deeper answer than just whether or not she was a killer.

"Whatever you think is going on here," she whispered back, "I'm not the bad guy."

He watched her for another moment from that intimate closeness, his breath warm on her face. "I hope that's true."

Then he stepped away and tugged her arm to direct her toward the cage door.

Chapter 20

Ty

TY SETTLED HIS prisoner in the suspect chair of interrogation room one. LaRosa was already waiting. He closed the handcuffs attached to the table around the woman's slender wrists, then circled around and took the seat next to LaRosa.

"Let's start with introductions." LaRosa set a hand against her chest. "I'm Detective LaRosa." She pointed to Ty. "This is Detective Williams." She looked across the table expectantly.

"Do you make a habit of arresting people when you don't know who they are?"

LaRosa's smile showed a lot of teeth. "We do when they're murderers."

The woman looked away. "I didn't kill the woman in the attic."

"I saw her die," Ty said. "You were the only other person in the house."

She met his gaze, and he finally placed what had been bothering him since they faced off in the holding cell—both her eyes were the same caramel brown.

"I *didn't* kill her." Her gaze never wavered. She was either telling the truth, or she was a psychopath. . . . Not out of the question.

"How about Rodney Temple?" LaRosa flipped open the folder in front of her and spun a glossy photo of Temple's mummified remains around for the woman to see. "Did you kill him?"

The woman didn't flinch. She didn't stare at the photo like a pervert admiring her work or shy away in horror. She looked at the picture. She looked at LaRosa. "Don't you need to read me my rights before you question me?"

"Depends."

"On what?"

LaRosa pursed his lips. "We know you were at the battle of

Arlington—a soldier IDed you off your sketch—and practitioners don't have the same rights as regular citizens."

The woman swallowed and sat up a little straighter. "Even if your ID holds up . . . that doesn't prove I had anything to do with your murder victim."

LaRosa tilted her head to one side. "We also know Mr. Temple was conscripted into the necromancer's army in Wilmington, so he was at Arlington, too. And thanks to your excellent choice in drinking companions"—she glanced at Ty—"we know you were in the neighborhood where Temple was killed within minutes of his death."

Their suspect's gaze darted to Ty, and a small crease appeared between her eyebrows. "Circumstantial."

"Look, I get it, I do. You're just cleaning up the rifters who escaped Arlington. It's a public service, really." LaRosa folded her hands over the open folder. "The thing is . . . we can't find any record of you. And since we know you're a practitioner, that means you're not registered." She shook her head. "The PTF doesn't look too kindly on that."

"But maybe we can make a deal," Ty chimed in. "You tell us what we need to know, and we'll put in a good word with the PTF, tell them how cooperative you've been. They're grateful for your help at Arlington. I'm sure they could forgive the death of an escaped rifter."

"So instead of getting executed, I can look forward to spending the rest of my life in a cell with one of *these* around my neck." She lifted her chin to bring their attention to her control collar. "No thanks."

"You're going to end up in PTF custody one way or the other," Ty said. "Help us help you."

LaRosa leaned forward. "What do you know about Rodney Temple's death?"

When the woman didn't respond, Ty asked, "Why did you visit Anton Nowak at KBU Construction?"

"And where is he now?" LaRosa added.

The woman folded her fingers together on the tabletop and leaned back in her seat. "I have nothing to say to you."

"Fine." Ty pulled LaRosa's folder toward him and flipped a page to reveal another case file. Paperclipped to the top was a picture of a young girl. "Let's talk about Mirana Fuentes."

Mira

MIRA FROZE. HER heart stuttered, stalled, then started racing.

She glanced at the picture attached to the file under Mr. Yummy's hand. Her hair had been longer than it was now, falling past her shoulders. It had been lighter, too. And her eyes were that same light-brown color. Mira had been nine years old when that picture was taken. Steve had taken her and her mother to the Anna Scripps Whitcomb Conservatory. That was before the abuse started, when he was still pretending to be her mother's hero. When they still believed his promises about marriage and a comfortable life.

"We pulled your prints while you were sleeping," Mr. Yummy was saying. "Imagine our surprise when they matched a missing person case in Detroit from fourteen years ago."

He flipped a page. The words printed on the next sheet were too small for Mira to make out.

"Mirana Fuentes, eleven years old, disappeared after a house fire destroyed the building where she and her mother were living. Mother, Maria Fuentes, suffered third-degree burns over eighty percent of her body." He turned another page.

Mira looked away, but not before catching a glimpse of red, angry flesh in the next photo.

Her mother's screams filled her head. She didn't need pictures to remind her of the way skin bubbled and melted . . . the way it smelled when it burned.

"Steven Holbrook—the owner of the house and Maria's boyfriend at the time." Another page turned. "He wasn't so lucky."

Mira glanced sideways, seeing a new picture out of the corner of her eye. Steve's skin wasn't red. It was black. Not melted but charred. He hadn't screamed nearly as long or as loud as her mother. He'd been with her at the very center of the fire. His suffering was over too fast.

"The fire was deemed accidental, and it was assumed that young Mirana ran off to escape burning with her parents."

Mira bit the inside of her cheek to keep from correcting him. Steve was *not* her parent.

Mr. Yummy tapped his finger on the file. "But to me . . . this looks like the result of a new practitioner coming into her power. Bad timing—what with the Faerie War in full swing and magic users being rounded up. Must have been terrifying for a child who'd just killed a man and maimed her own mother."

Mira resisted the urge to shift in her seat. She *had* been terrified. Not just of being captured by the authorities and having to face what she'd done, but of doing it again. She didn't remember much from the time immediately after the fire—the demon had been in the driver's seat—but she remembered thinking that anyone who got close to her was going to die. She'd run until her legs gave out. Then she'd crawled. She'd gotten as far from the city as she could, and when she woke up . . . she was alone. She'd been alone ever since. Just her and her demon.

The emptiness ringing in her head was like a silent scream. She could almost feel the magical anchors that tethered the demon to her soul . . . but without drawing on the energy that was currently denied her, she had no way of knowing if those anchors were still intact.

"The police and FBI searched for months, but . . ." He shrugged. "Then one day, four years later, little Mirana shows up on her grandmother's doorstep in Florida." He closed the file. "No explanation given. Claimed she couldn't remember what happened that night. The police didn't pursue the matter. The girl was home, case closed." He leaned back in his seat and crossed his arms. "Except that isn't the end of the story . . . is it, Mirana?"

Mira ran through her options. It was a short list.

Whether she talked or not, the end result would be the same—a PTF prison. There was only one person who *might* be able to get her out of it.

"I need to make a phone call." The words were out of her mouth before her brain had time to register them, almost like her demon had taken the wheel for a moment. She hated to drag Garrett into this mess—especially after her speech about not needing him—but she had no choice. She wasn't getting out of this one on her own.

"Practitioners don't get phone calls." The female cop shrugged. "At least not the unregistered ones. You've done a fine job of erasing yourself from the world. Which means no one will notice your absence."

The words stung because they were true. *Abuela* would write more emails, but eventually she'd give up. The handful of contacts she'd developed around the country might notice that she hadn't passed through town in a while, but they wouldn't waste much time wondering why. Now that Garrett was working with the PTF, maybe he'd see a report with her name on it . . . but that would be too little too late.

They were right. She'd erased herself from the world.

"Not so cocky now, hmm?"

"Let's try this again." The man leaned forward so his arms rested on the table. "What were you doing at Reed Decker's house last night?"

Mira pressed her lips tight.

"What's your relationship with Gemma Murphy?"

Mira stiffened. "Why are you asking about her?"

He raised an eyebrow. "Finally feel like talking?"

"Look, Detective . . . Williams, was it? Decker's the one you need to be looking into. Not me."

The lady cop clasped her hands and rested her chin on top. "Is that why you were dating Mr. Decker's assistant?"

"What? No." She shook her head.

"Security footage has you going up to Decker's office to talk to her."

"I was there to see Decker."

"And witnesses place you together at a restaurant called"—the man glanced at the paperwork under his elbow—"Tir Na Nog the night before last."

"Gemma and I are friends." Mira flinched at the word but pressed on. "Just ask her."

"We'd love to." Williams spread his hands wide. "If anyone could find her."

Mira stared at the detectives for a moment, unable to wrap her mind around the words. "Gemma's missing?"

"No one's seen her since she left work yesterday." Williams shrugged. "So, yeah. She's missing."

Mira stared at her bound hands, mind racing.

The silhouette arguing with Decker was too short to be his wife. . . .

She straightened and studied the cops across from her. The woman, LaRosa, had shifted back and crossed her arms. Her narrowed eyes and tight mouth did not look friendly. The guy wasn't much better. Mr. Yummy—a.k.a. Detective Williams—had a closed expression. Would their night of passion make him more open-minded? Or would he see this turn of events as a personal betrayal, however indirect, and lash out. Both cops were watching her like a caged rat in a maze, waiting to see what path she would take.

She chewed her lower lip, wishing hers wasn't the only voice in her head.

If Gemma was the woman arguing with Decker in his house last night, maybe *she* was in the duffel bag he'd hauled out. In which case she was probably dead. There hadn't been much time between the lights going out and Decker emerging with the bag, but a rifter wouldn't need a lot of time to kill a helpless mortal.

Mira glanced up. The speckled-cream tiles of the ceiling were no comfort.

I need you here to think through this with me.

The crushing weight of the silence in her head pressed against her like an ocean.

She sighed and met LaRosa's gaze. "I think Decker may have killed Gemma."

Williams shifted in his seat. "Is that why you were at his house last night? To confront him?"

"To get revenge maybe?" LaRosa chimed in. "Except you found his wife instead."

Mira was shaking her head.

"She tried to hide in the attic," Williams picked up the story. "You followed."

"No."

"And when you caught up to her . . ."

"No!" Mira flattened her palms against the table. "I didn't kill Mrs. Decker."

LaRosa met her gaze. "Then why don't you paint us a different picture?"

Mira sighed. She was as good as outed as an illegal practitioner anyway after her reaction to the control collar in the holding cell.

"You're right about me being at Arlington." She glanced up and met the dark brown of Williams's eyes boring into her, thirsty for truth. "I did fight in that battle, and I did follow Temple when he fled, although I didn't know his name."

Neither cop spoke. Maybe they were worried about breaking Mira's flow now that she'd finally started talking. She shifted her arms. The chains on her cuffs scraped against the table.

"I followed a trail of violent murders—mostly homeless victims—to a shelter here in Midtown. I laid an ambush and . . ."

She sucked her lower lip. Did she want to mention Nowak? How could she explain the chain of events that led her to Decker without revealing that there were rifters who didn't fit the universally accepted mold? That people could be possessed without going berserk? That Decker was, in all probability, just like her?

She closed her fists on the table. She couldn't tell them about her demon. Being an unregistered practitioner was bad enough. Being a rifter would guarantee a one-way ticket to the afterlife as soon as the words left her lips. But how could she convince them Decker was a threat without revealing the truth?

"And?" Williams prompted.

"When I confronted him . . ."

Both cops leaned forward.

". . . there was another practitioner at the site," she blurted.

"Another practitioner." Williams echoed. He and LaRosa wore matching, flat expressions.

"I didn't get a good look at him, except that it *was* a *him*. He attacked Temple, and me, then fled."

LaRosa frowned. "So you're claiming you didn't kill Temple? It was this mystery practitioner?"

Mira licked her lips. If she wanted them to believe her, she had to give them something. "I finished Temple off. He was a dangerous rifter who would have killed a lot more people."

"Where does Decker fit in?" Williams asked.

"I tracked the practitioner from the construction site through his magic. That's how I ended up at Decker's office the day I met Gemma."

"You can track magic?" LaRosa looked at her partner.

Williams pursed his lips. "It *is* possible to tell different magics apart . . . but it's subtle. Only a handful of fae and even fewer practitioners can mark the difference, let alone trace it back to its source." He braced his elbows on the table and raised one eyebrow. "You can do that?"

She swallowed and nodded. Better they believe she had a rare gift than demonic assistance. She just hoped they didn't ask her to demonstrate.

"You went to Nowak first." LaRosa gestured to Mira's hair and face. "A little cosmetic work, but that was you on the security footage."

Mira shrugged. "He was another potential for the source of the magic."

"So what happened?" She spread her hands, palms up. "Where is he?"

"I don't know. He wasn't in his office when I got there. I went out the back door, thinking he'd stepped out for some air. When I didn't find him, I left."

Williams narrowed his eyes. The corners of his mouth turned down.

"And then you went to Decker?" LaRosa prompted.

"Yeah, but I couldn't get past his secretary."

"Gemma Murphy."

She swallowed, trying to work more moisture into her mouth. "She was friendly. I thought if I was friendly back . . ."

"She might let you in to see Decker?"

Mira nodded.

Williams drummed his fingers on the table. "So where is she?"

Mira shook her head. "I told you. I think Decker killed her."

"Why would he do that?"

"When we were hanging out, I might have let my suspicions about Decker slip. Gemma was excited about the mystery. She wanted to help." Mira tried to raise her hand, forgetting for a moment that it was chained to the table. The cuff drew tight, biting into her wrist. She let her hand drop. "I think she went to the house that night to confront Decker, or maybe just to gather intelligence. Either way, Decker caught her snooping and . . ."

A new thought struck her. If Decker thought Gemma was working with Mira, perhaps he'd have kept her alive as collateral in case the trap in the attic failed to stop her. Gemma might still be alive.

Williams leaned over his arms. "What about the wife?"

Ay, coño! How can I explain the dead woman?

Mira opened and closed her mouth twice. Then said, "All I can say is that she was already dying when I got there. I was searching the house, found the stairs to the attic already open, went up and . . ." She spread her hands, rattling her chains. "The woman was bleeding out." She looked at Williams. "You came in a minute later."

"Why'd you run?" he asked.

"I'm an unregistered practitioner and you found me standing over a dead body." She raised her handcuffs for emphasis.

LaRosa jabbed an elbow into her partner's arm and jerked her chin toward the door. Both cops stood. "Sit tight while we confer."

Williams opened the door, followed LaRosa through, and pulled it shut.

Mira clasped her hands together and bowed her head. *Hail Mary, blessed mother, have pity on us poor sinners. Please watch over Gemma Murphy. Protect her if you can; give her peace if you cannot. Saint Jude, I beg of you in this moment of hopelessness, let my words ring true.* She glanced at the closed door. *Please, please, please let that be enough to convince them.*

Chapter 21

Ty

"YOU BUYING HER story?" LaRosa crossed her arms and leaned back against the hallway wall.

Ty glanced at the closed door behind which they'd left Mirana Fuentes. "Not entirely."

He'd felt like she was telling the truth at least some of the time, but her mannerisms, the way she hesitated or fidgeted during certain parts of the story, made him think she was still hiding things. Maybe she'd only given them enough truths to make her lies convincing. She'd seemed adamant that she hadn't killed Mrs. Decker, but Ty had seen her standing over the woman as she bled out. There was no one else close enough to have stabbed her and fled without passing Ty in the house . . . unless Decker really *did* have magic.

"What do you think about Decker being a practitioner?"

LaRosa pursed her lips. "Not sure. Seems fishy to me, and I'm not gonna take her word on it, but we could poke around. Ask some questions." She shook her head. "Even if she's right about Decker, she's definitely not telling us everything."

"Agreed."

She tipped her chin. "That magic tracking thing she was talking about is really real?"

He nodded. "Though as I understand it, it's not so much tracking as comparing. Like how no two people smell exactly alike so a dog can tell them apart."

"So she smelled magic at the construction site, then went to sniff Nowak and Decker to see if they matched?"

"Something like that."

"Could we use someone like that to sniff out if she was the one who used magic in Nowak's office?"

Ty frowned. Mirana had definitely not been telling the truth about Nowak. "In theory, yes. But like I said before, there aren't many practitioners with that discriminating a sense. And considering the current social climate, I don't think the PTF is going to be bringing practitioners out into the field again any time soon." He shrugged. "With the exception of their experiment in Colorado."

"So we're stuck with regular police work—facts, evidence, and instincts." She pushed away from the wall. "What's your gut telling you about Ms. Fuentes?"

Ty studied his shoes and tried to ignore the knots in his insides. A year ago he would have said he thought Mirana was on their side, however gray her methods, despite the evidence stacked against her. And a year ago people would have listened. Now. . . .

"She seemed genuinely concerned for Gemma Murphy. I think I believe that they were friends." He grimaced. "That doesn't mean she's not responsible for her disappearance, but I'm inclined to question Decker before I make that call."

LaRosa nodded. "We'll need to transfer her to PTF custody, but once they have her we probably won't get another crack at her. You think we can get any more out of her?"

"It'll take a while to arrange transport. Let's let her cool her heels for a few hours and contemplate her fate. That'll give us time to check some of her story. Then we hit her once more to see if she comes clean. Otherwise"—he shrugged—"we turn her over to the PTF and hope they have better luck."

"I'd rather close this case ourselves, but yeah, let's do it."

She led the way back into the interrogation room but didn't sit. Neither did Ty. He didn't bother to close the door.

"You're still not being honest with us, Ms. Fuentes," LaRosa said as she walked around the table.

Their suspect was sitting with her head bowed over her clasped hands. She sagged at LaRosa's words, deflating like an old balloon until she seemed even smaller than she had when he lifted her limp form last night. She looked up and . . . were those tears in her eyes?

LaRosa hooked a thumb at Ty. "Williams here will take you back to holding." She collected the various photos and files on the table, snapped her folder shut, then stared down at Mirana. "It'll take a few hours to arrange your transfer to PTF custody. I suggest you use that time to think about what kind of report you want me to give them. Misguided hero . . . or dangerous vigilante. And keep in mind what the PTF does to magic-users branded with the word 'dangerous.'"

She picked up her folder, nodded to Ty, and walked out of the room.

Mirana's gaze followed LaRosa, then snapped to Ty. "Are you going to look into Decker?"

"We'll see." He uncuffed her from the table and led her out of the interrogation room.

"Gemma might not be dead."

Ty stopped, pulling her to a halt as well. "I thought you said—"

She twisted to face him fully. "The woman in the attic, Decker's wife . . . I think she was a trap."

He raised an eyebrow. "A trap?"

"For me. He wanted to stop me from poking around, learning his secret. What better way than to get me arrested?"

"So he stabbed his own wife and left her to bleed out slowly on the off chance that you'd show up to take the fall?"

"How did you know to come to the house last night? At that exact time?"

Ty frowned. "Anonymous tip."

"Someone called and told you they saw me entering Decker's house?"

Ty recalled that the tipper hadn't been routed through dispatch, they'd called directly to *his* department. Uneasy tension slithered through him, souring his stomach. "Something like that."

"The woman in the attic was already stabbed when I found her. I thought she was dead. But when I touched her to check there was a . . . a magical booby trap." She frowned and looked him up and down with narrowed eyes. "Do you understand how magic works?"

"I know enough."

"Well the magic in that attic got instantly tapped out when I touched her, like her body was a heat sink for magical energy. Why do you think I dropped boxes on you instead of casting a spell?"

Ty suppressed a shiver. "I assumed you were still trying to hide the fact that you were an unregistered practitioner."

She nodded. "Fair enough. But the woman didn't actually start bleeding until I touched her." She raised her chin. "I think she was being held in a stasis spell that was designed to shatter when someone with magic touched it. It burned through the ambient energy and left me weak enough for you to catch me."

"You think I need a handicap to take you down?" He tugged her arm to get her walking again. "I was tracking magic-users back when you were still popping pimples."

She stopped again. "You were an agent?"

"Not just an agent, an investigator." He gave her another push.

"Then what are you doing here?"

"*Trying* to get away from magic and all the bullshit that goes with it."

"Yeah? How's that working out?"

He pursed his lips.

"Look, I know you don't trust me, but I'm telling the truth about Decker. He's dangerous and he's got my friend. If she isn't dead already, he might have her in a stasis spell like the one he put on his wife. There might still be a chance to save her."

"Assuming Decker is the bad guy in this scenario, why would he keep Gemma on ice? You're already out of the way." He pulled open the holding room door and directed her into the cage.

"Maybe in case you didn't manage to catch me the first time. Or as a bargaining chip in case I escape." She shrugged. "I don't have any actual proof, but . . . don't you ever just trust your gut?"

He stepped out and closed the steel door with a *clang*. The bolt locked in place. "No."

She scowled. "Then you must have been a piss-poor investigator."

He turned away.

"Call my friend," she shouted.

He glanced over his shoulder, waiting for more.

"I have a friend who works with the PTF. He'll vouch for me."

"What's his name?"

"Garrett."

He waited a beat. "That's it? No last name?"

"Not that he's ever told me, but he's the practitioner liaison for the new paranatural coalition they're building in Colorado."

He sighed, turned, and walked out.

Ty

AN HOUR LATER Ty was sitting across the conference table from Reed Decker, listening to a very different story.

". . . then I put my gym bag in the trunk and left." Decker's voice hitched. He ducked his head, pinching the bridge of his nose between thumb and forefinger as though fighting back tears. "If only I hadn't gone out that night . . . she might still be alive."

"And you're sure the attic door was closed when you left?" Ty asked.

"Yes." Decker shifted, looking up at the two detectives. "My wife was getting ready for bed. She would have had no reason to go up there except to hide. I've told you all this before. I don't understand why we have to keep going over it."

"Just being thorough, Mr. Decker."

"But," LaRosa interjected, giving Ty a sharp look, "I think we've heard enough. Thank you for coming in."

"Anything to find justice for my wife and perhaps save poor Ms. Murphy from a similar fate." He stood and offered his hand first to LaRosa and then to Ty, who shook it reluctantly. He hadn't spotted any holes in Decker's story, but something felt off about the man. Touching him made Ty's skin crawl.

"Officer Patel here will escort you out." Ty nodded to the waiting officer and watched Decker leave. He wore the expression of a grieving husband trying to hide his pain—but he wore it a little too well for Ty's liking, as though the emotions had been scripted and rehearsed.

Once Decker was clear of the conference room they used for less formal interviews, Ty asked LaRosa, "Do you think there could be any merit to Mirana's accusation?"

"As far as Decker being a practitioner?" She shrugged. "You'd know better than I. But as for being a murderer . . . I think Fuentes spun that story as a ploy to deflect suspicion, not to mention splitting our time and resources. Speaking of which, I need to get on the horn to arrange that prisoner transport. Looks like we'll be handing her over sooner rather than later."

Ty nodded and followed her out, veering off to his own desk. He looked at the paperwork piled at his station without really seeing it, comparing Decker's explanation of events to Mirana's. The evidence definitely sided with Decker, but Ty couldn't shake the compelling way Fuentes had spoken. Had she really made it all up?

Criminal Psychology 101—give the cops a plausible story. All most people needed to walk was reasonable doubt, and a well-told story could create that even in the face of a mountain of evidence.

Of course Mirana Fuentes wasn't most people. She wouldn't be making her claims in front of a jury with a lawyer to advise her. She was a practitioner. Under the current law, she was as good as owned by the PTF for as long as she drew breath. If they deemed her a threat, they could lock her away for the rest of her life . . . no trial needed. And if the stories he'd heard from Arlington were any indication, she was definitely a threat.

Ty stared at the phone on his desk. He shifted in his chair and bounced his knee. He glanced at LaRosa, who was already on the phone arranging the prisoner transfer. Once Mirana Fuentes got in that truck, Ty would lose any chance of verifying her story—he'd never know if his instincts were right about her.

He sighed, ran both hands over his hair, then sat forward and grabbed the phone. He punched in the number for the PTF call center and shook his head. *What am I doing?*

"Paranatural Task Force, Baltimore. How may I direct your call?"

"I need you to transfer me to a liaison named Garrett in Colorado."

"One moment, please."

Tinny music filled the line.

Ty tipped his head and stared at the ceiling. The melody was hypnotic, lulling him into a dream-like trance.

"This is Garrett."

Ty jerked in his seat, snapping back to reality. "Mr. Garrett—"

"Just Garrett. Who are you?"

"My name is Ty Williams. I'm a detective with the Baltimore PD in Maryland."

There was a sigh and a *thump* from the other end of the line. "I take it this is about the request for information sent with your BOLO? I'm afraid I haven't had time to—"

"We found her. Mirana Fuentes. She's in custody."

There was a long pause. "If she's already in custody, why call me?"

Ty glanced at LaRosa. She was still engrossed with her own conversation. Billy was standing guard in the holding room with the tranquilizer gun. Two uniforms were chatting by the coffee maker. The door to Captain Holtz's office was closed.

Ty sank a little lower in his seat and pitched his voice low. "She seems to think you'll give her a character reference."

"She asked you to call me?"

"You sound surprised."

"I am."

Ty rubbed a hand over his eyes. She'd played him. "Sorry. She said you were friends. I—"

"No, no, we are. At least insofar as Mira has any friends."

"Mira? Is that what you call her?"

"Tell me, detective . . . how much trouble is she in?"

Ty pursed his lips. "Two counts of murder, breaking and entering, resisting arrest, and involvement in two missing persons cases." He shook his head. "Top that off with being an unregistered practitioner, and it's not looking good."

There was a moment of silence, then, "Is there anything you can do for her?"

"I'm doing it right now by calling you."

"Even if I was to claim she was working under the new paranatural coalition, we're only sanctioned to work in Colorado. She's way outside our jurisdiction."

"She says the man she admits to killing was a rifter who evaded capture at Arlington."

"I don't doubt it."

"And that the man whose house we caught her in was an unregistered practitioner who, she claims, murdered his own wife to frame her and either killed or captured an acquaintance of hers."

"Look, detective, I don't know you and you don't know me, but I *do* know Mira. She may not always play by the rules, but she is one hundred percent on your side. If she says a man is bad news, he's bad news. And if he's the kind of bad that she's hunting, you're better off letting her handle it."

"So she's what, a criminal with a heart of gold?"

"She does the job the PTF claims it's here for—protecting people from magical dangers."

We're going to protect people. Jamal's voice echoed in his head.

LaRosa stretched, stood up, and walked toward him.

"If there's anything at all that you can—"

Ty hung up, cutting Garrett off mid-sentence.

Ty's desk squeaked as LaRosa propped her hip against it. "We're all set with the transfer. We'll drive her over in an hour." She nodded to his phone. "Who were you talking to?"

"Just making sure all our i's were dotted, t's crossed."

She arched one eyebrow. "Mm hmm. Well we've still got two missing people to track down. Though I doubt we'll find either Nowak or Murphy alive at this point."

"I'm still not ruling out Decker's involvement."

"She really rattled you with that story, huh?"

He opened his mouth but couldn't find a way to voice his conviction that Mira was telling the truth without sounding like an idiot. He could tell her about Garrett's assessment of Mira's motives, but what was the worth of a stranger's word? No, ultimately it came down to a gut feeling, and Ty was no longer confident enough to argue on that alone.

He sighed. "I just want to make sure we're putting the right person behind bars."

She put her hand over his on the desk. "We are."

He didn't reply.

She slid off his desk and headed for the captain's office. "I'll bring Holtz up to speed."

He leaned back in his chair and pressed his laced fingers to his lips. In the PTF, the military, even as a child, Ty had gone out on a limb plenty of times on instinct alone—even when it meant breaking rules or standing against a crowd. He'd always done what he thought was right . . . until his gut got Jamal killed.

I should follow LaRosa's lead and let it go.

But he couldn't shake the look in Mira's eyes when she claimed Gemma might still be alive, or the tone of Garrett's voice when he begged Ty to do what he could to help her. His gut was telling him that he and Mira were on the same side . . . despite all evidence to the contrary. If he handed her over to the PTF, whatever work she'd been doing would go unfinished.

He closed his eyes and rested his forehead against his clasped knuckles.

There was nothing he could do. She'd be in PTF custody in an hour. She'd have to convince them her story was legit, that Decker was a threat. Except they wouldn't listen. Maybe, just maybe, before that mess with the sorcerer rebellion . . . but now? No chance they listened to what she had to say.

He *thump, thump, thumped* his knuckles against his forehead. The watch on his wrist caught his eye. It ticked away his seconds of indecision.

Unstrapping the watch, he held it in his lap and popped off the back. A little button battery sat in the center of the mechanism. Setting his jaw, he yanked open the top drawer of his desk, grabbed a handful of paperclips, and tried to remember everything he'd ever learned about how control collars worked.

Chapter 22

Mira

MIRA NIBBLED AT the turkey sandwich that had been left on a tray in her cell and washed it down with a sip of room-temperature water from a plastic cup. The guard by the door, the one who'd chased her into the Goodwill the day before, watched her in silence—but the silence in the room was nothing compared to the silence in her head. It had been hours now since she'd experienced a thought that wasn't her own, and the emptiness was making her twitchy. She jumped at every noise and scanned the room constantly as though she might find her demon floating just beyond reach, but all she found was the steady gaze of her guard.

She rocked back and forth, her thoughts turning darker as the day stretched on. *How pathetic. Done in by a dart and a dog collar.* She pulled her knees to her chest and wrapped her arms around them. *You'd laugh if you could see how lost I am without you. All my high and mighty talk of independence and self-sufficiency, and I fall apart after a few hours on my own.*

But it wouldn't be just a few hours. She was being transferred to the PTF, where she'd be tested and charged as an unregistered practitioner. The collar might prevent them from discovering she'd been a rifter . . . but the silence would never end.

All because of Decker. She bunched her fists.

Mira had felt a twinge of guilt when she blurted her suspicion about Decker being a practitioner—outing another paranatural was a big no-no in the magical community after all. And Decker wasn't just any paranatural. He was a sustainable rifter, like her. But she was over that. Decker had killed his wife, maybe killed Gemma, and landed her in this silent, lonely prison. Whatever he was, he was *not* like her, and she wouldn't waste another second of regret on him.

The door to the holding area opened, and Detective Williams walked through. His tan work boots scuffed against the concrete floor. A collection of chains and handcuffs dangled from his hand.

"Hey, Billy." He slapped the young guard's back. "Anything to report?"

Her guard shook his head. "She's just been sitting there. Mutters sometimes, but nothing else."

Williams nodded. "The transport's nearly ready. Time to get her prepped." He lifted the chains in his hand and gave them a jingle, then moved to the cage door. He cleared his throat and waited for her to make eye contact. "I'm going to put these on you now so we can transport you to the PTF facility." He tipped his head toward the guard behind him. "Billy here is going to have you covered with the tranquilizer gun, but you're not going to give him any reason to shoot you, right?"

Mira glanced at the guard, then back to Williams. She set her feet flat on the ground, sat up straight on the hard metal bench, and shook her head.

"Good." He unlocked the cage and stepped inside.

Mira watched Williams approach, trying to gauge his mood, looking for any indication she'd gotten through to him. "Did you call my friend?"

His lips compressed. Was that a good sign—that he'd talked to Garrett and was now conflicted about her fate? Or was he feeling guilty because he'd ignored her request and was now wondering if he'd made the right call?

He knelt beside her leg, back to the guard, and snapped one metal ring around her ankle. Then he leaned in to reach the other leg. His shoulder bumped her knee. He kept his gaze down, focused on what he was doing.

"I'll help you."

Mira froze. The words had been a mumbled whisper, nearly inaudible. Had she really heard them? Or was she so desperate for hope that she'd imagined them?

His hands rose, sliding up the inside of her calf to where her hands rested between her knees.

When his knuckles brushed against her leg, a tingle rippled through her that had nothing to do with her current predicament. Mira could imagine the demon's voice, taunting, teasing, as all the secret places in Mira's body tightened in remembered pleasure of that touch.

She scrunched her eyes shut and swallowed. This was *so* not the time for that kind of thinking.

Williams snapped a cuff around her right wrist. "Promise me no one will get hurt." He looked up and met her gaze.

She stared into those dark eyes. Shadows of doubt danced in their depths, but also a steely resolution that made her breath catch. He believed her. Against all odds, he was going to help her.

She gripped his fingers and squeezed, promising with her eyes and her touch as she whispered, "I promise."

He squeezed back, then snapped the second cuff in place around her left wrist and tucked something into her jacket pocket. When he straightened he shifted so his body blocked her entirely from the view of the guard by the door. Metal scraped her neck as he slipped something between the control collar and her skin. Whatever it was, it circled half the collar around the back of her neck, further constricting the already tight choker.

"One large jolt, as much power as you can manage, and it's gonna hurt like hell." His breath shivered across her skin as he whispered the words in her ear. "Wait till we're away from the building, and take the evidence with you." He pulled her to her feet, and again she could feel herself sinking into the depth of his earnest eyes. "Don't make me regret this."

She nodded, giddy anticipation tying her tongue. She wouldn't end up in a PTF cell after all. She was getting out. She was going to be free.

Williams hauled her out of the cell, one hand wrapped around her upper arm. Her chains jingled and scraped as she shuffled along, but even their weight couldn't counter the lightness in her step. The guard by the door followed them out, the tranquilizer gun at Mira's back.

They stopped in front of the scuffed chrome doors of an elevator. Williams glanced at the nearby stairwell, sighed, and pressed the call button. The door opened with a *ding* to a wood-paneled interior. The skin around Williams's eyes and mouth tightened. He stuffed his free hand in his pocket, then hauled Mira inside. The guard stepped in beside them. The doors closed. The grip on Mira's arm tightened, and Williams's breath came faster.

The guard cast Williams a concerned look. "You all right?"

"I'm not a fan of small spaces."

As soon as the elevator doors opened, he tugged Mira into the concrete parking garage.

Orange overhead lights created an artificial twilight in the man-made cavern—an illusion heightened by the chill, damp air. Their footsteps echoed off the close ceiling and thick pillars that supported the station above. Another officer, an older man with graying hair and a paunch that strained his uniform, stood beside Detective LaRosa in front of the open back of a police van. Bench seats lined the sides with an aisle in the middle. The front seats were blocked off by a wall of metal mesh.

LaRosa patted the van. "Last chance. Anything you want to tell me?"

Mira met LaRosa's gaze. "Nothing you'll listen to."

LaRosa pursed her lips and jerked her head toward the windowless interior in silent command. Williams and the holding cell guard supported Mira as she climbed in. The guard sat down across from her, tranquilizer gun pointed at her chest.

Mira smiled at him. "Keep your finger off the trigger, will you? I don't want to get shot accidentally if we hit a pothole."

The second uniformed officer climbed in, attached the chain between her ankles to a steel ring in the floor, and sat down beside her. The back doors closed. A lock clicked into place. Muffled conversation drifted into the van, but Mira couldn't make out the words.

The doors to the front cab opened a moment later. LaRosa climbed into the driver's seat. Williams settled on the passenger side and strapped on his seat belt. He held another tranquilizer gun, currently pointed at the floor mat between his feet. Guess they'd been arguing about who was the better shot.

LaRosa turned over the engine and shifted the van into gear. The vehicle lurched. Mira bumped shoulders with the officer beside her, but his solid mass absorbed the impact without moving. Maybe he was there for the sole purpose of making sure she didn't roll around the back seat. The younger cop swayed with the van, the barrel of the tranquilizer gun swinging.

That would be Mira's opening. She'd wait for the van to make a turn and strike while the Boy Scout was off balance.

The van's shocks squeaked under its passengers' weight as they crossed a drainage dip at the garage entrance. Weak daylight filtered through the windshield, making Mira blink after the dim lights of the garage. She wasn't entirely sure what time it was. Her stint in the holding cell had been like a timeless limbo under artificial lights.

LaRosa pulled into traffic.

Mira wasn't sure which PTF facility they were taking her to, or how long it would take to get there, but she wanted some distance between the van and the police station before she made her move.

A handful of intersections later, LaRosa took a sharp right that pressed Mira's back against the van wall and made the guy across from her lean into the aisle. The tranquilizer gun was pointed at the floor.

Taking a deep breath, Mira said a prayer and yanked at the ambient energy around her like an imploding star. Electricity surged through her, lighting up her nervous system, and a ribbon of burning agony seared the back of her neck. She tried to gasp, but her lungs froze in place as her muscles seized. The man beside her stiffened, noticing the change in her, but she couldn't deal with him . . . not while the collar was still active.

She continued to draw power despite the pain. Her limbs shook. Her neck was on fire. The collar was overheating. There was a crackle, like the static pop of a radio, then the electric currents surging through her body cut off. Mira sagged. Her eyelids fluttered open, but she didn't have the energy to move. Her muscles were toast. Her heart raced like the flutter of a hummingbird's wings. Sweat cooled against her back, making her shiver.

The man beside her grabbed her arm. The one across from her raised his gun.

She blinked and exhaled. The world was moving in slow motion.

When she breathed in, a familiar presence filled her, following the lines of power she'd opened and hadn't yet closed. Energy surged through her, breathing new life into her abused muscles and fading thoughts.

<Finally!>

Mira choked on a sob as relief washed through her along with the demon's presence.

Her consciousness drifted into the background as the demon took control, shoving Mira to the side. They weren't equals right now. Mira was tired, weak, and totally vulnerable.

A new wave of pain enveloped her. Not the electrical jolt of the collar or the burn of Williams's short-circuit device, but the agony of unraveling as every cell in her body was pulled apart.

Mira knew this sensation, though it had been years since she'd felt it this bad. This was the fate of a possessed body—a mortal being used as a human battery to fuel its demon rider. This was what happened when Mira and her demon were out of balance with the demon in the driver's seat. This was how she felt right before her world exploded and the people around her turned to ash.

Mira could feel the lines of darkness seeping from her eyes and fingernails, cracking her skin, tracing her veins like rivers of decay spreading through her body. The energy draining from her physical body collected and was released in a single moment, like a pebble dropped in the center of a pond. By the time she refocused on the world outside her body, the two officers in the back with her were on the floor.

Are they . . .?

<Just sleeping.> Mira grabbed the collar around her neck and, with a burst of magically enhanced strength, tore it free. The two halves fell to the floor with a metallic clang.

LaRosa slammed on the brakes. Tires screeched. Horns blared. The smell of seared rubber on asphalt filled the air. Mira's shoulder, followed quickly by her head, slammed against the mesh grate that separated her from the front. Blood trickled into her eye, warm and sticky, gumming up her lashes.

"Shoot her!" LaRosa screamed the words.

Williams raised the tranquilizer gun, lining the narrow barrel up with a gap in the mesh.

Their gazes locked.

His dark eyes were screaming a message as loud as LaRosa's command. *Take me out.*

Mira hesitated. The demon didn't.

A wave of compressed air rippled out from Mira's body. The mesh warped, twisting and tearing. Williams slammed against the dashboard. The gun fell, unfired. LaRosa's forehead connected with the steering wheel. The windshield and side windows blew out.

For a moment, there was no sound in the world. Then Mira's senses came rushing back. Horns and voices took the place of road noises as traffic stalled in both directions—the vehicles behind the van because there was no safe way around, the cross traffic because people were people and couldn't resist staring.

Mira wiped blood from her eye.

Williams's chest rose and fell, as did LaRosa's.

She knelt and pressed two fingers against the neck of the nearest officer, then the other. Both had steady pulses. She exhaled.

Were you with me the whole time?

<I couldn't access the anchors within you, but I could follow them from within the Rift. I've been watching.>

Good. We need to—She shot out a hand to steady herself against the van wall as her vision swam.

<We're out of whack. We need energy.>

Mira shook her head. *I'm not a vampire. We don't feed on the innocent.*

<We do today.> Energy flowed through the hand still pressed to the young officer's neck.

No. Mira tried to pull her hand away but failed. *I promised no one would get hurt.*

<A little late for that.> Mira's gaze darted toward the front, where LaRosa was draped on the steering wheel and Williams was slumped across the center console.

<Don't worry. I won't do any permanent damage.>

The dizziness receded. The cracked skin on her hands sealed, and the dark veins faded. Mira moved to the second officer and repeated the process, drawing energy from him the same way she drew demons from rifters, except in this case she was tapping directly into his life force—the energy that kept his mortal machinery running.

Mira's stomach churned. This wasn't the first time she'd had to resort to feeding from mortals. . . . Her mind flashed to an old woman in an alley back in Detroit—or maybe she'd just seemed old to Mira's child eyes with her hunched back, matted hair, and layers of tattered clothing. They'd both hunkered among trash bins in an effort to hide from the bitter cold of the wind and the freezing temperatures of the winter night. Mira had been exhausted, starving, and scared. She didn't have the magic or the mass to stay warm.

When the morning sun crept down the opening of that alley the next day, Mira walked out. The woman was found much later—a vagrant who'd frozen to death on the winter streets. But Mira knew it wasn't the cold that had killed her. She'd sworn then and there, never again.

<That was a foolish promise born of guilt and regret, and I never agreed to any such limitation. My priority was, and is, to keep you alive.>

She lifted her hand off the second man's neck. He was pale, and sweat slicked his skin.

<A few days of flu-like symptoms. Nothing they can't survive.>

She glanced toward the front.

We have enough. Let's get out of here.

<Fine.>

Mira rose and teetered unsteadily for a moment. She was healed enough to function, and to pass for human, but their internal balance was still off. She could feel the push and pull of power inside her as her own energy and that of the demon struggled for dominance in their shared body.

If her demon had been like the others of its kind, Mira wouldn't have been able to maintain even a fraction of control in her present condition. She would have been a walking meat puppet like the rifters she put down. Even with the demon doing its level best not to overwhelm Mira, they'd have to take some time to reset their anchors and find their equilibrium, or they were going to self-destruct like every other rifter she'd come across. . . . Every rifter until Nowak and Decker.

Focusing on escape, Mira sent a ribbon of heat into her cuffs that melted the locks. The chains fell heavily to the van floor. She set her hands against the locked door and pushed. Metal groaned and screeched as the lock tore free. The doors jerked on their hinges, flying fully open, bouncing, then swinging back. For the instant they were open, Mira saw motorists gathered on the street around her, squinting and pointing, backlit by the ambient glare of the overcast sky. Then she was blocked from sight as the broken doors sagged shut, hiding her in the windowless compartment.

Think we're balanced enough to hide in plain sight? She lifted her hand and tugged at her magic, testing. It came hesitantly, as though it was half-asleep and resented being woken.

<Doubtful. You're not terrific at illusion magic even at the best of times.>

Then we run for it. She tested her injured ankle. The ache was gone. *God, I love magic.*

Sirens were screaming in the distance, growing closer. A few brave souls had left their vehicles and were drifting toward the wreck, either out of curiosity or a sense of civic duty to see if the cops inside were okay.

The evidence!

Twisting, Mira grabbed the broken control collar off the van floor. A thin piece of wire and what looked like a metal button were melted to the inner curve. She also snagged the tranquilizer gun her guard had dropped and tucked it into the waist of her pants at the small of her back.

She glanced once at Detective Williams, said a silent prayer that he would escape blame for her prison break, then burst out of the back of the van.

The nearest observers jumped away from her abrupt appearance.

Mira pivoted, scanning the stopped vehicles and surrounding area. Buildings stood shoulder to shoulder along both sides of the street, trapping Mira in a canyon of bricks and mortar. The sirens were getting closer, echoing off storefronts to create the illusion they were right on top of her. Flashing red and blue lights reflected off windows a block away. The traffic jam gave her a head start, but she wouldn't make it far on foot.

A woman in stretchy black pants and a puffy purple coat called out from the sidewalk to ask if she was okay. A large man with windswept black hair, sunburned skin, and a leather biker jacket took a step toward her, hands raised like he was calming a spooked horse. A Harley-Davidson was parked in the left-hand lane, just visible behind a blue Prius.

Mira charged forward. Onlookers scattered, taking cover behind stopped vehicles. She swung her leg over the Harley and sent a prayer to Saint Jude that the owner left the ignition unlocked and was close enough for the security fob to work.

The bike rumbled to life.

Mira grinned.

"Hey!" The man in the leather jacket started toward her, but she was already letting out the clutch.

She peeled out between the blue Prius and a white Accord.

Chapter 23

Mira

BRANCHES DOTTED with the first signs of spring buds scratched at Mira's arms as she moved away from the hiking trail she'd followed into Gwynns Falls Park—an enormous nature preserve nestled along the western edge of the city. She'd ditched the Harley in front of a bar a mile or so from her escape, then ducked into the wooded park in search of a secluded place to catch her breath. Damp mud smeared underfoot, and she sat down hard in a pile of decomposing leaves near the sluggish current of a stream. Even without their summer greenery, the trees and bushes in this area were packed tight enough to hide her from view.

Mira scooped a handful of shockingly cold water into her palms and splashed it on her face. She gasped and shook. Icy drips trickled down her neck, soothing the raw skin where the collar had burned her. The distorted reflection on the tumbling surface of the water threw back swathes of color with little detail, but Mira could still see that half her hair was white and her left eye shone a brilliant gold. She and her demon were matched equally at the moment, or near enough, each with one hand on the steering wheel—which might seem like a balanced partnership but was a sure recipe for a wreck.

Because her demon was naturally so much more powerful than her, their balance needed to be far from even, like a heavy-handled knife balanced on a fingertip. There was a lot more material on one end because the other was so dense. In Mira's case, the demon could only keep the smallest portion of herself manifested or the body they shared would be torn to pieces by the force of her presence. Even now, after the feedings that had temporarily stabilized her, Mira could feel the strain on her cells. Purplish stains were starting to form around her fingernails and trace up her fingers like ground cracking in advance of an earthquake.

She pressed her palms to the damp earth and took a deep breath of moist air.

<We need to reset the anchors.> The demon's voice swelled and

faded, as though she was rapidly changing positions, flitting about Mira's mind unable to hold still—the incorporeal equivalent of pacing.

Nodding, Mira shifted so she was sitting in a more comfortable position. They hadn't had to reset their anchors in years, and she wasn't sure how long it would take. She relaxed her neck and shoulders until her chin rested against her chest, closed her eyes, and took another long, steady breath.

She opened herself up to the energy around her—not in unshielded abandon as she had in the police van, but by allowing a thin trickle to funnel through a specific point that she controlled like a sluice gate. She could feel the rift energy, the energy her demon was made from, seeping into her, filling her reservoirs. At the same time she could feel the pull of the demon's power, tearing away the energy that kept her alive, the physical bonds of her mortal form.

This was the balance they maintained—the cannibalistic partnership—each devouring the essence of the other for the power they needed to perform magic. While the demon could channel vast amounts of rift energy—far more than Mira could handle without risking a burnout—she relied on Mira to manifest that energy in the physical world.

Mira found the first of the dozen or so anchor points buried deep within her body—places where her practitioner magic and the demon's rift energy balanced in perfect harmony... usually. The anchor was tearing into the physical matter of Mira's body, searing and spreading like an infection as the pure rift energy of the demon sought to overwhelm its human host. The demon was there with her, throttling back the surge of rampant energy as best she could without pulling out entirely.

Drawing off some of that energy, Mira shifted it through the magical filter that transformed it from chaotic potential to useful fuel. Then she pumped it back into the anchor. The balance shifted, Mira and her demon each pushing harder or pulling back as the anchor flickered between existing in the Rift between worlds and a point on the physical plane. When both Mira and the demon could affect the anchor evenly, they tied off the magic, sealing the anchor in place.

They moved on to the second, and the third, each time pushing and pulling to find their balance. With each anchor that snapped into place, Mira could breathe a little easier. The shaking in her limbs subsided. Her sense of being out of control faded. The anchors didn't exist only to connect Mira with her demon, they were the firewall that kept them separate and distinct. As those walls went up, the demon shifted further into the background, present but no longer overwhelming.

As Mira continued to set anchor after anchor, her mind wandered once again to the possibility that other rifters might have found this balance, learned to share control in such a way that they wouldn't burn each other out and self-destruct. She thought of Decker. She'd only seen him from a distance, but he hadn't worn gloves or glasses—nothing that would hide the effects of long-term demon possession. If he was a rifter, he'd found a way to bypass the usual relationship . . . just like Mira.

She clenched her jaw. Even if Decker *had* learned how to survive with his demon, he and Mira were *not* the same.

Her thoughts shifted to the policemen she'd fed from in the back of the van and LaRosa draped over the steering wheel with blood running down the side of her face. Threads of doubt slithered into the cracks of her self-righteousness.

Was she any better than the rifters she put down? Than Decker? He'd killed his wife. He'd kidnapped and maybe killed Gemma. But she still didn't know *why*. And reasons aside, Mira's hands were hardly clean.

<Focus!>

The levels of Mira's magic were wobbling like a drunk juggling Jell-O shots. She cleared her thoughts of Decker, and doubts, and what it meant to be a rifter, and concentrated on evening out the flow of her power. The last anchor clicked into place like a key turning in her soul.

She fell back against the soggy bank, panting. She could tell without looking that the white in her hair had returned to a thin strip and her eyes would be as close to the same color as they ever got. She had both hands on the wheel again with the demon safely parked in the passenger seat until she was needed.

<Let's not do that again any time soon.>

She nodded and shifted her weight. Her right leg had gone numb below the knee, and the backs of her legs were damp from the wet ground. Metal clinked in her jacket pocket. She reached in and pulled out the two segments of the broken collar.

She turned them over in her hands. The hinges and lock were twisted and sheared where she'd snapped them. Each segment had a narrow strip of wire melted to the otherwise smooth inside curve. The wire formed an irregular pattern, as though it had been hastily straightened but refused to lay quite flat. She traced her finger along the wire's path, imagining the line of pain around her neck that would match that pattern perfectly.

Her hands started to shake.

She set the collar pieces aside and dug her fingers into the muddy bank, scraping away handfuls of earth.

<What are you doing?>

Mira continued to dig, her mind focused on the feelings of isolation and helplessness that welled up inside her when she touched the collar. She'd been trapped, at the mercy of the police, with no recourse, no power to stop them, entangled by secrets and lies, afraid to tell the truth for fear of the repercussions. Then there'd been the gaping hole in her soul where the demon had resided for more than half her life—an aching emptiness she never wanted to feel again. Her heart raced. Her breath came in short, sharp bursts. The tremor in her hands spread to her limbs.

She dug until water seeped into the bottom of her hole. Her fingers, stiff with cold, fumbled the collar when she tried to pick up the pieces, but she managed to toss them in. Then she pushed the soggy ground back in around and over them. She packed and patted the mound—a shallow grave for her fears.

Mira sat back on her heels and took a deep breath. She tipped her face toward the overcast sky, closed her eyes, and listened to the melody of the burbling stream.

<Are you meditating now? I really think we can find a more practical use of our time.>

The corners of Mira's mouth tugged up. The demon was back, annoying commentary and all. She was whole. She was powerful. She was safe.

But once again she'd been saved by the kindness of a stranger. Williams had saved her from a life of imprisonment or worse at the hands of the PTF, just as her demon had saved her from her mother's boyfriend all those years ago. The realization made her want to puke. Grateful as she was to be free, the weight of debt and her own inadequacy was a hard pill to swallow. She'd spent years trying to be independent, self-sufficient, but in the end . . . she hadn't been enough on her own. Had anything really changed since she was a kid?

She reached into the pocket where Williams had tucked something during their chat in her jail cell and pulled out a slip of paper. There was a phone number scribbled on one side. No name. No other information. Just a number.

<Looks like Mr. Yummy wants to reconnect.>

Mira stared at the paper for several long moments, then jammed it back in her pocket, shoving it all the way to the bottom.

"We'll rest here a little longer, then head back to the motel."

Ty

"KNOCK, KNOCK."

Ty peered past the nurse taking his blood pressure and spotted LaRosa in the doorway of his hospital room.

"How's the wrist?"

Ty waited until the nurse removed the inflatable cuff from his bicep to flex his fingers. Stretchy strips of gauze wrapped his palm and forearm. "Sore, swollen, but nothing broken." He tipped his chin. "How's your head?"

LaRosa lifted a hand to the white bandage that was taped over half her forehead. Below it, the skin around her left eye and the bridge of her nose was discolored. "I'll live."

Guilt and anger twisted in Ty's chest, strangling his lungs. Mira had promised no one would get hurt. Granted, he and LaRosa were being discharged, but Billy and Collins were staying in the hospital. The doctors assured him they'd both recover, but they looked to be on the brink of death when the ambulance brought them in, and they both remained unconscious. Mira had definitely done *something* to them.

He looked away from LaRosa, focusing on the nurse who was now tucking away the blood-pressure cuff. "Dr. Singh should be in to release you in a few minutes."

Ty nodded and shifted to look out the window as the nurse squeezed past LaRosa and out of the room. The overcast sky had grown darker in the past hour, threatening rain. Somewhere out there, Mira was free . . . because of him. Because he'd followed his instincts. Had he made the right decision?

"Captain got a call from the PTF." LaRosa raised a hand as though she was going to run it through her hair but stopped with a wince when her fingers brushed the bandage. She put her hands on her hips instead. "Since we hadn't finished the transfer, they're holding us responsible for Fuentes, which is bullshit. They should have had jurisdiction as soon as she was IDed as a potential practitioner."

Ty sighed and eased his arm onto his lap. "They're probably happy to have an excuse to push the case off on us for now. I'm sure they're scrambling to find enough agents to cover their current case load. They'll need at least double per call if they're responding without magical backup."

"It was their decision to bench *all* the practitioners during the rogue uprising." She sighed and looked at the ceiling. "How long do you think they'll keep them benched?"

Ty shook his head. "Guess that depends on how things go at the test site in Colorado."

"In the meantime we're stuck picking up the PTF's slack." She sucked her teeth. "We're not equipped to handle magic-users. That's why the PTF was formed in the first place. And how the hell did she get out of that collar? Aren't those things supposed to be magic-proof?"

Ty continued to study the scene out the window and kept his expression carefully neutral. "For the most part. But the electrical transfer can only handle so much. Some practitioners, powerful ones, can channel more energy than the collar can contain. That kind of overload can short out the system."

"Great, so not only did we lose our murder suspect, she's a crazy-overpowered practitioner that even a PTF collar can't contain." She dropped onto a steel-framed folding chair with a beige cushion and slouched with her elbows braced on her knees. "So what do we do now, Mr. ex-PTF? Put her picture on the news and start a tip hotline? Call in SWAT? Wait for another body to turn up?" She deflated as she exhaled until her head hung low enough that her hair blocked her face. "We don't even know if she's still in town."

"She seemed pretty convinced Decker was up to no good."

LaRosa peered through the curtain of her long, black hair. "You think she'll go after Decker?"

"I think he's worth checking out. Might be there's some merit to her story, and he *is* connected to both our missing persons. Even if he's not the culprit, he's still our best lead to tracking Mira's whereabouts."

LaRosa lifted one eyebrow. "Mira?"

Ty cleared his throat. "Mirana Fuentes." He shrugged. "I shortened it."

"Uh huh. Well I still say she was feeding us a story with Decker, making accusations to keep us off balance until she saw a chance to escape."

"In which case she's likely skipped town." Ty glanced at his cell phone, piled on the bedside table with his wallet, badge, and gun. Mira had seemed so adamant about Decker's guilt in his assistant's disappearance, but LaRosa was right; criminals lied all the time. Had she been playing off his fears and sympathies to get him to break her out? If she ghosted him, he supposed he'd have his answer. He looked away from the silent phone. His instincts were still on Mira's side, but as the clock ticked off the passing hours since her escape, the logic of the situation screamed that he'd made a mistake. And if he had . . . whatever happened next would be his fault.

LaRosa pushed to her feet. "Either way, you're right about Decker being our best lead." She opened the door to his room. "Let's find that doctor and get you released so we can track this witch down."

Chapter 24

Mira

THE DUMPSTER beside America's Best Wings offered a decent if foul-smelling cover for Mira as she watched her motel. A few cars were parked in the restaurant's lot. None *looked* like cop cars. Across the street, most of the motel's parking spots were empty. Business clearly wasn't booming in this area.

She'd paid for the night before but had missed the noon deadline for tonight's rent. Would the clerk have checked her room already? Claimed her few possessions in place of the missing cash? Or worse . . . had he recognized her picture from a police bulletin and called them to set an ambush?

She chewed her upper lip, thinking.

<Let's just burst in on a wave of magic. Anyone hiding inside will be knocked unconscious.>

And anyone hiding outside *will be alerted.* Mira rubbed a hand over the healing burn on the back of her neck. *We need to do this carefully.*

<When did you get so timid?>

I'm being cautious, not timid.

<Is there a difference?>

Mira pursed her lips. She wasn't going to learn any more from watching her room. So what was she waiting for? She was cold, tired, and hungry enough that even the restaurant discards in the bin beside her were starting to smell appetizing.

<You could always call that number in your pocket and just *ask* if the police are waiting in our motel room.>

Mira closed her eyes. Her demon wasn't wrong, but the memory of her inability to escape the police on her own was still fresh in her mind. The idea of asking for help again so soon stung her pride and made her all the more determined not to contact Williams. She clenched her fists. *We don't need him.*

<What's the use of having an inside man if you aren't going to use him?>

I did use him . . . to get out of that collar.

<He put that number in your pocket for a reason. He clearly wants more. Maybe he can be, like, your secret partner.>

You're *my secret partner.*

<So we can have a secret threesome. I'm okay with that.>

Mira shook her head, trying to rid herself of the image of Williams, naked above her, sweat shining like diamonds on his dark skin.

One complication at a time. The first step is to get in the hotel room, and we can handle that on our own.

<If you say so.>

I do. She straightened, stepping out from behind the dumpster. *We go in quiet. No use drawing attention if the police aren't looking for us here yet. But keep your guard up. I don't want to take another dart in the ass if we need to run away.*

No one jumped out at Mira when she crossed the road and entered the motel parking lot. No one sniped her when she set her hand against the door to her room. Pulling a thread of magic that made her giddy with the sheer joy of being able to do so again, she shifted the bolt in the lock and turned the handle. She shoved the door open and waited with her back pressed to the outside wall beside the frame. No hail of bullets erupted from the room.

She peeked around the door frame. Her laptop was closed on the nightstand. Her backpack sat on the floor at the foot of the bed. The photo strip of her and Gemma was untouched on the dresser.

She stepped inside, waited another moment, then kicked the door shut behind her.

"So far so good."

Mira grabbed the TV remote, switched on the small flatscreen, and started scrolling through channels. She found several conflicting news reports about the police action that afternoon, but the reporters seemed oddly short on details. Only one report mentioned the possibility of an escaped prisoner, and none provided her name or description.

Switching off the TV, she sat on the bed and pulled her laptop open. A quick search showed online sources had little more to say about the incident than the television. She found one article citing bizarre police drills interfering with civilian traffic and another with a witness statement claiming a policewoman stole his Harley. Mira smiled.

"Looks like the cops have decided not to make us famous, at least for now. Considering I escaped in the middle of a transfer, the police and PTF are probably arguing over who has jurisdiction . . . and who takes the blame if I get away."

A small icon at the bottom of her screen alerted her to a waiting message from the PI job board—which reminded her that the last of her cash was still in her wallet at the police station and well beyond reach.

She groaned and rubbed her forehead. No matter what she did next, she'd need cash, and that meant finishing her side job . . . or robbing a bank. She opened the message and quickly skimmed over Shaquana's request for an update, then sat with her fingers hovering above the keyboard.

<What are you gonna tell her?>

Sighing, she closed the laptop lid. "Nothing yet."

<At least the cops keeping quiet about our escape gives us some breathing room while we go after Decker.>

Mira shook her head. "Screw Decker. A quick chat with Angela to earn some cash and we're getting out of here, like we should have done from the beginning." She unplugged her laptop and shoved it in her backpack.

<Seriously? You're just gonna dump it all on Mr. Yummy and run?>

"Tactical retreat. And don't call him that. He has a name now." For a moment Mira felt herself sinking into those deep, piercing eyes in the holding cell. He'd believed her. He'd helped her. The weight of debt settled over her like the collar he'd freed her from, choking her. She shook her head and forced herself to swallow past the tightness in her throat. "He can deal with this shit show on his own. He's a cop. That's his job."

<Well unless you want those puppet lines to come back, we're going to need a rifter to drain. Anchors aside, we've got almost no buffer between us right now. If we don't get more energy soon, I'll have to—>

"I know." They'd had long stretches between feedings before. Some long enough that Mira barely survived the toll of carrying a hungry demon within her body. She wasn't eager to repeat the experience. "We'll rely on my practitioner abilities until we can track down a regular rifter. There are still plenty unaccounted for from Arlington."

<Not in *this* city.>

"Exactly."

<We don't have any leads right now. We'd have to start from scratch.>

"We've done that plenty of times."

<Yeah, but *after* a good feeding. In our current condition we'll be lucky to make it a week before you show symptoms. So unless you want to start draining mortals like the vampires you find so repulsive—>

"Not gonna happen."

<—we need a fast meal from a known source. And Decker's the only one on that menu.>

"We'll manage." She zipped her backpack shut. "We always do."

<You're scared.>

Mira slammed the backpack onto the bed. "Damn right I'm scared. I just spent a day cut off from my freedom, my magic . . . from you. I was alone, powerless, and if Williams hadn't helped me I would have been that way for the rest of whatever life the PTF decided to grant me." Her pulse was thundering. Her chest grew tight. Her limbs started to tingle. She sank onto the edge of the bed and cradled her head in her hands. "How could I *not* be afraid to risk that again?"

<You should at least tell Mr. Yummy you're leaving.>

"Don't call him that."

<You owe him that much.>

She owed him so much more . . . and that was part of the problem.

She sighed. "Fine. I'll call, but only to tell him he's on his own."

<And thank him.>

Mira clenched her jaw and reached into her pocket, digging around for the note she'd crammed in there. Paper crinkled between her fingers. She pulled out the slip Williams had given her, but a second piece of paper came with it—the scrap of waxy trash she'd picked up during her stakeout at Decker's house. The cops must have missed it when they'd patted her down. She separated the trash from the note—not easy because the trash was sticky—and noticed there was something printed on it.

Setting the phone number aside, she flattened the wrinkled, translucent paper and turned it over. A pale double spiral decorated one side of the square scrap. It was a candy wrapper . . . saltwater taffy . . . from Gemma's favorite store.

She stared at the wrapper for a moment, then looked over at the strip of black-and-white photos propped on the motel dresser. Gemma's smiling face beamed out beside her own.

"She must have hidden under the same tree, waiting for Decker to arrive."

<It *was* the only decent hiding spot near Decker's house.>

"Then she confronted him."

<She must have gone in just before we got there, since we saw them arguing.>

"Or she started off talking about regular work stuff and it took a while for her to work up to accusations." Mira shook her head. "Either way, we missed it. She was definitely in that duffel Decker dragged out . . . and it's my fault."

<You didn't kill her.>

"But I piqued her curiosity."

<You told her to back off.>

"And because of that she was alone when she faced Decker. A helpless mortal looking for intrigue and adventure against a demon rifter powerful enough to sustain a possession." She turned the candy wrapper over and over in her hands.

<She might not be dead.>

Mira continued to flip the wrapper, hypnotized by the spiral logo as it flashed past again and again.

<Decker could be holding her as leverage against you. Either as a hostage, or to frame you for another murder.>

"Or just to keep the police focused on me as the prime suspect in her disappearance."

<But Mr. Yummy knows better. He believes you.>

"So far." She lifted the number Detective Williams had given her in her left hand and held it beside the wrapper in her right. How much use would he be without the whole truth about Decker? But if she told him, how long would it take for him to uncover her own secret? And how long would Williams's trust last if he discovered she was a rifter?

She chewed her lip. *Leaving is the smart option.*

<Doesn't mean it's the right one.>

She looked again at the photos of her and Gemma from their night at the harbor and pressed her lips into a grim line. *This is why I don't have friends.*

<People would get hurt regardless.>

But I wouldn't care.

<Liar.>

Mira sighed and rubbed her fingers across her forehead. "Fine, we'll stay. We'll rescue Gemma, or by God we'll make Decker pay, but we can't risk telling Williams that Decker is a stable rifter. It's too likely he'd figure out about us."

"He broke you out of prison. What's the poor guy gotta do to prove himself?"

She stared at the note with Williams's number on it. "Let's see what we can do on our own first. If we need help . . ."

<You'll call him.>

"I'll think about it." She tucked the note back in her pocket.

Mira

MIRA TURNED THE shower knob with reluctance, cutting off the flow of near-scalding water far sooner than she would have liked. Depending on how the next few hours went, she might not have access to running water again for a while. But she was clean. That was enough. She didn't have time to let the heat soothe her tense muscles. The skin on the back of her neck was still raw. Mira was never a great healer, so they tended to rely on the demon for that . . . but that required energy. Energy Mira didn't have to spare at the moment unless she wanted to sport some new puppet lines. So she slathered lotion on the burn like any normal mortal and did her best to ignore it.

"We need to decide how to approach Decker."

<I'm thinking with a truck . . . at high speed. *Bam!*> The demon took control long enough to punch Mira's fist into her open hand with a wet slap. <Then we finish him off while he's collecting his insides off the pavement.>

Shaking her stinging palm and wishing their level of physical control wasn't quite so even, Mira grabbed a towel off the rack. "While I appreciate the imagery, I doubt we'll get a good opportunity for vehicular assault. We'd have to know where he'd be at a given time."

<Well I'm not going back to that house. Who knows what other booby traps Decker planted there.>

Mira scrubbed the towel over her wet hair. "I'm pretty sure his wife was the only one . . . but I agree. Even if Decker went back there and the cops weren't still crawling around the crime scene, that spell we triggered burned through a crazy amount of energy. I wouldn't be surprised if the magic in that area was thin enough now to qualify as a waste—like the dead zones created during the Faerie Wars."

<Can you call something that only covers one house a waste?>

Mira flipped her damp hair. "A mini-waste then. Anyway, the house is out."

<That leaves the office . . . unless you know somewhere else he hangs out?>

Mira sighed and moved the towel down to her body. "There are a lot of potential casualties in that office. I'm not willing to start a magic firefight there." She pursed her lips, thinking. "We could wait in the lobby, then tail him when he leaves and—"

<Hit him with a truck!>

Mira rolled her eyes.

<I like this plan.>

"*Or* . . . we could follow him to his car, ambush him, and force him to take us to Gemma. He's got to be keeping her *somewhere*."

<Unless he's already killed her.>

"In which case we hit him with a truck." She tucked the towel back on its chrome bar and grabbed her underwear off the neatly folded pile of clothes on top of the toilet seat.

<You sure you don't want to sip off a few mortals first? We're not exactly at the top of our game, and Decker's clearly high level.>

"Hence the *ambush* part of the plan. If we land the first shot, I think we can take him. But first things first. Let's pack up. I doubt we'll be back here." She wiggled into her jeans, pulled a navy-blue sweater over her white cami, ran her fingers through her damp waves, and stared at herself in the mirror. "We'll need a face change before we go out in public, just in case."

<What did you have in mind?>

"We went pale last time, so . . ." She narrowed her eyes and concentrated on her reflection. A tweak here, a shift there; she didn't need the demon's help for this level of magic. She darkened her hair till it was glossy black and tightened her waves to ringlets. Then she shifted the color of her skin, like sliding the marker on a color wheel, until her reflection was a warm chestnut.

<Now you're you but darker. Mr. Yummy and his partner might still recognize you.>

Bracing against the sink, Mira drew more energy. She lifted the bridge of her nose until it was a sharp, straight line. She thickened her lips and added some weight to her cheeks. "How's this?"

The demon nodded Mira's transformed head, making her damp curls bounce. <Not bad.>

Mira shifted her jaw side to side, noting the way her false features stretched slightly out of sync with her actual movements. "I envy how easily disguises come to the fae."

<They've had centuries of practice. It's built into their genes at this point.>

She scrunched her nose and frowned at the way her skin wrinkled. "Tweaking colors is one thing, but changing shapes . . . I feel like I'm wearing a layer of playdough on my face."

<Then I suggest you not move so much or it might slide off.>

She looked down. "If only I could make myself taller."

The demon chuckled.

Mira took a moment to collect her toiletries from around the bathroom. She shoved them into her backpack, pulled on her socks and shoes, and looked around to make sure she hadn't missed anything. The photos of her and Gemma were still on the dresser, beside the room key she was insanely grateful she hadn't been foolish enough to carry with her. She stared at the photos for a moment. She glanced at the trash can. She grabbed the pictures, shoved them in her back pocket, slung her backpack on, and marched out the door. She left the room key in place—the clerk would find it eventually.

Chapter 25

Mira

MIRA RUMBLED through Decker's neighborhood in her home-on-wheels, which she'd altered to look like an HVAC truck, grateful that too many instances of losing her keys had prompted her to create a more permanent solution to starting her vehicles. This prevented pesky little problems like catching on fire, falling in the ocean, or in this case being frisked by the police from impacting her ability to get around.

She didn't strictly *need* to drive down Decker's street to get to the place where she'd left her bike, but she was curious. Wastes were dead zones, empty of more than just magic. The energy practitioners used to cast magic was the same energy that flowed through the world and everything in it. Wastes were barren, lifeless. If Decker's trap had been powerful enough to create one . . .

Wipers swished across the windshield, but the cleared moisture was quickly replaced as more raindrops speckled the glass. She spotted the drooping branches of the tree she'd sheltered under the night before—the same tree Gemma must have crouched beneath, sucking her taffies as she waited for Decker to arrive.

Mira eased off the gas pedal.

Decker's house looked just as it had last night, except for the boards and police tape blocking off the attic window. Mira pictured Decker's wife bleeding out on the floor. The way her fingers had clutched Mira's hand until her grip finally slipped.

The house itself was pale gray with dark trim—not a lot to indicate whether the building contained a waste—but the grass in the front yard sported splashes of green among the yellows of the winter lawn. As much as it might have felt like it to Mira, Decker's trap hadn't completely drained the area.

She turned the corner, taking one last glance at Decker's house in the mirror. Then she continued until she found her motorcycle—parked where she'd left it, thank God. She eased to the curb in front of it and cut the engine with a twist of magic.

Mira waited in the cab just long enough to be sure no one was curious enough to ask why an HVAC truck was parking in front of their house, then she climbed out, circled around, and opened the back. Rain pattered against her, but the drops were small and scarce—more a mist than a downpour. Still, she worked quickly to avoid getting soaked.

She extended the small ramp tucked under the bed and rolled her bike into the back of the truck. Her motorcycle was fast and convenient, but far too conspicuous for what she needed next. Besides, whether she killed Decker or blew the leeway Williams had given her, she'd need to leave town fast.

She attached straps anchored to the truck walls to the bike's handlebars, wheels, and behind the seat to keep it from shifting. There wasn't much space with the motorcycle in the back, so sleeping in the truck was out of the picture for the time being. She scowled at a puddle forming on the floor. She'd also need to mop before laying out her futon.

Once the bike was secured, she locked up the back and returned to the cab. The clock on the dash read 3:42. Plenty of time to reach Decker's office before he called it quits for the day.

She gripped the steering wheel and started the engine. "Let's get the bastard."

Mira had to drive six blocks past Decker's office to find a lot that still used an older meter rather than the newfangled license plate tracking system that her magic wasn't precise enough to fool.

Damn technology making everything more complicated.

She placed a crumpled grocery store receipt in the windshield and altered it to look like a payment slip, turned the collar of her coat up against the rain, then started the long walk back to the building that housed Bressett International.

Mira paused in the small plaza across the street from Decker's office. Red and gray bricks made a zigzag pattern around a concrete fountain at the plaza's center. Rain continued to fall, bringing life and movement back to the fountain that had been drained for winter. Mixed with the rain were tiny flecks of white. If the temperature dropped a few more degrees, the rain would shift fully to snow.

The edges of the plaza were lined with boutique shops and jewelry stores that filled out the lower levels of high-rises that rivaled Decker's. Mira had to crane her neck to catch a glimpse of the clouds above. There were also a handful of street vendors desperate enough to make a profit that they hadn't abandoned their posts despite the ragged weather. Steam rose from a cart advertising pulled pork and bratwursts. Beneath the stand's blue-and-white umbrella, a man with flushed cheeks and squinted eyes puffed into his hands to keep his fingers warm. At the next cart a woman with a frayed bun of blond hair handed a large, paper-wrapped pretzel to a man in a suit and tie. The rich aroma of coffee rose from a stall near the end, and Mira about fainted with desire.

Scanning the ground she spotted a paper receipt plastered to the side of a building, blown there by the wind and glued on by the rain. She moved to the paper and knelt as though tightening the laces on her sneaker. She quickly snatched the damp paper off the bricks.

<Seriously? You're worrying about litter again? Don't we have more pressing issues at the moment?>

In this case my motives aren't entirely selfless.

Holding the paper behind her back, she funneled a strand of energy into it. When she lifted her hand to inspect the results, a twenty dollar bill was pinched between her fingers.

<I thought we weren't doing that anymore.>

Needs must. That cop took the last of our cash and I'm running on fumes.

She stepped under the white canopy of the coffee cart. The man who greeted her was beanpole thin, towered over her by a good foot, and wore a black apron.

"What can I getcha?"

"Café con leche and a scone." She slid him the counterfeit bill.

He shoved her payment in the register with barely a glance and handed back her change, then started making her drink with the boredom of repetition.

Mira dropped the coins in his tip jar to ease the twinge of guilt stinging her conscience about the magic money. The few other people in the plaza either huddled under the various awnings as they waited for food or scurried between doorways and cars under cover of umbrellas or upturned coat collars.

"Here ya go."

Mira picked up her paper cup, taking a moment to warm her hands on it before sipping. Liquid heat scalded her mouth and traced a line down her throat until she could feel the warmth pool in her stomach. She closed her eyes and smiled. The coffee wasn't as good as hers, but it went a long way toward soothing her jangled nerves.

She grabbed her scone off the counter and headed across the street.

The security guards in the lobby seemed a little more alert than on her previous visit. *Think Decker told them to watch for us?*

<Even if he did, this is a pretty good disguise.>

Mira strolled over to one of the many chairs arranged in clusters around the lobby and took a seat that offered her a good view of both the lobby elevators and the front door. A pile of magazines with crumpled covers and bent corners were spread across a natural wood table beside her. An Asian woman in a business suit with feathers of gray at her temples sat in the chair on the other side of the reading material with her nose buried in a copy of *Cooking Light*.

Mira bit into her scone. A cascade of crumbs tumbled into her lap, and she brushed them carefully into the napkin the scone had been wrapped in.

<How long do you think we'll have to wait?>

She glanced at an analog clock mounted high on the wall behind the security desk. Its narrow second hand glided around the circle at a smooth, even pace.

Assuming he keeps a normal office schedule, he should be down in about an hour. Till then, we'll just sit tight.

She took a gulp of warm coffee and finished off her scone. Men and women wearing expensive clothes and salon-styled hair continued to pass through the lobby. Mira nursed the last of her drink, savoring the flavor even as the liquid cooled. She pushed the magazines around on their table like a kid pushing peas around their dinner plate—feigning interest without paying any real attention.

<Head's up!>

Mira's attention snapped into focus at the demon's alert. She scanned the room from the tiled floor to the vaulted ceiling, the glass entrance to the chrome elevators. And there she saw him.

Decker stood beside the elevators, having moved to let the other riders exit, but he wasn't alone. Detective Williams looked a bit ill as he stepped stiffly from the elevator, and Mira recalled his dislike of small spaces. He walked with one hand stuffed in his pocket. His partner, LaRosa, took no notice as she chatted with Decker, her glossy red lips moving soundlessly from this distance.

Guilt shot through Mira when she spotted the white bandage taped to LaRosa's forehead.

<I told you Mr. Yummy was on our side. They're following up on the information you gave him.>

Maybe.

She slouched lower in her seat and sipped her coffee, watching the little group in front of the elevator bank. Decker spoke and gestured toward the front doors. The three moved in that direction. Decker continued to speak as they walked.

Can you make out what they're saying?

<Not from this distance in this crowd.>

Mira grunted and downed the final drips of her coffee, sucking in fruitless disappointment at the empty cup.

LaRosa stopped short and shook her head, the long dark braid of her hair whipping like a snake against her back.

Williams looked surprised. Decker waved a hand as though shooing a fly, and Williams and LaRosa both seemed to relax.

This doesn't feel right.

LaRosa reached out, but she didn't slap a cuff on Decker's wrist as Mira would have liked. She shook his hand. Williams nodded and smiled.

Mira's scone squirmed in her stomach. *They're treating him more like a friend than a suspect.*

<You think he enthralled them?>

She sank lower in her seat and grabbed a fitness magazine from the stack to hide behind. *If he even needed to.*

<What do you mean?>

You put too much faith in people. Decker is rich and successful. He's getting a freaking humanitarian award from the mayor, for goodness sake. People like that . . . they don't need magic to get what they want, and why waste magic when mortal means will do? A little cash to grease the wheels and anyone can be convinced to see things a certain way.

<Not Williams. He believes you.>

A big enough donation could change that.

Mira's thoughts spiraled back to her mom's boyfriend, with his big house and fancy car. She flashed back to dinner parties where he drank and laughed with the city's elite while Mira and her mother cooked, served, and cleaned up after. She recalled his promises and his threats, made in equal measure. No, people like that didn't need magic to keep others in line.

Williams and LaRosa passed through the big glass doors of the office building. Mira glared after them as they walked to a silver pickup parked across the street and climbed in. A jumbled knot of vindication and disappointment twisted inside her. For a moment she'd almost let the demon convince her that Williams could be an ally, but she'd been right. She couldn't count on him.

<Don't write Mr. Yummy off yet. We don't have all the facts.>

Mira set the magazine aside and watched Decker as he strode back across the lobby toward the elevator. His back was to her.

<Let's grab him now. He won't be able to fight us without revealing what he is.>

She was halfway out of her seat before Mira squashed the impulse and forced her butt back into the chair, turning the motion into an odd hop. The Asian woman glanced at her, then went back to her magazine.

Neither could we. Have you forgotten about the tranquilizer guns? We can't risk approaching him while the cops are here. We stick to the plan.

The silver truck remained at the curb across the street. They hadn't even started the engine.

<I don't think the cops are going anywhere.>

Mira bit her lower lip. *They're staking the place out.*

<Keeping an eye on Decker?>

She considered LaRosa's handshake and the way Williams had smiled. *More like watching for us. They're probably hoping we'll do something stupid, like attack Decker here in the lobby.*

<Hey!>

She glanced at Decker again as a *ding* announced the arrival of the elevator.

<We could slip into the elevator with him. Even if the cops recognized us, they'd never get to him in time.>

And if we just wanted to kill him that might be enough. She glared at Decker's back as he stepped into the elevator. *But we need to know what he's done with Gemma, and extracting information takes time.*

The chrome doors slid shut, blocking Decker from view.

Mira resisted the urge to crush the paper cup in her hand.

She swung her attention back to the silver truck. Williams had believed her. He must have or he wouldn't have helped her escape. So why was he being all chummy with Decker now? Why was Decker still free? Threat, bribe, or magic? She wanted to march across the street, pull Williams from the truck, and shake him until he gave her an answer. She couldn't of course, but maybe she could still find out what was going on.

She fingered the slip of paper in her pocket and glanced at the woman in the seat beside her with the *Cooking Light* magazine in front of her face. Her gaze wandered down to the black purse on the floor beside the woman's high-heeled pump. The glossy corner of a smartphone stuck above the edge of one of the purse's many pockets.

Bending at the waist, Mira pretended to peruse the magazines again and slipped the phone free. She tucked it into the cuff of her jacket, stood, tossed her empty coffee cup and crumb-filled napkin into a black trash can with a swinging silver top, and walked to the other side of the lobby. When she was confident no one had noticed the theft, Mira pulled the little slip of paper with Detective Williams's number out of her pocket, let the woman's phone drop into her hand, and positioned herself near the corner where a concrete column would block her from view.

Please don't be locked.

The phone's screen lit, displaying a basic desktop with widgets for the local weather, a dozen time-killing games, and the woman's calendar.

<Lucky.>

Mira smirked. *Only about half the people in this country bother to password-protect their phones.*

<As opposed to you, who just throws your phone away after every use and buys another . . . No wonder we're always running out of money.>

I don't throw them away every *time. Just when I think someone might be looking for me.*

She typed in the numbers and pressed the call button.

Ty

TY SETTLED BEHIND the steering wheel of his truck and stared through the rain-splattered windshield toward the office building across the street. The rain that had been threatening when he and LaRosa arrived to interview Decker had fulfilled its promise, but as the temperature dropped, flakes of snow were thrown in the mix. Some drops erupted in wet explosions against the windshield while others clung to the glass in perfect fractal forms for a moment before melting away.

LaRosa climbed in beside him and pulled the passenger side door closed, sealing them together in the small space. Between the moisture from their clothes and their warm breath, the glass quickly started to fog. LaRosa tugged at the collar of her shirt where her half-zipped jacket had failed to protect, pulling the wet fabric away from her skin and jiggling it as though that might make it dry faster.

"What did you think of Decker's story?" LaRosa asked, giving up on her shirt.

"I think he's full of shit."

"He has the travel receipts to prove he was out of town on business."

"But back with plenty of time to kidnap or kill his assistant."

She shook her head. "I still don't see the motivation there."

Ty rested his head against the top of his seat and watched raindrops explode against the windshield through half-lidded eyes. LaRosa had only grudgingly agreed to consider Decker as a suspect in Gemma Murphy's disappearance, but at least she'd agreed. After Decker's speech however . . . the guy was a smooth talker, no doubt. And what evidence could Ty offer besides his own questionable instincts and the testimony of an unregistered practitioner who'd fled custody?

"You heard the talk around that office. What's his name at the front desk insisted Gemma was sleeping with Decker."

"Which Decker denied," LaRosa countered. "He said those two were competing for the same job. That guy was just a sore loser looking for some excuse why a woman got hired instead of him." She crossed her arms and stared out the window. "He couldn't accept the fact that she might be more competent."

Ty pressed his lips closed over all the things he dared not say and continued to watch the rain.

A deep rumble echoed through the cab.

For a moment Ty thought the sound was thunder, that he'd just missed the flash of lightning. Then LaRosa set a hand over her abdomen and said, "'scuse me."

He stared at the color creeping into her cheeks. Then he glanced out his window at the food vendors dotted around the plaza. "You want a pretzel, hot dog, sandwich, or—"

"I'm fine."

"Well I'm not," he lied. "If we have to sit here for the next few hours, we might as well get something to eat."

LaRosa rolled her eyes but smiled and said, "Grab me a salty pretzel with cheese."

Ty opened his door.

"And a soda," LaRosa added.

He stepped into the rain, closed the door, and trotted to the shelter of the pretzel stand's umbrella. The woman behind the cart wore a red-and-white striped apron that matched her umbrella. Her white-blond hair was collected into a frizzed bun.

He grinned at the woman. "Hi. Can I get—" His phone buzzed.

Lifting one finger both in apology and a signal to wait, Ty turned away from the pretzel-seller and pulled out his phone. He didn't recognize the number, but then that was exactly the sort of call he'd been hoping for. He lifted the phone to his ear. "Hello?"

"Why didn't you arrest him?"

Ty stiffened and glanced around the plaza. LaRosa was slouched in her seat, staring at the office building. A few people were dashing between cars and buildings, trying and failing to avoid the rain. He squinted toward the lobby of Decker's office building but couldn't make out the details of the people inside.

Mira was there . . . somewhere.

"You certainly took your time making contact," he said. "I was half convinced you'd skipped town."

"What did he offer you?"

He shook his head, trying to make sense of Mira's question. "What are you talking about?"

"You wouldn't have been smiling if he'd threatened you. More likely a little palm grease to make you look the other way."

Anger flooded through Ty, temporarily chasing back the cold. "I've never taken a bribe in my life. And I sure as hell—"

There was a clatter behind him.

He glanced over his shoulder to find the pretzel vendor staring at him.

He offered her a weak smile, turned away again, and hissed in a strangled whisper, "Where do you get off accusing me of something like that?"

"I saw you when you left Decker just now, all buddy-buddy."

He stepped farther from the pretzel stand, preferring a soaking to the pressure of the vendor's prying gaze on his back. "What did you expect? That we'd arrest him on an unsubstantiated hunch? I can question him, which I did, and I can watch him, which I am. But unless you've got some evidence up your sleeve that you haven't shared yet, that's all I can do until he gives me a reason to act."

Silence stretched across the line.

Ty ran a hand over his hair, knocking water droplets loose. "Look, we need to coordinate so we can—"

"I can't trust you."

The words were a slap in the face. He'd freed Mira because it felt right at the time, but he'd had to betray his partner, his department, and his badge to do it. "I went way out on a limb for you," he growled. "I'd think you'd be a little more grateful."

"So you think I owe you now?" Anger crept into her voice to match his own. "I don't need you. I don't need anyone."

"Yeah, you were doing a great job in that holding cell."

There was a moment of silence when he could hear deep breathing on the line, then, "Fine. I did need your help, and I *am* grateful, but going against Decker won't be as simple as slipping a wire in my collar. There's more going on here than you know."

"So tell me."

"I can't. Even if your moral compass is rigid enough not to take a bribe and your backbone strong enough not to back down from a threat, you and your partner are too susceptible to magic. I *can't* trust you."

"I'm PTF trained, and special ops in the war before that. I've faced my share of magic."

"Then you know even the best training isn't one-hundred-percent effective. A strong enough enchantment and Decker could have you eating out of the palm of his hand."

"If he's that strong you can't take him alone. You need backup."

"Not if I can't trust it. I'll take care of Decker. You should back off now, before you or your partner gets hurt."

"Don't do anything stupid." Ty waited for a response. Silence stretched across the line. Ty shivered as the rainwater finally saturated the last layer of his clothing and found his skin. "Hello? Hello?"

He looked at the screen. The call had been disconnected.

Ty dropped his arm to his side, phone still clutched in his hand. He'd thought Mira sticking around would be a good sign—proof that she stood behind her convictions about Decker, that her PTF contact was right to recommend trusting her. Now he wasn't so sure.

He blinked snowflakes out of his eyelashes and stared at a crack in the wet concrete where a twisted sprig of green was trying to grow. He'd freed Mira knowing she was a vigilante, knowing she'd move faster and more decisively than the police with all their rules and red tape. Maybe she was right; maybe the best thing he could do at this point was to stay out of her way and try to keep LaRosa clear of the fallout zone.

Ty stood in the plaza as the rain pattered down around him, feeling that his instincts had once again led him down a dangerous path.

Leave now . . . before you or your partner gets hurt.

He glanced at LaRosa, waiting for her pretzel in the cab of his truck. He hadn't wanted a partner, but he hadn't been given a choice. He had one now, and he was stuck with her until this mess was resolved. The question was: Which was the greater danger, knowledge or ignorance?

He tipped his face into the storm and squinted at the sixth floor of the office building across the street. Was Mira up there at this very moment? And was she serving justice or exacting revenge?

Garrett was adamant that Mira could be trusted, that she was trying to protect people from forces beyond the purview of regular cops—doing the job the PTF promised but fell short of actually doing.

If he's the kind of bad that she's hunting, you're better off letting her handle it.

Ty wasn't a part of the PTF anymore. He didn't have their resources . . . or their obligations. He was just a regular cop. Domestic disputes. Drunk and disorderly. No more magic. He was nobody's hero. Not anymore.

He turned back to the woman behind the pretzel stand, who quickly looked away and busied herself filling tiny plastic containers with Day-Glo cheese in an effort to hide the fact that she'd been staring at him.

He'd watch. He'd interview. If the opportunity arose, he'd arrest. But he'd let Mira handle the magic. That's why he'd let her out after all.

Chapter 26

Mira

<WHAT IN THE Rift was that?>

Mira leaned back against the rough concrete of the pillar and closed her eyes.

<I get that there'd be risk involved, but he can help us. He *wants* to help us. Why won't you let him?>

She rolled her head side to side against the pillar, wishing she could make her demon understand. Hell, wishing *she* understood. "I just . . . can't."

Somehow her worry over Gemma's fate, her anger at seeing Decker free and smiling, her frustration that she'd been unable to free herself from the police without help, and her confused feelings of guilt, debt, attraction, gratitude, and annoyance toward Detective Williams had all bubbled over, and she'd done what she always did. She'd withdrawn.

She thumped her skull against the concrete. *What is wrong with me?*

<Do you really want me to answer that? 'Cause I've been making a list.>

"Ha ha," Mira said flatly. She looked out the window. The slushy rain had turned mostly to snow, though it melted as soon as it touched the ground. Williams was buying a pretzel. LaRosa was still in the truck. "I don't think they're planning to leave any time soon."

<Is this because he's seen you naked?>

Mira jerked. "What?"

<Mr. Yummy. Is that why you don't like him?>

"No." She raked a hand through her hair, frizzing it. "Maybe. I don't know. And don't call him that."

<It's just that you're pushing him away even harder than you do most people, and I thought . . . you don't usually interact with anyone after you've slept with them.>

"He slept with *you.*"

<Ah. So *that's* the problem.>

Mira frowned. "What is?"

<You wish it had been *you.*>

"What? *Pfft.* You're crazy."

A man in a gray suit who was walking from the elevator to the front doors glanced in her direction.

Mira quickly glanced out the window again and pretended to be watching the snow. *I don't have any interest in that kind of complication.*

<Lie to yourself all you want, but you can't lie to me. You totally want Mr. Yummy. And who wouldn't? That build? Those eyes? And that thing he did with his tongue?>

Mira shivered at the memory.

You're being ridiculous.

<And you're being stubborn. I know you don't like getting close to people, but you *like* him. And he likes you.>

He likes you.

<He likes *us.*>

Mira shook her head, thinking about the crucial piece of information she'd withheld about Decker . . . and herself. *He doesn't know anything about us.* She pushed away from the pillar and strolled over to the security desk. *And we're all better off keeping it that way.*

She set the stolen cell phone on the counter and smiled at the guard who looked up. "Excuse me, but do you have a lost and found? This was lying on the floor over there." She indicated an area near the Asian woman. "It must have fallen out of someone's pocket."

"Thanks." The guard took the phone. "We'll try to get it back to its owner."

Mira smiled again, then turned and walked out the front doors. She stuffed her hands in her pockets, hunched against the cold, and kept her eyes on the sidewalk in front of her as she walked, careful never to glance across the street at Williams by the pretzel stand or LaRosa in the silver truck.

<You're giving up on the ambush idea?>

If we go after him while the police are watching, we'd *be the ones getting ambushed.*

<So you're going to leave him to the cops after that big speech you just made about taking care of Decker by yourself?>

Mira snorted. "Hardly. We just need to set up a situation where we can make a quick, clean grab." Mira's sneakers splashed through puddles on the sidewalk as she turned toward the parking lot where she'd left her truck. "Somewhere that the cops and any security Decker could bring to bear against us will have their attention split."

<A distraction?>

"A party."

<Decker's award banquet.> The demon sounded pleased.

"Politicians, business owners, philanthropists. If there's a danger to a group like that, security will have so many targets to keep safe they won't even notice us until it's too late." She used magic to unlock her truck's driver's side door. Once settled behind the wheel, she let her disguise fade. "We'll create a general threat, a bomb or something, and snag Decker during the evacuation. By the time the cops realize he's gone, we'll have him somewhere secure."

<Even if everyone else is distracted, Decker's not gonna go down without a fight, and we're not exactly at the top of our game after his dead-wife booby trap.>

"Then I guess it's a good thing *one* of us thought to snag a weapon specifically designed to take down practitioners." She shifted in her seat, remembering the sensation of having a dart in her ass. "We know from experience that it works fast."

<The party's not for another few hours. What do you want to do in the meantime?>

Mira started the engine. "Let's pay Angela Dougherty a visit. One way or another, we're getting that paycheck so we can split town as soon as this mess is over."

Mira

MIRA PULLED TO the curb in front of the Hermes Shipping warehouse and surveyed the area from the cab of her idling truck. A chain-link fence circled the property, broken only by a rolling gate where the main road turned onto the property. The ground inside the fence was a collection of interconnected lots around a gray, rectangular building. Anything not covered in concrete was muddy dirt with patches of snow starting to stick to the tallest clumps. Three eighteen-wheelers were parked with their tails to the loading bays on one side of the building, though only one of the garage doors was open. Three additional bays sat empty.

Two dozen cars were parked in the northernmost lot, which led to a set of double doors painted the same color as the rest of the exterior. Probably the employee entrance.

"We could ditch the truck and sneak in . . . but I don't want to waste any magic here if we don't have to. As it is, we're going to need every last drop of energy to match Decker if the tranquilizer plan goes belly-up."

She drummed her fingers on the steering wheel and glanced at the dashboard clock. It was nearly four thirty. The fragment of conversation she'd overheard at the farmers market had indicated Angela would visit the warehouse after four, when the vendor's friend came on duty, though Mira still didn't know what they'd be meeting about.

"They didn't spread my picture on the news," she mused aloud. "No one here should recognize us. I suppose we could just walk in the front door and ask to see Dave Rubens. Worst case, they turn us away and we sneak in at that point."

<What if Angela isn't there yet?>

She shrugged. "We'll wait. We've got nearly three hours till Decker's party."

<And we should probably arrive fashionably late, after people have had a few drinks and started to relax.>

"Plenty of time." She shifted the truck into gear and eased toward the warehouse gate.

A metal box was mounted on a pole at the side of the road. There was a numbered keypad where authorized personnel would type in a code. There was also a red call button and speaker at the bottom, which Mira pressed.

There was a scratch of static, then a woman's voice came out of the box. "Can I help you?"

"I'm here to see Dave Rubens," Mira said. "Paul sent me."

Another crackle of static. "Popular guy today. Park in the east lot. Check in at the front desk."

The intercom cut off. A second later a motor kicked in and the gate started its slow roll to the side. When there was enough clearance, Mira drove onto the lot and around the building to the far side. This area was a little less stark than the loading docks, but still utilitarian in design. The Hermes Shipping logo was on a large, plastic sign above a set of four doors. Large windows on either side of the entrance gave a glimpse of a white lobby with a reception desk and a set of backless benches.

She parked in the front row and crossed the short distance to the building's entrance, scuffing her sneakers on a doormat before stepping inside.

The woman sitting at the front desk glanced up, then waved a hand to the side.

A heavy-set man with a thick, brown beard was leaning against the wall to the right of the desk. He pushed off and uncrossed his arms as Mira approached.

"Not like Paul to send so much extra help," he said.

"You have another tonight?"

The man nodded. "I'm Dave." He extended his hand.

"Minnie," Mira said without hesitation.

The demon chuckled. <As in Mouse?>

He shook her hand then tipped his head in a "follow me" gesture and led her through a door. "How much experience you got?"

Mira shrugged. "A bit." They walked down a hallway of bare white walls and a dozen closed doors.

<Maybe you were right about the prostitute thing. This could be a brothel.>

"Who else did Paul send your way?"

Dave mimicked her shrug. Then he pushed through a door at the end of the hall and they stepped into the storage section of the warehouse. Rows of shelving filled the high-ceilinged room, each filled with cardboard boxes. Small forklifts hummed up and down the aisles with workers standing on their backs. Mira didn't see Angela.

"These are the orders." He lifted a paper off a stack in a black box on a table by the back wall. His voice echoed dully in the wide space. "Locations are here." He pointed to a letter-number combination in the left margin, then moved his sausage-like finger to the next column. "And this is the product ID. Check as you go. Once the pallet is full, wrap, label, initial, and load. Any questions?"

Mira shook her head.

Dave shoved the example paper into her hands, nodded, and walked off.

Mira stared after him.

<I don't get it. Angela is working at a fulfillment center? I thought she was an event coordinator?>

Something's not right here. You can't just walk into a warehouse and start packing orders. There are background checks, and liability forms, and orientations. This isn't normal.

<But Dave did say Paul sent him someone else, so Angela must be here somewhere.>

Right. Mira glanced down at the paperwork Dave had handed her. *Let's get to work.*

She walked along the back wall, glancing up the aisles. Men and women rode the forklifts like kids racing go karts, but Angela wasn't among them. As Mira walked she saw the letter-number combinations written on her sheet mirrored in the labels at the end of each set of shelves. But there was no convenient location marker for what she was looking for.

Beyond the final set of shelves was an open area where people with loaded forklifts deposited their boxes onto stacked pallets. Eight such works-in-progress were spaced out on the cement floor, each at a different stage of completion. About halfway down the row, a woman with spiky blond hair was wrapping her full pallet in what looked like a giant roll of cling film.

Found you.

Angela Dougherty was wearing baggy jeans and a loose, purple T-shirt with a white rabbit face on the front and a fluffy bunny tail on the back. Her white sneakers squeaked against the concrete floor when she moved.

<Guess she's not a prostitute.>

Mira walked along the final aisle, watching Angela work until she was directly across from her. Then she stepped into the open space and waved her paperwork in greeting. "Hey there."

Angela looked up and froze.

"I'm kinda new to all this. I was hoping you could—"

"It's you." She dropped the roll of plastic wrap and backed away from Mira. "Why are you following me?"

Mira frowned. "What? You must have me confused with someone else. I'm just here to work."

Doubt and confusion flashed across Angela's face as she examined Mira, turning her explanation over. Then she shook her head and her expression closed down. "You're the one in the drawing. I'm sure of it."

<Drawing?>

I don't know either.

Mira laughed, trying to ease Angela's suspicion. "Look, I'm not sure what—"

"*Why* are you *following* me?"

<So much for subtle.>

"Fine. I don't have time to beat around the bush anyway." Mira let the paperwork for her unfilled order drift to the floor. "Your girlfriend hired me to snap pictures of you having an affair."

Angela took another step back, the rosy glow draining from her cheeks. "But . . . I'm not—"

"I know. But Shaquana seems to be under the mistaken impression that you're still an event planner and has therefore explained away your long hours and lame excuses as a love affair." She indicated the warehouse and Angela's half-wrapped pallet. "That's clearly not the case. So what's going on?"

"She hired you to follow me?" Angela set a hand against her stack of boxes, as though suddenly dizzy. "She thinks . . ."

"Not to be insensitive, but I'm kind of in a rush and I can't get paid until you come clean. So spill."

Angela's crystal-blue gaze snapped up to Mira. She nodded. "Shaquana comes from a wealthy family, so she's never had to work, but I've always tried to be an equal partner in our relationship." Her expression stiffened, and she glared defiantly at Mira. "I don't take handouts."

Mira lifted her hands. "I get it. Independent woman. I'm all for it."

Angela nodded, her gaze growing distant. "But then . . ."

"You lost your job."

She looked away. "Me and a lot of other people. The economy takes a nosedive and businesses tighten up. Workers get tossed. It's an old story. Suddenly I went from an equal partner in my relationship to struggling to pick up the dinner bill." Her voice cracked, and she shook her head.

<But why all this cloak and dagger?> The demon's question jolted Mira out of Angela's story. <Why not just tell her girlfriend what had happened?>

Fear. Shame. I'm sure she had lots of reasons.

<That's stupid.>

People usually are when it comes to their pride.

"Can you believe I was actually planning to propose next month? I had it all planned out. Skiing in Aspen. A cozy cabin. Champagne by the fire." She shook her head again. "Then . . . poof."

"So all those visits the other day—the florist, the caterer, the vendor at the farmers market . . .?"

"Contacts I'd made during my years with the city. I've been making the rounds, working through my address book, looking for jobs." She waved a hand at the vaulted ceiling. "Day labor like this is about all I've been able to grab lately, and even that's scarce. It's terrible hours, crap pay, and not entirely legal . . . but I couldn't just sit back and mooch off Shaquana." She slumped against her loaded pallet like a puppet with her strings cut. "I love her so much, but"—she stared at her empty palms—"she deserves better than what I've got to offer right now."

<Does this mean we aren't getting paid?>

Mira ran a hand through her hair and exhaled noisily. "You love Shaquana, right?"

Angela continued to stare at her hands. "More than anything."

"More than your pride?"

She looked up.

"Because Shaquana loves you. That much was clear when we talked. She hired me because she couldn't quite bring herself to believe you were cheating on her, but she couldn't come up with any other explanation. You need to give her one. Tell her the truth—come clean about getting fired, the proposal, all of it."

<Look at you giving relationship advice.>

"Shh."

Angela frowned. "I didn't say anything."

Mira waved the comment away. "Look, if you love her and she loves you, that means you're in this together, right? Good times and bad? Anything less and it isn't really love. If that's the case, you should just break it off now and spare her the pain of uncertainty."

"So . . . you think I should still propose?"

Mira wrinkled her nose. "If you're sure that's what you want."

"What if she thinks I'm just after her money?"

"How long have you two been together?"

"Three years next month. I was going to propose on our anniversary."

"So it's safe to say she knows you fairly well?"

Angela nodded.

"Are you the kind of person who would marry for money?"

"No!"

"Then what are you afraid of?"

Angela chewed on her thumbnail, gaze skittering, sorting her thoughts.

"Hey!"

Mira and Angela both jumped.

Dave strode toward them from the far end of the aisle. "If you're not working, leave."

"Just finishing up," Angela said, and grabbed the roll of cling film hanging from her half-wrapped pallet.

Dave glanced at the order form Mira had dropped and pursed his lips.

"Yeah, I'm not sure this job is going to work out." She met Angela's gaze as the woman made another circuit of her pallet.

"Then I'll walk you out." Dave turned, took two steps, and looked back to make sure Mira was following.

"You don't get paid if you don't report back to Shaquana, do you?" Angela asked.

Mira shook her head.

Angela scrunched her face like she was swallowing something nasty, then said, "Wait for me out front. I'll meet you as soon as I finish this pallet."

Mira huddled in her jacket as snow slowly turned the muddy ground white, wondering with every passing moment if she wouldn't be better off just leaving. When Angela finally stepped out of the warehouse, she asked, "Dave okay with you taking a break?"

"I'm not on a break," Angela said. "I told him I had to leave."

Mira quirked an eyebrow. "From what you said earlier, I'd think twice before flushing even a gig like this down the drain."

"I did. But my relationship is more important. Plus I owe you. I knew things between me and Shaquana were strained, but I figured that was all coming from my side. It never occurred to me she might think I didn't love her." She clasped her hands in front of her chest. "I have to make this right."

"I agree you need to talk to your girlfriend, but I'm not sure what that's got to do with me at this point."

"You don't get paid unless you finish the job Shaquana hired you to do, right?"

Mira nodded.

"And she asked for proof of what I've been up to—an explanation for all the sneaking out and secrecy?"

Another nod.

"So you tell her you've got the proof. That you'll meet her at a hotel where you found me and show her exactly what's going on."

Mira raised an eyebrow. "You're going to pretend to get caught having an affair so I can get paid?"

Angela pulled back, eyes going wide. "What? No! I would never hurt Shaquana like that."

The demon laughed. <Good instincts on that one.>

Mira tried to ignore both the demon's mockery and the look of disgust on Angela's face. "Then what did you have in mind?"

"I want you to help me set up a romantic proposal. You lead Shaquana into the room, and I'll be waiting with flowers and a ring. I'll tell her the whole story, then I'll ask for her forgiveness and beg her to be my wife."

<Aw, see? That's sweet.>

Mira frowned. "How does this help me?"

"Shaquana hired you to find out my secret. I'm sure she'll be satisfied even if the secret turns out to be different than she thought. Hell, hopefully she'll be thrilled. Either way I'll ask that she pays you what she promised."

Mira glanced at the dull-orange patch of overcast sky where the sun was hiding. She still had time until Decker's banquet . . . and she *did* need the money. "One more question."

"Shoot."

"You said you recognized me from a picture?"

Angela laughed. "It makes sense now, but . . . see the cops came by my house and they showed me a sketch of you. They said you'd been following me—which I guess is true—and they wanted to know why."

<Must have been after that Boy Scout spotted us in the market. He must have realized we were tailing Angela.>

"Did Shaquana tell them?"

"She said she didn't recognize you. I guess she didn't want to admit to hiring you since I was standing right there. Still, lying to the police . . ." She shook her head.

Mira chewed the inside of her cheek.

<You worried she told the cops something?>

Actually I'm relieved. She didn't know anything about us that would matter even if she did tell the police, but for a second there I thought my likeness had been circulated to the general public after all. It's good to know it was just these two. And since the cops tracked me to Shaquana because I was following Angela, she'll assume it was about me being a stalker, which she hired me to do.

"All right, Angela," Mira said. "You've got yourself a deal. I'll help you lure Shaquana into a romantic ambush. You help me get paid." They shook hands. "Where do you want to do this?"

Chapter 27

Mira

MIRA STALKED down the supermarket aisle. Three dozen roses stuck out of her basket, hiding the box of chocolate-covered strawberries beneath. She scanned the refrigerated shelves until she spotted a bottle of champagne, then tucked it beside the flowers and headed for the checkout lines to pay with the cash Angela had provided. She felt like some kind of pathetic cupid playing matchmaker to a pair of insecure idiots who couldn't express themselves without a referee. But she had nothing else to do but worry until the banquet began, and Angela had her own errand to run if this plan was going to work. At least she was finally going to get paid.

<This is so exciting.>

Mira set her basket on the conveyor and returned the clerk's smile as he started swiping her purchases. *We risk our lives on a regular basis, but you think arranging a date for a couple of strangers is exciting?*

<Different kind of exciting. Risking our lives . . . that's just what we do. This is *romantic.*>

Mira rolled her eyes, handed over the cash Angela had fronted her, grabbed the plastic bags, and walked out the door.

<You should be taking notes . . . you know, in case you ever want to have a functional relationship.>

Like lie about my employment status? Or how about sneak around in such an obvious way that my partner thinks I'm having an affair? Or better yet, I could be the partner that gets so jealous she hires a stranger to take dirty pictures of my lover because I'm too much of a chicken shit to just flat out demand to know what's going on.

<Okay, maybe these two aren't the *best* role models for a functional relationship . . . but they *do* love each other. They just need to learn to communicate better.>

If communication is the framework for a healthy partnership, these two are screwed. Mira set her bags on the floor of the passenger side of her truck and started the engine.

<If you don't think they're good together, why are we helping Angela propose?>

"I'm in it for the money. So long as I get paid it doesn't matter to me if their relationship is all sunshine and lollipops or goes down in flames five seconds after I leave the room."

<That's cold.>

"That's life. Their business is their business, and none of mine beyond a paycheck." She pulled into traffic and headed toward the downtown hotel Angela had chosen for her romantic encounter. "I just hope Shaquana shows up on time. We've got another party to get to tonight, and that one I *do* care about."

Mira parked a few blocks away from her destination and covered the remaining distance on foot. Snow continued to fall, coating the sidewalks in a thin layer of white at the edges where the press of pedestrians hadn't trampled it to slush. Her fingers, exposed so she could hold her shopping bags, started to sting. She sniffed as the chill made her nose run.

The Renaissance Hotel was positioned to overlook the Inner Harbor. It sat directly behind Tir Na Nog—the restaurant where she and Gemma had shared dinner and drinks before exploring the nightlife of the harbor. The photo booth where they'd taken their pictures was only a block away.

Frustration and anger twisted in Mira's chest, choking off her breath and making her lungs ache. She longed to be doing something to help Gemma right now instead of counting off the seconds until her plan could begin.

<*I* wanted to rip Decker apart at the office,> the demon said in response to Mira's unvoiced anxiety. <*You're* the one who said we should wait.>

"Because waiting was the smart move. Waiting gives us a better chance of succeeding, and we have to succeed." Saying those words out loud eased the tension in Mira's chest so she could breathe easily again, but the lingering impatience was still there. *What if Gemma dies because we were too slow?*

<The way I see it, she was either dead before Decker shoved her in that duffel bag at his house or he's keeping her alive as a bargaining chip for when we face him. Either way, nothing's going to change until we talk to Decker.>

Mira squinted in the direction of the photo booth but couldn't make it out. "I once heard about this scientist who put a cat in a box so no one could tell if it was alive or dead."

<Whose cat was it?>

"That doesn't matter."

<I bet it mattered to whoever's cat it was.>

"The point is, you couldn't know for sure until you opened the box."

<At which point you either get a face full of freaked-out cat or a pile of decomposing guts. That's messed up.>

"Look, I just meant you're right about nothing changing with Gemma until we talk to Decker."

<Then just say, "Yeah, you're right." No need to drag dead cats and mad scientists into the conversation.>

Mira sighed and shook her head. She turned away from the Inner Harbor and the ghosts of her memories and walked through the revolving glass doors of the Renaissance Hotel.

Angela was waiting near the front desk, her own bags of supplies in hand.

"All set?" Mira asked as she walked up.

"So far so good, as long as you sent the message."

After parting ways at the warehouse, Mira had replied to Shaquana's update request with instructions to see the desk clerk at the Renaissance Hotel at five o'clock, money in hand, to collect her proof. The clerk would give Shaquana a room key. "Five isn't far off. You sure she'll get the invitation in time?"

"Shaquana is glued to her phone. She's incapable of ignoring a notification. She'll be here." Angela hefted her bags and headed for the elevator. "Let's make sure we're ready."

Ty

LAROSA SCARFED her pretzel in record time and was draining her soda when her cell phone rang.

"Go for LaRosa."

Ty glanced over.

LaRosa's expression was pinched in concentration. "You're sure?"

He frowned. Then his own phone buzzed, making him jump. He set his half-eaten pretzel on a napkin in his lap, wiped his fingers, and dug in his pocket. Cyber had sent him a text.

Target made contact, but connection came from a TOR exit node. Impossible to trace.

He stared at the text, pretzel turning to cement in his gut. He'd completely forgotten to call off the forum trap. At least they hadn't found her . . . though on the heels of his relief was disappointment that he'd been outmaneuvered.

"See you soon." LaRosa tucked her phone in her pocket and swiveled toward Ty.

"Cyber couldn't trace Fuentes from the PI forum," Ty said, finally looking up from the text.

"Good thing we didn't have all our eggs in one basket. The tail I put on Angela Dougherty paid off. She and a woman matching Mirana Fuentes's description just checked into the Renaissance Hotel on Inner Harbor."

Ty frowned. "She followed Angela up to a room?"

LaRosa shook her head. "McNally says they met in the lobby, talked for a minute, then went up *together*."

He leaned his head back against the rest and stared out the window. "That doesn't make sense."

"Sense or not, we know where she is." LaRosa snapped her seat belt in place. "I told McNally to keep his distance until we arrive."

Ty gestured to the building across the street. "What about Decker?"

"If Fuentes is at the Renaissance, Decker's not in danger. But we don't know how long she'll stay put, so step on it."

Ty pursed his lips. The last thing he wanted was Mira getting arrested again before she brought Decker down, but with LaRosa sitting right beside him there was no way to warn her. He just had to hope whatever brought her to the hotel was over quickly and she was gone by the time he arrived. Reluctantly, he put the truck in gear and headed downtown.

Mira

OF THE THREE dozen blood-red roses Mira had purchased, only twelve kept their heads—the rest had their petals plucked and strewn about the room in a romantic flower massacre. Streamers of red, white, and purple hung from the ceiling in swooping drapes, pinned at the ends by strips of masking tape. Sparkling strands of silver and gold tinsel—discounted overstock from New Year's—exploded like glittery fountains around the room.

Angela shoved the champagne into a bucket of ice Mira had just returned from filling at the machine down the hall. She set two fluted glasses beside it on one side and a plate of chocolate strawberries arranged in a sunburst pattern on the other. "What do you think?"

Mira considered the decorations they'd whipped together. *It looks like Valentine's Day barfed in here.*

<Be nice.>

She forced the corners of her lips up. "I like it. Do you think Shaquana will?"

"I hope so." Angela lifted a small package from the nightstand. She started to sit, glanced at the murdered flowers on the bed, and moved to a chair in the far corner of the room. There she opened the package and pulled out an over-sized candy Ring Pop. She turned the ring over, studying the red candy as though staring into the facets of the diamond it represented. "I hope she gives me the chance to buy her a real ring someday."

Angela sniffed. Her eyes were starting to water.

Mira pursed her lips and looked away, staring at the speckled-gray carpet in front of her sneakers.

<Say something.>

Like what?

<I don't know. Tell her everything is going to be all right.>

Do you really believe that?

The alarm on Angela's cell phone buzzed, announcing the appointed time for Shaquana's arrival.

Mira cleared her throat. "Come on." She pulled Angela to her feet. "She'll be here any minute."

Angela took her place, down on one knee, in front of the door.

Mira stepped into the bathroom and closed the door until only a small gap remained through which she could observe the scene. Her job had been to get Shaquana to the room. Once Angela had her say, Mira could collect her money and be done with all this mixed-signals romance bullshit.

One minute ticked by. Then five. Angela began to squirm. She switched knees and rolled her shoulders, arms clearly tired from holding up the ring. She glanced at Mira through the crack in the door. The tears were back in her eyes.

"Maybe she's not coming." Her lower lip quivered. She sat on her heels and stared at the Ring Pop cupped in her hands.

Mira started to open the bathroom door but heard the *snick* of a bolt sliding in a lock. She pulled back just as the room door opened.

Ty

"IF I COULD give you a ticket for granny-driving, I would," LaRosa snarled as she unstrapped her seat belt and jumped out of the truck.

Ty took his time shutting off the engine. As soon as the passenger door closed, he pulled his phone from his pocket and redialed the number Mira had called him from. He watched LaRosa's angry stride as she entered the hotel.

"Hello?" A woman's voice, not Mira's, answered the phone. Her pitch was higher, and she had an Asian accent.

"Um . . . hello," Ty stammered. "I need to speak to Mira."

There was a moment of silence, then, "I think you've got the wrong number."

Ty wrapped the fingers of his free hand around the steering wheel and squeezed until his knuckles went pale. "She called me from this number less than an hour ago."

There was another pause.

"I do see a number I don't recognize in my call log, but I don't know any Mira."

"Did you let anyone use your phone?"

"No, but it fell out of my purse earlier. I just collected it from the lost and found."

Choking back a curse he disconnected the call, stuffed his phone in his pocket, and headed inside.

LaRosa was deep in conversation with McNally, punctuating her statements with hand gestures. He stepped up beside her and had to dodge a backhand that came a little too close to his face to be an accident.

"You took your time," she snapped.

"What's the sitrep?"

"Your suspect and the woman I was tailing went upstairs about twenty minutes ago. Haven't come down." McNally, a wiry man in his mid-fifties, scratched the gray stubble along his narrow jaw. Rather than a uniform, he wore a pair of faded blue jeans and a white tee topped with an unbuttoned, gray-and-blue plaid shirt with worn cuffs. His badge flashed briefly on his belt when he shifted. "My partner's around back, but there are too many exits for him to cover alone."

"Do you know which room they're in?" Ty asked.

"If you'd been here for the first part of the conversation you'd know he hasn't spoken to the desk clerk yet."

"Didn't want to start the staff gossiping before we were ready to move," McNally added.

"Good work, McNally," LaRosa said. "Hold here. If you see our suspect, follow discretely. She's extremely dangerous, so don't engage unless absolutely necessary."

"Ten four." McNally lowered himself into the upholstered chair he'd chosen to observe the lobby from.

LaRosa smacked Ty on the arm and tipped her head toward the front desk. "Come on."

A woman with long brown hair dyed pink at the tips smiled when they approached the counter. She wore a red shirt with a white collar and the name of the hotel embroidered on the left breast pocket. "Welcome to the Renaissance. How may I help you?"

Ty flashed the clerk his badge and said, "Two women came through here about twenty minutes ago. One was named Angela Dougherty. She has short blond hair and a fair complexion. The other may have looked like this." He nodded toward LaRosa, who pulled the sketch of Mira out of her back pocket.

"Sure, I remember them." The clerk beamed like a puppy looking for a pat on the head. "Miss Dougherty left instructions for another friend to join them. I sent her up a few minutes ago."

Ty shared a look with LaRosa, whose frown matched his own, then turned back to the clerk. "What friend?"

"Let's see . . ." She rummaged through some loose papers behind the desk. "Shaquana Jones."

He and LaRosa shared another look.

"Why would Shaquana be here?" she asked.

He shook his head. "This is making less and less sense."

LaRosa stuffed the sketch of Mira back in her pocket and pinned the clerk with a narrow glare. "What room are these ladies in?"

"Um." She tapped a few keys on the computer. "Room 618."

Both cops looked toward the elevators at the back of the lobby.

"We need a key to that room," LaRosa said.

"How do you want to approach this?" Ty asked.

"We've only got one tranquilizer gun now, so our best bet is to surprise her in the room. I'll target Fuentes. You cover the other two. We'll figure out if they're hostages or accomplices once Fuentes is down."

Ty lifted the plastic key card the clerk pushed across the counter. An uneasy knot tightened his chest. Mira would be cornered in the hotel room, and he was sure she wouldn't let herself be captured again. Would she attack if she felt threatened? He'd helped her because he thought they were playing on the same side—if by slightly different rules—but how much did he really know about her? How far could he trust her? He studied LaRosa from the corner of his eye as they made their way to the elevator. Was he leading another partner into an ambush?

Chapter 28

Mira

ANGELA LOOKED UP as the door opened, wiped her eyes, and rose again to one knee. "I'm sorry I haven't been around much lately, and that I made you worry. The truth is that I got laid off and I've been working odd jobs to earn enough that you wouldn't find out, because I wanted to propose but I didn't want you to think that I couldn't pull my own weight. I was embarrassed, and proud, and stupid. I should have just told you the truth from the beginning." She lifted the Ring Pop like Lancelot offering up the Holy Grail. "This isn't exactly the proposal I'd been envisioning, but I love you and I can't wait any longer. Will you marry me?"

Silence filled the room.

Mira shifted, peeking out the crack. Shaquana was standing in the open doorway in a teal ski jacket and black velvet sweatpants. She was still holding the door handle. Her jaw was slack. Her eyes were wide and red rimmed. The mascara smudges on her cheeks showed she'd been crying, probably on the drive over as she imagined what she'd find at the hotel. Her mouth closed, opened, closed. She blinked. Then she dropped to her knees in front of Angela and threw her arms around the other woman, sobbing against her neck.

The door swung slowly shut and latched in place.

"I th-th-thought you were ch-ch-cheating on me," Shaquana wailed.

Angela hugged her girlfriend tight, tangling the Ring Pop in her curls. "I would never, ever, in a million years cheat on someone as absolutely amazing as you."

Ugh, what a sob-fest.

<It's called having feelings. Maybe you should try it sometime.>

This coming from a demon, who by her very nature can't experience human emotions.

<At least I'm trying. Would it kill you to make a connection?>

Might kill them.

Shaquana snuffled and sniffed, then sat back on her heels. She wiped purple-nailed fingertips under her eyes, further smearing her makeup. Then she glanced around the room as though seeing the decorations for the first time. "This isn't at all what I expected to see when I walked in here." She stiffened and looked around again, this time searching. "The message telling me to come here . . ."

"Mira," Angela called.

Mira stepped out from behind the bathroom door.

"You—" Shaquana's head jerked back and forth as she looked from one woman to the other. "When? How?"

"You hired me to find proof that Angela was having an affair."

Shaquana winced and glanced at her girlfriend, but Angela just smiled.

"But she wasn't," Mira continued. "I brought you here to give you the proof you needed." She gestured to the Ring Pop in Angela's hand. "Proof that your girlfriend still loves you."

Shaquana worried her lower lip between her teeth. "The police are looking for you."

"Because she was stalking me," Angela said.

Shaquana shook her head. "I went to the station after they visited the house to explain why she was following you." She looked at Mira. "They wanted to talk to you about something else."

Mira tried to smile reassuringly, but it felt more like a grimace. "Yeah. They caught up with me yesterday. We had a talk."

"So it's all good?" Shaquana asked. "You're not mad I let Detective Williams trace your account through our job board messages?"

Mira froze her expression to keep from showing her surprise, swallowed to make sure her voice would come out normal, and said, "All good."

<If they've been tracing our messages we definitely can't go back to the motel.>

The onion router should have kept them chasing their tails, but you're right, we can't go back there.

<Good thing we packed before we left.>

But our last message named this hotel. If they read it . . .

She stepped closer to the kneeling women. "If you'll just pay me what I'm owed, I'll get out of your hair so you can—" She tipped her head toward the petal-strewn bed.

Ty

THE SIXTH-FLOOR hallway was empty when Ty and LaRosa stepped out of the elevator.

Hooray for small miracles.

As they approached the door to room 618, Ty pulled his service pistol but kept it down at his side. The key card that would give them access was clutched in his other hand.

LaRosa drew the tranquilizer gun, checked the cartridge was loaded, and moved to the far side of the target door.

Time seemed to slow as Ty approached the door. If Mira was caught, would she expect him to help her again? Would she blackmail him with his previous questionable actions? Would she hurt LaRosa to save herself? Would she drop this whole damn building on them to avoid getting caught?

His palms grew sweaty, and his breathing sped up. He couldn't seem to get enough air. How could he stop this from happening without alerting LaRosa to the fact that he was playing both sides?

An itch twitched inside his nose. He sniffed, smothering it. Then he got an idea.

He took a deep breath . . . and sneezed. Not exactly a clear warning, but Mira might realize there was someone outside her door. Hopefully it would make a difference.

LaRosa glared daggers at him.

He shrugged, trying to appear sheepish, and mouthed, "Sorry."

She shook her head, then pointed to the lock and held up three fingers.

Ty positioned the key card above the lock.

LaRosa lowered one finger . . . the second . . . she raised the tranquilizer gun. When her last finger fell, Ty dropped the key in the lock.

Mira

A SNEEZE SOUNDED in the hallway just outside the hotel door. Mira tensed, searching for footsteps, voices—any additional noises that would mark the passage of another hotel guest going about their business. *Check for—*

<On it.>

Mira stepped back into the bathroom as the demon's magic rose. Angela and Shaquana became two fluttering heartbeats, their movements stirring the ether of the Rift. Outside the door two more heartbeats pounded.

<We're about to have company.>

Mira caught Angela's gaze and said, "I'll explain after, but please *please* tell them I'm not here." She stepped into the bathtub and pulled all the magic she could muster around herself to hide.

Angela and Shaquana stared at the place where Mira stood—from their perspective, she'd just vanished. They looked at each other, eyes wide. Then the door to the hotel hallway swung open and slammed against the wall. Both women jumped and fell back, hugging each other.

LaRosa swung the long barrel of the tranquilizer gun over the cowering women, then around the rest of the room, poking into corners and behind furniture.

Detective Williams stepped up beside her and pointed his gun at the floor in front of Angela. "Don't move."

Shaquana's eyes went wide and watery. She broke out in sobs.

Angela hugged her girlfriend and glared at the cops.

LaRosa turned toward the bathroom.

Mira's pulse raced. She did her best to breathe slow and even so no sound would give her away. She held the magic like a child hiding behind a sheet in a game of hide-and-seek.

LaRosa's gaze slid past the seemingly empty tub and around the rest of the small bathroom until she got to the mirror. Her gaze flicked to Mira in the reflection, catching something that registered as not quite right. She frowned and turned back.

The demon's magic swelled, layering Mira in a second illusion and wrapping her tight. Mira's knees shook as energy was sapped from her body. Energy she couldn't afford to lose. She stiffened her legs and held her breath as LaRosa moved toward the tub, searching for the glitch she'd spotted in the mirror. The gun barrel hovered inches from Mira's nose.

"Clear." LaRosa stepped back, holstered her weapon, and joined Williams in front of the women sitting on the floor. "Mirana Fuentes, a.k.a. Mindy Perez. We know she came up here with you. Where is she?"

Angela raised her chin. "She left . . . about ten minutes ago."

LaRosa growled and kicked the dresser.

"You told us you didn't know her," Williams said. "What were you doing with her?"

"She came to see me earlier today and told me Shaquana had hired her to spy on me because she thought I was having an affair. But she realized I wasn't. She agreed to help lure Shaquana here so I could propose." She glared. "Which is what you just interrupted."

LaRosa pursed her lips and shifted her focus to Shaquana. "Is this true?"

Shaquana sniffed and wiped her nose. She glanced toward the bathroom, then quickly at the floor. She nodded. "I got a message from Mindy telling me to meet her here at the hotel, that she had the proof I'd asked for. But when I came in Angela was down on one knee in front of the door." She looked at Angela and smiled. "And the answer is yes."

Angela grinned, slipped the Ring Pop onto Shaquana's finger, and kissed her fiancé.

<See? They just needed to clear the air. Honesty. It's the most important element of a healthy relationship.>

How would you know? The longest "relationship" you've ever been in was a three-day orgy with that yoga instructor in Maine, and she didn't even know what you are.

<I'm just saying secrets cause problems.>

Relationships cause problems.

Detective Williams finally holstered his gun. He put his hands on his hips and frowned at Shaquana. "Why didn't you let me know she'd contacted you?"

"I'm sorry." She snuffled again, and LaRosa reached into the bathroom to grab a few tissues for her. She dabbed her eyes and blew her nose. "You said you didn't think she intended Angie any harm, and I didn't have much time to get here according to the message, and I . . . I just needed to know . . ." She looked at Angela. "I'm so sorry I ever suspected you of cheating on me."

"And I'm sorry I lied about getting laid off, so we're even." Angela looked up at Williams. "What exactly is it you think . . . er, Mindy did anyway?"

Ignoring the question, LaRosa asked, "Do either of you expect to see her again for any reason?"

Angela shook her head. "I paid her the rest of what Shaquana owed in exchange for helping me set this up." She gestured to the decorations. "The job's done. There's no reason she'd contact us again." Keeping her eyes on the police, she rose to her feet and pulled Shaquana up beside her. "Now if you don't mind, my soon-to-be-wife and I have some celebrating to do."

Williams looked at LaRosa, who glanced once more around the room. She squinted for a moment into the bathroom and Mira held her breath. LaRosa pursed her lips, sighed, and jerked her head toward the door. She and Williams left more slowly than they'd entered.

Mira let her awareness bleed into the Rift on the demon's power. The two eddies of energy that were Williams and LaRosa paused outside the door, then moved away.

Mira exhaled and released her magic. Her knees buckled as she stepped out of the tub, and one shin smacked against the edge before she grabbed a towel rack for balance. She shuffled to the doorway. "Thank you."

Angela and Shaquana stood so close together they were practically one person. Shaquana's eyes were wide. Her makeup was a hopeless mess of dark smears beneath her eyes and streaks down her cheeks. Angela's expression was pinched with concern and maybe a little fear.

"Are you a fae?" she asked.

Mira shook her head. "Practitioner."

Angela glanced toward the door through which the police had left. "Unregistered I take it?"

Mira nodded. "But I don't mean you any harm, I swear." She stepped forward and both women stepped back. She froze.

"If I thought any different I wouldn't have lied just now. And we're very grateful for your help, but you, um . . . you don't look so good." Angela pressed her lips tight and indicated a mirror on the wall.

Mira turned. Her reflection made her take a step back as well. Tendrils of dark veins decorated her eyes and cheeks just as Shaquana's melted makeup covered hers. Her eyes were more gold than brown, and the white stripe in her hair had spread to nearly a third of her head.

"*Ay, coño*. We burned through our buffer."

<I told you we didn't have much.>

Mira ground her teeth, hating the truth of the situation. *We're going to have to sip someone if we want to get to Decker at the party tonight.*

<We've got two right here, and a private room.>

I just told her I wouldn't do them any harm.

She turned back to Angela and Shaquana. "I need to get out of here."

Angela nudged Shaquana. "Pay her."

Shaquana nodded and opened the brown leather purse she wore slung over one shoulder. She rummaged for a moment, then pulled out a thick wad of cash and held it out.

Mira took the money.

"I don't blame you for hiding," Shaquana said, finally finding her voice. "The way they treat practitioners and all."

Mira smiled grimly. If being a practitioner was all she had to worry about she might have turned herself in years ago.

"Wait a second." Shaquana dug around in her purse once more and came out with a set of large, amber-tinted sunglasses with tiny rhinestones set in the frames. She offered them to Mira, who took them gladly.

"Thanks." She slipped them on to hide the puppet lines and the unnatural shine of her eyes. "I'm sorry the cops interrupted your proposal"—she gestured to the rose-covered bed—"but at least it's not a total loss."

Mira opened the door, checked the hall, and stepped out. She gave one last wave to Angela and Shaquana, who stared at her until the door closed, then she walked in the opposite direction the police had gone, toward the hotel's back stairwell.

<I can't believe Mr. Yummy was tracking us.>

Believe it. He's changed his mind about us. Mira's sneakers dragged along the carpet. Lifting them was too much effort.

<Maybe he set the trap before he decided to help you.>

If that was the case he would have canceled the trace.

<Then he must have changed his mind because you said you wouldn't work with him back at Decker's office.>

She pulled open the heavy stairwell door and started down the first flight. Her footsteps echoed up and down the concrete box. She pictured Williams as he'd been that first night—gentle, insatiable, desperate to lose himself in the moment. Then in the holding cell he'd been conflicted but earnest. He clearly cared about helping people, even if it meant bending a few rules. A dull ache filled her chest. She couldn't quite reconcile that man, whom she'd thought she might actually be able to trust, with the one smiling at Decker, or standing over Angela and Shaquana with his gun drawn. "Better he betray us now than later when we might actually be counting on him."

She pushed through the outer door on the ground level and stepped into a parking lot behind the hotel. Beyond the asphalt to the left was a gas station. To the right, framed by a short, stucco wall and a trash compactor, was the back door of the hotel's attached restaurant, La Jouissance. A man in his mid to late thirties with a stained white apron tied over his paunchy gut was leaning against the wall near the trash compactor. He pulled a long drag from a cigarette, then exhaled a slow, steady stream of smoke.

<Oh look, curbside service.> She took a step in the direction of the man.

No. She turned and stumbled, catching herself with a hand on the wall.

<We need it.>

She braced her back against the wall and looked at the man she was having a hard time not thinking of as a meal. She shook her head. *We can find someone else—a drug dealer or something.*

<You can barely walk straight. If we don't feed now, we may as well give up on stopping Decker and avenging Gemma, because we're worse than useless in this condition.>

She pushed away from the wall and took a few more swaying steps toward the restaurant, unsure which of them was driving.

The man watched her approach.

With the way we're weaving, he probably thinks we're drunk.

<Good. We want him to think he's about to get lucky.>

"Hey, baby." Her voice slurred a bit, and she played that up to sell the drunk party girl character. "Know where I can find a good time?"

The man flicked the stub of his cigarette on the ground and crushed it under his shoe. He exhaled one last cloud of smoke, then pushed away from the wall. "You look like you've had plenty of fun already."

Now that she was closer she could make him out a little better, though the light above the back door cast sharp shadows across his features. His skin was a leathery brown, and she bumped her age estimate up a little when she noticed the lines around his eyes. His hair was silky black and pulled into a ponytail. A thin, black mustache traced his upper lip and dipped toward his jaw, framing full lips. The light-blue, button-up shirt he wore under his apron was rolled up to his elbows despite the snow clinging to the ground and the dropping temperature. One arm was decorated with the bold, black pattern of a tattoo.

She closed the distance between them, stumbling at the end so she could reach out and grab him without it seeming odd.

He gripped her upper arms, helping her keep her feet. "Are you a guest in the hotel? We should get you back to your room."

She leaned into him so their bodies were pressed together. "Who needs a room when I've got everything I need right here?"

She rose to her tiptoes and moved toward his mouth, but he turned his head at the last second so she caught the edge of his jaw.

"Miss, I really think you should go back inside."

<Seriously? Is this guy dead from the waist down?>

Maybe he doesn't like women. Or maybe he's too decent a person to take advantage of a drunken stranger. Her mind flashed to Detective Williams arching against her, his fingers kneading her flesh. *Unlike us.*

<He enjoyed that as much as we did. And we don't have time for decency right now.>

She cupped the man's cheek with her hand and found his lips with hers.

His eyes went wide, then slid closed as he responded to the kiss. The sudden pressure against Mira's abdomen proved her physical appeal hadn't been the problem.

I'm so sorry, she thought as the first tendrils of energy flowed between them. Physical contact made the transfer easier. The tremor in her limbs subsided. Her dizziness faded. It only took a few seconds for Mira to take what she needed, then she tipped her head back and gasped a deep breath of freezing air that burned in her lungs and made her feel alive.

She felt terrific . . . and terrible.

She lowered the man to the ground as gently as she could, cradling his head against his arm. She checked his pulse, made sure he was breathing, then reached for her pendant, feeling the need for forgiveness. Her fingers bumped the flat space against her sternum where her necklace should have been.

"Holy Mother, hear my prayer and forgive my failings. Lead me to do better and not repeat these mistakes. And I beg of you, watch over this man and see that no harm comes to him because of my actions." She kissed her fingertips and pressed them against the unconscious man's forehead. "Why did you have to be such a nice guy?"

She knocked on the restaurant's back door and jogged off into the night. Hopefully, someone would find her victim before he froze.

Chapter 29

Ty

TY OPENED THE station door for LaRosa, who stomped past without looking up. His one attempt at conversation on the drive from the hotel had resulted in a growl about him dragging his feet and an assurance that if *she'd* been driving, Mirana Fuentes would be back in custody. The rest of their ride to the police station had passed in tense silence.

Sighing, he followed her through to the homicide department, pausing to wave to the officer behind the front desk who had her hands full with a large group of men. Two were sporting bloody noses. They all smelled like the bottom of a bottle.

LaRosa had her hand on the knob to Captain Holtz's door by the time Ty reached the open area with the detective desks. Sandy Shuster was on the phone in the far corner. A young man stood with his back to the room adding sugar packets to a paper cup. Guilt twisted in Ty's chest. Billy should have been covering the night shift. Instead, he and Collins were in the hospital.

They'll recover. He took a deep breath and lifted his chin. Mira hadn't done any harm since her escape. In fact she seemed to have *helped* Angela and Shaquana. She'd take out Decker, a dangerous practitioner, and be on her way. After that, she wouldn't be his problem anymore.

Ty followed LaRosa into the captain's office but pulled up short. Aside from LaRosa and the captain—who sat behind his desk rubbing two fingers back and forth across his forehead like he was trying to smooth out the wrinkles there—another person was in the room, and the man was unexpectedly, unpleasantly, familiar. From his polished shoes to his slicked-back hair, his gray, silk suit to his contemptuous smirk, everything about Andrew Chen screamed, "I'm better than you, and we both know it." Ty had despised the man since their time together at the training academy.

"What are you doing here, Chen?"

"Williams." One side of Chen's perpetual smirk lifted higher. "I hear you've lost a potentially dangerous witch, not once but twice now." He spread his hands in an ostensibly friendly gesture. "I'm here to clean up your mess."

LaRosa crossed her arms. "And where were you earlier when we requested PTF backup for the prisoner transport?"

Chen shrugged. "Guatemala. But I'm here now, and that's the important thing." He lowered himself into one of the two chairs in front of Captain Holtz's desk. "The PTF is spread thin these days, what with our sorcerers out of commission. Agents aren't currently being assigned with less than a three-person team. But between my track record and Williams here having PTF training, it was decided I could utilize your local assets to get this job done." He glanced at Ty. "Though it looks like you might be rustier than we thought."

Ty clenched his fists, opened his mouth—

"No matter." Chen waved his hand. "Your presence is an unnecessary precaution in this case. Just stand where I tell you and try not to get anyone killed."

Ty went cold. He swayed, dizzy. Then his veins filled with fire and he lunged at Chen. He landed one hit. Then LaRosa was on his back, pinning his arms. Chen took a cheap shot to Ty's gut that knocked the wind out of him. Captain Holtz was up and circling the desk, yelling for them to break it up. He grabbed Chen by the arms and yanked him back. LaRosa dragged Ty, gasping and sagging, to the second chair and dropped him in it. She kept a hand on his shoulder.

"I take it there's a history here?" Holtz said.

Chen swept aside a strand of hair that had fallen out of place. "No more than you'd expect between a precision operator and a cowboy."

Ty glared daggers at Chen, but he couldn't get enough air in his lungs to respond.

"Well, work it out or lock it down." Holtz pointed a finger at Ty. "The PTF will only give us Chen if you're on the team."

"We don't need him," Ty spat.

"Like hell we don't. A month ago this whole mess would have been PTF jurisdiction, plain and simple. I've already got two men in the hospital with some kind of magically induced anemia. I want this case off my desk, pronto, so you and Chen play nice. Get that practitioner back in her collar and off my streets."

Ty gripped the sides of his chair and swallowed his first response. Chen was an ass, but he was a solid agent. Like Ty and Jamal, he specialized in magical target apprehension, and his close rate was near perfect. Maybe Ty could convince him to look into Decker. Otherwise he'd need to run interference until Mira finished her work. Either way, Holtz was right. Ty had to play nice.

Ty stretched his lips over his teeth in an approximation of a smile. "Happy to have you on the team, Chen."

LaRosa squeezed his shoulder, then stepped away so the four of them were more evenly spaced. "Fuentes—that's the target—seems to be stalking a man named Reed Decker. Her first victim was on his construction site. The second, though his death is unconfirmed, was the foreman for the job. Third, though again unconfirmed, was Decker's secretary. The last was Decker's wife, murdered in their home while he was out."

Chen frowned. "Why this fixation on Decker? Who is he to her?"

"She believes he's a practitioner with an evil agenda." Ty met Chen's gaze when he spoke.

"You believe her?"

"No," LaRosa said at the same time Ty answered, "Maybe."

LaRosa shook her head. "There's no hard evidence against Decker. Unlike Fuentes." She gave Ty a meaningful look. "I say she was just trying to shake us."

Chen pursed his lips, looked at Ty, and raised an eyebrow. "Your impression of Decker?"

Recalling the way Decker had made his skin crawl that first day they met, Ty lifted his chin. "The guy's hiding something." He glanced at LaRosa. "That doesn't prove he's an unregistered practitioner, but I think it's worth considering that Mirana Fuentes might have been telling the truth." He shifted his focus back to Chen. "She wouldn't be the first practitioner to turn against her own kind when she thought someone was stepping over a line."

"Seems to me," Chen said, "whether Decker is a practitioner or not, he's where the action is. We should shadow Decker, find out what, if anything, he's hiding, and set a trap for when Fuentes shows up to finish him off."

"Our thoughts exactly," LaRosa said. "We're heading to a banquet Decker is attending tonight. Figured we'd join the security detail."

Chen smoothed the lapels of his suit jacket. "Then by all means, lead the way."

Mira

MIRA ADJUSTED the straps of the classy black dress she'd chosen for the banquet. Swoops of fabric draped off her shoulders and plunged to her cleavage. The waist was form-fitting, then flared into a split-panel, ankle-length skirt. Stepping out of a side street, she merged with the men and women heading toward the double-door entrance of the three-story brownstone where Decker would receive his award.

Two men in monkey suits were collecting invitations on the front steps. Both wore earpieces and had bulges under their jackets that suggested they were armed.

<Security.>

Which we expected.

She zeroed in on a middle-aged woman in a mink coat walking toward the venue on impractical heels that *click-clacked* against the sidewalk. She held a sparkly gold clutch in one hand and her invitation in the other.

Mira sent a small tremor through the ground, making the woman stumble. Both the clutch and invitation fell as the woman struggled to keep her feet.

Mira snatched the invitation and pressed it against the sheet of heavy card stock she'd brought with her. A quick burst of energy and the contents of one paper were copied to the other. Then she scooped up the clutch and handed both items back to the shaken woman. "Are you all right?"

The woman nodded, pink creeping into her pale cheeks. "Yes, thank you." She took back her possessions and hurried up the steps to the entrance.

Mira looked down at the paper in her hand and smiled. A quick trim and a change of name and she was on her way to the party.

When she reached the front of the line, the guard looked at Mira's forged invitation, then gave her a slow, assessing, down-and-up with his eyes. Mira did her best to keep her expression neutral so as not to smudge the glamour she'd caked over her features. With any luck the usher would see a woman with pale skin, slightly Asian features, dark eyes, and black hair tied up in a bun.

The man's gaze lingered for a moment where the collar of Mira's dress dipped low, then he handed back the invitation and tipped his head toward the open door behind him.

<Guess we didn't need to spend so much energy on changing your face. With this neckline, no one's going to look above your collarbone.>

Mira tucked the invitation into her purse beside the tranquilizer dart she'd taken out of the policeman's gun and entered the building.

Most of the guests checked their coats at a station just inside the door, then crossed the carpeted foyer to the entrance of the banquet hall. Mira, however, having chosen to brave the cold rather than risk losing her jacket, headed straight for the service hallway that bordered the ballroom. She passed the first two doors, marked as bathrooms, and continued up the hall. Caterers bustled back and forth to the kitchen, which lay behind the third and fourth doorways, carrying trays of fancy finger-foods, drinks, and chrome-covered plates. A few glanced her way, but they were too busy with their work to pay her much mind.

She continued past the kitchen to a utility closet at the end of the hall. When the coast was clear, she flipped the lock with her magic and slipped inside. Wire-rack shelves lined one wall, stacked high with cleaning supplies. A damp mop sat inside a big yellow bucket with wheels, dreadlock tendrils draping the sides like the tentacles of a sea creature trying to escape.

<Have you noticed how often we hide in closets?>

Mira shrugged. "Last time we hid in a bathtub."

<True.>

She shifted the wheely-bucket with its mop-squid passenger and rapped a knuckle against the exposed wall behind it. Based on the floor plan she'd looked up online, the banquet hall was on the other side of those boards and plaster. If she placed her "bomb" here it *should* blow a hole through to the other side.

Just enough to scare people into running. Not so big that anyone gets hurt.

<Materials aside, it's a bomb. We can't guarantee there won't be someone leaning against the wall on the other side when it goes off.>

We can try.

Channeling her magic, Mira wove a spell with air and fire. It was slow, delicate work—not her favorite type of casting. Minutes ticked away as she fitted the various components into place, adding enough fuel to keep the spell burning long enough for the finale.

When she was satisfied the spell would detonate as she intended, she tied off what could loosely be described as a stick of magical dynamite and set the countdown fuse. Ten minutes—that's how long she had to get in position. Then the magic "bomb" would go off and all hell would break loose in the ballroom. She needed to be right beside Decker so she could hit him with the tranquilizer while he was off balance. Then she'd slip an illusion over him while security was distracted, "help" him out in the ensuing chaos, and take him back to her truck for a private chat.

<We should assume Mr. Yummy and his partner are here since they

were watching Decker earlier. When the bomb goes off, they might stick to him.>

"Then we'll have to go through them. But there are enough politicians and city influencers here that I'm hoping Decker won't be their highest priority."

After double-checking to make sure her spell was stable, she opened the closet door a crack and waited for the hall to be clear of caterers. Then she slipped out and closed the door behind her. She passed the first set of doors leading to the banquet hall—the one being used by the servers as they scurried back and forth—and headed to the main entrance where the other guests had entered.

". . . being here tonight to celebrate the impactful works being carried out around our city." The voice, strong and sure as only a practiced public speaker can be, drifted through the open doors of the main room as Mira rounded the corner. A short man shaped roughly like a bowling ball—whom Mira recognized as the mayor from his picture on the event announcement website—was giving a speech in the open area at the center of the room. Williams's partner LaRosa was guarding the entrance, but the glammed-up cop had her hands full with an overly friendly gentleman, and Mira was able to slip past unnoticed.

Two chandeliers hung from the banquet hall ceiling, reflecting a bright double-halo on the polished wood floor that faded as it spread across the tables. The outer edges were cast in shadow by a second-story gallery that ringed three quarters of the room. The mayor clutched a shiny, brass plaque against his white suit jacket and droned into a microphone about the importance of giving back to the community. He turned a slow circle as he spoke, catching gazes with his dazzling blue eyes, trying to engage the guests who sat at their tables spearing vegetables or cutting steak as the welcome speech wore on.

Flashes of light snapped around the edges of the room from cameras set on tripods. Reporters stood with voice recorders raised or pens furiously scribbling on tiny paper pads. Men and women who were dressed like guests but moved like soldiers were evenly spaced around the room. Caterers continued to circulate, trading out plates and topping off glasses. The second story was empty except for two men who patrolled the gallery like circling hawks preparing to strike. The stairs leading up had been cordoned off by a black ribbon.

Shifting her attention back to the seated guests, Mira stalked slowly past tables of the city's wealthy elite, the policy makers—most of whom would order her put down in a second if they discovered what she was.

<We don't have to save them.> The demon's voice was a quiet echo in her thoughts. <We can just walk away, let them suffer whatever Decker's planning for them.>

Except these wouldn't be the people who'd suffer. These are the people sipping champagne on fiberglass yachts while the rest of us drown.

Her gaze continued to drift as she circled the room, slipping between waiters and photographers along the outer wall where the shadows were deepest.

How long have we got?

<Rough estimate? Three minutes.>

Applause erupted around the room, making her jump. Her focus snapped back to the mayor, who seemed to have finished his speech. She followed the line of his outstretched hand and found Decker, rising from a table on the far side of the room. He was headed for center stage.

Mira eyed the open space around the mayor—a no-man's-land guarded by the circling security. She moved toward the innermost tables, stopping just shy of the empty floor as Decker wrapped one hand around the microphone. She was going to have to time this just right.

Chapter 30

Ty

"WILLIAMS, YOU TAKE the bird's eye." Chen pointed to the stairs leading up to the second-story gallery. "LaRosa, you stick by the door. With all these cameras I doubt she'd use a standard illusion, but no magical disguise is perfect. Look for lags in expression, distortions around the mouth and eyes. You get so much as a funny feeling about someone, you call it in."

LaRosa nodded.

"I'll stick to Decker." Chen tightened his tie and met Ty's gaze. "Don't be a cowboy."

Ty and Chen left LaRosa at the entrance. Chen moved to the far side of the room, crossing the bright patch of empty floor where the speeches would take place. Ty hung to the outskirts, steering wide of the bustling guests looking for seats. Blue napkins boxed in by polished silver sat like little swans atop the white tablecloths of the dozen or so tables spaced around the room. Men and women in hand-tailored outfits circulated, drinking and chatting with their peers, while those in off-the-rack suits like his own stood behind cameras or carried trays.

Mayor Mitchell's voice droned from the middle of the room as he expressed his pleasure at the night's turnout and name-dropped a few prominent attendees—no doubt contributors to his reelection campaign.

Ty stepped over the black ribbon that had been stretched across the gallery stairs to block access. From above, the split between light and shadow was even more pronounced. The chandeliers created a bright patch in the center of the room where the mayor stood. That light illuminated the first row of tables, including Decker's, but the overhang of the gallery cast Chen—who stood only a few steps behind Decker—and those beyond into shadow.

Ty circled the gallery then started back, watching the mayor as he gave his speech, the servers as they distributed covered trays, the diners as they tucked into their meals. Decker chatted with his tablemates, drinking and laughing, the picture of social comfort. He certainly wasn't acting like a man overcome by grief at the loss of his spouse, and once again that sense of *wrongness* settled over Ty.

A few stragglers and guests who'd stepped out for a moment trickled through the main doors. LaRosa studied each like there was going to be a quiz at the end of the night, not even trying to mask her inspections. A silver-haired man in a dark suit stopped to talk to her. LaRosa tried to wave him on as other guests slipped in behind him, but the guy just leaned closer. Ty chuckled. Even from this distance he could tell LaRosa was having trouble staying polite. If that guy wasn't careful, his appreciation would earn him a black eye. Not that he could fault the man's taste.

While LaRosa's demeanor was far from covert, her outfit certainly fit with the in-crowd of tonight's event. Truth be told, the shimmery, maroon fabric that clung to her hips like a second skin made it hard for Ty to look at her as a fellow officer. Braided spaghetti straps and a thigh-high slit that showed off the curve of her tanned calf turned his thoughts in a direction that might have earned him his own black eye if she could read his mind. Ty had fancied up for the occasion, but he would have been happier in his jeans. LaRosa more than looked the part; she wore it comfortably—which made him wonder what she did in her off-duty hours.

Applause broke out around the room, bringing Ty's attention back to the moment. Mayor Mitchell was holding out Decker's award.

Decker rose from his table. Chen took a step forward, but Decker said something, too quiet for Ty to hear, that resulted in a localized fit of laughter from the men and women seated around him. Chen stiffened, then clasped his hands and settled back on his heels. Decker trotted to the center of the room like a quarterback taking the field, smiling and waving as he wove between tables. From up in the gallery Decker was little more than a head of fluffy, blond hair styled to cover the thinning patch that was clearly visible from above. He had a bounce in his step and a nod for everyone he passed.

When Decker reached the central space between the two chandeliers, he accepted the award from the mayor, patted the shorter man on the back, and took the microphone. "Thank you so much for that kind introduction, Mayor Mitchell." He hugged the award against his chest. "I'm both humbled and honored."

As the mayor made his way out of the limelight, Decker turned a slow circle, as though assessing his audience. Forks and knives continued to clatter against plates while Decker observed the crowd. More and more faces looked up as the silence stretched. The sounds of eating and the whispers of hushed conversation died away. When Decker seemed satisfied that he had the attention of every person in the room, he raised the microphone.

"As I'm sure you're all aware, poverty, displacement, and vagrancy have been an ongoing issue in our city, our country, and our world. Too often people are content to ignore this problem and those affected by it, or pass laws to shuffle them off our streets and out of sight. The goal of my development was to bring those scattered people suffering alone in this city to a safe, central location." He paused, glanced around the room, then smiled. "And we've succeeded. I'm thrilled to say that every one of the hundred and fifty beds in our new homeless shelter has been filled, and every low-rent apartment we've constructed has a family living in it. We've even got families ready to move in to the final building once it's complete. Let's get those kids off the streets." He punched his plaque into the air and the room burst into applause.

"This development isn't just about having a place to sleep," he continued as the noise died down. "The business center will help with job searches and resume building. The athletics facility and cafeteria will improve health." He turned another slow circle but stopped halfway, staring into the crowd. "This isn't just about getting people off the streets. It's about changing the world. It's about creating a future we can *all* be a part of."

Ty moved along the balcony to see what had caught Decker's attention. When the chandelier was no longer blocking his view of the far crowd, he spotted a petite woman standing under the overhang of the gallery on the far side, just at the edge of the shadows. She looked too old to be Mira, and too Asian, but his instincts were screaming that it was her. The way she held herself, the way her steady gaze followed Decker . . . it was Mira.

Static crackled in Ty's earpiece and Chen's voice cut through his thoughts. "What's the matter? Did you spot her?"

Ty gripped the balcony railing.

Mira had come—just like Chen and LaRosa assumed she would. She was there to kidnap or kill a prominent businessman and philanthropist who was even now being honored for his selfless contributions to the city. She had to know Decker was being watched. Why choose such a prominent venue? If she started a fight here it could result in incalculable collateral damage. Didn't she realize that? Didn't she care?

His gaze shifted back to Decker, who was talking about building a community the likes of which had never existed. Decker was being stalked by a dangerous woman. His assistant and the foreman of his project were missing, presumed dead. His wife had been murdered. He was the victim in this scenario . . . so why did Ty feel like the world would be a safer place if one of these chandeliers fell on his head?

If he's the kind of bad that she's hunting . . .

There were some evils humans just weren't equipped to handle—evils you couldn't even see until it was too late.

Ty couldn't deny the evidence stacked against Mira, or the possibility that she was just an off-her-rocker practitioner with a Decker obsession who was playing him . . . but he couldn't ignore that twisting wrongness he felt around Decker or the earnestness in Mira's voice when she insisted she was on his side either. She'd sounded just like Jamal when he convinced Ty to join the Army—desperate to make the world safe—back when Ty still believed he could make a difference.

"Williams." Chen's sharp rebuke drew Ty's focus to Decker's dinner table, where Chen stood behind the seated guests.

"What's the call here?" LaRosa asked through the earpiece. She'd stepped away from the door. Her right hand was hidden in her purse, ready to pull the tranquilizer gun as soon as she had a target.

Ty looked at the woman he believed was Mira. She was circling the room, keeping to the shadows, her attention centered on Decker.

The *clink* of glasses below echoed the beer bottles Jamal had stolen from his father's stash on the sweltering summer afternoon he convinced Ty to enlist. Jamal's voice rang through his head, and he felt the sting of a phantom slap against his back. *I can't do this without you, man. I don't have your instincts.*

Ty swallowed his doubts and prayed he was making the right decision. "False alarm."

Chen scanned the room, searching the faces of the guests, servers, and media representatives who were moving around. His gaze swept over Mira, passed her by, then swung back. Ty started toward the stairs.

He made it three steps when a concussive blast popped his ears. The balcony bucked under his feet, knocking him off-balance. The chandeliers jangled and swung, throwing a kaleidoscope of light around the room. Plaster chunks fell from the ceiling. Muted screams filtered through the ringing in his ears, but it was Jamal's voice that filled his mind.

The building's coming down.

Fear and panic dropped Ty to his knees. He clutched the railing with one hand and plunged the other into his pocket, groping for the smooth comfort of his focus stone. He traced the fissure in its surface, willing himself to see beyond what was in front of him, fighting the wash of memories as his chest constricted and his heart raced.

He'd followed his instincts, and he'd chosen wrong . . . again.

Mira

MIRA'S MAGIC TORE a hole through the back wall of the building, shattering windows and toppling bricks. There was a moment of stunned silence during which all the guests seemed to inhale. Then Mira shouted, "Bomb," and the room erupted into chaos. Those already on their feet ran for the nearest door. People who'd been sitting jumped up, toppling chairs and tables. Dishes clattered to the floor. Glasses shattered, covering the hardwood with jagged shards. Several guests went down in the crush of people near the exits.

Decker, who'd been knocked to his knees by the initial blast, was climbing to his feet.

Mira pulled the tranquilizer dart from her purse and let the accessory fall. Gripping the small glass tube in her right hand, she stepped up behind Decker and thrust the needle at his exposed back.

Time seemed to stretch. The shouts of the crowd grew distorted. Debris fluttered like snowflakes around them. The air became thick as syrup, slowing Mira's attack.

With the needle two inches from the black fabric of Decker's suit, he turned. Mira tried to shift, to redirect her attack, to pull back even, but her body was committed to its current path. Unlike her and the rest of the room, Decker moved with the fluid confidence of a man with time on his side, sure and relaxed. He spun so they were facing each other, slipping one arm around her waist while the other gripped her wrist to redirect the tranquilizer. If anyone had seen that frozen moment it would have looked like they were dancing.

<Oh your God, oh your God, oh your God . . .> The demon's magic began to build in response to her panic, but the flow was lethargic. <He's manipulating time. He must be a sovereign!>

Mira struggled to make sense of what was happening, but even her thoughts seemed slow.

Sovereign. . . . That was the highest level of demon in the Rift. She'd never actually met one. To the best of her knowledge, neither had her demon. They were practically myths.

Are you sure?

<Time-manipulation is kind of a giveaway. Who else can wield that much power?>

Mira closed her eyes in slow motion as Decker's face came closer, brushing her cheek with his.

"What was your plan?" he whispered, and his voice was the only sound in the eerie silence of their stolen moment. "Drug me and steal me away in the chaos of the moment?"

He shifted again, pulling her slightly off-balance. Visions of being pulled around, unable to fight back, filled Mira's head, confusing her thoughts. A tight ache built in her chest as her body refused to respond. Decker was in complete control. It was all Mira could do to keep the panic and humiliation of her inadequacy from overwhelming her.

She inhaled and opened her eyes.

Decker was assessing the scene around them—the settling dust, the screaming people, the overturned tables. A man in a gray suit with black hair and eyes was frozen mid-stride just a few steps away, and unlike most of the crowd, he was moving toward Mira and Decker rather than an exit. As she watched, his front foot touched down on the wood floor and his back heel lifted. Time was still moving, however slowly.

She glanced up and found Detective Williams huddled against a rail post on the gallery, eyes squeezed shut, too preoccupied to be a threat . . . or a help.

"Not a bad plan," Decker said. "But a little lackluster as far as distractions go. If you really want to hold someone's attention, you need to make it personal." He pressed closer, his lips brushing her ear. "Your friend is waiting for you. Come to my office at midnight so we can have a *real* talk."

He stepped to the side and spun her out like the dance partner he resembled, and as they turned, time regained its hold on the world. The screams rose in volume, coming back into focus. The man in the gray suit completed his lunge and tackled Decker around the waist, tearing his grip from Mira's wrist.

"LaRosa," the man shouted as he and Decker crashed to the floor and skidded across the polished wood.

Mira spun and found Mr. Yummy's partner raising the now familiar long barrel of a tranquilizer gun. Her vision constricted to that single point. The panic that had been building inside her since Decker took control of the moment overflowed its banks, mixing with the feelings of helplessness and isolation she'd experienced the last time one of those darts found a home in her flesh. The demon's magic flooded through her, tearing through their buffer as fear and anger washed away Mira's control.

No, she thought weakly, but she'd already lost her grip on the wheel.

Magic burst from Mira in the form of an explosion. Fire engulfed her for no more than a second, then shot toward the threat on a wave of force. LaRosa was tossed into the air like a feather on the wind. She slammed into one of the balcony pillars, then landed with a thud on the hardwood floor. The tranquilizer gun lay beside her, its barrel twisted and glowing a dull red.

Mira took a stumbling step back. *No.* She shook her head and covered her mouth with one hand as the scent of charred flesh brought visions of her mother's melted face drifting up from her memory. Once again the world seemed to slow, but this time there was no magic involved.

Williams, still kneeling in the gallery, was screaming LaRosa's name. The man in the gray suit was up on one knee, pulling a twin to the melted gun from a holster at his waist. Decker smiled at her from his position on the ground.

Mira took it all in. Then she turned and ran.

Chapter 31

Mira

MIRA RAN TO THE parking structure where she'd left her truck, which now sported a logo for J and P Plumbing. She wrenched open the back, climbed in, and slammed the door. She stood panting in the darkness for a moment, shaking with every gulp of air. Then she shouted into the black—the inarticulate howl of a wounded animal. She smashed her fists against the cabinets and the counter, kicked the back tire of her motorcycle, which claimed most of the interior, and tore at the bands holding it in place. She stomped and wriggled past the bike until she was in the small cube of clear space that butted up to the cab. There she turned her back to the wall and slid to the floor. She dropped her head in her hands and sobbed.

<I know you're frustrated Decker got away, but—>

"Decker?" Her voice hitched and cracked. "You think I'm pissed about Decker?"

<Well, we *had* hoped to finish him off tonight.>

Mira shook her head, trying to clear the image of LaRosa flying across the room after being hit by that fireball. "How could you do that?"

Irritation bubbled through her. <Sure, blame me for LaRosa. Just like you blame me for your mother and her boyfriend, and that homeless woman, and every bad decision you've ever made.> The demon's anger was rising to match her own. <You're not a kid anymore, and you've had more than enough experience with magic to know how it works. So how about you take a look at what really happened before you go pointing fingers.>

"What really happened? You blasted LaRosa with a fireball and sent her flying." Mira pounded her fists against the floor. "You were so scared of being hit by that dart, of being stripped away and locked out by the collar, that you overwhelmed me."

<Have we really gotten so muddled that you can't even tell the difference anymore?>

Mira stiffened.

<Yes I was scared of being separated from you, and yes my magic rose in response . . . but I wasn't the only one. Your panic was just as strong as mine, and when it comes right down to it, it was *your* fear that let loose. All I did was help direct it.>

She squeezed her eyes closed.

<If I'd used that much energy in our current, fragile balance . . . there'd be evidence.> She raised their shared hand and a small, orange glow formed in her palm. <Take a look.>

Mira opened her eyes. The skin around her fingernails was intact. She reached up with her free hand and felt her smooth, tear-streaked cheeks. She stood, yanked open an upper cabinet, and pulled out a small mirror. Makeup streaked her face, smeared by sweat and tears, but there were no puppet lines. Her left eye was honey gold, but her right remained the deep brown she'd been born with. The pale streak in her hair was only three fingers wide.

"It was me?" A fresh tear streaked her cheek.

"It was us," the demon said into the mirror. "I'm not exactly a stabilizing presence, but that doesn't mean every impulse is my fault."

Mira lifted her palm and pinned the ball of glowing light to the ceiling with a thread of magic, casting the interior into sharp contrasts of flickering orange and deep black as though she stood in the heart of a flame.

<Come on,> the demon said. <We need to get ready for our date with Decker.>

Mira shook her head. "We can't fight him."

<Like hell we can't.>

The corner of Mira's mouth twitched, then fell. "Let me rephrase that. We can't fight him *and win*." She leaned her back against the wall again but kept her feet. *A sovereign . . .*

<So you're giving up? Just skip town with your tail between your legs?>

Mira crossed her arms and stared at the textured metal of the floor.

<Abandon Gemma?>

She shifted her weight, uncomfortable in her own skin. "All I've done since getting involved is make things worse."

<And your solution is to crawl under a rock and throw yourself a pity party?>

"What do you want from me?" Mira shouted into the empty room. "He's stronger than I am, than both of us together. I can't win this on my own!"

<I agree.>

Mira pulled back from her tirade.

<Which is why we need to call Mr. Yummy.>

Silence filled the truck for a moment, then Mira burst into laughter. "Seriously? *That's* your plan? Call the guy whose partner we just killed?"

<You don't know she died.>

"Even if she didn't, I *barely* convinced him to help me before; there's no way he'll trust us now."

<Then call Garrett and have him bring the PTF down on Decker's head.>

"You know he can't. Even if he could mobilize a team on such short notice, and ignoring the fact that his jurisdiction ends at the Colorado border, there's no way he could get here in time."

<Then Mr. Yummy is your only option.>

"Would you please stop calling him that?" She paced from side to side—which in the confined space was basically step, turn, step, turn, step.

<Do you know why I came to you all those years ago?>

Mira frowned. The demon had been with her so long, she didn't really think about her possession much—it was just a part of who she was, like having brown eyes and unruly hair. "Because I was powerful."

<There are lots of powerful practitioners.>

"Because I was young and didn't have a Church-appointed paladin waiting to chop my head off at the first sign of possession."

<It's because you were good.>

"I was eleven. I'd never even done magic before I met you."

<That's not quite true. And I didn't mean because you were good at magic. I possessed you because you were a good person.>

Mira snorted.

<As a resident of the Rift I can see the energy pulled from it by the practitioners in your world. Magic-users light up like beacons in the dark, and any demon close enough to see that light is drawn to it. Through the link between practitioner and Rift, we can see what's happening in your world. Most of what we see is sorcerers attacking people. Sometimes we see healers making money off their ability. The day I possessed you, you were trying to save your mother from a beating. You were pounding your little fists against a grown man's back.>

Mira swallowed the lump in her throat, pushing back against the memory.

<You didn't have any chance of winning, which you knew from past experience, but you fought anyway. You fought because you couldn't just

stand by and watch. You fought because, despite all that had happened to you, you weren't a victim. You fought . . . and you won.>

"Because of you," she whispered.

<You're a good person,> the demon repeated. <You do what's right, even when it's hard. But everybody needs a little help sometimes.>

She shook her head. "Williams isn't going to help us."

<You won't know that until you ask, but you have to be honest . . . about everything.>

Mira's jaw dropped. "You want me to—"

<Remember in the hotel? Angela's secret nearly destroyed her relationship, but when she came clean . . .>

"Telling a law enforcement officer I'm a rifter isn't as simple as admitting to my girlfriend that I was laid off. That kind of secret could destroy my whole world."

<It already is.>

"What's that supposed to mean?"

<You wander from city to city, sleeping in motels and parking lots. You won't visit your family. You have no friends. You keep yourself so closed off you may as well be a demon yourself for all the contact you have with this world.>

She stumbled back a step. Her hip bumped the counter. Heat bloomed in her chest. "I hadn't realized you thought my life was so meaningless."

<I'm just saying maybe it's time you tried living *in* the world instead of just on it.>

"And your solution is to trust my deepest, darkest secret to a near stranger?"

<I like him. You like him. He likes us. I think he's the closest thing you have to a confidant at the moment, and he's in a position to help.>

Mira pulled open the drawer where she kept her burner phones and lifted the slip of paper she'd stashed there when she changed for the banquet. The scrawled number was smudged and hard to make out in the dim, orange light.

"I don't fight because I'm a good person," she said. "I fight because I don't know any other way to live." She reached in the drawer, pulled out her second-to-last phone, and made the call.

Ty

TY PACED FROM one side of the beige waiting room to the other. Glassy-eyed men and women sat in padded chairs nursing paper cups of drip coffee and the contents of the nearby vending machine. Occasionally a nurse or doctor would step through the swinging doors at the end of the hall that led to the ER. When that happened, everyone's focus zeroed in like a targeting laser. Bodies tensed. Coffee sloshed in shaking hands. Sometimes the staff just walked by. Sometimes they'd approach a person or group in the waiting area and speak in hushed tones. Sometimes there was shouting. . . . There were almost always tears.

Andrew Chen stepped into Ty's path. "Any word?"

Ty pulled up short. He hadn't seen Chen arrive. The PTF agent had been organizing a search net to catch Mira when Ty left the scene at the banquet hall to follow LaRosa's ambulance to the hospital. She'd been rolled out, unconscious on a stretcher, and taken straight to the ER.

"No," he said in a choked voice. "Any luck finding Fuentes?"

Chen shook his head, lips pursed. "You saw her, didn't you? Before that blast went off. That's who you were looking at from up in the gallery."

"I couldn't be sure."

Mouth drawn tight Chen thrust one finger in Ty's face. "But you *suspected.* You could have had LaRosa or me move in to verify, but instead you claimed it was a false alarm."

"I made a judgment call."

"A bad one"—he swung his finger toward the closed doors behind which LaRosa had been wheeled—"and it's cost you another partner."

Ty jerked as though zapped by a stun gun.

"I thought maybe you left the agency to avoid bad memories, but I guess the rumors about you were true . . . your instincts really have gone sour." He shook his head and let his arm relax to his side. "I've requested the next available PTF team be dispatched to Baltimore. In the meantime, I'll be conducting a manhunt using local LEOs. Do everyone a favor and just stay out of the way."

"Tell the public there's a rogue practitioner on the loose and you could start a panic."

"She blew up a building. She's not just an unregistered practitioner, she's a terrorist. The public needs to know."

Ty clenched his jaw and tightened his fists. Despite his own panic when the bomb had gone off that he was about to have another building dropped on his head, the damage hadn't actually been that severe. The explosion originated in an empty utility closet adjacent to the main room. While it had blown a hole in the wall and destabilized the gallery, most of the actual injuries were inflicted by other guests during the mad press to evacuate. The only serious casualty was LaRosa, but now the PTF had a poster child for why practitioners were dangerous if unchecked—a rallying cry to stand against the paranatural coalition experiment in Colorado. All because of Mira . . . and by extension, him.

Chen glanced over his shoulder toward the ER doors. "I'm sorry about LaRosa, but I can't stick around here. Need to get back to the hunt." He slapped Ty on the arm. "You understand."

Ty shrugged off his hand.

Chen offered a grim smile and walked out the waiting-room doors that led to the parking lot.

Ty dragged both hands over his scalp. Then let loose a punch on the side of the vending machine.

"Hey!" yelled a man in green scrubs behind the check-in desk.

"Sorry, sorry." He backed away from the vending machine, both hands raised.

Ty made three more circuits of the waiting room, obsessing over his choice to shield Mira. Should he have sicced Chen on her at the banquet? Would that have saved LaRosa? Or should he have thrown in with her to take Decker down before LaRosa ended up in the crossfire? He dropped into a vinyl-covered chair and cradled his head in his hands as though trying to physically contain his swirling thoughts.

A year ago he would have backed Mira from the outset, loud and proud. He would have launched an investigation into Decker and to hell with what anyone else thought. A year ago he'd thought of himself as a human lie detector, able to see through people's bullshit to the truth of a matter. But since he'd followed that halfer boy like a rat after the Pied Piper . . . since Jamal . . .

"Detective Williams?"

Ty jerked upright in his seat.

A tall woman with upswept blond hair and red-framed glasses stood in front of him. She hugged a clipboard against white scrubs dotted with multicolored ice-cream cones. "I'm Doctor Ross."

Ty pushed to his feet, and the woman took a step back to give him space. "How is she?"

"Ms. LaRosa is out of surgery and stable. We've moved her to the ICU. There was severe damage to her ribs and spine from her impact, and she suffered third-degree burns on her right arm."

"Can I see her?"

"We're keeping her sedated for now."

"She doesn't have to be conscious; I just need to see her . . . please."

The doctor's mouth pulled to one side. Then she gave a brisk nod and said, "You'll need to turn off your phone in the ICU."

Ty hesitated, then pulled his phone out of his pocket and shut it down. Chen was on point now. The case was out of Ty's hands.

LaRosa was in a private room. Her right arm was bandaged all the way to the sleeve of her blue hospital gown. Her left arm had tubes taped to it through which clear liquid flowed from a hanging IV bag. A monitor attached to her index finger sketched jagged lines and filled the room with a rhythmic beep. Her skin was pale and streaked with sweat. Her hair clung in damp strands against her forehead. She couldn't have looked more different from the woman who'd been guarding the ballroom door.

"I'll give you a moment." The doctor stepped out and closed the door.

Ty dragged the only chair in the room over to the bed and fell into it. He couldn't take his eyes off LaRosa's pale face. Jamal never made it to the hospital—he'd left that building in a black bag. Still, Ty couldn't shake the feeling of déjà vu.

"I'm so sorry," he whispered. "This is all my fault." Thinking of the Saint Jude medal he'd first seen on Mira the night they met and later found in Nowak's office, Ty clasped his hands, lowered his head, and closed his eyes. "I'm not sure what constitutes a lost cause these days—seems to me the whole world is pretty lost right now—but if there's anything you can do for LaRosa . . . She was just doing her job, trying to keep the streets safe. It was plain bad luck that she got saddled with me."

He sighed. "Guess I've been a pretty shitty partner all around. I wasn't straight with LaRosa. I didn't fully back Mira. I was so conflicted about who was right and so worried about choosing wrong that I ended up playing both sides, and because of that . . . everyone lost.

"I should've convinced LaRosa to trust Mira, or seen if she could convince me not to. Before Jamal, I never doubted my instincts. I saw a path and I took it. This wishy-washy shit"—he shook his head—"it's not me. But how am I supposed to trust my instincts when they landed Jamal in the morgue and LaRosa in the ICU?"

He opened his eyes and looked up to the office-panel ceiling, searching for answers.

The steady beep of the heart monitor was the only sound in the room as the seconds ticked by.

"Yeah," he said finally. "That's what I thought."

Chapter 32

Mira

AFTER TWO RINGS Mira's call was sent to Detective Williams's voicemail. Grumbling, she lowered the phone and reached for the end button. Her gaze caught on the bag of saltwater taffies on the counter across from her. She hesitated. Gemma might still be alive, and if the banquet was any indication, chances were slim Mira could take Decker on her own. If she failed . . . Williams might be Gemma's only hope, but he had no idea what he was up against.

She brought the phone back to her ear just as the tell-tale *beep* signaled the start of her recording. She set the fingertips of her free hand against her chest where her Saint Jude pendant should have hung and sent a silent prayer that Williams would hear what she had to say with an open mind.

"Williams, I . . ." She stalled out. Her gaze roamed the truck's interior, searching for inspiration—or perhaps trying to pin down her flagging courage. "I'm sorry about your partner. That . . . that was a mistake. I panicked. I . . ." Again words failed her.

She blew out a noisy sigh and ran a hand through her hair, pulling her waves loose from their short ponytail. "I'm calling because it turns out Decker is even more dangerous than I thought. I wasn't totally honest with you before. He's not just a practitioner. He's a very special kind of rifter—one that can hide inside his human host for a long time. I know this because—" She hesitated, trying to swallow past the lump in her throat.

<Go on . . . you'll feel better.>

"—I am too."

She exhaled a shaky breath as the words she'd held close for so long flowed into the world. Her secret was out. A tight ache swelled in her chest, threatening to cut off her air.

"I know you've got no reason to trust me." Her words came out strangled. "But I really am on your side. I hunt beings like Decker—

magic-users even the PTF doesn't know about and are ill-equipped to handle. I'm good at what I do, and my unique nature means I'm usually a match for whatever I'm up against, but not this time. Right now I don't have the power, the resources, or the tactical advantage to give me a leg up on Decker. Honestly, I'm not sure I can take him . . . so I'm asking for your help."

She cringed, hating the way the words tasted. This was the second time she was pleading with Williams, the second time she was admitting she was out of her depth and vulnerable. She hated how weak it made her feel, but she gritted her teeth and pressed on. "I'll be at Decker's office at midnight tonight. You can come alone and back me up, or you can call in a SWAT team to take me down. The choice is yours. Either way I wanted you to know about Decker. Someone should . . . in case I fail."

She pressed the button to end the call, dropped the phone, and gulped in a big breath of air as though she'd just finished a sprint.

<See? Don't you feel better getting that off your chest?>

Mira braced her hands against her knees. "I think I'm gonna puke."

<Oh come on, it can't have been that bad.>

Mira glared at empty space, wishing not for the first time that her demon was outside her body so she could have a physical target for her frustration. "We just handed him a confession that we're a unique form of rifter. If he goes to the PTF with that recording—"

<He won't.>

"I hope you're right."

Mira stepped out of her strappy sandals and stripped off the fancy dress she'd worn to the banquet, bumping twice into the motorcycle and nearly falling over in the tiny space. She smoothed the fabric, sighed, and folded it on top of her laundry pile. Then she pulled out a fresh pair of dark jeans and a long-sleeved, navy-blue shirt. She let the magic clinging to her features melt away, removed the remaining pins from her hair, and shook her head so her waves swung loose. "Much better."

Squeezing past the motorcycle, she took her can of Cafe La Llave and her propane stove out of their respective cubbies.

<You're taking a coffee break? Now?>

"The cops will be swarming this area by now, scrutinizing anyone trying to leave. So we'll lie low for a bit, then head over to Decker's office once the police have finished their sweep. In the meantime, we might as well dose up on caffeine. I have a feeling it's going to be a very long night."

Ty

TY STARTLED AWAKE. An alarm was sounding somewhere nearby. Disoriented, he looked around for his clock before realizing he was still in LaRosa's hospital room. He must have dozed off in the chair beside her bed. Another thought hit him and he sprang to his feet, fearing the alarm meant LaRosa's heart had stopped. Then he registered the steady spikes on her monitor and the doctors and nurses rushing past the small window in the door. It was someone in another room, some other unfortunate soul, who'd taken a turn for the worse.

He sighed, then cringed as a wave of guilt rolled over him on the heels of his relief.

He looked down at the chair he'd so abruptly vacated, then at LaRosa. Her chest rose and fell, but her face remained pale and slack. He reached for her hand but pulled back when his fingers encountered the bulky black cube sealed over her finger.

"Stay strong," he whispered. "I'll be back."

He stepped into the hallway outside LaRosa's room and rubbed his eyes, trying to clear the cobwebs from his thoughts. The last thing he remembered was sitting beside LaRosa's bed, turning his choices, past and future, over in his mind—looking for some kind of sign. How long had he been asleep? Why hadn't the doctor returned to chase him off? Or maybe she had and, seeing him passed out, had chosen to leave him be. He shook his head and pushed through the double doors to the waiting room, pulling out his cell phone to check the time.

A quarter to midnight and one missed call.

He continued through the waiting room, past the desk with the blurry-eyed man in green scrubs who'd yelled at him for hitting the vending machine, out the doors Chen had taken when he walked away. The cold, damp night slapped him in the face, giving him a much-needed jolt that shook the sleep from his brain and brought his senses to full alert. He breathed deep, enjoying the sting in his lungs and the scent of wet grass. Then he lifted the phone again and tapped the icon that would bring up his voicemail.

"Williams, I . . ." Ty stumbled as Mira's voice drifted through the line. "I'm sorry about your partner."

He moved to a white bench at the edge of a small sitting area beside the hospital and collapsed onto the cold metal. Tipping his face up, he stared at the stars as Mira's words washed over him. Her apology. Her explanation. Her plea. He listened to the whole message, then replayed it twice more, and the whole time he watched the twinkle of the stars as they played hide-and-seek in the drifting clouds at the tail end of the evening's storm. When Mira's voice cut off for the third time he lowered the phone to his lap.

A rifter . . .

He closed his eyes, shutting out the bright pinpricks in the sky so there was only darkness and the spiraling of his thoughts.

He had three choices—back her up, shut her down, or pretend he never got her call.

He already knew he couldn't do the last. He'd been on the fence for too long already, and that indecision had caused nothing but trouble. It was time for him to make a choice. Evidence or intuition.

She could be lying about the whole "special rifter" thing. There's never been a case of a rifter surviving in a human host for more than three months . . . unless that host became a necromancer. He shuddered. There were only four documented necromancers in all the histories hidden in the Church's archives, and those were spaced hundreds of years apart. Having just put down a full-blown necromancer attack on Washington, the idea that not one but two more could be walking around was inconceivable.

But why would she make something like that up? What would she gain? And if she really is some new kind of rifter, did the friend who vouched for her know? Or is she lying to him, too?

He dialed the PTF switchboard and once again asked to be transferred to the Colorado office. When the call connected, he told the woman who answered, "I need to speak with Garrett."

"At this hour?"

"It's an emergency. Patch me through to his cell."

"One moment." After a brief pause, she came back on the line. "It seems Mr. Garrett is currently on a plane. Would you like to leave a message?"

Ty squeezed the phone until the plastic creaked and blew out a frustrated breath.

"Never mind." He ended the call.

So much for verifying the information.

Ty dropped his head into his hands. The edge of the cell phone dug against his forehead.

Mira had sounded sincere when she asked for his help. More than that, she'd sounded scared.

In case I fail . . .

She was asking him to take Decker down if she couldn't. But the only evidence he had that Decker was even a threat was her word . . . the word of a liar. She'd lied about who she was, what she was, what she'd done. How could he justify believing her now, even with every instinct he had telling him she was worth believing?

Just like when I led Jamal into that ambush.

He shook his head. He couldn't risk making that kind of mistake again. No matter what his instincts said, he had to look at the evidence. He had to use his head, and the facts said Mira was an illegal practitioner, a liar, and a murderer. He could worry about whatever secrets Decker might or might not be hiding later. Right now it was his duty to bring Mira in . . . before anyone else got hurt.

Opening his eyes, he looked at the glowing display on his phone. Ten minutes to midnight. Not enough time to organize an ambush. Maybe not even enough to intercept Mira before she met with Decker.

Taking one last deep breath of the revitalizing night air, Ty jumped to his feet and jogged for his truck, dialing Chen as he went. This time he'd play by the book. No more cowboy heroics, no more trusting his gut, no more blood on his hands. This time he'd make the right choice.

"What is it, Williams? I'm busy."

"I've got a lead on Fuentes."

There was a beat of silence, then, "What've you got?"

"She'll be at Decker's office building at midnight."

"Who's your source?"

Ty sucked his teeth, fighting against the sickening twist in his gut that said giving Mira up was the wrong thing. But his instincts had landed LaRosa in the hospital. His instincts were wrong—soured, as Chen put it.

"Fuentes called me. Said she was going after Decker."

Another moment of stunned silence stretched across the line. "Why would she call you?"

"She's maintaining her story that Decker is a threat, powerful and magical . . . that she's trying to keep the city safe."

Chen laughed. "That's what the PTF is for."

Ty pulled open the door to his truck and slid behind the wheel. "What's your call?"

"I've got units spread all over the city, trying to box her in. It'll take a minute to pull them back . . . and this might be a decoy so she can slip my net."

"I don't think so."

"Because your instincts are always so reliable." Chen sighed. "I'll scramble who I can and meet you in front of the office building in fifteen."

Ty tucked his phone in his pocket and checked the magazine in his Glock—the only weapon he was carrying since Chen commandeered all the tranquilizer guns for his blockade. Then he plugged his key in the ignition and headed for downtown. Chen's ETA put him five minutes past Mira's deadline, but Ty just might make it in time. The question was, what would he do when he got there?

Mira

THE PLAZA ACROSS from Decker's office building was deserted. The stalls were closed, the vendors snug in their homes for the night. An occasional car passed on the street, flashing its headlights over Mira's hiding place, but traffic was light. The snow from earlier clung to bushes and tree branches, but the concrete and bricks of the man-made structures had retained enough heat to melt it, coating the world in a dark, reflective sheen. Puddles collected in uneven patches along the sidewalk, and streams gurgled through the gutters.

Mira shivered. Even though the rain and snow had stopped, the damp seemed to seep through her, turning her skin clammy and cold. Her breath puffed in barely visible clouds.

<I don't see an ambush.>

It wouldn't be much of an ambush if we could see it.

Mira continued to scan the shadows from the narrow alley that fed into the empty plaza. Decker's invitation was most definitely a trap. But what kind? And then there was Detective Williams. She'd staked out the building well before the appointed hour but had yet to see any sign of the policeman. On the one hand, that might be a good thing, since there was a fifty-fifty chance he'd show up with the PTF, SWAT, or US Marshals to take her down before she reached Decker's office. But as midnight approached and the area remained clear, a sinking sense of isolation settled over Mira.

Williams not working actively against her was a good thing . . . but he'd apparently decided not to back her up. As she'd feared, her mistake with LaRosa had destroyed what little trust there was between them.

She blew a puff of breath into her chilly hands and looked up at the dark windows on the sixth floor of Decker's building.

I just hope that mistake doesn't cost Gemma her life.

<He could still come.> The demon's voice was quiet, subdued. She understood Mira's isolation better than anyone. After all, she'd caused it. Perhaps that's why she was so adamant that Mira try to connect with other humans.

Mira shook her head. *We're on our own. Now and always.*

Creeping along the storefronts, keeping to the shadows, she made her way to the edge of the plaza. Once she stepped into the street she'd be an easy target for any waiting sniper.

She took a deep breath and moved away from the wall. The yellow glow of the iron, Victorian-era street lamps that dotted the plaza spilled over her, stripping her cover.

No one shot her with a tranquilizer dart. No swarm of armored men rushed out of hiding to tackle her.

So far, so good.

She waited for a truck to pass, splashing slush over the sidewalk when it hit a puddle. When the taillights vanished at the next intersection, she crossed the road and approached the front of Decker's office building. The glass doors of the main entrance were unlocked.

Odd for the middle of the night.

<Except we're expected.>

But Decker doesn't control the whole building. His business only fills one floor, and the security for the lobby was separate. Speaking of which . . . do you see any guards?

Mira crossed the empty lobby and peeked behind the security desk. A heavy-set man with a bushy beard was lying on the polished floor. His dark-blue uniform and the patch on his shoulder marked him as the security guard on duty. There was no blood, and no obvious injury.

Mira glanced at the computer monitors on the desk. They were all blank. The building's security cameras had been turned off.

Decker must have taken out the guard and security system to hide our meeting.

<Or he's setting you up again. Remember his wife?>

She shuddered. "Except this time it's *me* who tipped off the cops. Let's just hurry and get this over with."

Bypassing the elevator, Mira opened the door to the stairwell and began to climb. She eased open the door on the sixth-floor landing and scanned the waiting room where she'd scrambled that receptionist's brain when she first came looking for Decker . . . when she first met Gemma.

I wish I'd listened to you and just charged in, magic primed, that first day. This would all be over. Gemma would be safe. LaRosa wouldn't be in the hospital.

<Remember that the next time you think we should play it safe.>

She crossed quickly to the door to the back offices. Her sneakers brushed soundlessly down the hall. The big, glass meeting rooms were empty, illuminated only by a handful of emergency lights that broke the darkness like dim stars set in the ceiling.

The small waiting area in front of Decker's office was empty. A thin bar of light spilled under the door to the inner office, reflecting off the corner of Gemma's desk and the glass bowl of her saltwater taffies.

Mira tensed her jaw and slipped inside. She wrapped her fingers around the handle to the last barrier between her and Decker.

You ready?

<Always.>

Gathering her magic, she yanked the door open and burst into the back office.

Chapter 33

Mira

MIRA BLINKED IN the bright light of the back office. Shelves lined one wall. A liquor cabinet rested against the other. A large rectangle of plush, gray carpet covered the space in front of the polished oak desk that dominated the room. Behind the desk was a swiveling, wingback chair, turned to hide its occupant. Beyond the desk, a wall of plate-glass windows looked out over the glowing lights of the city, but the darkness beyond was overlaid with a reflection of Decker's office—and the face Mira found in that mirrored surface did not belong to Decker.

"I'm glad you decided to come." The chair turned, and Gemma Murphy stood. "After that debacle at the banquet, I thought you might have lost your nerve. Tell me, how is Detective LaRosa faring?"

Mira stared at Gemma, open-mouthed, magic forgotten. Her anger and conviction had been replaced by confusion the second she saw Gemma's face. "But . . . what . . . how . . .?"

Gemma stepped around the desk, slowly so as not to seem threatening. Her green gaze stayed steady on Mira. A sad smile played on her mouth.

"You're not dead," Mira finally managed.

"Very astute."

"Or kidnapped."

Gemma nodded.

<Holy shiznit . . . *she's* the demon.>

"You're—"

"A friend. At least I'd like to be." Gemma completed her trip around the desk and leaned back so her butt and hands rested against the front edge, as if to say, *See, there's no threat here. We're just two women talking.* "I'm sorry I had to lie to you, but with a secret like mine . . . well, I'm sure you can understand."

Mira shook her head slowly from side to side, sorting her thoughts, trying to arrange them in some kind of order. She stared at the woman before her—barely into her twenties; petite; glossy, red-blond hair; bright, engaging eyes; a cream-colored blouse with a pale-green camisole peeking from the unbuttoned collar; loose black slacks; polished boots with just a bit of heel. Gemma looked exactly like the young professional she'd pretended to be.

How did you not notice?

The demon remained silent.

Can you sense the demon inside her now?

<No,> came the quiet response. <If she really is a sovereign, she's found a way to mask even the shadow of a tether that I found in Nowak . . . that I'm sure she can see in us.>

So she knew from the beginning what we were.

"What about Decker?" she asked. "He froze time at the banquet."

Gemma tipped her head to one side. "Technically I did that."

"But you weren't . . ." She trailed off as she realized her mistake. They'd never actually sensed a demon within Decker. They'd just assumed. And a sovereign who could alter time and hide its presence would have no difficulty manipulating the scene from the shadows.

"Decker is a useful thrall, and I occasionally speak with his voice . . . but he's not a practitioner. If I were to inhabit him for any length of time, he'd ignite like a match before the union was complete." She traced one hand over the curves of her body. "Think of this form as a marionette, handcrafted and well maintained. Decker is a finger puppet I sometimes use to deal with the mortal riffraff who might not take a woman seriously." One corner of her mouth lifted, and she peered at Mira from beneath the curtain of her eyelashes. "He also makes a tempting target for anyone poking around where they're not wanted."

Heat rose to Mira's cheeks as she imagined Gemma watching her chase after Decker, laughing inside as Mira gobbled up every crumb she dropped in her path. Mira had gone fishing for minnows and ended up swimming with a shark. Now she was frantically treading water with no land in sight.

"Why the act?" Mira's voice was barely more than a whisper, a flat gray sound that fell from her lips without the energy to carry. "That night on the harbor, you . . ." She laughed at her own stupidity. "Of course. You were gauging my strength, trying to decide if you could control me like you had Nowak. Especially since Nowak was gone." She shook her head. "When you figured out I wasn't a pushover, you set me up at Decker's to get me out of the way. A magic-draining trap and one phone call, and your problem was taken care of."

"You're not wrong," Gemma said. "But you're not quite right either. I wasn't pretending when I invited you to the harbor. Remember how we talked about traveling from place to place to complete our work, and how it was lonely? That was all true." She raised one hand and brushed a strand of hair that had fallen loose back behind her ear. "Yes, I knew what you were. And yes, I knew what you'd done to Nowak. But I wasn't angry or afraid . . . I was excited." She pushed away from the desk so she was standing straight. "I know you have some inkling of what it feels like to be the only one of your kind—always forced to hide and lie among people who'd just as soon kill you as look at you if they knew what you were."

The echoed pain of memories stabbed through Mira. Running from the flames of her home in Detroit, not yet sure what had happened but positive she'd be punished if the authorities found her. Hiding on the streets as the Faerie Wars heated up and humans began hunting magic-users like dangerous animals, fitting them with muzzles and collars, or worse. Keeping her distance from her family for fear that the only people who still loved her would turn their backs like the rest of the world and leave her truly, completely alone. Avoiding relationships that lasted longer than a single transaction while at the same time searching desperately for a sense of connection. Wishing there was even a single other person like her in all the wide world.

Gemma sighed and looked at the floor. "The honest truth is, I invited you out that night because I was lonely." She brought her gaze up to meet Mira's. "I really did want you to be my friend . . . and I still do."

"You've got a funny way of showing it." Mira balled her fists. "Do you have any idea what wearing one of those PTF collars is like? How . . . naked it made me feel?"

She shrugged. "Honestly, I hadn't expected you to go down so easily to a couple of humans, but after you made it clear you were going after Decker, I used that as a way to keep you occupied while I wrapped up my business."

"You were in Decker's house that night. It was you I saw him arguing with through the window."

"A puppet show put on for your benefit. I was actually hiding in the same tree as you, just a little higher up, waiting for you to arrive."

Mira shivered. The demon she was hunting had been within striking distance, and she hadn't even known she was there.

"But the duffel bag—"

"Supplies."

"And Decker's wife? Why kill her? And why pretend to be missing?"

"I told you. I had business to complete, and I couldn't very well do that with you hanging about." She made an off-hand gesture. "Between the evidence that you'd killed Decker's wife—a horrible shrew of a woman, by the way—and suspicions that you'd murdered me, I figured the attention you were getting from the police would keep you well out of my way." She placed one hand on her hip and gave Mira a steady stare. "I half expected you to skip town once I turned up the heat, but you're damn stubborn."

<She has no idea.>

"So why'd you change your mind? Why invite me here, confess who you are?"

Gemma pursed her lips. "I thought you were a bit sharper than this."

<She said she needed us out of the way while she finished her work . . .> The demon's words trailed into silence, but Mira's mind picked up the thread.

"Whatever you were planning . . . you're done."

Gemma leaned back against the desk again. "Not quite, but there's really nothing you can do to upset my plans at this point."

"Don't be so sure." Mira started drawing in the magic she'd let dissipate in her surprise at seeing Gemma alive and well.

Gemma frowned. "I don't want to fight you."

"I don't blame you."

The frown deepened. "You're no match for me, and I'd hate to see you permanently damaged."

"Your concern is touching." Mira flicked her wrist and sent a blazing ball of liquid fire toward Gemma, who batted it aside as though swatting a fly. The bluish-white flames snuffed out in a puff of smoke.

"I want you to join me," Gemma said, as though Mira hadn't just tried to incinerate her.

Mira took a step back.

"We both know how rare we are." Gemma gestured to Mira, then indicated her own body. "A fully integrated human-demon rifter? It's unheard of. It's impossible. Yet here we are." She spread her arms wide. "Freaks of nature, alone in all the universe."

<Don't let her get inside your head. She's just trying to throw you off balance.>

She's a sovereign. She doesn't need us off balance to wipe the floor with us.

<Then she's doing it for her own perverse pleasure. The point is, you shouldn't listen to anything she has to say.>

Except that she's right. Mira countered. *In all the years we've searched, she's the first evidence we've ever seen of another melding like ours.*

"Your demon doesn't like me, does she?"

Mira refocused to find Gemma smiling at her. Had she been responding out loud? Sometimes she didn't even notice when she did that.

"Not surprising," Gemma continued. "Do you know how demons grow stronger?"

Mira met her gaze. "By absorbing others of your kind."

She nodded. "We're cannibals, like fish in the sea, living and feeding in a closed ecosystem." She stepped away from the desk and began pacing the room.

Mira turned to keep her in sight.

"In the Rift we're endlessly torn apart and reformed by the chaotic currents of energy—it creates us, sustains us, and destroys us. But a few of us are strong enough to hold that energy in focus. Not perfectly of course. Reigning in the chaos of the Rift is like trying to trap the ocean in your hands, and many a fool has died trying. But a sip here? A sip there? If you're patient and not too greedy, you can learn to navigate the currents . . . feel the rhythm of the tides. You can collect more than is stolen from you." She reached the bookcase and turned back toward Mira. "As your companion well knows."

Mira had never heard the chaos of the Rift described quite like that before, but she was aware her demon sustained itself and grew stronger by feeding off the energy of other demons. That was the main reason they hunted rifters. Any demon strong enough to manifest in the physical realm would offer more than a light snack. The more powerful the rifter, the more satisfying the meal. But they'd bitten off more than they could chew this time around.

"How far back can your demon remember?" Gemma asked.

"None of your business."

"I can remember a time, thousands of years ago, when humans were little more than a curiosity scattered in tiny pockets across the world. That's how long I've been 'sipping' at the Rift." She stopped in front of the desk and crossed her arms. "But it seems you've found a faster way. I admit it never occurred to me to cross to this realm and feed as the vampires do."

Mira stiffened at the comparison. She wanted to shout that she didn't drain the innocent, but the memory of the cook behind the hotel restaurant was too fresh in her mind.

"But that's beside the point." Gemma waved the comment away.

"What's important is that you and I are both strong enough to exist in and interact with the physical realm over an extended period. Long enough to make plans and see them through."

"Which is what you've been doing here in Baltimore."

"And elsewhere, but yes." She tipped her chin up and sighed wistfully. "It's been a long and lonely road, with no one to share the burden or the triumphs."

"You had Nowak," Mira pointed out.

Gemma rolled her eyes. "A nattering imbecile with a mayfly existence. He was potent enough to last a single job, but the effort of keeping him in line almost outweighed his usefulness. And the standard riffraff I can drag onto this plane is even worse. But you . . ." She took a step forward. "You're different. You could be a *true* partner."

Mira frowned. "What is it exactly that you're doing here?"

A wide smile broke across Gemma's lips. "Acceptance. Inclusion. Unification."

Mira stared at her. "I don't get it."

"Do you know what runs under the construction site?" She pointed at her feet. "What's beneath us right now?"

Mira shrugged. "Power lines, pipes, sewers—"

"Ley lines."

Mira blinked, then laughed. "You've got to be shitting me. You actually believe magical conduits of power run through the earth?"

Gemma scowled. "I told you a person could learn to read the currents of the Rift given enough time and practice. Well I've had centuries . . . millennia."

Mira's smile melted. "You're serious." She shook her head. "So what, you're tapping into the ley line to boost your power? To get even stronger?"

"Don't think so small." She crossed the hardwood floor and stepped onto the plush carpet where Mira was standing so they were within touching distance. "What is it that every being craves . . . even demons?"

"I don't know. A home? A family?"

<Contact.>

"Demons are the only species in the universe that's been denied the ability to form basic connections. We're shadows and phantoms, trapped beyond touch—a collection of thoughts and feelings held together by sheer will and under constant threat of being ripped apart and scattered. It's exhausting. Meanwhile we watch humans use and abuse their bodies, completely unaware of the gift they've been given."

"But what do ley lines have to do with making physical connections?"

"Demons can interact on the physical plane by inhabiting a human body—and there are billions of bodies over here, more than enough for all the demons in the Rift—but that connection isn't stable. Most don't even have the strength to cross on their own, and those who do will burn out within months, taking their hosts with them. The two planes are just too different to reconcile, except in very rare cases like ours." She reached out and took Mira's hand.

The demon inside tried to pull back, but Mira refused to hand over control.

We need to know exactly what she's planning.

<No we don't. Whatever it is, it's nothing good. That's enough.>

She hasn't made any move to hurt us. We can hear her out.

<She was just getting close enough to drain us!>

Did you see her deflect that fireball? She could have overpowered us the second we walked in the door if that's all she wanted. Mira clenched her jaw. *I think . . . she really is lonely.*

<I don't doubt that she is. That doesn't mean—>

You're the one who's always telling me I should try to connect with people.

<*People* people. Not more demons and rifters.>

"You don't have to be afraid," Gemma said, drawing Mira's focus back to their clasped hands. "I have no intention of destroying you." She squeezed her fingers. "That would be like burning the Mona Lisa."

"You said the two planes were too different to reconcile, but that's exactly what you're trying to do, isn't it? You want to make it so more rifters can balance like us . . . so you're not alone."

Gemma tapped a finger against the tip of her nose.

"But how?"

She released Mira's hand and held her palms facing each other a few inches apart. "By bringing the planes closer together." She shrank the space between her hands until they were nearly touching.

"That would require a monumental amount of magic." Mira stiffened. "That's how you're using the ley lines . . . focusing and amplifying your magic to cast a spell on a planetary scale."

Gemma smiled and nodded like a proud teacher. "I've been setting anchors at strategic points around the world for"—she puffed her cheeks—"well, a long time now. And I'm close to done. A few more and I'll be able to drag the Rift and physical plane into alignment." Her eyes glinted with longing. "I'm going to create a world where humans and demons can live together."

<That . . . actually doesn't sound so bad.>

"You're crazy."

<Hey, you're the one who wanted to hear her out. And you're always whining that no one understands you. Gemma's plan would fix that.>

"I'm ambitious," Gemma replied, mistaking Mira's outburst. "And you should be, too. Together we could usher in a new era. One where everyone can be *exactly* who they are."

"That kind of shift . . . even if you succeed, there's no telling what damage it would cause. You're talking about changing the very fabric of reality. Who's to say humans could even survive that kind of energy infusion? Or the demons, for that matter?"

"We'd adapt, evolve." Gemma waved the concern away. "If the fae could break free of the Rift, we can too. And humans are only using a tiny percentage of their potential. This would force them to expand. We'd be doing them a favor."

"And how exactly are you setting these anchors? That level of magic would require an insane amount of energy—more than even a sovereign could channel."

"More than I can manifest on my own, but I don't need to produce the energy . . . I just need to focus it."

Mira raised an eyebrow, struggling to fit the pieces together. The construction site was on a ley line, so she would have access to a higher-than-usual amount of ambient energy, but why take the time to develop it? And why change the construction plans from condos to low-rent apartments?

<More people.> The words were tinged with horror and respect. <Hundreds of desperate people with nowhere else to turn, grateful for a roof over their heads. And each one is a battery just waiting to be drained.>

Mira's gut clenched, and a cold hollowness washed over her as the demon's words sank in. She met Gemma's gaze and saw the truth in her eyes. "You're going to kill them all."

"Sacrifices must be made." Gemma spread her hands. "The bigger the sacrifice, the stronger the anchor. Decker's there right now, finishing the preparations."

Mira shook her head, wishing she could deny what she was hearing. "If you want humans to coexist with demons, murdering hundreds of innocents is hardly the way to convince them."

"It's the *only* way to convince them."

"Inviting the chaos of the Rift into the mortal realm will only divide us more."

"And what's your solution? Asking nice? Humans can't even accept other humans who do magic, and look at what they've done to the fae. Do you really think they'd ever be able to accept beings as different as demons? But once the planes are merged, they won't have any choice."

"Some humans are trying to change things . . . to make Earth more inclusive."

"Convincing people with hippie logic is like trying to patch the Titanic with chewing gum. They'll never let us join them on their pedestals. The only way we'll ever be on equal footing is to bring them down to our level."

"And what happens to the humans once they're down in the mud? Given an abundance of accessible bodies, do you really think the demons will share control with the original owners?"

"Not many, I'll grant you, but the humans won't be helpless. Whoever possesses the stronger psyche will control the body." She shrugged. "Survival of the fittest."

We can't let her do this.

There was a moment of silence in Mira's head as she waited for the demon's response.

Agreed? Tension sang through Mira's muscles. She couldn't fight Gemma without her demon's support. Hell, she probably couldn't win even with it.

<Yeah, okay. I like this world well enough the way it is, even if it is a bit lonely sometimes.>

Mira exhaled. Then she once again started drawing energy.

Gemma was looking out the window, surveying the lights of the sleeping city. "You and I can set the foundation . . . and the ground rules. We can decide how the new world works." She turned to Mira, a wide grin on her face. "Think of it, Mira. Join me and we can be gods."

"There's only one God." Mira unleashed the full force of her combined magic at the rifter before her—the only being she'd ever met who was like her. Maybe the only one there ever would be.

Gemma stumbled, collided with the desk, and tumbled over it. Waves of energy rippled across the air in front of her and ricocheted around the room. She dropped from sight for a moment as she rolled off the back of the desk, toppling the wingback chair.

Mira cut off the flow of her attack and took a cautious step forward.

She peeked over the edge of the desk, ready to unleash her magic a second time.

Heat and pain slammed into her chest. She flew across the room and collided with the far wall. Framed certificates and a landscape painting crashed to the floor, but Mira stayed in place, suspended by the force pressing against her body. The drywall around her cracked. Fissures shot out around her in fractal patterns.

She opened her mouth to scream, but there was no air in her lungs and the crushing pressure stopped her from finding more.

Then the most disturbing sensation spread over her—a numbing cold that started in her fingers and toes and seeped toward her center. She flopped and thrashed, but couldn't break free of the weight pinning her to the wall. Every thread of magic she managed to call was snatched away by the leaching cold.

Gemma was draining Mira, just as Mira had done to so many other rifters, despite the women being on opposite sides of the room. Such a thing shouldn't have been possible—it certainly wasn't for Mira—but there was no denying what was happening. All the energy and power Mira's demon had gathered would become a part of Gemma. She would be that much stronger, and Mira would be a mummified corpse like the one she'd left at the construction site.

The demon flailed and raged within her but had no better luck focusing her magic than Mira had. An ameeri was no match for a sovereign in a straight battle of strength. Before the drain started, maybe— with the element of surprise and a lot of luck—but now? Every drop of energy was being ripped away before Mira had a chance to shape it. Every spell she channeled became fuel for Gemma.

"I really didn't want it to come to this," Gemma said. Tension filled her face as she concentrated on her spell. Strings of black, white, and gold drifted between them, lifting from Mira's body and vanishing into Gemma's.

The numbness passed Mira's wrists and ankles. Only a few seconds had passed since this torture began, but every shred of energy torn from her body felt like years of lost life. Tears leaked from her eyes and trickled down her cheeks. She was going to die here, helpless and alone. What would her *abuela* think? Would she ever find out, or would she imagine Mira was still out there somewhere and just didn't want anything to do with her? Would anyone else even notice she was gone?

The demon continued to strain against the pull of Gemma's energy drain, but Mira relaxed. She was tired of fighting.

Chapter 34

Ty

A LIGHT SHONE from the sixth floor of Decker's office building, a beacon in the night. Ty glanced through his truck's windshield at the empty street, then at the plaza on the far side. The only movement was a sheet of newspaper as it tumbled end over end across the sidewalk. He pulled out his cell phone and checked the time. Two minutes past midnight. Had Mira already gone in? He scanned the area again. No sign of Chen or the backup he'd promised. Chewing his lower lip, he craned his neck to look once more at the glowing light so far above him. Then he cut the truck's engine and stepped out.

Soft lights were on in the ground-floor lobby, but the security desk was empty.

Anxiety twisted in Ty's gut as his instincts screamed and his senses went on high alert.

Maybe they're taking a bathroom break.

He looked up and down the street again. Still no sign of Chen.

Setting one hand over his holstered gun, he crossed the street to get a closer look. Other than the missing security guard, nothing seemed out of place. He walked along the bank of windows, peering in. Chairs, tables, magazines. . . . A dark shape caught his gaze—a boot sticking out behind the security desk.

"Shit." Casting one last glance at the empty street, Ty yanked on the front door. He stumbled slightly when it opened without resistance but pushed the thought aside as he raced behind the desk.

A security guard was sprawled on the floor, hidden almost entirely from view by his station.

He knelt and checked for a pulse. The man was alive but pale and drawn . . . like Billy and Collins after Mira took them out in the back of the transport.

Pulling the phone from his pocket, Ty called dispatch. "This is Detective Williams, reporting an active threat situation at the Bergquist building on Lexington. Security officer down in the main lobby. Requesting ambulance."

Ty looked at the elevator he'd ridden in with Decker earlier that day, then out the lobby windows. Chen was on his way with whatever backup he'd been able to scramble. They'd be there any minute, along with the EMTs. He glanced at the man beside his knee. He should wait with the injured man, keep the lobby secure. Chen had lead on the investigation now—he'd have troops and tranquilizer guns. He looked again at the elevator. But Mira might be done and gone by the time the cavalry arrived. Or if she was telling the truth about Decker, she might be a corpse. Either way the next few minutes might make the difference between an arrest and a coroner's report.

He scraped his palm over his scalp, trying to push away the voice screaming in his head that he needed to get his ass upstairs and see this thing through.

Don't be a cowboy.

He looked out the big, glass windows again, then back to the elevators. The urge to act growing until it was a flame in his nerves.

"Screw it," he growled. Bypassing the elevator, he pulled the gun from his holster and headed up the stairs.

The sixth-floor reception area was dark, as were the offices and meeting rooms beyond, but a line of light shone beneath the door of the back office.

Ty paused in front of the closed door. Voices filtered through from the other side, but—he frowned and leaned closer, pressing his cheek to the smooth wood—neither voice was deep enough to be Decker's.

Pointing his gun toward the ceiling, he reached out with his left hand and twisted the knob by the most minuscule of increments until the latch pulled back. Then he eased it open a crack, moving slower than a glacier etching out a canyon.

A seam of light outlined the door.

". . . really think the demons will share control with the original owners?" With the voices no longer muffled, Ty could make Mira out as one of the speakers.

"Not many, I'll grant you." Ty couldn't place the second voice. It was high and nasal—definitely not Decker's. "But the humans won't be helpless. Whoever possesses the stronger psyche will control the body. Survival of the fittest."

Were they talking about creating *more* rifters? Ty's blood ran cold as the implications of the eavesdropped conversation settled over him.

He pushed forward slightly, widening the gap until a sliver of the office beyond came into view. Floor-to-ceiling windows, a wide desk, a woman's back. Too tall to be Mira, though not by much. Long, reddish hair swung in a ponytail down her back.

Ty frowned, recalling a recent photo he'd seen. Gemma Murphy, Decker's missing assistant, had hair like that.

"You and I can set the foundation . . . and the ground rules. We can decide how the new world works."

Were Mira and Decker's assistant planning to bring about some kind of demon apocalypse? But why would Mira have called him if she and Murphy were working together? And where was Decker? He was supposed to be there.

Ty's muscles were singing with the need to act and the strain of resisting.

The woman Ty had pegged as Gemma Murphy turned to face the center of the office, where he assumed Mira was blocked from sight by the still mostly closed door. A cold smile stretched her lips. "Think of it, Mira. Join me and we can be gods."

An offer? An ultimatum? If Gemma was trying to convince Mira to join her, that meant Mira had been telling the truth about her purpose in the city. Ty's instincts sang a chorus of "I told you so." He'd been right to believe her against all logic. Then he remembered the call he'd placed to Chen and his short-lived sense of vindication withered.

"There's only one God." Mira's response rang through the silent night. Then the room on the other side of the door erupted in flames.

Mira

MIRA'S EYELIDS drooped. She could no longer feel her arms or legs. Her skin felt tight, stretched thin over her bones. The demon continued to struggle, but with the pitiful hopelessness of a fish on the shore as its gills dried out.

Bam. Bam. Bam. Thud. Then the tinkle of shattered glass.

Mira dropped like a rag doll. She tried to catch herself, but her legs couldn't hold her, her arms didn't respond. Her cheek hit the polished wood hard enough to bruise.

What . . .?

<Wake up!>

I'm not asleep. But a groggy film clung to her thoughts.

"Mira?"

Hands gripped her shoulders and rolled her onto her back.

<He came.> The excitement in the demon's voice ricocheted around Mira's skull like a pinball. <He actually came.>

Mira blinked to clear her murky vision and bring the dark figure above her into focus. Detective Williams's expression was strained. The deep pools of his eyes bore into her. His full lips were forming words.

"Can you move?"

She didn't want to move. She was tired, and having his arms wrapped around her, supporting her, felt so good. But . . . Gemma. She tensed and tried to sit up. "Where—"

"She's gone." He looked away, at something over Mira's head. A muscle twitched in the side of his neck. "I shot her."

Mira shook her head, struggling against him now, pulling away so she could twist enough to see the space where Gemma had been standing. A cold gust of frost-kissed air whistled through the missing windowpane.

"She went out the window," Williams confirmed. He pushed to his feet. "My backup is on the way." He glanced down at her, clearly torn. "You should be gone before they get here."

Mira wiggled her fingers and toes. Now that Gemma wasn't draining her energy, the feeling was coming back on an unpleasant wave of pins and needles.

"We need to check." Her voice was ragged. She cleared her throat to smooth it.

Williams offered her a hand.

She stared at his pale-brown palm for a moment, then reached out and slipped her hand in his. His warm, soft fingers closed, and he pulled her to her feet. She wobbled, and he set a hand against her hip to steady her. Heat crept up her neck and into her face.

She stepped back, took a deep breath, and pulled her hand out of his tender grip. "Thanks for coming." She couldn't look at him when she spoke. The pull of his gaze was too distracting. "I wasn't sure you would."

"Don't thank me yet, I . . ." He trailed off as Mira moved toward the shattered window. "She fell from the sixth story with four bullets in her chest. She's—"

"Gone."

"Exactly."

"No." Mira turned back from the window, pinning Williams with a glare. "The body. It's gone."

"What?" He trotted to the gaping hole and looked down at the stretch of sidewalk below, illuminated by streetlamps. A dark smear marked the concrete . . . but there was no body. "That's impossible."

"Not for a sovereign-level demon." Mira raked her hands through her hair. "I underestimated her."

He set his hand on her shoulder. "We all did."

"But *I* should have known better. I know what it's like to be underestimated—how people like us use it to give us an edge—and I fell for her 'young and innocent' act just like all the idiots I ever played to get close to."

Williams stiffened.

She frowned, wondering why his mood had suddenly changed.

<Jeez, you're dense.>

What are you—Then it struck her, the way her words must have sounded. "I didn't mean . . . what happened at the bar wasn't . . ."

"It's fine." His voice was gruff and tight. She'd definitely stepped in it.

Sighing, she looked at the blood streaks on the sidewalk below. "It must have taken a massive amount of energy to heal that much damage, so there's some good news. She'll be underpowered for a while."

Speaking of . . . how's our reserve looking?

<Bare banks in a summer drought, but the reservoir's not empty yet.>

She'll probably try to finish her plan before I get the chance to interfere again.

<So she's headed for the construction site.>

To kill all those people . . .

<And she won't be alone.>

Mira cast a sideways glance at Williams, studying his profile. *Neither will we.*

"I know where she's going. If she's allowed to complete her plan, a lot of innocent people will die." She set her hand on the taut muscle of Detective Williams's bicep, drawing his heady gaze. She swallowed past the sudden lump that lodged in her throat. "Will you come with me?"

His lips pursed, drawing her attention to the soft, puckered skin. "I only overheard part of the conversation, but . . . is she really trying to make more rifters?"

Mira snapped her gaze back to his eyes. "Worse. She's trying to force demons and humans to inhabit the same space—the same plane of existence."

Confusion danced in his eyes.

"The Rift will overlap the Earth." She held up both hands, then laced her fingers together. "*Everyone* will become rifters."

Sirens echoed through the night, rising in pitch as they drew closer.

"The ambulance I called for the security guard," Williams muttered. His gaze never wavered from Mira's face. "The police and Agent Chen will be right behind them."

"Then you'd better choose quickly," she said. "Do you trust me, or not?"

He continued to stare at her, searching. His lips parted. "I do."

The words were a whisper, but they rocked Mira back on her heels. She exhaled the breath she hadn't realized she'd been holding. "Then let's go."

She and Williams raced down the stairwell, skipping steps and careening around landings until they burst into the lobby. Williams thrust out an arm, pushing Mira back into the shadow of a pillar. Blue and red lights flashed through the large front windows. The security guard was still on the floor behind the desk.

"I didn't do that," Mira blurted.

He glanced at her, searched her face, and nodded.

A knot loosened in Mira's chest. She wasn't sure why it mattered to her that Detective Williams knew she hadn't attacked the guard—it wasn't like she wasn't guilty of harming other people—but having him believe her made it easier to breathe.

<It's because you like him.>

She shoved the demon's teasing voice to the back of her mind. *I need him.*

<Yeah you do.>

To take Gemma down, she clarified.

"Wait here." Williams was peeking out from behind the pillar, his back to her. "I'll direct the EMTs to the guard. You sneak out while they're distracted and wait in my truck across the street. I'll be there in a minute." He handed her a set of keys and, without waiting for a response, stepped out from behind the pillar and jogged to the front door.

Mira stared at the keys in her hand and worked her mouth.

<Very take charge. I dig it.>

I don't.

<You're just used to being the bossy one.>

Williams called the EMTs over and led them to the security guard. As soon as the medical team ducked behind the desk to examine their patient, Mira grabbed a handful of shadows for a quick coat of camouflage and slipped outside. She skirted the flashing lights of the ambulance, circled the silver truck across the street, and let herself in. A moment later Williams came out of the building, alone, and crossed the street.

He stepped up to the driver's side door, but Mira had locked it behind her. She turned the key in the ignition and tipped her head to indicate the passenger seat.

Williams stared at her through the window for a moment, muttered something she couldn't quite make out, and rounded the truck.

<That was childish.>

I thought you liked it when people took charge, she teased.

Williams snapped his seat belt and glared at her. "I don't usually let strangers drive my truck."

"Then you shouldn't give them your keys." Mira smiled and stepped on the gas.

Chapter 35

Ty

TY'S TRUCK TIRES skidded as Mira slammed the brakes in front of the homeless shelter Decker had just received an award for erecting—the shelter where he'd managed to gather hundreds of people that were about to become a demon's meal. She jumped out of the driver's side, leaving the key in the ignition and the door open.

Ty hung up on dispatch and stuffed his phone in his pocket, having called in a bomb threat on the homeless shelter as the fastest way to ensure an evacuation. They'd decided on the way over that while quietly removing the threat was the best-case scenario, they couldn't risk the spell being completed and catching the targeted residents unaware. He snatched the keys from the ignition and joined Mira on the damp sidewalk in front of the shelter and four high-rise apartments, the nearest one still under construction.

"That's a lot of ground to cover." He rubbed his hands over his sleeves as goosebumps broke out over his skin. "Murphy and Decker could be anywhere."

"No." Mira's gaze had taken on a faraway quality, and maybe it was just the yellow glow of the street lamp they stood under, but her eyes seemed more gold than brown. "Can't you feel it? Like an electric charge in the air." She turned slightly, shifting her focus to the northeast. "She's channeling magic . . . charging the spell." Her voice wavered, and Ty wondered if she was afraid. She'd already been beaten once.

Ty's own nerves were a bundle of jagged knives. This rifter had gone out a sixth-story window with four slugs in her chest and walked away. Any mortal in their right mind would be terrified to face her.

"I'll handle Gemma. You start the evacuation." She took a step, but Ty grabbed her arm, his hand fully encircling her slender wrist. She jerked to a stop and glanced at the point of contact.

He loosened his grip but refused to let go. "I should go with you."

"We agreed the evacuation was top priority."

He nodded but still didn't let go. "The police are on their way. Murphy wiped the floor with you last time. You need backup."

"Thanks for the vote of confidence." Annoyance simmered in Mira's gaze. She yanked her arm free. "I know I might not be able to handle Gemma. That's why you have to get these people moving." She met his gaze. "I can't be in two places at once. I need you to handle the evacuation so I can focus on the rifter. Even if I can't beat her, I can buy time. As long as one of us is successful, tonight will be a win."

"But . . ." Her argument was sound, so why was he wasting time? All he knew was he didn't want to let her walk away and risk never seeing her again.

She turned and bolted, charging over the muddy ground toward a small park at the north end of the lot.

Shoving aside the complicated emotions watching her leave stirred up, Ty headed for the homeless shelter. The front door was unlocked. A woman with steel-gray hair, thick glasses, and freckled skin that sagged from her cheeks and jaw sat behind a curved oak counter. She tugged her maroon sweater tighter, hugging her thin frame as a gust of frigid air blew in with Ty. She gave him a once-over and frowned.

"You looking for a bed?"

He flashed her his badge. "There's a bomb in this building. We need to get everyone out." He glanced around and found a small red box on the side wall next to a door marked *Dormitories.* He crossed the room in three strides while the woman behind the desk stood gaping like a fish, eyes as round as her glasses, and pulled the fire alarm.

Lights flashed near the ceiling. A siren blared.

That should at least wake them up.

He didn't waste any more time with the shocked woman behind the counter. There were three more buildings to alert.

He burst back through the front door and into the night. When he rounded the side of the shelter, he caught a movement out of the corner of his eye.

He skidded to a stop and squinted into the dim space between the buildings. A man with a tall, slim build crossed from the back of the shelter to the unfinished apartment. He was moving quickly but not like he was panicked. There was a large duffel bag draped over his shoulder.

No way.

Ty watched Reed Decker slip into the back of the unfinished building.

If Decker wasn't done placing the bombs, or if Ty could stop him from setting them off. . . . Maybe stopping Gemma Murphy wasn't the only way to prevent this tragedy from happening.

He glanced at the shadowy silhouettes of the occupied apartment buildings. Had Decker already set devices in them? Should he ignore Decker and try to alert the residents?

But already he could see lights coming on in some of the windows as people looked out to see what the noise at the homeless shelter was about, and the police and firemen were on their way. The distant wail of sirens was growing closer as emergency vehicles responded to his call.

Praying that the natural curiosity of people to know what was causing a scene would be enough to spread word of the threat, Ty raced to the front of the unfinished apartment where Rodney Temple had been found dead only days before. He unholstered his gun, tore off the yellow police tape, and slipped inside.

Sawdust, spackle, tool oil . . . and under it all the clinging scent of decay. Temple's body had long since been removed and the crime scene scrubbers had come through, but still the smell of death remained, sharp and rank. Or maybe that was just his imagination.

Shafts of light from the nearest street lamps cut across the floor through empty window frames, painting the wood-framed rooms in orange-tinted shadows. Sections of hung drywall reflected as pale panels in the darkness. The broken sections had been cleared away but not yet repaired.

Ty crept through the ground floor, pausing at each opening, leveling his gun at shadows as his heart raced and his mind found shapes in the darkness.

Floorboards creaked above.

He moved to the stairwell near the center of the building. A cement rectangle rose up beside the stairs—the shaft that would one day hold an elevator. The stairs were open, without rails or walls to block them in, probably to make moving equipment to the upper floors easier during construction. It also meant Ty had no cover as he poked his head above the second-story floor.

Like the first level of the building, the second was only partially complete. Electrical wires and water pipes were visible between patches of unfinished drywall. Less light made it inside at this height, so the shadows were deeper.

A scuff sounded to his left.

He eased the rest of the way onto the second floor and down a hallway toward the sound. Whispered voices drifted on the air—more than one. Did Gemma have other henchmen working with Decker?

A circle of dull-orange light flashed against a wall up ahead, then swung away. A pale glow continued to emanate from the doorway through which it had shone.

Pressing his back to the drywall, Ty took a deep breath and steadied both hands on his gun. He could hear someone moving just inside the door. Exhaling, he spun toward the opening, leveled his gun on the source of the light and shouted, "Baltimore PD!"

Three high-pitched shrieks filled the night. Something small and white streaked past Ty's ankle. A flashlight hit the floor and rolled, sending shadows dancing crazily across the walls. When the light stopped, Ty was staring into three wide-eyed faces, not one of which could have been more than twelve years old.

Ty raised his gun so it was no longer pointed at the two boys and girl huddled together on the floor in front of him.

The largest of the boys wiped his nose on his sleeve and stood up. Balling his fists at his sides, he stepped in front of the other two and glared at Ty. "We ain't done nothin' wrong."

"Shh." Ty pressed a finger to his lips. He looked back up the hall the way he'd come. "Have you seen anyone else in this building?"

"Just the kitty," said the little girl, her words hitching as she struggled to stop crying. "But you scared her."

"Shut up, Meg." The second boy gave her a withering look, though his voice shook slightly too. "He doesn't care about a cat."

"You need to get out of here." Ty motioned for them to get up and move toward the stairs, but they all just sat or stood where they were. "Now!"

The kids startled, looked at each other, and the remaining two climbed to their feet.

"We didn't mean any harm," said the smaller boy. He had mousy brown hair and eyes that matched the girl's. "We were just exploring."

"Don't tell him nothing," snapped the older boy. He had lighter skin than the other two, and his hair was buzzed to near non-existence save a two-inch stripe down the center of his scalp.

"There's a dangerous man in this building," Ty whispered. The little girl shrank closer to the boy who was probably her brother, fresh tears brimming in her eyes. He didn't want to scare the children, but he needed them to be quiet, and most importantly he needed them to move. "I'm going to take you downstairs. Do you live in one of these apartment buildings?"

The siblings looked at each other. The older boy looked at his shoes, which were cracked and faded.

"You're staying at the shelter?" Ty amended.

The smaller boy nodded.

"The shelter's being evacuated. When you get outside, I want you to wait on the sidewalk by the road for your parents. Other police will be here soon. Ask them if you need help."

"Can't *you* take us to our parents?"

Ty stared at the little girl; she was maybe eight years old.

The older boy shook his head, looking disgusted. "We should never have let her tag along."

"She would have pitched a fit if we didn't, and then *none* of us would have gotten out."

"I wish we hadn't," the girl whimpered.

"Come on." Ty led the trio back down the hall toward the stairwell, gun once more swinging toward every shift in the shadows. The concrete column of the elevator shaft came into view, and Ty breathed a sigh of relief. Then he stepped around the corner and came face-to-face with Decker.

Mira

MIRA SLOWED AS she approached the bare trees that marked the edge of the community park to the northeast of Decker's development site. She'd followed the ribbons of energy that flowed into the doomed site like the currents of a river, fighting upstream back to the source, back to Gemma. The hairs all over her body were standing on end, as if lightning were about to strike.

<This is a massive spell.>

Let's just hope we reach Gemma before she's done casting it. Who knows, maybe she's channeling enough that interrupting her will trigger a backlash.

<A backlash on this scale might level a city block and take us with her.>

Mira tightened her jaw and crept between the trees. *Still better odds than a fair fight against a sovereign.*

<Who said anything about fighting fair? She's not likely to abandon her plan after all this effort to set it up, and breaking off the spell mid-cast would be just that. So rather than disrupting her spell, if we go after her *while* she's casting . . .>

She won't have enough spare energy to defend herself. Mira smiled. *That just might work.*

Mira stopped at the edge of the park's open space, taking cover behind the trunk of a wide oak. Gemma stood in the middle of the clearing. To any normal human, she'd look like a young woman standing in a field looking up at the night sky, though closer inspection would reveal the dark stains on her clothes to be blood. Mira, however, could see the intricate patterns of the ritual spell Gemma had etched in magic over the ground. She wasn't standing at the center of a patch of grass, she was standing at the center of an energy focus. Magic swelled up from the ground, drawn from the ley line Gemma had tapped into. She then channeled that energy into fine strings and sent them out to connect to the matching energy sinks Mira had seen at the development site.

Any moment those rivers of energy would reverse, and the magic Gemma was channeling to create her spell would become a highway for the energy of hundreds of murdered souls that would then charge the ley line and provide the power Gemma needed to set her dimensional anchor.

"I've never seen someone channel that much energy," Mira whispered, staring at the spectacle. She shook her head, despair seeping through her chest. Even if everything worked out in her favor. . . . *The only way to truly stop her is to kill the demon.*

<And the only way to do that is to drain her.>

It's too much energy.

<Probably.> The demon and Mira were both silent for a moment, weighing their choices. <Do you want to leave?>

Yes. She closed her eyes for a second, then opened them. *But we can't.*

<Well . . . we *could.*>

Mira shook her head.

The equivalent of a sigh echoed through her thoughts. <Then let's go be heroes.>

I wish we could drain from a distance like Gemma did in the office.

<Yeah, that was crazy.>

Although . . . Mira looked at the threads of magic woven through the night around her. *We've never had access to a sustained spell like this. Do you think it's connected enough to—*

<I see where you're going.> The demon's excitement bubbled up in Mira. <Let's try it.>

Mira wrapped her fingers around one of the strings of magic. She could feel the pull of the energy seeking its target, but that wasn't the direction she wanted to go. Feeding her own energy into the thread, she sent her magic like a vine twisting around a fence post, winding ever closer to Gemma.

When her magic reached the overflowing pool of Gemma's power, that scouting tendril dipped into the reservoir and began to drink.

Strength flooded Mira. Her aches and exhaustion vanished. She felt as thought she'd just woken from a good night's sleep, refreshed and ready for anything. But the power kept coming. She wasn't just ready for action . . . she was eager for it. Her muscles were screaming to move. Her mind was racing with schemes and plans. She could do more than just stop this one event. She could fix what was wrong with the world. She could do anything.

"I was wondering when you'd show up." Gemma's voice cut through Mira's spiraling thoughts. "You almost missed the finale."

Mira stepped out from behind her cover before she even realized she was going to move.

I feel drunk, she realized with awe. Because of the healing effects of being partnered with a demon, she rarely felt the effects of alcohol.

<Drunk on power!> The demon cheered in her head. <Even the endless smorgasbord of zombies we absorbed last month didn't feel this good.>

A wide smile broke out on Mira's face as her thoughts became hazy.

Gemma lowered her gaze from the sky. Her expression matched Mira's. "Isn't it glorious?"

Mira continued to sip energy off Gemma, reveling in the heady power, but the younger woman didn't seem to mind. She still had enough to hold her spell. Mira had never met anyone with such a capacity. Her mind reeled with the implications. Gemma wasn't just a kindred spirit—another stable rifter, which Mira had believed an empty hope before this week. She'd seen and done so much that Mira was still just figuring out, things Mira had barely imagined possible.

"Now do you see what I'm offering?" Gemma tipped her head back once more and spread her arms wide. "We can remake the world and rule it side by side. No longer outcasts, rejected by humans and demons alike. Neither of us will ever have to be lonely again."

Images and emotions flowed through Mira's mind. At first they seemed to belong to her demon . . . but then she realized they were the thoughts of the demon possessing Gemma. Tapping into Gemma's energy pool had created a connection between them. Now all four consciousnesses were beginning to blur.

Memories of green hills and the crash of waves against steep cliffs filled her mind. A stone-and-wood cottage at the edge of a two-street town. Sheep grazing in the fields. Half-a-dozen red-headed siblings running circles around their mother as she hung laundry on a line, coarse fabric blowing in the cool breeze.

This is Gemma . . . before her demon.

A little girl twirled in the garden beside the town church. Flower petals popped off their stems to dance on the wind like faeries. The other children clapped and laughed. The adults did not. A man who wore the black cap and cassock of the English clergy and had too much red in his cheeks and nose grabbed her arm and dragged her toward the church doors. The adults whispered. The girl struggled.

If this continues . . . I'll lose myself.

Mira squeezed her eyes shut and shook her head, but the images continued to drift through her consciousness. The whispers. The accusing looks of people she'd known all her life. They called her a changeling and kept their distance. That was the beginning of her isolation. Then came the voice in the darkness.

<Mira . . .> The demon's call was oddly muffled, dampened by the other two presences.

Mira opened her eyes. She was standing right in front of Gemma, close enough to touch. She didn't remember moving.

"Join me." Gemma offered her hand, palm up. Her gaze met Mira's, no longer the blue-green of a mortal but the bright, swirling silver of the being within.

Mira's demon was thrashing in the back of her mind. Speaking with words too distant to hear clearly.

Mira raised her hand.

Gemma smiled.

But Mira continued past the symbol of Gemma's invitation. With a sudden burst of speed, Mira wrapped her fingers around the other woman's throat.

Gemma's eyes went wide. "You da—"

Mira tightened her grip and called to her demon, but her partner was already working. She opened herself up, no longer sipping from the tendril of energy she'd dipped in Gemma's magical reservoir but gulping it down, drowning in it.

The shared memories vanished as Gemma's demon tried to pull back, but they'd overextended, swelling beyond the capacity of Gemma's body in a final effort to convert Mira.

Energy poured into Mira. The manic feeling she'd experienced previously compounded until it felt like a swarm of insects were crawling under her skin. Her veins burned. Her skull felt like it would split open from the pressure, and her heart beat so fast she was sure it would burst.

Gemma tried to shift some of the magic she was channeling into a spell to protect herself, but the ritual she was casting was in full swing, and she no longer had the control to redirect the river of energy she'd created. She was no longer a conductor but a conduit held rigid by the current.

A smoky shape encased Gemma's body as Mira continued to draw power. Silver eyes burned in the darkness.

"You cannot contain me." The demon spoke with Gemma's voice, but not through her mouth.

"Guess we'll find out." Mira gritted her teeth against the sensation that her body was breaking apart. Cracks appeared around her fingernails, creeping over the back of her hand and up her arm. Purplish light leaked from the breaches in Mira's skin.

<You've reached your capacity. If we draw any more, you won't survive it.>

If we stop now, she lives. We have to keep going or this will all have been for nothing.

Ty

TY CENTERED HIS gun on the man on the stairs, but before he could squeeze the trigger, Decker lifted the duffel bag he was holding in front of his chest.

"Don't! Unless you want to go *boom*."

Ty hesitated. Many bombs could withstand a gunshot . . . but some couldn't. He had no idea what kind of explosives might be in that bag.

The smaller boy who'd been following right behind him bumped into Ty's back.

Ty rocked forward slightly onto the balls of his feet.

That was all the opening Decker needed. Throwing the duffel into Ty's face, Decker tackled him around the waist. The kids screamed. The patter of running feet scattered in all directions. Then Ty's back hit the floorboards, and Decker's weight came crashing down on top of him.

The gun went off next to Ty's head, and he couldn't hear the kids anymore. He couldn't hear anything but the ringing in his ears. Decker's bony knuckles bit into Ty's side as he struggled to dislodge the duffel suffocating him. A knee dug sharply into his upper thigh, just missing his groin.

With a grunt of effort, Ty bucked his hips and threw all his weight to the side.

Decker rolled off him, and he followed, riding the momentum. The two of them rolled right off the second-floor landing and onto the stairs.

Grunts and growls punctuated their descent as the two men tumbled end over end in a tangle of arms and legs. The duffel bag fell away. The gun was knocked from Ty's grip as his wrist came down on the edge of a metal stair, sending a ripple of tingling numbness up his arm. Together they dropped down one flight, then continued off the lower landing when the stairs doubled back.

Ty flailed in open space for a moment, kicking out to get clear of Decker. Then his back hit the ground for the second time and all the air was forced from his lungs.

He gasped as shadows danced dizzily in his vision. Red and blue strobes flashed across the ceiling. Shouts echoed from outside. His backup had arrived. The buildings would be evacuated. All he had to do was subdue Decker.

Pain flared to life all over his body as a million different bruises made themselves known when he rose. Decker stirred beside him. Ty took a cheap shot at his exposed side, driving the toe of his boot into Decker's ribs.

The CEO yelped and rolled away, but Ty didn't let up. He closed again, bringing his fist down on the side of Decker's face when he tried to stand a second time.

"Stay down," Ty said between short, sharp breaths.

Decker shifted, pulling inward like a child curling around his knees. Then all at once he lunged, springing at Ty like a jack-in-the-box.

Decker's shoulder hit Ty in the solar plexus, once more stealing his breath, and lifted him clear off his feet. This time he didn't hit the ground, however. This time Decker charged him like a bull straight into the opposite wall, smashing through the drywall and cracking the studs. Ty's head flew back on impact, and a burst of light sprayed across the inside of his eyelids.

Decker, unrelenting, slammed punch after punch into Ty's ribs. The CEO was wiry but strong, and he didn't seem to be feeling any pain, whereas Ty was already a bundle of bruises after his fall down the stairs.

Ty tried to guard, but there was nowhere to move, no space to counter.

Resigning himself to a few cracked ribs, Ty turned his body into the next blow so he could pivot his hip and bring his foot to bear on the side of Decker's knees. Blinding pain arced through Ty's side, but a second later he was rewarded when Decker's leg bent, throwing his assailant off balance. Ty followed up by raising his knee to meet Decker's dropping chin.

Decker's head snapped back, and he pinwheeled away in a desperate attempt to keep his feet.

Ty took a step in the opposite direction, buying a moment to regroup, and spotted a dark shape at the base of the stairs—his Glock.

Ty lunged for the weapon and, grabbing it, twisted to face Decker.

Seeing the gun, Decker stopped in his tracks. His chest rose and fell in heaving breaths. A sneer curled one side of his mouth. "Go ahead. You can't stop what's coming."

"Wanna bet?" Ty panted, the ache in his ribs screaming. "My partner's kicking your secretary's ass as we speak."

"You think this is the only anchor? The only chance? You've stumbled into something your pathetic mind can't even comprehend." Decker reached one hand toward the breast pocket of his jacket.

"Don't," Ty warned.

Decker's fingers dipped into the pocket.

Ty squeezed the trigger, then he squeezed it again and again until half his clip was buried in Decker's chest.

Decker stumbled back with each shot, eventually hitting a wall. Blood oozed from the corner of his still-sneering mouth. He slid to the floor, leaving a dark streak on the drywall. He looked down at his hand, the one that had reached in his pocket, and Ty followed his gaze. A small, black device rested on his palm. Decker's thumb touched the center of it.

A fast, high-pitched beep sounded behind Ty, and he twisted to find the source—Decker's duffel bag, lying at the base of the elevator shaft.

Chapter 36

Mira

A BURST OF SOUND and light from the construction site shocked Mira into glancing over her shoulder as a series of explosions shattered the night.

Pain stabbed through her wrist and the flow of energy into her body cut off. In the split second she'd looked away, Gemma had driven a small knife between the bones in her arm.

Gemma took a stumbling step back.

Mira yanked the blade from her arm, dropping it in the grass.

"Next time . . ." The shadowy form encasing Gemma dissipated into the night, splitting apart and fading like steam from a cup.

The spell Gemma had been casting snapped. The river of energy flowing away from the park rushed back, crashing into a conduit no longer solid enough to hold it. Gemma screamed. Her physical body, no longer supported by the demon, fell limp to the grass. Her cheeks sank in, skin stretching thin over bones. She shuddered and spasmed as the excess energy tore through her body, shredding the paths she used to channel magic, burning out her core in the same way Mira had been about to do by taking the last of the demon's energy.

Gemma's eyes dimmed, the aqua-blue turning glassy, as one final explosion punctuated the night.

Mira took a stumbling step back and stared at the fractured skin on her hands. Seams were splitting open, healing, and splitting open again as her own demon tried to shore up the crumbling structure of Mira's body. Even without taking any more . . . Mira couldn't contain the energy she'd absorbed. She was going to have a burnout.

The sound of crumbling brick and shattering glass filled the night, along with screams and the wail of sirens that she now dimly recalled hearing during her trance-like state. Plumes of smoke rose into the sky, blotting out the stars above the city. The top half of one of the apartment buildings visible above the trees tipped sideways and started to slide as its bombed-out middle floors buckled.

<Remember the banquet?>

Mira frowned, trying to follow the demon's thought but too stunned by what she was seeing. *All those people . . .* She glanced at Gemma's withered husk. *And the demon got away.*

<Those people aren't dead yet.>

Mira, driven by her demon, took two steps in the direction of the screams. Magic poured from her body, coating her in a shimmering cloud of oil-slick darkness. When her third step came down, she was standing in front of the homeless shelter.

How did—

<We've got the power of a sovereign right now.>

The demon's words slammed through Mira's scattered thoughts, sharpening her focus.

The banquet. The power of a sovereign. She raised her arms and called on every drop of the raw energy that was ripping her apart. She couldn't contain it . . . but maybe she could *use* it.

The crumbling roof of the homeless shelter froze in place. The left-most apartment building hung in the air at an impossible angle. The remaining buildings paused in their collapse. The world muted as Mira and her demon turned their combined focus on the structures. Nothing organic. Nothing living. Those had to be free to move. The crowd of people trampling the mud and grass around her faded away. The shouts of emergency workers and the wail of the sirens vanished. She stood in a void, alone, with five broken buildings frozen in time.

Ty

TY'S EYELIDS FLUTTERED open. His ears were ringing. He was on his side. Thin shafts of warm light fell around him, crisscrossing the darkness. Particles of dust danced like millions of tiny insects. Ty coughed and pulled his collar over his mouth to filter the air.

Moving hurt.

He blinked to clear the dizziness blurring his vision. Debris pinned him on every side—chunks of concrete from the elevator shaft that had protected him from the direct blast, twisted strips of metal that used to be stairs, drywall, two-by-fours, pipes, and plywood. A thick wooden beam had wedged at an angle, caught against a vertical piece of concrete on one side to create the small cave in which Ty found himself. Beams and bent metal formed a sort of cage on which the other debris rested.

No, no, no . . . This can't be happening. Not again.

The dim light that shone through the chinks in his tomb cast deep shadows that shifted and coalesced into the shape of a man.

No.

Jamal stared at him—battered, blood-streaked, and oddly translucent. Ty's mind began to spiral. His pulse raced.

No. He clamped his eyes shut, stuffed his hand in his pocket, and found the smooth surface of his anchor stone. He traced the familiar scratch with his thumbnail and whispered, "This isn't real. This isn't real. This isn't—"

A muffled cry sounded from somewhere beyond his tiny world.

His eyes snapped open.

He was still trapped, debris pressing in on every side. The image of Jamal continued to stare at him.

"Did you—"

Another shout cut him off. Jamal's mouth hadn't moved, and the voice was too high-pitched to be his, regardless. Then Ty recalled the children he'd been escorting when he came across Decker on the stairs. They'd scattered when the fighting started. Where were they when the bomb went off?

"This *is* real."

Ty twitched. This time it *had* been Jamal's voice, just as he remembered it, and the apparition's mouth *had* moved.

"You're not."

"But you're still talking to me."

Ty started to laugh, then stopped when a sharp pain stabbed his side. "Am I finally losing what's left of my mind, or did I just hit my head really hard?"

The ghost of Jamal shrugged, a shaft of light cutting through his shoulder. "Does it matter?"

"Guess not." Ty rested his head against a chunk of concrete. "All that running, second-guessing myself, and I end up right back in the same damn mess." He let his eyelids close as despair settled over him like a shroud. "I'm so tired."

"I know. But they need you."

He shook his head, shame and guilt welling inside him. "I can't."

"You can. You're strong, Ty, and the strong should protect the weak."

Ty opened his eyes and looked at his friend. "You were the strong one."

Jamal frowned. "You have to be strong enough for both of us now."

Another shout, closer this time.

"It's okay if you take the wrong path sometimes. What matters is that you keep moving forward." A phantom hand settled on Ty's shoulder. "Don't let your road end here."

Ty clutched his anchor stone until his fingers ached. He wanted to lay down his load, to close his eyes and join his friend, but that was the coward's way out. He and Jamal had promised to be heroes together. Now it was just him. He couldn't afford to be a coward.

Pulling his feet under him in the tight space, he braced his shoulders on one of the beams blocking him in and lifted. Chunks of drywall fell around him. Scraps of splintered wood and a few pieces of twisted metal clattered to the floor. The flickering orange light illuminating his prison grew brighter. Dust and smoke filled his lungs, making him cough, but he continued to straighten, muscles straining, until the debris shifted enough to create a gap for him to slip through.

With one final effort, Ty shoved the beam as hard as he could and dove through the opening in his cage. The debris he'd shifted came crashing down, collapsing the space behind him. He looked back at his almost-tomb. The specter of his friend hovered in his vision for a moment. The ghost nodded, a small smile on his lips, and faded away.

The room Ty stood in had changed dramatically. Decker's body was coated in dust and debris. Half his face had been turned to pulp by shrapnel. The elevator shaft had channeled the explosion, protecting Ty's side of the room, but large chunks of concrete had been blown loose and now lay scattered across the floor. The area in front of the shaft's open side was charred black, and small fires burned at the edges of the initial damage. The biggest change however, was the staircase. The second-story landing ended in a mangled mess of warped, jagged metal, and two flights of stairs were tangled with wood and plaster in the scrap pile Ty had just crawled out from under. A gaping hole yawned in the second-story floor. There was no way up, and no sign of the kids.

Ty cupped his hands to his mouth and shouted, "Hey! Come to the stairs if you can."

He listened to the crackle of the spreading fire, the pop of warping metal, thuds from somewhere far above, and the wail of sirens and frightened people filtering in from outside. Then the face of the oldest boy came into view in one of the hallways that dead-ended at the stairwell hole. A moment later, the siblings appeared as well.

Ty exhaled then choked a bit when he tried to refill his lungs. "We need to get out of here before the fire spreads or the rest of the building collapses."

"But the stairs are gone," the little girl pointed out.

The older boy's gaze fixed on a point behind Ty. His eyes grew so wide they were circled with white. "Did you kill him?"

Ty glanced over his shoulder at Decker's body, remembering how it jerked when the slugs hit it. He spared a thought to wonder where under all that rubble his gun had ended up, then shook his head and turned back to the children.

A terrible crack sounded above. Ty looked up to see the ceiling above the kids start to cave in as the weight of the upper floors came down on top of them.

He thrust his hand into his pocket once more, but his anchor stone couldn't help with this. This wasn't a dream or a memory. This time there was no escape from his nightmare. Fate had finally caught up to him.

The children turned, following his stare, and saw death coming for them. They screamed and ducked, huddling together with their arms over their heads as if such a fragile shield might somehow save them.

But as Ty watched, the wood and paneling slowed . . . then stopped. The broken elements of the floor above hung in midair above Ty and the terrified children.

The kids continued to scream for a long moment while everyone waited for an impact that didn't come. Then, out of breath and finding themselves still alive, they lifted their heads. Tears and soot streaked their faces, and the light of the fires burning around them danced in their eyes as they took in the impossible scene above.

"How in the heck?" mumbled the oldest boy.

The girl looked at Ty. Snot dripped from her nose. "What did you do?"

Ty shook his head. It had to be Mira . . . somehow. He'd never heard of a practitioner strong enough to freeze objects in time. A few fae, maybe, but never a human. Was this the power of a rifter? Even so, there was no telling how long she could hold it. "We need to get out of here *now*."

The oldest boy scrambled to his feet while the younger pulled his sister up.

"You're going to have to jump." Ty said. He moved as close to the hole as he could, but the wreckage of the missing staircase shifted under his feet, keeping him back. Spreading his stance, he reached out his arms as he'd seen parents do at the pool when encouraging young swimmers to take the plunge. "I'll catch you."

"Are you insane?" the middle child shrieked. He backed away from the edge.

"You see any better options?" Ty snapped.

The older boy glanced at the debris hanging precariously above his head, then down at Ty. "I'm out." Bunching his legs, he supermanned off the landing.

Ty managed to catch the boy around his middle. He stumbled back with the impact, but didn't fall. As soon as the boy's feet touched the ground, he bolted for the door. Ty called after him, thinking there might be other hazards on the way out, but the boy was already gone and he had two more to deal with.

"Okay," he said, regaining his stance at the base of the rubble. "Next."

The remaining boy took another step back from the edge, shaking his head.

"Come on, Jake." The girl tugged her brother's hand. "He'll catch us."

"What if he doesn't?"

"He will." She turned to Ty. "Won't you?"

"I promise." He fought to keep his voice steady as every nerve in his body screamed at him to run, to follow the first boy to fresh air and safety. The smoke was growing thicker. Even if the building's collapse had been halted, the fire hadn't. He glanced at the ceiling. How long would this miracle last?

The girl flung herself from the second story without warning, but her jump was too short. Ty lunged to intercept her, crashing to his knees on the mangled wreck of the stairs, and reached out his arms. She was smaller and lighter than the first boy, and he was able to pull her against his chest and twist to take the impact before she hit the ground.

He yelled out as the angled edge of what used to be a stair dug into his side, and all his previous aches screamed out with renewed awareness.

"Megan!" The boy's face popped into view over the edge of the landing. "Are you alive?"

The little girl pushed back from Ty's embrace, sitting on his abdomen, and waved to her brother, then she looked down at Ty. "Are you okay?"

He tried to smile, but grimaced instead. "I'll be fine." He sat up, shifting his grip to lift the child in his lap, and picked his way clear of the broken stairs. He set her down on the first available space of clear floor.

"Wait here while I help your brother."

She nodded.

He turned back to the remaining child.

"I can't," the boy said before Ty even opened his mouth.

Ty coughed and waved a hand in front of his face in a vain effort to clear the air. He didn't have time to coax this kid . . . and he had the girl to think about. He could take her out, then come back for the boy with help. There'd be firemen with ladders and oxygen tanks. He looked again at the dark opening where the first boy had run. But if the building came down in the meantime. . . . He couldn't face losing anyone else like that, not even a stranger, and definitely not a kid.

Turning back to the wreckage, he carefully began to climb. The debris slid and shifted under his weight. Jagged shards and sharp angles tore and scratched at him. When he reached the point directly below the boy, he braced one foot against an angled piece of metal and the knee of his opposite leg on a chunk of concrete.

"Okay," he called up. "Now you don't have to jump. Just hang off the side and drop."

The boy's lip trembled. "You'll catch me?"

Ty nodded.

The boy's face vanished. A second later, a pair of sneakers with worn- out soles popped into view. The boy bent at the waist, then slid a little farther so his chest was braced at the edge.

"Come on," Ty prompted, glancing at the ceiling once more. Was it closer?

The boy dropped the last few feet into Ty's arms.

Ty grunted at the impact but didn't stumble. Setting the kid on a slab of broken concrete he turned and said, "Climb on my back."

The boy complied without comment, wrapping his arms around Ty's neck just short of choking him.

As soon as his feet were on solid ground, Ty scooped up the little girl—who'd been clapping her hands since her brother was successfully rescued—and bolted through the open doorway toward the front of the building.

"I can walk," the boy bouncing against his back yelled in his ear, but Ty didn't stop or even slow. Duty done, there was only one thought left in his head.

I have to get out of here.

Chapter 37

Ty

WHEN TY BURST through the open door frame at the front of the collapsing building, he stumbled from one nightmare into another. The area was in chaos. Police were directing streams of frightened people to a cordoned-off area in the street. Firefighters aimed hoses at the worst blazes and raced in and out of buildings to evacuate the injured. And in a clear space at the center of it all stood Mira.

Her feet seemed barely to touch the mud. Her arms were spread wide. Pale smoke laced with black, white, and gold rose around her and streamed off her arms like wings. Her dark hair was almost completely bleached of color, and her eyes shone a bright, molten gold without focus. Jagged lines cracked the skin beneath her eyes and the palms of her hands like shattered glass. She was deathly still, unblinking; she didn't even seem to be breathing.

Three officers stood around her, well back, with their sidearms raised, but none seemed certain what to do. Glancing behind him, Ty saw that all five buildings, including the one he'd just run out of, were frozen in a state of collapse. The roof of the homeless shelter had caved in. One of the apartment buildings was tipping toward horizontal halfway up. Another looked as though one side of it had melted. The unfinished building he'd been in had sustained the least damage, though it seemed two or three levels had been compressed out of the middle.

Approaching the nearest of the three officers, Ty shouted, "Don't shoot or those buildings will fall."

"Detective Williams?"

Ty recognized one of the cops as a new recruit at his own precinct but couldn't remember his name. He set the little girl down and crouched so the boy could slide off his back. "Help these kids find their mom."

The familiar-looking man nodded, holstered his gun, and took each child by a hand. He seemed happy to be reassigned from guarding the glowing woman, which was clearly way above his pay grade.

Ty stepped in front of Mira, staying far enough back not to brush the smoky energy curling around her. "Mira?"

She didn't react to her name. Her eyes remained unfocused, as though she was in a trance.

"She hasn't responded to anything since showing up like this," said one of the cops. "Not even when we threatened to shoot."

"Lower your weapons," Ty said.

"All due respect, Detective, we need to keep this suspect secure until the PTF arrives."

"Speaking of . . ." Ty spotted Agent Chen forcing his way through the crowd and moved to intercept.

"Williams," Chen shouted to be heard above the chaos. "EMTs said I just missed you at Decker's building. Then I got a call from your captain about a bomb threat." He looked past Ty. "More than a threat it seems." His gaze shifted to Mira's back, and his eyes narrowed. "Caught in the act."

"She didn't collapse the buildings. Decker and his assistant, Gemma Murphy, did."

"The missing secretary?" Chen frowned. "Then what's *she* doing here?" He pointed at Mira.

"Saving lives." Ty turned to inspect the scene again. The buildings did seem to be moving . . . just very slowly. "She's giving us time to get everyone out."

"More like she's holding them hostage," Chen said.

"What?" Ty spun to stare at Chen.

"Clearly the police arrived before she was able to clear out, so she made herself indispensable to avoid being shot on sight—which were my standing orders. She thinks this . . . spectacle . . . will give her room to negotiate." He glared at Ty. "But I don't negotiate with terrorists."

He took a step to the right, but Ty shifted to match him, keeping himself between Chen and Mira.

Chen frowned. His gaze narrowed even further. "Stand aside, *Detective.* This is outside your jurisdiction."

"She didn't plant the bombs, Chen. I told you it was Decker and Murphy."

"You saw them do this?"

Ty pointed to the unfinished building he'd escaped. "Decker's body is in there. I watched him press the detonator."

Doubt flickered through Chen's expression, then smoothed away. "Then they're in it together."

He stepped to the side again, and again Ty moved to block him.

"She's not a threat," he shouted.

Chen's eyes widened, and purple crept into his cheeks. "I knew you had a screw loose after what happened to Jamal, but how can you possibly see that"—he pointed at Mira's back, at the tendrils of white, black, and gold swirling off her—"and claim she isn't a threat?"

"We can trust her."

"Says who?"

Ty lifted his chin. "My gut."

"Well excuse me if I need more than indigestion from a greasy lunch to inform my decisions." He tried once more to step around Ty.

This time Ty didn't move with him. This time he reached out and grabbed Chen's collar, spinning him around, and planted a fist on the agent's temple.

Chen's head snapped to the side. His eyes rolled up. Ty let go of his collar, and he fell to the mud.

"Turns out my instincts are just fine," Ty said to the unconscious man, "and I'm done second-guessing them." He clipped his handcuffs to Chen's wrists.

The remaining two cops guarding Mira had witnessed the whole exchange. Ty had disobeyed, then assaulted, a PTF agent. They looked at Chen, each other, Mira, and Ty, clearly at a loss as to how to proceed.

Ty stepped into the space between them. "I'll take full responsibility for my actions when this is over. Right now the priority is getting everyone evacuated from these buildings, and that means making sure this woman is *not* disturbed."

The policemen shared another long look. Then the man on the right holstered his gun. "The buildings were already falling when this woman showed up. She stepped right out of thin air, raised her arms, and the buildings stopped."

The second cop took one last look at Chen, unconscious on the ground, then holstered his gun as well.

Ty nodded his thanks and stepped around Mira to get a clearer look at the evacuation progress. The trickle of people from the homeless shelter had tapered off. A fireman exiting the front door raised his arms and crossed them over his head. The building was clear. Residents of the three in-use apartments continued to spill out into the night, some supported by emergency workers, some draped over the shoulders of firemen.

He glanced at Mira. The white that had dominated her hair before seemed to be fading back to brown. Even as he watched, the darker section spread like a stain to cover nearly a quarter of her hair. A sheen of sweat coated Mira's face. Her arms were shaking. She seemed too small and frail to support the weight of those buildings, and yet she was. He knew from his experience with the PTF that magic had more to do with the strength *inside* a person than their physical form. Still he wanted to move closer, to take her in his arms and help her bear this burden, but he dared not touch the energy spilling off her and disrupt her concentration. He simply had to trust that she was up to the task.

He turned back to the evacuation, willing the people to move faster as the broken building tops sank closer to the ground. "Just a little longer, Mira. You can do it."

Mira

SHADOWS MOVED through the smoky darkness around her, without detail or substance. They were shaped vaguely like people. They ran to and fro, some piling together in a massive cloud, others flowing like streams into the distance. A few remained distinct, just at the edge of her perception.

Am I in the Rift?

<Not quite,> her demon replied. <You're sort of . . . in between.>

Why?

<I needed access to *all* my energy. The only way for you to survive was to force your consciousness out. Temporarily, of course,> she added hastily.

Is this what it's like for most rifters? The ones who get completely taken over?

<I'm not sure.>

One of the apparitions stopped right in front of Mira. The shape seemed vaguely familiar . . . but then "vague" was the operative word.

Are these demons?

<They're humans as demons see them.>

The smoky shape in front of Mira moved closer and waved the trailing ribbons of its arms back and forth.

I think it's trying to get my attention.

<What is?>

The person-shadow-thing in front of us. Can't you see it?

<I can't see anything but the buildings I'm holding up right now.>

Mira recalled the strange void where she'd seen the buildings for a moment before they too vanished and left her in this smoky limbo.

Wait, if you can't see what's going on . . . how are we supposed to know when the buildings are clear?

<Um . . .>

Seriously?

<Well excuse me for not planning ahead when I cast this entirely experimental spell using a massive amount of wild energy I'm not used to channeling. I didn't hear you offering any great ideas.>

Right. Sorry.

The figure in front of Mira moved closer, hesitated, then reached out. About a foot away from Mira's body . . . or consciousness . . . a bright light flared, creating a pale aura around her. Where the figure passed through the aura, the indistinct smoke became a hand with a wide palm, scraped knuckles, and dark skin.

Someone's . . . uh . . . coming through.

<Through what?>

I don't know.

The hand was followed by an arm, then a shoulder. Finally the face of Detective Williams resolved before her. His expression was pinched, as though the effort of reaching her was painful. His hand settled on her shoulder. Suddenly the rest of him snapped into focus.

"—are clear." The words cut in mid-sentence, as though she'd just tuned in to his station. "You can let go."

The buildings? She tried to say the words out loud, but no sound emerged. She was still too distant from her body, which was tied up with the demon's spell.

<What about them?>

I think it's safe to drop them now.

<Are you sure?>

The someone coming through was Detective Williams.

<You can see him?>

He says to let go.

<If you're wrong . . .>

A lot of people will die.

<I don't have the juice to cast this spell again. As it is, I'm barely maintaining it.>

"Mira? Can you hear me?" Williams leaned in. His second hand closed on her other shoulder. His lips were inches from hers when he spoke. She felt herself once more being pulled into the gravity well of his deep, brown eyes. "It's time to let go."

Is it safe for me to come back to my body?

<Should be. I've burned through most of the sovereign's extra energy.> There was a slight hesitation in the demon's voice.

You don't want me to come back?

Another, longer hesitation. <This is the most alone I've ever been in our body—fully corporeal while you're the one tethered by a paper-thin anchor. It's . . . different.>

Mira held her breath.

<But of course I want you back.>

She exhaled.

<Dealing with the minutiae of day-to-day living would grow tiresome very quickly. And bodily functions? No thank you.>

Then let's do this.

She felt a tug from somewhere deep in her chest, as though a leash had been attached to her soul and the demon was yanking on the far end. Then the darkness around her began to resolve as details and colors bled back into the world around her. Gravity took hold as she regained mass and the exhaustion of the spell the demon had been holding slammed into her. Her knees buckled.

Detective Williams slipped one hand behind her back, slowing her fall and supporting her just above the ground.

Buildings crashed to earth around them in a cacophony of shattering glass and concrete. A rush of air thick with dust washed over them, and she scrunched her eyes shut. Williams curled his body over her, taking the brunt of the shock waves as each building found its way to the ground.

The impacts faded to the sporadic *thuds* of fluttering debris. Mira's ears were ringing. Blue and red lights flashed against the dust cloud that blotted out most of her vision.

"Are you all right?" Williams pulled back enough to see her. Keeping one arm under her back for support, he used his other to brush her hair from her face and wipe at whatever grime he found there.

Mira wanted to thank him. She wanted to pull away from him. She wanted to snuggle up against his chest. She wanted to run from his closeness.

She opened her mouth, but the demon got there first.

"Well, well . . . if it isn't Mr. Yummy." She gripped the collar of the detective's shirt and crossed the last few inches to his soft, warm lips.

Mira considered pulling away, but she didn't want to. Instead she let herself sink into the kiss.

It was Williams who eventually drew back, though not far.

Mira exhaled and realized the demon had withdrawn at some point during the kiss, leaving her in control. "That was—"

"You have to go," he said against her cheek.

The dust was beginning to settle, and Mira could make out figures moving through the cloud like the smoky images she'd seen from the edge of the Rift.

Williams pulled her to her feet, keeping his hand on her waist until she was stable.

"Can you make it?"

She nodded.

He leaned in once more, and she lifted her chin, thinking he was closing for one last kiss, but his jaw brushed past hers. He whispered in her ear, "Meet me at Skipper's Point when you're clear. I'll come as soon as I can."

He pulled back and stared into her eyes, but she couldn't find any words. Without accepting or rejecting his request, she turned and ran through the settling dust and raining debris, away from the crowd that was growing more distinct by the second.

Chapter 38

Ty

". . . AND THAT'S when the buildings came down," Ty said for at least the twentieth time that morning. "Ms. Fuentes vanished in the ensuing chaos and hasn't been seen since."

"Thank you, Detective Williams." Captain Holtz stepped up beside him to address the gathered officers. "Fire crews report the situation is contained. We're maintaining a two-block radius around the site. Patel, you'll be in charge of the perimeter teams. Edwards, I want you to coordinate with the rescue workers looking for survivors."

Ty shuddered. There were still eleven people unaccounted for . . . that they knew of.

"Dismissed."

The officers fresh on shift pushed back their chairs and filed out of the briefing room.

When the room was nearly clear, a man in a wheelchair rolled up to the front. He wore well-pressed slacks, a blue knit sweater, and sneakers so white they practically glowed. His hair was cut in a "high-and-tight" similar to Ty's—black curls fading to bare brown skin on the back and sides. Based on the creases around his eyes and mouth, Ty placed the man in his late forties.

"Sounds like you had quite a night."

"And you are?" asked Holtz.

The man extended his hand. "Garrett. I'm in charge of the new practitioners department at the PTF."

A jolt of shock ran through Ty's body as a myriad of questions tumbled through his mind.

Garrett shook Holtz's hand, then turned toward Ty. "You must be Detective Williams. It's nice to meet you."

Ty glanced at Holtz, then shook Garrett's hand. "What are you doing here?"

"As I said, practitioners are my department." Garrett smiled. "And it sounds like you've got a very unique one on your hands."

"Not anymore," Holtz said. "Mirana Fuentes fled the scene, and likely the city if she had any sense, early this morning. She's the PTF's—and I guess your—problem now."

"Indeed. Which is why Detective Williams and I need to have a little chat."

Mira

MIRA TURNED HER truck, masked to look like a brown-and-white RV, at the weathered wooden sign that marked Skipper's Point Campground. Detective Williams's silver pickup sat at the far end of the parking lot. There was also a short, white van a few spaces away.

She stopped near the entrance, pulling across several spaces so her truck was angled for an easy escape if it came to that. She almost hadn't come, but she owed Williams a goodbye at least. And despite the risks, she found she wanted to see him.

Sighing, she turned off the engine and stepped into the cool, crisp morning, wincing slightly when her jeans brushed the fresh cut on her thigh—the one she'd made for Gemma.

Detective Williams slipped out of his truck. His shoes crunched gravel. When she was halfway across the lot, he said, "I wasn't sure you'd come."

She shrugged. "Neither was I."

"I'm glad you did."

She tried, and failed, not to smile. She stopped a few feet away and glanced at the unmarked white van. "Are there guys with guns in there?"

"One guy," he said. "No guns. This isn't an ambush."

"At least," said a strong, deep voice from behind the van, "not the kind you're imagining."

Mira stared as her friend Garrett rolled out from his hiding place, his strong arms working the wheels of his chair. His dark eyes fixed on her, and he smiled a wide, toothy grin that shone in bright contrast to his brown skin.

Mira blinked. "What are you doing here?"

"I caught a flight out as soon as I heard about your 'terrorist act' last night at the awards banquet. Mr. Williams here was kind enough to let me tag along to this meeting." His wheelchair crunched across the gravel lot. "I thought I'd have a hell of a job trying to put out your fires this morning, but it seems you've found another champion." He glanced at Williams. "The detective has been an impressive advocate to both the police and PTF on your behalf."

"I just told the truth."

<Not all of it, I hope.>

Mira met the detective's gaze. "Thank you. Truly. Not just for speaking up for me this morning, but for everything you did last night, and even before that. The fact that I'm still breathing free air is . . ." She waved one hand, indicating the campground and the world in general. "Just . . . thank you."

<Wow. I'm not sure I've ever heard you so sincere.>

Yeah, well, don't get used to it.

<We do owe him a lot though.>

We owe him our gratitude. That's enough.

<Even after what we did to his partner?>

Mira cringed. "How's LaRosa?"

Williams looked away, staring into the winter trees. "She's on bed rest for now, and she'll have some scarring, but she should make a full recovery."

Mira clasped her hands together. "Thank God."

"That reminds me . . ." He reached into his pocket and pulled out a familiar silver pendant. "You can have this back."

Mira watched Saint Jude flash in and out of view as the medallion spun on its chain. She crossed the space between them and lifted the pendant on her palm, staring at the cast figure—the symbol of her hopeless situation.

"I didn't mean to hurt her, I just . . ." She closed her fist around the necklace, forcing the words out. "Sometimes I get overwhelmed and lash out without thinking." Her voice faded to a whisper. "And the people around me get hurt."

"Like your mom and her boyfriend?"

Mira nodded but kept her gaze focused on her closed fist.

"I can't say I'm okay with what happened to LaRosa . . . but I believe you didn't mean to hurt her."

She glanced up and found him staring at her.

"And you saved a lot of other people," he said. "Don't forget that."

"On that note," Garrett broke into the awkward silence that followed, "I'd like to ask again that you work with me at the PTF. You *and* Detective Williams."

<He's persistent.>

Mira kissed the image of Saint Jude and tucked the broken necklace in her pocket. "Nothing has changed."

"A great deal has changed," Garrett said. "And continues to change.

The partnership between humans and paranaturals is a worthwhile goal, as proven by your cooperation with Detective Williams last night. Hundreds of people would have died if not for the two of you."

<He's got a point. You and Mr. Yummy make a pretty good team.>

She looked at Williams. "What do you think of all this?"

"I've already accepted PTF reinstatement and turned in my resignation with Captain Holtz."

She raised an eyebrow. "Just like that?"

He rubbed one hand over the back of the other, glanced at Garrett, then focused on Mira. "I left the PTF because I lost someone, but last night reminded me why I joined in the first place. I want to help people."

"Cops help people."

He nodded. "But there are enough cops. I think I can do more good with you than with Baltimore PD." He set a hand against his chest. "Every instinct in my body is telling me this is the right choice, and I'm going to listen."

"Detective Williams—"

"Agent now, actually. But please, call me Ty."

<That's a nice name.>

She smiled. "Ty." The word filled her mouth, reminding her of their kiss—not from the first night they met, but surrounded by mud and dust as buildings fell around them, when the demon withdrew and Mira had truly kissed him for the first time. She shook her head. "I'm glad you've found your calling or whatever, but you don't want to work with me."

"Yes, I do."

She huffed a bitter laugh. "What part of 'the people around me get hurt' do you not understand?"

"The part where it matters," he replied. "I know a thing or two about hurting the people around me. I'm hardly in a position to throw stones." He took her hands in his. "You're not perfect, neither am I, but I'm willing to risk trusting you if you'll do the same."

<Well, damn.>

She opened her mouth but couldn't find words. His hands were so warm and strong, and soft except for a few calloused spots on his palms and fingertips. She stared into his midnight eyes and found hope staring back at her.

She licked her lips. *So much for avoiding complications.*

Tearing her gaze away from the curves and angles of Ty's face, she looked past him to Garrett, who was wearing one of his infuriatingly smug smiles. She pulled her hands free. "Even if I agreed to join you, which I'm not, your experiment of paranaturals and humans working together is restricted to Colorado." She shook her head. "That won't work for me. There aren't enough—" She glanced at Ty and closed her mouth.

<If you're going to work with him, he'll need to know eventually.>

Knowing I'm a rifter is bad enough. Finding out I eat people to survive . . .

<You don't *eat* them.>

Drain them. Whatever. He's got this whole lofty goal of helping people—

<We help people.>

We kill to live.

<Not every case we take involves a rifter. We helped Shaquana and Angela.>

For money.

<So you're not a saint. Who is?>

This guy, apparently.

<You think he didn't get paid to be a cop?>

"Are you okay?" Ty was leaning close to her face, studying her.

She pulled back. "What? Yeah, I'm fine."

"You kinda zoned out there for a second."

Garrett pursed his lips and nodded. "I had a feeling that might be the case. Which is why I very much want you to work with Agent Williams. He's an experienced PTF investigator cleared for global deployment now that his . . . hiatus . . . with Baltimore PD is over. I'll ensure he's given the necessary leeway to follow any and all leads as he sees fit, with the full backing of the PTF."

"Which is all well and good for him," Mira said, glancing sideways at Ty. "But after last night, everyone knows who and what I am. I'll have to go far off the grid to slip this noose."

"Not necessarily." Ty smiled at her.

She found herself wanting to smile back but smothered the impulse.

"With Garrett's help, all the records of one Mirana Fuentes were misplaced or corrupted."

"And after Williams's eloquent speech this morning about how you exposed the rifter in the city's midst and prevented the tragedy at the development site, it's been determined that one unregistered practitioner is not worth the time and resources to track down with the PTF currently stretched so thin—as long as she doesn't continue to make a spectacle of herself."

"So you want me to keep working from the shadows."

Garrett nodded. "But with the trust and backing of a PTF agent and all the resources available to him."

She pressed her lips together and looked down as a choking tightness spread through her chest.

<What's the matter? You didn't want to become a traditional agent. This seems like a good compromise.>

I don't know, I just . . . "Sometimes it feels like I'll never escape the shadows."

"I wouldn't be so sure about that." Garrett pulled out a newspaper that was folded next to his thigh and tossed it at her. "Morning edition."

Mira opened the paper and found a full-color image of herself on the front page. The picture had been taken from the back, so her face wasn't visible, but it was definitely her. A hazy cloud of white shot with black and gold enveloped her, coiling off her raised arms like wings. The suspended buildings were visible in the background of the image, crumbling and licking flames as firefighters herded people out. Above the image was the headline: *An Angel in Baltimore.*

She skimmed the article, which conveyed the city's gratitude to the mysterious practitioner who'd risked exposure to save so many lives and the mayor's public endorsement for what he called the "Colorado Experiment," saying he looked forward to a day when paranaturals could be employed in Baltimore.

"Times are changing," Garrett said. "But for now people like you are the only ones who can keep the rest of us safe from the darkness."

Ty set his palm against Mira's back and leaned in to see the paper over her shoulder. His closeness made her want to squirm, though she couldn't tell if she wanted to get closer or farther away.

He smiled. "Angels always find a way to shine."

Want more?
Continue the adventure with
Personal Demons
Book 2 of the Rifter series.

About the Author

L. R. Braden is a bestselling, multi-award-winning author of dark-yet-hopeful urban fantasy stories. Her published works include the *Magicsmith* series, the *Rifter* series, and several works of shorter fiction. A bit of a recluse, she enjoys collecting skills that may (or may not) prove useful in the event that she is suddenly transported to an inhospitable alternate reality. Since that hasn't happened yet, she mostly spends her days weaving fantastic tales, playing with her family, and getting lost on purpose. Her writing has won many awards, including the Eric Hoffer Book Award for Sci-fi/Fantasy, the Next Generation Indie Book Award for Paranormal Fiction, and the Imadjinn Award for Best Urban Fantasy.

Connect with her online at lrbraden.com

www.ingramcontent.com/pod-product-compliance
Lightning Source LLC
Chambersburg PA
CBHW021002260626
47169CB00006B/1900
9781968414153